Critical acclaim for the captivating novels of Julia London

JULIA LONDON

THE BOOK OF SCANDAL

POCKET BOOKS

New York   London   Toronto   Sydney   New Delhi

Pocket Books
An Imprint of Simon & Schuster, Inc.
1230 Avenue of the Americas
New York, NY 10020

This book is a work of fiction. Any references to historical events, real people, or real places are used fictitiously. Other names, characters, places, and events are products of the author's imagination, and any resemblance to actual events or places or persons, living or dead, is entirely coincidental.

This Pocket Books paperback edition September 2023

POCKET and colophon are registered trademarks of Simon & Schuster, Inc.

For information about special discounts for bulk purchases, please contact Simon & Schuster Special Sales at 1-866-506-1949 or business@simonandschuster.com.

The Simon & Schuster Speakers Bureau can bring authors to your live event. For more information or to book an event, contact the Simon & Schuster Speakers Bureau at 1-866-248-3049 or visit our website at www.simonspeakers.com.

Interior design by Erika R. Genova

Manufactured in the United States of America

10 9 8 7 6 5 4 3 2 1

ISBN 978-1-6680-2657-1
ISBN 978-1-4165-7947-2 (ebook)

*This book is dedicated to women
who have loved children and lost them.*

chapter one

EASTCHURCH ABBEY
GLOUCESTERSHIRE, ENGLAND
1806

The remains of the abbey at Eastchurch sat upon one of the rolling green hills of the Cotswolds in Gloucestershire, England. Judging from the breadth of the foundation it had been quite a large abbey, but all that remained was a few walls, a stairwell that led to nothing, and heaps of rubble. Only sheep and cattle inhabited the abbey now, but one could imagine what it looked like when the hills had been dotted by white-robed monks working in the fields.

The abbey was emptied along with dozens of others in the sixteenth century, when Henry VIII broke from the Catholic Church, and its lands were leased to the king's friend, Lord Lindsey, for only a few shillings per annum for as long as the Lindsey heirs survived. The abbey itself fell into ruin.

Yet it was not the ruins that were noted by denizens and visitors to the shire, but the house down the hill, a large, sprawling mansion situated in a dell, with a river and hills at its back, and fields and forests flanking it. It had been built sixty years ago with the grand confidence of a new earl.

Nor was it the mansion's neoclassical architecture, the style favored by the venerable John Soane, or the mansion's grounds, which were designed by the equally venerable Capability Brown, that captured the attention of people in the shire.

It was what went on inside.

Grayson Christopher had heard rumors in the last few years, and he heard them again at the public house where he'd stopped for a pint, having ridden all night from London to reach the abbey.

"You'll not find your sort there," the innkeeper told him as he placed the ale before him. "Not a fine lord like yourself, sir. There's naught but women and drink at the abbey."

Grayson smiled a little. "I have been known to enjoy women and drink, sir."

"Aye, milord, but I'd wager not *that* sort of woman. Or that sort of drink, really. The Libertine of Lindsey is a congenial man, I'll give you that, but what he allows to go on at the abbey?" He shook his head. "It's not proper behavior for an earl, if you don't mind me saying."

Grayson knew that things had gone a bit awry for his old friend, Nathan Grey, the Earl of Lindsey. He assured the innkeeper he did not mind his remarks, paid his bill, and continued on to the abbey.

The road was remarkably clear, given the rain. He rode past fields where cattle grazed and beneath towering pines and beech trees. He rode past the abbey ruins and the small lake Nathan kept stocked with carp. He rode past the small church where the tenants of Eastchurch Abbey attended services, and its small graveyard.

He rode through a massive gate, down the lane, and into the drive. A groomsman was quick to greet him and take his horse. Grayson's knock on the door was answered only moments later. Benton, Lindsey's longtime butler, stood just inside. He was a thin, nervous man, with a wide, round countenance and hair that was combed to frame his face, as was the style.

"My lord Darlington," he said, bowing low. "Please do come in."

Grayson swept inside, quickly shrugging out of his soaking cloak. The foyer smelled of tobacco smoke, he noted as he handed off his cloak and hat. "I regret calling without sending notice, Benton, but I must speak with Lindsey."

"Of course, my lord. This way."

As Grayson followed the butler along a corridor, he noticed the consoles that had once graced the halls and held vases of hothouse flowers were missing. The corridor looked a little barren.

Benton reached a door and opened it slightly; Grayson's nose was instantly assailed by the stench of smoke. He walked in behind Benton; the smoke was hanging like a cloud over the room. Furniture was scattered haphazardly about, save a card table in the middle of the room, where one chair had tipped over.

Lindsey sat at the card table with his back partially to the door. Lord Donnelly, whom Grayson knew as well, was seated at the card table across from Lindsey. In addition, there were three women, clearly harlots, judging by the immodest way they were dressed and the way one smiled brazenly at him.

One of the women sat on Lindsey's lap, idly watching the card game. Another sat on Donnelly's lap and smiled saucily at Grayson. The third was lying on a settee, her feet dangling over the arm. She was sleeping.

"My lord?" Benton said.

Lindsey did not acknowledge his butler but continued to study his hand, chewing on the end of a cigar.

"My lord."

This time, Lindsey responded with a grunt of warning and a flick of his wrist—a signal that he was to be left alone. Donnelly seemed not to notice the butler either; he was as engrossed in his hand and the considerable pile of coins in the middle of the table as Lindsey.

Benton, a steadfast and loyal butler, was not to be deterred. "My *lord*," he said, a little more forcefully. "There is a gentleman here to see you."

"Benton, on my word I shall put you out on your arse today!" Lindsey groused. "There is always one gentleman or another here to see me. Show whoever it is to the salon or a bedroom, but leave me be—I am on the verge of divesting County Cork's Donnelly of a considerable amount of money and I cannot be interrupted." He looked up and grinned at Donnelly as he laid down his cards. He had three of a kind, and a cry of disbelief went up from his opponent.

"*My lord!*"

"*What?*" Lindsey snapped as he raked the coins toward him. He glanced at Benton, then started upon seeing Grayson.

"Good morning, Lindsey."

Lindsey pushed the girl from his lap and came to

his feet. "Christy, I cannot believe you've come!" he exclaimed.

Donnelly looked up with surprise. "Darlington!" he said jovially. "Come, come, and have a tot of good Irish whiskey—"

"Lord no!" Nathan laughed. "That is widow-maker poison, Declan, guaranteed to fox a man at first sip, and the Duke of Darlington will *not* be foxed." He grinned at Grayson, swaying a bit unsteadily. He looked like hell—his shirt was rumpled, his neckcloth nowhere to be seen, and his dark brown hair mussed from the fingers of a harlot.

"What time is it, Benton?" Lindsey demanded.

"Half past ten, my lord."

Lindsey blinked.

"In the morning," Benton added.

Lindsey glared at the butler. "Now that was hardly necessary, sir." He looked at Grayson and smiled again. "Good God, Christy, what am I thinking? Come in, will you? Are you up from town to avoid the inconvenience of all the social engagements?"

"Were I to leave town to avoid society, my lord, I should choose a place more restful than the den of iniquity the Libertine of Lindsey presides over at Eastchurch Abbey."

That earned an appreciative laugh from Donnelly.

"A den made by Wilkes, Donnelly, and that Scots scoundrel, Lambourne," Nathan said jovially. "Were it not for them, I should pass each night at a warm hearth with a good Christian book, would I not, Benton?"

"Undoubtedly, my lord."

Donnelly snorted; the woman Lindsey had dumped off his lap giggled.

"The three of them have been in residence at East-church for two months now . . ." Lindsey paused, thinking. "Or perhaps three?"

"Devil take me if I can remember," Donnelly added cheerfully.

"What brings you so far afield, Christy? Are we at war? Have I lost all my money? Has my title been revoked?" Lindsey laughed at his jest.

Grayson did not. He was a man who took the responsibilities of his title and his position in society to heart. There was a time Lindsey had, too, but he had seemed to forget them the last few years. Donnelly, from Ireland, was far more interested in horseflesh than in his title. Specifically, the racing of horseflesh and the wagering on it.

Benton stepped forward and announced, "I shall have a bath drawn at once, my lord."

Nathan looked surprised, but then waved a hand at the man's swiftly departing back. "Bloody butler," he said with a grin. "He'll be sweeping floors if he's not careful. Come, Christy," he said, gesturing to the door. "To the study, where we may speak frankly while my bath is drawn," he said, in a voice mimicking Benton.

"What, you're going?" Donnelly asked idly, but his attention was on the harlot who was stroking his ear.

In the study, Grayson picked up a decanter.

"I'd have a care with that, were I you," Lindsey said, gesturing to the decanter as he eased himself onto a settee. "Bloody Irish whiskey. The devil brewed it, I swear it. Come now, Darlington—what's brought you to Eastchurch? I'm on tenterhooks! You must have a very good reason to ride all night from London in this deluge."

"I won't deny that it is a matter of grave importance,"

Grayson agreed as he poured a tot of whiskey and tossed it down his throat. "I heard something quite disturbing and thought you should know straight-away. You are aware of the Delicate Investigation, as it has been dubbed, into the conduct of the Princess of Wales?"

Lindsey shrugged. "Bits of gossip here and there. Why? What has it to do with you?"

"Not me," Grayson said dispassionately. "Allow me to explain. As you may or may not know, Caroline, Prin-cess of Wales, adopted a boy a few years past. There are some who swore that the princess was with child around the time the boy would have been born. Caroline did not deny it, and reportedly said to more than one person she would claim the pregnancy was the result of a night or two spent in Carlton House, thereby insinuating the child was the legitimate offspring of George, the Prince of Wales."

Lindsey laughed at that—it was no secret the Prince and Princess of Wales had been estranged since the early days of their marriage in 1795. Their dislike for one another was so intense that it was thought nothing short of a miracle they had managed to produce Prin-cess Charlotte from their brief but disastrous union in the marriage bed. Since then, both had been rumored to have had numerous adulterous affairs. The prince had sired more than one illegitimate offspring.

"Naturally, the allegations were cause for great con-cern," Grayson continued, "for it appeared as though Caroline would put a bastard son on the throne ahead of Princess Charlotte."

"You must be joking," Lindsey said.

"Not in the least. The king had no choice, really, but to

convene a commission from the House of Lords to look into the matter. If they were true, it was high treason."

Lindsey nodded.

Grayson continued, "While the Lords Commissioners could find no evidence that Caroline's boy is anyone other than an orphan the princess did indeed adopt, they did find quite a lot of evidence to suggest that the princess had often engaged in questionable and repulsive behavior with a number of men . . . and perhaps even women."

"Good lord," Lindsey muttered. "You surely didn't come all this way to tell me this."

"Not this precisely," Grayson said. "Hear me out. Caroline's behavior was such that she was removed from the king's favor and the Prince of Wales believed he at last had his grounds for a parliamentary dissolution of his marriage, which, as you know, he has long wanted. The king has not as yet decided if the dissolution will be put forth. But Caroline is canny. If the king does not intercede on her behalf and restore her to favor, there is speculation she will publish her correspondence with the king during the investigation in order to prove her innocence. In publishing this volume, which some have taken to calling *The Book of Scandal*, she would reveal some of the prince's more egregious behavior."

"Accusations that are probably true," Lindsey said wryly. "Or were true when we were members of his inner circle."

"Yes," Grayson said. Ten years ago, when they'd been young men. Even then the prince had been a glutton for food and drink and women. Grayson considered it a tragedy, really, for the prince was extraordinarily well educated and knowledgeable. But his talents were wasted by his lusts, and the public disapproved of his extravagant, debauched behavior. Now, there were many in Parliament who feared that a closer look into the prince's life might lead to a call to bring down the monarchy.

"The princess has hinted at rather sensational scandals involving other members of the royal family, as well," Grayson added.

Lindsey smiled. "The prince has fourteen siblings, so there is quite a lot of room for it, I suppose. What sort of scandal would she allege?"

"Secret births. Murder. General disloyalty and mayhem," Grayson said with an insouciant shrug. "But the point of it is, Nathan, if Caroline publishes these letters, there will be a scandal the likes of which London has never seen."

Lindsey chuckled.

"Lindsey, listen to me. There are members of the *haute ton* who are expected to be named in the book as being witnesses or participants to scandal and potential acts of treason."

Nathan laughed. "Are you implying *me*, Christy? Has the pastoral debauchery at Eastchurch Abbey suddenly become so important in London?"

"No, Nathan . . ." How could he say it? "Not *you*, but your wife."

The smile melted from Lindsey's face. "I beg your pardon?"

Grayson sighed and ran a hand over his head. "Shall I speak plainly?"

"I rather think you must," Lindsey said, his voice calm, his demeanor sober, "but *speak*."

"There is some . . . speculation . . . that Lady Lindsey is involved with Lord Dunhill—"

"Who?"

"Dunhill. Young and new to London, but a close acquaintance of the prince and his inner circle."

Lindsey's expression darkened.

Grayson tensed. He didn't want to open old wounds—everyone knew of the chasm between the Greys. He glanced at his hands. "Nathan . . . some advisors to Caroline believe that as a result of Lady Lindsey's . . . *association*, she has been privy to the unlawful conduct of the prince. She has been in his company at Carlton House, and at the country races, and at Buckingham and perhaps St. James's. She might be called to testify in a public trial, and certainly the details of her association would become public as well."

"Well," he said, folding his arms. "I suppose I can hardly feign surprise, can I? But I rather imagine Evelyn can fend for herself."

"*Your* reputation would be ruined. And indeed, anything granted your family or your title by the crown could be called into question if your wife is implicated in a scandal against a royal. It is best—for *your* sake—that she be removed from London. It is best if it appears that the Earl and Countess of Lindsey have been reconciled, as the king will look more favorably on you, should anything come to light."

Lindsey stood and walked to the bank of windows that overlooked the deer park. "Is it true?" he asked. "Does she know something?"

"Personally, I have no knowledge," Grayson said, and that was true. But he'd heard enough to suspect she might know something. She was a frequent guest at the prince's apartments at Carlton House, and he'd heard what went on in the prince's private apartments—ribald pageants, even orgies. It was impossible to say what she might have seen or heard. "But it is rumored rather fervently among the *ton*."

"Then I will send her to her mother—"

"That will appear to all the world as if you believe the rumors. If the king believes *you* believe your wife's innocence, he will try and help you. But if he does not believe it . . ."

"If he does not?"

Grayson frowned. "Eastchurch Abbey is granted to you on a lease from the crown, is it not?"

Lindsey nodded. "For almost three hundred years."

"Think of it, Nathan. If it appears that your wife was involved in a treasonous offense against the Princess of Wales, or privy in any way to treason against the crown, that lease may very well be revoked. For your sake, you must appear to believe in your wife . . . and remove her from London."

Lindsey bowed his head and rubbed the bridge of his nose. "Bloody hell," he muttered at last. "It would seem the witch must come back to roost at Eastchurch." He glanced at Grayson and smiled a little lopsidedly. "You have done me a great service, old friend."

Grayson shrugged. It was no more or less than Lindsey would do for him.

Lindsey sighed. "This calls for several tots of Declan's poison," he said, picking up the decanter of whiskey.

Nathan could not believe he was about to leave for London to bring Evelyn back to Eastchurch. He'd rather have a bone broken and reset. Or be speared and roasted on a spit.

He and Evelyn had not parted on good terms three years ago. He could now admit to himself that perhaps he'd not been a proper husband, but it didn't change the fact that the rift between them was deep. They had hardly communicated in three years, and even then, only through letters. He remembered only an angry woman who found fault with everything he did.

But here he was, waiting for the coach to be loaded so he could go and fetch her.

If he was going to London, he was going to at least make it worth his while. He had some business, and he had promised young Frances Brady, the son of his game-keeper, that he would show him the city.

Nathan had stumbled upon Frances last year when he had been playing in the gardener's shed without per-mission. He was eight years old, and after a good scold-ing, Frances had followed Nathan about the estate like a puppy. Nathan had taken an instant liking to him, with his moppish brown hair and bright brown eyes. The boy's father was a widower, and while his grandmother often looked after him during the day, the lad had run wild. He was a ruddy child with a thirst for life, and with his father's permission, Nathan had taken it upon him-self to show the lad as much of life as he could.

Privately, Nathan wished for a son like Frances Brady. But as he would never have his own son—not with the chasm that stretched between him and his wife—he could at least be a decent godfather of sorts.

He was taking Frances to London to be fitted for proper clothing.

Benton walked out to the coach with him and handed the coachman a leather satchel to include with the luggage.

"Have a care with things while I'm away, Benton, or I will see you sowing winter crops in the fields," Nathan said as he fastened his cloak at his neck.

"Yes, my lord," Benton said, without missing a step.

"My lord!"

Nathan turned toward the sound of Frances's voice. The boy bounded across the lawn, waving a red hat in his hand. A warm smile lit Nathan's face as the lad reached his side.

"My lord, one of our plants is sick!" Frances exclaimed breathlessly, referring to some lavender he'd helped Nathan plant. "It is turning brown and Mr. Milburn said it's not taking root properly."

"Oh my," Nathan said.

"My lord?" the coachman said, opening the door to the coach.

Frances looked anxiously at the coach, then at Nathan.

Nathan put his arm around Frances's shoulders. "Hold the team," he said to the driver. "We've a sick plant to attend to." He winked at Frances. "We best have a look, eh?"

What was one more hour after three long years?

chapter two

After only a few days in London, Nathan felt the undercurrent of scandal—the city was a little more ruthless, a little more jaded. The morning newspapers were full of innuendo and speculation from the most important issues to the most inane. How much ale Princess Caroline might supposedly drink in a night was put up against the amount of whiskey Prince George might imbibe. It seemed that everyone had taken sides in the dispute between the Prince and Princess of Wales. There was also a good deal of speculation as to what the scandal might do to the king's precarious health—the madness he'd suffered several years ago had not returned, but there were many who seemed to think he was on the precipice, and this scandal was precisely the sort of thing that would push him over the edge. Some snidely claimed that the madness had already returned, for it was well known that the king favored Caroline over George.

Even more unsettling, Nathan learned, influential people from both the Whig and Tory parties were banking on the prince becoming king sooner rather than later. The result was a fiendish jockeying for position and favor, depending upon one's view of how the scandal would play out.

Because of the rumors and innuendoes swirling around him, Nathan did not call on Evelyn at Buckingham House, where she served as a lady of the bedchamber to the queen and her daughters. He preferred to apprise himself of the lay of the land before he spoke to his wife for the first time in three years.

Now, as he entered Carlton House to attend a ball, Nathan observed that the scandal had done nothing to dim the Prince of Wales's taste for social frolicking. He guessed there were at least six hundred intrepid souls crowded into the mansion's ballroom. Hanging just below the dozen chandeliers that illuminated the dance floor were gilded cages, the symbol for a prince who felt caged by his marriage.

No expense had been spared for the ball; champagne flowed from fountains, chocolate sculptures of women in Greek dress stood on pedestals with paring knives nearby. Predictably, the breasts of the sculptures had been carved away and presumably eaten.

But it seemed to Nathan as if everyone was looking over their shoulder. He moved through the crush, smiling and speaking to acquaintances.

He spotted a familiar face in the crowd—Lady Fiona Haines, the younger sister of Jack Haines, the Earl of Lambourne. She was in the company of two young women, the three of them whispering urgently about something. The moment Fiona saw Nathan, her face broke into a lovely smile. "My lord Lindsey!" she exclaimed, dropping into an elegant curtsy. "I'd no' heard you'd come to London."

"As I am in town only for a few days, it did not bear mentioning."

Fiona introduced him to the two young women, Miss Clark and Lady Martha Higginbotham. They eyed him closely, smiling coyly over the tops of their fans.

"Mind you have a care, ladies," Fiona said. "My lord Lindsey has quite a reputation, he does."

"Pardon?" Nathan asked playfully, taking Fiona's hand. "Why, that is purely conjecture and rumor, my lady, for I am lost in the hope of you," he said, bowing gallantly over her hand.

One of the young women tittered, but Fiona smoothly removed her hand from his grasp. "You are *married*, my lord."

He smiled. "A mere distraction, I assure you."

Now both young ladies tittered with delight.

"You are worse than my bonny brother." Fiona laughed. "How does he fare? I've no' seen him in a fortnight."

"He is well, indeed."

"I am glad to hear it. Now you must tell us, sir—who do you side with?"

"Side with?"

Fiona exchanged a glance with her companions and leaned forward to whisper, "Who do you side with, Lindsey? Your friend the prince? Or the princess?"

"Ah," he said, and laughed. "I am on the side that best suits me," he whispered back.

"*Aye?*" Fiona reared back. "And which side would that be, precisely?"

"I've not the foggiest notion."

The three ladies laughed.

He chatted a bit longer with them before moving on through a crowd that seemed to be growing. He happened to bump into Lord Fawcett, who expressed surprise to see Nathan in London. "Why ever should you come here to this bloody mess? I've heard Eastchurch is filled to the rafters with women and horseflesh."

"That's ridiculous," Nathan said. "It holds only as many women and horses as a mortal man can handle."

"And how many might a mortal man handle, my lord?" Fawcett laughed.

"As many horses as I have stables, but only one woman at a time. It takes all my energies to pursue the one thing I desire while she pursues my purse."

Fawcett laughed heartily. "Good to see you, Lindsey. I hope you aren't mired in this awful to-do between George and Caroline."

"Not in the least," he lied. Yet he sensed the entire ballroom was mired in it, and the sooner he could be done with his business and gone, the better. Unfortunately, finding his wife was not unlike finding the proverbial needle in a haystack.

It was, therefore, something of a small miracle that he managed to spot his wife a quarter of an hour later, under the glittering light of what seemed like a thousand beeswax candles. She was moving through the crowd, talking and smiling. He watched the familiar sway of her hips, how her hands fluttered like little birds when she spoke. Her golden hair seemed to glow in the candlelight, her smile was angelic, and her countenance as lovely as he'd remembered it—no, *cherished* it—in his mind's eye these last three years.

She was beautiful. He'd always thought so, but tonight she seemed especially so.

Nathan followed her meandering path through the crowd, trying to catch up. He saw her pause to speak to a gentleman, and something the man said made her laugh.

Nathan's heart lifted a little; he moved without thought, as naturally drawn to her as any man would be to his wife.

But as he progressed through that crowd, he watched her lean in to the man as if confiding something, and it slowly dawned on him that she was engaged in an intimate *tête-à-tête*.

His heart sank back into the cold darkness from which it had dared to rise.

By the time he reached her, Nathan felt nothing but a numbing distance. He stood at her slender back, admired the way it curved into her hip, and said, "*Evelyn.*"

His voice was alarmingly rough; it was a moment before she turned toward him, but when her eyes met his, he could sense the tension in her body. "My lord?" she said uncertainly.

His gaze moved over the top of her head and the thick, blonde, wavy hair he used to liken to honey, to remarkably expressive eyes, to her lush mouth, and down, to the low décolletage of her gown.

Evelyn's skin pinkened at his scrutiny.

"I beg your pardon, sir, but the lady is engaged in conversation," the gentleman said coldly.

Nathan did not spare the man a glance—he could not take his eyes from his wife. Nor could she take her eyes from him, eyes gone wide with surprise and filled with dread.

"Lady Lindsey? Are you all right?" the gentleman demanded, putting his hand on her arm.

Nathan looked at that hand and imagined breaking each finger, one by one. "Perhaps you should introduce us," he suggested.

"I . . . I . . . Yes, of course. Where are my manners?" Evelyn said, and nervously cleared her throat. Without taking her gaze from Nathan, she said, "My lord Dunhill, may I introduce . . . May I introduce m-my . . ."

She couldn't say the word.

"*Husband*," Nathan finished for her, and looked at her lover. "I am her *husband*, the Earl of Lindsey. If you would be so good as to remove your hand from my wife, I should like a word with her."

Dunhill eyed Nathan as if he didn't quite know what to make of him.

Nathan, on the other hand, knew precisely what to make of this ass. He stepped forward, forcing Evelyn to step away from Dunhill's side. "Perhaps I was not clear," he said coldly. "I should like a *private* word with my wife."

Dunhill looked at Evelyn, whose cheeks had turned crimson. "Lady Lindsey?"

"I had not . . . I did not know," she stammered.

"Sir," Nathan said, drawing the man's attention back to him. "Allow me to speak plainly. Walk away now, or I will dispense with the formality of calling you out and happily break your neck here and now."

Evelyn gasped. "My *lord*!"

Dunhill at least had the grace to recognize there was no easy out for him. He pressed his lips together and exchanged a look with Evelyn before giving Nathan a curt nod and turning on his heel.

She watched Dunhill go, her horror plainly evident in her expression, and then shifted her gaze to Nathan. Her eyes were hazel, almost green with flecks of gold. In his memory, they always sparkled, but they didn't sparkle now. Her nose was appealingly small and straight, and her lips were dark pink and enticingly wet.

She shifted self-consciously.

Nathan remembered himself. "Would you care to dance?" he asked, extending his arm.

She looked at him as if he were mad. "*Dance?*"

"Yes. Dance," he said, his eyes on her mouth. "It is a rather common occurrence for a man and his wife to dance at affairs such as this, and given how a host of souls is scrutinizing us now, I suggest you take my arm and pretend all is well."

Evelyn stole a quick look around and frowned slightly. "Good Lord," she muttered. But she put a gloved hand on his arm.

Nathan covered her hand with his. Her fingers were small and fine-boned, the feel of them fragile. They brought back a rush of memories—the last time he'd held his wife's hand, they'd walked behind a coffin.

"Do at least try not to look as if you are headed to the gallows," he murmured as he led her through the crowd.

Evelyn instantly lifted her head and forced a smile at a pair of gentlemen who watched them walk past. "Frankly, I'm uncertain where I am headed," she admitted. "I am a bit confounded and . . . and *surprised*," she said, and turned her forced smile to him. "Could you not have sent word you were coming?"

"Did you need to be warned of my arrival?"

Evelyn's smile deepened below a pair of marvelously daggerish eyes. "What's happened, Nathan? It's so unlike you to come to London," she said sweetly. "Have you perhaps come to petition the banker for a loan to support your gambling?"

He smiled. "Were I to petition for a loan, madam, it would be to pay for your extravagant tastes in clothes and millinery."

With a brazen smile, she inclined her head and daintily indicated the gown she was wearing. It was dark green with dozens of roses embroidered in red and white. He had to admit, she was truly lovely. "If not the gambling, then it must be a mistress that has brought you here," she continued as they stepped onto the dance floor. "Poor thing probably wants out of the country."

"If I had a mistress, she would be content to live where I put her . . . unlike my wife."

"Mmm," she said, ignoring his remark as she studied his face. "Then perhaps it is your friends from whom you refuse to be parted. My guess is that the sport at Eastchurch has run its course, and they seek new diversions."

"Wrong again," he said cheerfully, and turned to face her.

Evelyn curtsied very grandly; Nathan quickly lifted her up, and with her hand firmly in his, he led her into the steps of a waltz, just as in the days long gone. They moved together as if they'd never parted, as if they had danced this way a thousand times.

It hadn't been a thousand times—perhaps not as many as a dozen. But once, on a wintry cold afternoon, Evelyn had insisted they practice this very dance, the waltz. *"You stepped on my toes at the Farmingham gala, you know,"* she'd said, poking him playfully just above his belt. *"Didn't they teach you at least a bit of dancing at school?"*

"We were boys!" he'd playfully scoffed. *"The only sort of dancing with a woman that interested us was another sort of dancing entirely."* He'd given her a wolfish grin, grabbed her up in his arms, lifted her off her feet, and twirled her around and around as she laughingly begged for mercy. And then they sank onto the floor before the hearth—

"Shall I continue to guess, or will you tell me what brings you to London after all this time?"

He realized his hand had slid down her back to the more familiar spot on her waist, just above the curve of her hip. Evelyn was watching him closely. There was something different about her, he realized. She looked wiser. Her beauty seemed deeper, more natural. It suddenly struck him—Evelyn had matured. She was a twenty-eight-year-old woman now, more confident and courtly than the girl he'd married.

He wondered how he looked to her.

"Very well, I shall guess. I guess that the buckets and buckets of whiskey they say are consumed at the abbey have given you a malady that only a London doctor can cure."

He smiled. "Buckets and buckets of whiskey? Evelyn, you know me better than that. Buckets and buckets of ale, perhaps . . . but not whiskey."

She smiled wryly. "Well, then, it seems I cannot guess," she said pertly. "You must tell me after all."

She had changed in more ways than one. The Evelyn he'd married had been a diffident young woman. This one was self-assured and bloody well bold.

"I think it must be obvious." He twirled her to the right, then to the left. "I came for you."

Damn her if she didn't look perturbed. "For *me*? But why? I have written you every other month, as we agreed," she said, as if that should have satisfied him and kept him forever in the country and away from London.

"And I have received all of your missives," he said with an incline of his head. "Should I ever be called upon at a moment of crisis to name the number of toast points her highness Princess Mary prefers with her morning tea, I shall not fail the lady of the bedchamber who has dutifully reported them to me."

That earned him a bit of a laugh; Evelyn's eyes

warmed. "I think all of England will rest comfortably knowing such valuable information is in your hands," she said.

A chunk of ice broke away from Nathan's heart. He pulled her closer, recalling again the feel of her in his arms. She was so slight compared to him, so soft. He hadn't understood that softness was missing from his life until this very moment. He could not resist letting his gaze drift down her body. Her curves had deepened; she wasn't as thin and girlish in figure as she'd once been. She was every inch a woman, voluptuous, and God, very alluring. When he looked up, she wore an expression that suggested she knew very well what she did to men.

"You look very well, madam," he said softly. "Very well indeed. Better, in fact, than I recalled."

Evelyn gave him a softly lopsided smile at the compliment, and Nathan could only imagine the number of gentlemen who would be charmed into dangerous desire by that smile. "Thank you," she said. "You look very well, too. It seems Benton is taking good care of you."

"*Benton.*" Nathan rolled his eyes. "On my word, the man fancies himself my jailer. He rarely lets me out of his sight."

Evelyn laughed, the sound of it sending a wave of unexpected longing through him. "He has long tried to save the Libertine of Lindsey from himself, has he not?"

Nathan grinned. "I suppose he has."

She smiled and cocked her head slightly as she gazed up at him. "Tell me, Nathan—are you well?"

"Nothing that a pint or a good hunt won't cure."

"Ah . . . it would seem some things never change," she said, still smiling.

Oh, but she was wrong. Everything had changed

dramatically—there were times he wondered if he'd actually lived that life with Evelyn or just dreamed it. "You seem to be favorably situated here," he said, seeking his footing. "Lady of the bedchamber seems to suit you."

"It suits me very well," she said as he twirled her into the center of the dance floor. She had relaxed; her body felt more supple in his arms now. "Princess Mary and I have become good friends."

"Has the scandal not troubled you?"

Evelyn looked at him curiously. "The scandal between the Prince and Princess of Wales?"

"The Delicate Investigation," he clarified.

"No," she said with a shrug, "other than the entire affair is distasteful. The Princess of Wales is obviously unhinged."

Was it possible she didn't know she was mentioned in the princess's book or the rumors flying about London? "That's all?" he asked.

"*All?*" she repeated uncertainly. "It's rather vile to have it all in the open, if that is what you mean, but you can thank Princess Caroline for that. She has spread awful lies about the royal family. Discord between a husband and a wife should be left private . . ." She colored slightly when she realized what she'd said—the discord between them had been anything but private.

"It is no longer a private affair between a husband and a wife, but a very public one that could end in trial, or at the very least, in Parliament, if George has his way," Nathan said.

"But that has nothing to do with me or my position here."

"Evelyn—have you not heard?" he asked. "Many expect *you* to be named in the scandal."

The news stunned Evelyn so badly that she stumbled; Nathan held her up, pulled her into step again. *"Me?"* she demanded in an angry whisper. "How could I possibly be named? With regard to *what*, pray tell?"

"You are truly unaware?" he asked, surprised. "Granted, the princess's papers have not been made public, but I would think the contents would have been leaked and devoured by the *ton*."

"Much of it has, obviously, but I've heard *nothing* about me, nor has anyone suggested such a thing! What have you heard?"

He twirled her around. "By virtue of your associations," he said tightly, "you may have been privy to certain unlawful and immoral acts by the Prince of Wales."

"My associations. With Princess Mary?" she asked, confused.

Nathan frowned at her. "No, Evelyn, not Mary. Your associations with men."

Evelyn blinked. And then colored. "That's absurd!" she cried, oblivious to the startled look of a couple dancing nearby. "That . . . that *book* is nothing more than an attempt by Caroline to sully the prince's name! If she has said anything about me, it is because she knows I wait on Mary and that Mary cannot *abide* her!"

While he was mildly intrigued by his wife's self-assurance, he spun her away from the curious gazes. "Whatever the reason you are mentioned, you must come home now," he said. "I will not allow scandal to touch the good name of Lindsey."

"Scandal will not touch my name," she said adamantly. "It is ridiculous. Caroline is . . . is *quite* the philistine. Do you mean to say you came to London based on *her* accusations?"

"I came," he said evenly, "to protect my name and my honor. You may think her accusations are empty, but others do not—there are vultures lurking everywhere, waiting to pick over the carcass of this scandal." He cast a quick look around before continuing. "If and when a trial begins," he added low, "you could be called to testify, and I don't need to tell you the scandal that will erupt with it. Everyone knows the king is sympathetic to Caroline, and if he knew that my wife was privy to unlawful acts against Caroline by the prince—that is treason, Evelyn—he might exact his displeasure by recalling Eastchurch to the crown. I shouldn't need to remind you that any *personal* scandal would remove you from the Queen's House, if not society altogether."

His wife looked suitably concerned.

"The best thing is for you to come home—"

"Impossible," she said instantly.

Nathan took a steadying breath. "You are involved, Evelyn. We must appear to be happily reconciled, and even that may not be enough."

"No," she said, and adamantly shook her head. "*No.*"

"Evelyn—"

"I won't go back, Nathan! I won't go back to that . . . that *place*," she continued heatedly. "There is nothing you can say to entice me."

Dancing among the *ton*'s most exalted members at Carlton House was not the place for this conversation, Nathan realized. He had not expected Evelyn to argue with him—frankly, he wasn't certain *what* he'd expected. "That *place*," he said tightly as he waltzed her to the edge of the dance floor, "is a rather large and grand house, filled to the rafters with the finest furnishings money can buy—all for you, remember?" With his hand firmly on the small of her back, he escorted her off the dance floor.

Evelyn hardly seemed to notice they'd stopped dancing and were now moving through the crowd. "It may be a grand house to *you*, but to *me*," she said, pressing a hand to her breast, "it is a place of very painful memories."

"Do you think you are the only one with painful memories?" he asked sharply. "At least I have known a measure of peace since you left!"

"I, too, have known peace, sir, since I left you!" She came to a halt mid-step and glared up at him. "*Nothing* will entice me back! Not time, not distance, not even death! My life is here, in London! Not at Eastchurch Abbey, and well you know it. You've been perfectly content to keep me at a distance."

"Indeed I have," he said angrily. "Do keep your voice down," he said, and nodded at a pair of noblemen watching them curiously. He steered his wife through the crowd, toward a small drawing room that was located at the end of the crowded reception hall. "I understand your reluctance, but the potential for damage is too great in London. I must insist you come home for a time until the scandal has subsided."

"*No*," she said again, defiantly. "I am a lady of the bedchamber in the queen's house, and I cannot simply pick up and leave."

He was beginning to understand that bloody wild horses could not drag her back to Eastchurch Abbey, and that angered him. They'd had their share of troubles, and he was mindful of her feelings—but she was his wife. He'd never denied her a bloody thing and she was not in a position to deny *him*, not after all the concessions he'd made to her.

"Evelyn—"

"I will not leave," she said again. "And you cannot force me."

Something snapped inside Nathan. Suddenly oblivious to the people around them, Nathan paused and took her firmly by the elbow, prompting her to look at him. "Perhaps I should state it another way," he said coolly. "I am your *husband*, madam, and I have allowed you quite a lot of liberty. More, I dare say, than any husband in England would allow his wife. And now, I am not *requesting* your return to Eastchurch, I am *demanding* it."

"I beg your pardon?" Evelyn retorted, shifting to face him fully. "I am not your chattel to be ordered about as you please!"

"*Chattel?*" he echoed with incredulous anger. "You've been given free rein!"

"Oh *no*," she said, yanking her arm free of his grasp. "Do not pretend that you have been some benevolent master!"

He caught her elbow again and leaned in close. "I am *indeed* the master, Evelyn, and if you have any doubt of it, you may consult the law. You are my *wife*," he said through gritted teeth, "a fact you have apparently forgotten."

"Oh, and *you* have lived like a monk all this time, is that what you'd have me believe? I have always had the misfortune of knowing what went on at Eastchurch Abbey, but now it would seem the whole country knows of it! I've heard of the women, Nathan, and the gambling, and the soirées!"

"You are coming home," he snapped.

She tossed her head back and stared at him defiantly. "Do you intend to force me? For I will not go willingly."

His gaze hardened. "Is that a threat?"

"Take it as you will! You dare to waltz into my life after three long years and think you can tell me what to do, particularly based on something as absurd as the accusations of the Princess of Wales!" she said. "Now kindly let go of my arm and allow me to return to the ball!"

But Nathan did not let go. He was aware that several people watched them, feeding on the spat between the Earl and Countess of Lindsey, but he hardly cared. The only thing that concerned him at the moment was the infuriatingly stubborn and open way his wife defied him. "I will say this once, *wife*. Gather your things, say fare thee well to your lovers, and be prepared to travel to Eastchurch Abbey by week's end!"

Evelyn's eyes narrowed in a way Nathan recalled all too well. "I will say this once, *husband*," she said, yanking her arm free of his grasp once more. "I will *not* return to Eastchurch Abbey! Not now, not ever! You cannot force me against my will!" With that, she whirled around and marched into the crowd, her head high.

Nathan forced down an overwhelming desire to snatch her back and take her now. To take her in more ways than one. She'd riled his blood in a way it hadn't been riled in a very long time.

Instead, he watched her disappear into the throng, and when he could no longer see her, he turned and strode out the door, signaling to a footman to have his coach brought round at once.

Bloody hell, Evelyn.

If she insisted on making this difficult, he would certainly oblige her.

chapter three

Evelyn's heart was still pounding, her hands still shaking, and it was two hours after her encounter with her estranged husband.

She paced the floor in her rooms at Buckingham House, where the queen and her six daughters currently resided (the king preferring St. James's Palace), trying to rid herself of the feelings of confusion and anger.

Horrible, wretched man!

Oh, but she'd forgotten how blue his eyes were, as blue as a cloudless October sky. She'd forgotten how little lines fanned out from the corners of his eyes, indicating his easy smile. He'd had an easy smile once. It was one of the things she'd loved about him when she was young and naïve and far too trusting.

And his hair, so darkly brown it was almost black, thick and shining. He wore it a little too long for London, but then again, he'd not been to London in years as far as she knew. He was impeccably dressed, his figure commanding in formal black tails. His shoulders were a little broader than memory served . . .

How *dare* he suddenly appear in London without as much as a word of warning and command her home? She was *furious* with him!

Evelyn was determined not to return to Eastchurch Abbey—it was not to be borne! She *couldn't* go back there, not after everything that had happened.

Mary would help her. Princess Mary would never allow her to be whisked away! On the morrow, she would seek Mary's help.

But tonight . . . tonight, she had to get word to Pierce. She hurried to her secretary and withdrew a piece of thick vellum. In her haste to dip the pen in ink, she spilled a bit from the well. She muttered under her breath as she dabbed at the stain. If nothing else, her husband's sudden appearance had finally forced her to admit that she was developing feelings for Pierce.

That realization appalled her, titillated her, and frightened her. It was precisely the reason she hadn't wanted to attend the ball at Carlton House tonight, and it was precisely the reason she could not stay away.

When she'd first escaped to London, she had found great relief in a Carlton House ball. She could lose herself among the hundreds of guests, dance until she was dizzy, drink punch spiced with whiskey until she was numb. A restless nervousness had pervaded her that could only be quenched with exhausting social activity.

But things had changed since her first year as a lady of the bedchamber to the queen and the princesses, and in particular, to Mary, the Prince of Wales's favored sister. Now, Evelyn wanted to avoid the crush and prying eyes, to avoid the man who had captured her attention so completely of late: Pierce Fielding, Lord Dunhill.

Evelyn could scarcely say how it had even happened. She'd met the dashing Lord Dunhill at a supper party and had found a bit of common ground: an intense dislike for peas.

Pierce had noticed Evelyn absently pushing them around her plate, and had remarked on it.

"I beg your pardon," she'd said with a smile, "but I cannot abide peas. I couldn't tolerate them as a child, and I cannot tolerate them now."

"Really?" he'd asked, arching a golden brow high above the other. "Even the *duke's* peas?"

Amused, Evelyn had looked around the room then whispered, "*Especially* the duke's peas."

Pierce had laughed and moved closer to her.

They chatted all evening, and she'd left Lord Cumberland's that night feeling as light as a feather, as if she were floating out to the carriage the queen had sent for her and the other ladies in attendance. Evelyn hadn't felt that way since . . . since a time she could no longer bear to remember.

Her affection for Pierce had grown since then. She saw him at this party, or that soirée. She was acutely aware of his increasing interest in her, and she was certain he was aware of her interest in him. How could she not find him agreeable? He was witty; he was handsome, slender and golden-haired. He was a gentleman, well regarded by most. And the way he looked at her . . . Lord, but it made her feel all fluttery inside.

And then one morning he'd come to Buckingham and asked Evelyn if she would join him in a walkabout in the gardens. As the heady scent of lilacs enveloped them, Pierce had let it be known how much he enjoyed her company . . . but how much more he could enjoy her company were she of a mind. And then he made a very romantic and stirring speech as to how he would enjoy her—and she him—even more in his bed.

Evelyn had managed to maintain her composure, even though her heart was racing. She refrained from telling him how much she liked his company, too, how she would very much like to be in his bed—she'd fantasized about it often enough. Instead she'd said, "Surely you must know that I am married, my lord."

He'd laughed at her naïveté. "It has hardly escaped my notice," he said, glancing at the finger on which she wore her wedding ring. "But it is a marriage in name only, Evelyn. You cannot claim otherwise—you have been waiting on the princess for three years."

It was true and everyone knew it. Evelyn had heard the whispering about the demise of her marriage in the hallways of Buckingham House. Her wedding to Nathan Grey, Earl of Lindsey, had been a notable event. Even the king and queen had attended the ceremony. But their very public marriage had dissolved after the death of their son.

She and Nathan had failed one another miserably after Robbie's death, and Pierce wasn't the first man to have eyed her lustfully since then.

But he was the first to have captivated her.

"I believe, with all my heart, that you have feelings for me, as well," he'd said boldly that sunny morning.

"Sir! I would never own to such a thing!"

"Wouldn't you?" he'd asked, and dismissed any more protest with a kiss behind a lilac bush—a soft, sweetly tender kiss that conveyed his regard and his desire for her.

That was the second time Evelyn had floated to her rooms.

Since that morning in the queen's garden, she'd been at sixes and sevens. She'd lain awake more than one night, considering his proposition. Could she *really* have an affair with him? Toss aside all her moral convictions? The Lord knew she desired him—oh yes, she desired him. She missed a man's touch. And really, why shouldn't she accept his offer? She was young; she had her own physical needs that had gone unmet for far too long. Besides, everyone in the prince's circle engaged in adulterous affairs, and rather openly at that—it was common knowledge that the prince particularly made a habit of it.

Was it really so wrong? Wasn't it just as Pierce had said—people involved in marriages arranged for title and fortune were expected to find love elsewhere?

Perhaps . . . but what bothered her was that she hadn't believed that when she took her vows. She had believed in the marriage of fairy tales. Yet she had not laid eyes on her husband in three years.

Surely there was another alternative to adultery. *Parliamentary divorce?* It was the only route that seemed plausible, given that she could not prove any other standard for divorce, such as insanity or relation by blood. A parliamentary divorce was very expensive, she knew, but she fancied that her father—or even Pierce—would want to help her.

Perhaps . . . perhaps after all this time, her husband might be agreeable. The Prince of Wales sought a divorce—how could anyone fault her for doing the same?

But what if her husband wasn't agreeable?

Her confusion as to what to make of her feelings for Pierce had grown as quickly as her regard for the man. The more she saw him, the more she wanted to retreat, to deny her feelings. She was afraid to see him, afraid not to see him. She was afraid of what she might do, of what she might not do.

She'd told Pierce as much in a letter this past week. She'd expressed her fears and her doubts, laboring over the wording, careful to tell him of her regard for him, but imploring him not to call on her any longer. She was a married woman. She could not forsake her vows, not even in the privacy of her own heart. Even if her vows had been, for all intents and purposes, forsaken years ago.

Or *could* she?

After she'd written it, Evelyn had debated whether to send the letter, but in the end, she had given in to the need to reach out to him. From the moment she'd watched the footman carry the vellum out her door, she'd waited. And waited.

She imagined every footman she saw was bringing her a letter with Pierce's response; every messenger that arrived would surely ask for her. But at week's end, she'd heard . . . *nothing*. Her letter had been met with a deafening silence.

Where was he? Had he received her letter? Had it somehow been diverted? Or perhaps her letter had displeased him. Perhaps he'd merely been carrying on a meaningless court flirtation after all.

When Princess Mary had asked Evelyn to attend the Prince of Wales's ball tonight, Evelyn thought she might at last have her answer.

Mary had fallen in love, unfortunately, with Prince William of Gloucester, and as the queen rarely let her daughters out of her sight—particularly not to attend a social event with potential for scandal such as one of the Prince of Wales's balls—she had to rely on various ladies to communicate for her.

In other words, the only way Mary could communicate with Gloucester from under the watchful eye of her mother was to send a note.

Evelyn had seen her opportunity, for surely Pierce would be in attendance as he was a friend of the prince. She had gone, crowding into the ornate hall beneath a dozen crystal chandeliers and a dozen gilded cages, with a bulky letter in her pocket intended for William.

She'd been at the ball an hour without seeing any sign of Pierce or, for that matter, Gloucester, and was beginning to fret she'd not see either man when she spotted Gloucester chatting up the Prince of Wales—who, incidentally, looked rather well into his cups at only half past midnight.

Evelyn started in that direction—the sooner she had divested herself of Mary's love letter, the sooner she could take her leave. She moved through the crowd, smiling and greeting acquaintances by rote, her heart feeling a bit hurt by Pierce's silence.

But as she passed the door leading into the service area, someone caught her by the elbow. "My Lady Lindsey."

She recognized his voice instantly and whirled around; a smile instantly lit her face. She looked directly into Pierce's brown eyes, shining with pleasure and desire.

"Dunhill," she'd said demurely, conscious of the ears and eyes around them, as she sank into a curtsy. "I thought you hadn't come. I thought perhaps you *wouldn't* come."

He lifted her up and leaned forward slightly. "I debated it, in truth. I didn't relish the thought of having my fool heart crushed again."

Evelyn blushed. "I didn't crush your heart—"

"You did," he said, putting a hand to his chest. "Into pieces."

She quickly looked around and leaned forward slightly. "Don't tease me. The situation is impossible—"

"Not impossible, Evelyn," he'd urged her, and cupped her elbow, pulling her a bit closer. "You can come with me, now. Tonight."

She was mesmerized by his eyes and his offer, but torn with indecision. "Pierce!" she whispered. "Please have a care! There is enough scandal among the royal family without adding to it."

"You are the one who has created *this* scandal, by taking my heart and folding it up in that letter and sending it back to me."

"Now you are being overly dramatic."

"Am I?" he asked, leaning closer, his mouth almost touching her hair. "I can't sleep, I can't eat, for thinking of you. I long for you in my bed, Evelyn. I know you want it as much as I do—I can see it in the flush of your skin, in the shine of your eyes. Say you will come with me tonight. My town house is empty, save an old butler who cannot hear."

Come with me tonight . . .

Evelyn had been on the verge of saying yes. The word had been on her lips, her desire fanning out through her limbs—

And then *he* had come.

Now, pacing alone, she hugged herself. She felt restless. "What will I do?" she asked herself. She couldn't bear to return to Eastchurch Abbey. She couldn't bear to see the church graveyard where her son was buried, to face all those memories in every single room of that sprawling mansion. She couldn't bear to revive the pain of her marriage, always wondering where Nathan was, if he was with Mrs. DuPaul, the woman in whose arms he'd sought solace after Robbie had died.

Evelyn paused at the window and gazed up at the starry night. "Mary," she muttered. "Mary will not allow him to take me from here."

chapter four

Princess Mary didn't seem as keen to keep Evelyn close at hand as Evelyn had hoped. Frankly, the princess looked a bit uncomfortable with Evelyn's request to help her.

The princess was seated at her writing table, hard at work at her morning correspondence, prettily dressed in white muslin with a wrap of brown silk on her shoulders that matched the brown bandeau wrapped around her locks. She blinked large blue eyes at Evelyn. "Lord Lindsey is *here*? In London?" she asked for the third time.

Mary was two years older than Evelyn, but sometimes she seemed far younger. Evelyn clasped her hands tightly in a bid to be patient. "He is indeed, Your Highness."

"And he wants you to go home?" Mary asked again.

"To Eastchurch Abbey. In Gloucestershire."

"Yes, of course," Mary said. "I don't rightly know what to say. He is your husband, after all."

"In name only," Evelyn said quickly. "You've remarked it yourself."

"Yes, but I hardly expected him to *come* for you. That seems rather dramatic, does it not?"

Romantic, she meant, Evelyn thought. Mary loved tales of romance. Evelyn believed it was because she'd been cruelly robbed of romance herself ten years ago. She'd fallen in love with the Dutch Prince Frederick. The king and queen consented to an engagement, but Mary was not permitted to marry until her older sisters—three of them—had wed. That, of course, was practically impossible, as the king and queen were notoriously protective and kept their daughters at home, finding various reasons not to consent to a royal match that would send them to the Continent.

Three years later, while Prince Frederick and Mary continued to wait, he died from an infection.

Now, Mary harbored romantic notions about Prince William, Duke of Gloucester.

"How were you and Lord Lindsey married, if I may ask?" Mary inquired. "Was it something you and Lord Lindsey sought for yourselves, or did your families seek it for you?"

"I, ah . . ." It had been ages since Evelyn had thought of it. She glanced anxiously at the window, where gray clouds were beginning to cover what had been a pale blue sky.

At the time, Evelyn had been happy with the match. She knew of Nathan's reputation for sowing his oats, but he was three years her senior, and she believed he would settle down like most men seemed to do when they married. "Our families, actually," she said slowly. "I knew him, of course—but our parents are fast friends. I did not think of him in . . . in *that* way until my mother suggested it."

"Did your parents disregard your feelings, then?" Mary asked curiously.

"No," Evelyn said, looking guiltily at Mary once more. "That is to say . . . I had no feelings to disregard. I was eighteen years of age and fonder of the idea of being a mistress of a grand house than I was of being married. I agreed to the match."

"Ah," Mary said thoughtfully. "I always rather liked Lord Lindsey. He's very charming."

"Too charming by half," Evelyn snorted. "He's charmed *quite* a number of women, if you take my meaning."

Mary smiled. "He's handsome—you cannot possibly deny that he is."

"Passable," Evelyn said with a shrug, "if one prefers that sort of square build." If there was one thing that could be said for her husband, he possessed a very masculine build.

"And he's clever," Mary said, enjoying their little game.

"Oh yes, clever, indeed! I think he pays the luxury tax with his winnings at the card table."

"There, you see? That *is* clever!"

Evelyn smiled. "If one admires profligacy," she countered.

Mary laughed. "I think you are too hard on him, madam! Men like a bit of sport. And I hate to think of the poor man needing you at home while you are here with me."

A tick of regret registered in Evelyn's heart. "Our wedding was ten years ago, Highness. Unfortunately, we . . . we did not prove to be as compatible as one might have hoped."

"I think men and women are not naturally compatible," Mary said with all the authority of a courtesan, in spite of her woefully sheltered life. "We are all so different, really. Men and their sport, women and their children . . ."

"Your Highness, I don't want to go back to East-church Abbey. There are so many dark memories there. I want to stay in London—"

"Near Dunhill?" Mary asked with a sly smile.

Evelyn paused, weighing her response. Of course Mary knew about Dunhill, for Evelyn had told her. Yet she wasn't certain if Mary thought it another romantic adventure, or if she disapproved. "Near *you*," Evelyn said carefully. "I would miss your company dreadfully."

"Oh, and I would miss yours!" Mary cried. "But what can I do?"

"Perhaps if you had a word with the king. He won't deny you."

Mary didn't seem particularly keen on that idea, but she did reluctantly agree to intercede with the king on Evelyn's behalf.

That afternoon, Evelyn passed the time with Lady Harriet, the young daughter of Evelyn's friend and fellow lady of the bedchamber, Claire French, Lady Balfour.

Claire was a distant mother at best, and seemed to chafe at the inconvenience whenever Harriet was deposited at her door, which happened more frequently of late, as Lord Balfour did not approve of leaving poor Harriet alone in the country when he was in London. The lass often sought the company of her mother, but her mother preferred the company of adults, and particularly, gentlemen.

Feeling sorry for the girl, Evelyn had befriended her, taking her under her wing. She was a lovely ten-year-old girl, with light brown hair and blue eyes. She had confessed recently to Evelyn that she longed to dance. Harriet would have a dance instructor one day as all girls of good breeding had, but in the meantime, Evelyn delighted in teaching her. On those afternoons when Mary was napping and Claire was away, Evelyn taught Harriet to dance.

They were practicing that interminable afternoon while Evelyn waited for Mary to speak to the king. Harriet was learning the quadrille, and side by side they moved, Harriet matching Evelyn's steps, moving in time to the strains of a music box.

"When I am old enough to attend a royal ball, I am going to dance all night, and I shall wear a gown more beautiful than my mother's."

"I think you will be the loveliest girl on the dance floor," Evelyn said, winning a big smile from Harriet. "Tomorrow," she continued as she crossed behind Harriet, "we'll go to the ballroom and practice. The quadrille requires a lot of room."

Harriet snapped a startled look at Evelyn. "Mamma said I am not to go anywhere in the palace, that the queen doesn't like me underfoot."

"She doesn't like any of us underfoot," Evelyn clarified. "And she certainly does not like the ballroom opened. So it will have to be our secret."

"Do you mean it, truly?" Harriet asked, her eyes shining with excitement.

"Of course!" Evelyn said. "I should never jest about such a thing! Watch your right foot, Harriet."

"Pardon, madam," a deep voice intoned.

The footman's arrival elated Evelyn; she quickly moved to close the music box before breathlessly whirling about . . . and coming almost nose to shoulder with her husband.

She was expecting the footman to say Mary had sent for her—not deliver her husband.

His presence shocked her. He looked magnificent, wearing a coat of navy superfine and tan trousers. His waistcoat, embroidered in gold, hugged a trim waist, and his neckcloth looked as if it had just been pressed. He was as finely dressed as any member of the royal family, but that was not what caught Evelyn's attention. It was his expression. It was cool and dangerously determined.

"His lordship Lindsey," the footman needlessly announced from somewhere behind him.

"I would like a word, madam," he said, his blue eyes settling very firmly on hers.

"Unfortunately, I haven't time," Evelyn said primly. "I am expecting an audience with the king at any moment—"

"Ooh, the *king*," he said, sounding impressed. "Naturally, if the king calls for you, I will not delay you."

Evelyn eyed him closely. He raised one brow, silently challenging her. "Would you give the footman leave, madam?"

She reluctantly glanced at the footman. Then at Harriet. "Lady Harriet, please go with Thomas, will you? I shan't be more than a moment."

The footman stood back, waiting for Harriet to come along. She went reluctantly, tilting her head back to peer up at Nathan as she went.

If Nathan noticed her, he gave no indication—his gaze was locked on Evelyn.

When they had gone, Evelyn said, "Whatever you have come to say, please say it and go."

"Why the rush, love? Here we are, alone, in a room that connects to a room with a bed . . ." One brow rose above the other in invitation, and he smiled.

The very suggestion sent a tantalizing shiver down Evelyn's spine; she quickly folded her arms across her body.

"No?" he asked, still smiling. "I rather thought as much." He clasped his hands behind his back and glanced about the room, taking in the furnishings. The queen believed in economy—the rooms were sparsely appointed, but the furnishings were of the highest quality.

"So this is where you have lived."

"Obviously," she said. When in London, at least. Sometimes at Windsor and Frogmore. But she did not explain that to him.

He ignored her caustic remark and paused to touch the music box. When he opened it, a Limoges porcelain figurine of a dancing couple began to twirl around in time to a Handel piece. The box had been made especially for her—Pierce had commissioned it to commemorate the first time they'd danced.

Nathan lifted his gaze. "Yours?"

Evelyn hugged herself tighter. "Yes."

"My money? Or a gift?"

Oh, how she despised his intrusion! "A *gift*."

He smiled wryly. "I infer from your discomfort that it was not a gift from Princess Mary."

Evelyn suddenly moved forward. She swept past Nathan, picked up the music box, and moved it to the mantel and out of his reach. She turned around. "What do you want?"

His eyes were shining with amusement now. He casually took in her gray and white gown. "Frankly, what I wanted when I entered this room and what I want now are not the same thing."

His words stoked a familiar heat in her. "I have a day full of appointments, my lord," she said, trying to put some distance between herself and his words.

"You may return to your appointments when I am gone."

"Well, there is some news, at least. You will be leaving. Perhaps we might hasten that along if you will but tell me what you want."

He grinned and moved closer. *Too* close. "There are many things I *want*, love," he said to her breasts, and shook his head. "You are lovelier than I've ever seen you." He touched her collarbone just above her décolletage.

Evelyn drew a sharp breath. "Don't, Nathan. You have no right."

"No right to admire my wife?"

"You have intruded into my private chambers—"

"As is my *right* as your husband—"

"Perhaps at Eastchurch. Not here," she said angrily.

"Darling," Nathan drawled, and brazenly laid his hand against her neck. "I may have access to your private chambers whenever and wherever I please until one or both of us is dead and buried."

"I beg your pardon? What now, Lindsey? Will you resort to badgering me?"

"Badgering isn't precisely what I had in mind," he murmured.

Evelyn whirled away from him.

He chuckled low. "In all honesty, as much as I should

like to ravish you, I've hardly the time for it at the moment. I've come only to see if you have reclaimed your senses and see clearly the situation in which we find ourselves."

"Reclaimed my senses, as if my refusal to return to Eastchurch means I have lost my mind?" She laughed wryly. "How boorish, how very *male* of you, Nathan."

"Have you considered it?" he calmly pressed.

"Oh, I've considered it, yes I have," she said with mock cheerfulness that did not belie her anger. "And I find it is precisely the same situation in which we found ourselves three years ago. We are *still* on opposite ends, and always will be."

"Meaning?"

"*Meaning*, you betrayed me, Nathan."

"For the love of God," he said, and sighed heavenward. "Not *that* again."

"Yes, *that* again. Admit it—you abandoned me for Mrs. DuPaul."

"That is absurd! I did no such thing!"

"I *saw* you, Nathan, have you forgotten? I saw you with her! At the lowest point in my life, you were in the arms of another woman!"

"You saw nothing, Evelyn. At the lowest point in *my* life, you were cold and distant and would have dragged us all into hell if we'd allowed you!"

That admonishment drew Evelyn up.

"And what does it matter now?" he demanded. "Three years have passed and for better or worse, you and I are different. But need I remind you, Mrs. Grey?" he said angrily. "We are still married!"

"In name only."

Nathan's gaze darkened; he suddenly caught her arm

and pulled her so close that she had to tilt her head back to look at him. He studied her face. "I cannot help the fact that we are still married any more than I can help the fact that your name is *my* name. Your scandal is *my* scandal. Your actions are considered *my* actions, and I cannot protect us from ruin if you are in London consorting with God knows who! Is that clear?"

He must have thought she would crumble under his censure and his authority. Evelyn lifted her chin and looked him squarely in the eye. "I have not sullied your *name*. I do not *consort*. And I certainly do not fear the empty accusations made about me by the Princess of Wales. She has no credibility here."

"*Here?* Evelyn, have you no sense of the people? The Princess of Wales has widespread public support! The populace finds the *prince* at fault. There are many who have begun to question the necessity of the monarchy itself!"

"How can they? He wasn't accused of bearing a bastard child," she shot back.

"Don't be naïve," Nathan said curtly. "His by-blows are all over this town. And the Lords Commissioners found no evidence to support the claim that Caroline bore a bastard child, but they found plenty of evidence to support the claims of bad behavior, and adultery by the Princess of Wales, which is still a treasonable offense with or without a child!"

"What has that to do—"

"If the king so chooses," he continued brusquely, "he could have her tried in a true court of law for adultery, among other things. Not by the Lords Commissioners, but in a *court*, before a judge, where she may know details about the private lives of those who testify against her and may respond in her own defense. The longer the king delays in making that decision, the more frantic Caroline becomes. She stands to lose everything! She is mounting her defense *now*, Evelyn. There are spies everywhere. The slightest event might be turned round to suit her defense. In the meantime, if the prince can't obtain the evidence he needs for a trial of treason, he will at least have enough evidence to bring about a parliamentary dissolution of his marriage."

Evelyn turned away from him, trying to absorb that news.

But Nathan tightened his grip of her arm and forced her around. "This scandal will ruin everyone who comes near it, do you understand? It will echo across this nation and *you*, my darling, will be forever ruined, because you are suspected of witnessing or knowing of some debauchery in which the prince was engaged while in the company of your lover! Do you think Princess Mary will want you waiting on her then?"

"That's not true," she said, trying to pull her arm free of his grip.

"For some reason, Caroline seems to think you do know something. What do you know, Evelyn?"

"Nothing! On my honor, I know nothing!"

His eyes narrowed.

"On my word!" she said again.

He suddenly released her and turned away, pushing his hands through his hair. He looked over his shoulder at her. "Then there is nothing to be done for it."

"Pardon?"

He abruptly pivoted and took her face in his big hands, his fingers splayed across his hair and her ears. He was so close that she could smell the spicy scent of his cologne and see the little flecks of gray in his eyes. But it was his mouth that drew her attention. His lips . . .

"The troubles of the Greys are rather minor in comparison to those of the royal family, but there is nothing to be done for it. You must come home."

Damn it, she could feel tears suddenly begin to well. "No," she said, and wrapped her hand around his wrist. "I won't abide it, all the hunting and gaming and Lord knows what."

"And here in London you, my pet," he said, slipping one arm around her shoulders, drawing her closer, "will be no more than a step or two from the nearest fashionable salon or soirée, hoping to ruin me." He bent his head toward her. "It seems we cannot escape one another," he murmured, and kissed her.

His lips were soft and sultry on hers, sparking a deep, hot flame. But anger quickly followed; anger that he could provoke such longing in her, anger that he had come and ruined everything. Evelyn opened her mouth beneath his . . . and bit his lip.

"*Ouch!*" he snapped.

She slipped out of his embrace. "You don't know me anymore, Nathan. I won't go."

Nathan put his finger to his lip, then slowly dropped his hands to his side. "Pack your things, Evelyn," he said curtly. "We leave this week."

"Will you force me to return knowing my feelings?" she cried incredulously.

"It seems so," he said bitterly. "I wish that it were not this way, I wish I could trust you to conduct yourself properly, but as you give me no reassurance of that, I will do what is necessary to protect my name and holdings."

"You have such gall! The man everyone knows as the Libertine of Lindsey would lecture me?"

"I don't give a damn what you do, Evelyn," he said sharply. "But who here will protect you from scandal? The king? Your *lover*?"

Her blood began to race in her veins. She had trouble catching her breath. "Get out," she said evenly.

He strode for the door. But there he paused and turned to point a finger at her. "This week, madam," he said. With that, he pushed the door wide open and walked away.

chapter five

*D*idn't know her?

    Nathan wondered what nonsense filled his wife's head. Was that the sort of thing she had learned in London? Of *course* he knew his wife. He knew her very well, indeed! He knew that she took cream with her tea, liked long walks on summer evenings, and was diligent about correspondence. He *knew* her!

He abruptly stood from his desk in the private apartments he had taken and walked to the window.

"A woman would be my guess."

Nathan glanced at his old friend Sir Oliver Wilkes. Tall and lanky, and still as athletically inclined as he'd been in their youth, Wilkes had met him in London. Along with two more old friends who'd remained behind at the abbey, Declan O'Connor, Lord Donnelly of Ireland, and Jack Haines, Scotland's Earl of Lambourne, Wilkes had, for all intents and purposes, made Eastchurch his home in England.

"I've no idea what you mean," Nathan said irritably.

He was in no mood for idle chatter. He was too busy mentally listing all the things he knew about his wife. For example, her favorite color was blue. He was almost certain of it.

"I mean, sir, that I've not seen you in such a dour disposition since the night you lost four thousand pounds to that gent from London."

"Rundberg was his name," Nathan muttered. "I still owe him two thousand pounds."

"One might think your sour mood was due to a bad hand at cards, but I looked for you in the gaming rooms at White's and you were nowhere to be seen. Therefore, I have concluded it is a woman who must be the cause of your long face."

"It is not a *woman*, it is my *wife*."

"Lady Lindsey?" Wilkes said with surprise.

Nathan shot him a look.

Wilkes instantly raised a hand in a placating manner. "You cannot fault my surprise. Her name has not crossed your lips in months."

Her name may not have crossed his lips, but it didn't mean he didn't think about her. Or know that she had a small birthmark on the outside of her left thigh. He knew his wife, goddammit!

"I have had occasion to see her," he said shortly. "And I intend to take her back to the abbey—but she does not want to go."

"So? If you desire it, take her," Wilkes said, as easily as if he was suggesting Nathan go for a stroll.

Surprised, Nathan looked at him. "*Take* her?"

Wilkes nodded as he walked to the sideboard to pour two whiskeys. He handed one to Nathan. "It is well within your rights. You are her husband and she is answerable to you . . . and not some young buck fresh out of short pants."

So Wilkes had heard of her affair as well.

"Tell the king first if you must, or George," he said, referring to the Prince of Wales. "But *take* her. The longer you allow it to continue, the bigger fool you will become in the eyes of the *ton*."

Frankly, Nathan cared less about the way he was perceived by the bloody *ton* than he did Evelyn's adamant refusal.

"Surely I need not mention that another adulterous affair and scandal at this time could be disastrous for all parties involved," Wilkes added slyly. "The sooner you are at Eastchurch, the sooner the scandal surrounding her will die. Take her, and go by the road that runs through Cricklade. It is quicker if there is not too much rain."

Nathan studied his friend. Wilkes gave him a bit of a shrug, but it was enough that Nathan understood everyone—all of London, all of the *ton*—knew that he'd been cuckolded.

And Wilkes was right. Nathan would take her by force if he must, but he would take his wife away from London as quickly as possible and before she ruined them both completely.

Wilkes must have realized what he was thinking; he held up his tot for a toast. "To the Lady Lindsey," he said.

Nathan grudgingly clinked his tot against Wilkes's. "To my reluctant wife," he said bitterly.

The note that came back from Pierce in answer to Evelyn's plea to meet her had one word: *Yes*.

At half past one the following day, Evelyn held up a red ribbon and a gold ribbon to her hair. "Which one would you choose?" she asked Claire.

"Husband or lover?" Claire asked idly.

Evelyn stole a look at Harriet, who was busying herself in Evelyn's jewelry box.

"*Ribbon,*" Evelyn corrected her, and handed the gold ribbon to Kathleen, her longtime ladies' maid. She glanced again at Harriet and smiled. "And he's *not* my lover," she added with a wink for the girl.

Sprawled on a chaise, leafing through a set of fashion plates, Claire ignored her and asked, "Where is Princess Mary today? She's so loath to be without you."

Loath to be without her yet unsympathetic to Evelyn's plight. Mary had taken the issue to the king, but the king had dismissed her. "*He has much on his mind and his knee pains him,*" she'd said to Evelyn. She meant that the Prince of Wales was on his mind. The entire family was on tenterhooks, wondering what Caroline might reveal about them all.

So Evelyn had begged her to speak to the queen. Mary had shaken her head vehemently at that suggestion. "*The queen would never sanction it. She believes a woman's place is with her husband.*" Which was why, Evelyn thought wryly, the queen spent her time at Buckingham House and the king at St. James's Palace.

"Princess Mary is with the queen," Evelyn responded brightly to Claire.

"You're very lucky to get away, you know," Claire said. "I'm waiting on Princess Sophia, who is in *quite* an ill humor."

Sophia was notoriously ill humored.

"Harriet, do please stop touching everything," Claire

added without looking up from her fashion plates. "And take those earrings off. You look like a harlot."

Harriet's young face turned crimson. "But *you* wear them, Mamma," she muttered as she quickly pulled them off her ears.

"That's an entirely different matter, and you know it," Claire said as she rolled onto her belly and propped herself up on her elbows to watch Kathleen dress Evelyn's hair.

"What do you intend to do about Lindsey's demands?" Claire asked. "You should divorce him, you know. No one would blame you."

Kathleen snorted; Harriet looked at her mother, mortified.

Evelyn shot Claire a look in the mirror's reflection. She didn't really care to discuss her personal life in front of Harriet, but Claire never had such reservations. "You're much better suited to London," Claire added.

For a long time after she'd arrived in London, Evelyn had harbored a secret hope that Nathan would come for her and admit he'd wronged her. But when he didn't come . . . didn't even inquire . . . she had thrown herself into London's elite society, and had, at least in Claire's eyes, made quite a splash. Claire was constantly telling Evelyn who had noticed her, or had inquired about her.

"How long will you be this afternoon, Lady Lindsey?" Harriet asked.

"Why should you concern yourself, Harriet?" Claire snapped. "You bother Lady Lindsey endlessly as it is."

"At least she has time for me," Harriet mumbled.

"Pardon?" Claire asked.

"She doesn't bother me in the least," Evelyn said quickly to Claire. "I very much enjoy her company. We share secrets," she added, and Harriet smiled. Just this morning, they had stolen into the ballroom and, suppressing laughter, had twirled the entire length of it and back. Harriet had stopped in the middle, twirling slowly, her head tilted back, looking up at the empty chandelier. *"I will be a great lady someday, and Mamma shall have to come to me,"* she'd said. *"I'll be prettier, too, and my husband shall love me."*

"You shall, indeed," Evelyn had assured her. And then they'd escaped, lest a footman or underbutler find them and report them to the queen.

"In answer to your question, Harriet, I shan't be gone more than an hour or two," Evelyn said.

"Really?" Claire asked, and laughed silkily. "What if your *friend* schemes to whisk you away to someplace quite exotic to save you from Lindsey?"

"Such intrigue, Lady Balfour!" Evelyn scolded her. "I assure you I shall return this afternoon."

Claire shrugged as she studied the hem of her sleeve. "Were it me, *I* should be tempted to suggest it to him. Perhaps I shall do so on your behalf. Perhaps France."

"I enjoy my post here," Evelyn said, and saw Claire roll her eyes in the reflection of the mirror as Kathleen finished dressing her hair.

Evelyn admired herself in the mirror. She was wearing a camel-colored gown with red trim and a red underskirt that flashed color when she walked. It was her best walking gown and one she hoped Pierce would admire.

"Oh, my lady, you look so lovely," Harriet said longingly as Evelyn turned one way and then the other before the mirror.

"Thank you, Harriet."

"You should wear these," Harriet said, and held up

a pair of tear-shaped amber earrings she'd fished out of Evelyn's jewelry box.

"They're beautiful!" Claire exclaimed. "Dunhill has superior taste!"

Evelyn felt a tiny prick of guilt. They'd been a gift from Nathan. "An excellent choice, Harriet," Evelyn said, and donned them. She stood back to look at herself one last time.

She was nervous, so very restless. And it wasn't the same sort of butterflies she usually had before seeing Pierce. This was more a feeling that something wasn't right.

"Oh dear, you mustn't frown!" Claire advised. "You look so terribly grim."

Behind her, Kathleen rolled her eyes. "Come, Lady Harriet. You may give me a hand in pressing her ladyship's new ball gown."

"Oh yes, Kathleen, *do* teach her the household arts," Claire said with an impatient sigh. But she made no move to stop them.

"I don't mean to frown," Evelyn said low so that Kathleen, who clearly disapproved of her flirtation with Dunhill, couldn't overhear, "but my situation is rather complicated."

"No more or less complicated than the situations of half the people at court," Claire said as Kathleen and Harriet disappeared into the adjoining sitting room.

Evelyn ignored that and smoothed the lap of her gown. "What is the time?"

"A quarter of two," Claire said on a yawn.

"A quarter of two! I shall be late!" she cried, and swept up a reticule lying on her bed on the way out. She hurried into the sitting room, promised Kathleen she'd not be late, kissed Harriet's cheek, and went out.

At a quarter past two, Evelyn walked briskly in the direction of Duke Street, her mind and her heart racing as she thought of all the things she would say to Pierce. *I'm sorry, my husband has come and I cannot continue.* Or perhaps Claire was right and a simple *Take me from here!* might be in order.

She reached the corner of George Street, which led straight into the park, and paused there to allow some traffic to pass. When it cleared, she struck out. She'd not taken more than a step or two when someone put a hand on her arm. Evelyn pulled away. "I beg your—" But her words were lost the moment she saw Nathan staring down at her. "W-what are you doing here?" she stammered.

He pointed to the big, ornate coach bearing the Lindsey crest she had not noticed until that very moment. He slipped his hand to the small of her back and said, "We are going home, Evelyn," in a tone that would have shaken her years ago, and began to usher her toward the coach.

As she realized what he meant to do, panic swelled in her breast. She instinctively tried to move away from his hand. "You cannot order me home!"

"I most certainly *can*, love, and I *am*."

"Oh no you won't," she said, and turned away.

Nathan caught her arm, twirled her around, and easily yanked her into an unbreakable embrace. They were so close that she could see the glitter of determination in his blue eyes, the little lines that feathered his skin as he squinted down at her. "Do not fight me, Evelyn. I am quite determined and you will only tire yourself."

She brought the heel of her boot down as hard as she could on the top of his boot.

Nathan grunted in pain and his grip loosened slightly—enough for her to spin around and jerk away from him. But two men she did not know blocked her exit. She swung her arm, and her reticule connected with one man's nose. He cried out and covered his nose with his hand.

The second man looked quite startled and stared at her wide-eyed. "I will scream," she threatened him. "I will scream to high heaven and everyone will hear it and come running!"

Just behind the two men, she saw a pair of gentlemen who were watching the scene unfold with avid curiosity. "Help me!" she cried, trying to push past Nathan's minions. "I am being abducted against my will!"

The two gentlemen looked at one another.

"Pay her no heed, sirs!" Nathan said cheerfully. "My wife is often loath to leave Bond Street and my money in my pocket."

One of the men laughed; both of them turned away.

Evelyn gasped with outrage. Fury—consuming, white-hot, suffocating, indignant fury—filled her.

Nathan had his hand on her waist again, his fingers digging into her side. "Cause a scene if you like," he said calmly. "It will not deter me. You surely must understand that no one will come to your rescue, because you are my wife."

The truth of that statement sunk into her consciousness. Evelyn tried to struggle, but Nathan gripped her easily. She was powerless against him.

"Open the door," he ordered one of the men.

"Wait, *wait*!" Evelyn cried, trying to buy time so she could think. "I . . . I'll make a bargain with you," she said.

"You are in no position to bargain—"

"Nathan, Nathan! Hear me out!" she pleaded with him. "I will agree to leave the queen's house and . . . and go home to my parents."

"No. That will still be perceived as a continued rift between us, and, in fact, will look to all as if I believe the things being said about you."

"Then I'll go to Scotland. I can go to my father's hunting lodge, and you can go to Lambourne, wherever it is he lives, and no one will be the wiser!"

"Lambourne is at Eastchurch. Get in the coach."

"No!" she cried.

With one arm around her waist, Nathan lifted her off the ground and put her in head first, following her inside. She quickly came up and tried to throw herself over him and out the door, but he clamped an arm around her shoulders and yanked her back so hard that she collided with his chest. She could feel the shadow of his beard on her temple and his breath warm on her face. He held her so tightly she could not breathe.

"*Nathan*! Nathan, don't do this, *please* don't do this!"

"I would not if I did not think it necessary," he said a little breathlessly, and pulled her back on top of him at the same time he put a booted foot against the latch. "I am hardly excited about the prospect of having you mope about the abbey again."

"I swear by all that is holy I will *never* forgive you!" she cried, struggling against him.

"Yes, so you have said on more than one occasion."

"What of my things? Of Kathleen? Of *Harriet*?"

"Har—" he started, but Evelyn kicked like a mule, managing to make contact with his shin. "Bloody *hell*," he hissed. "Stop that!" He flipped her over, so that she was beneath him on the bench. Just then, she felt the weight of people stepping onto the coach; it lurched forward.

"No!" she cried, struggling to free her hands as tears began to stream down her face. "How can you do this? How can you treat me so abominably? The king will hear of this!" she shouted at him. "He will hear of it and you will be held responsible!"

"Good Lord, Evelyn! The king knows of it! The prince knows of it! I personally told them of my decision! When will you accept that as your husband, I can take you home if I so choose?"

Anger and raging frustration filled her. She suddenly stopped struggling and sagged against the squabs, her face turned away from him.

"Evelyn."

Nathan straightened up and loosened his hold as the coach rocked along the streets of London.

It was no use. It was done, and she was lost. Evelyn slowly pushed herself upright . . . and noticed the boy sitting across from her, wide-eyed, his legs drawn up beneath his chin and his arms wrapped tightly around them. He was gaping at her as if he'd just seen a dragon fly through the coach.

Evelyn jerked her gaze to Nathan.

"Ah," he said, in response to her unspoken question. "Allow me to introduce Master Frances Brady, the gamekeeper's son."

chapter six

On the outskirts of London, on the road to Gloucestershire, Nathan left the coach in favor of a horse. The trip was a full day's journey—they would not arrive at the abbey until well after midnight.

That was just as well with Evelyn. She was very cross, what with her abduction and all the bouncing and jostling of the coach. Her ill humor was made even worse by the fact that a boy, no more than eight or nine years old, had witnessed it all. And just who *was* Frances Brady and why was he in the coach? She would have asked, but she had far more pressing matters on her mind.

Kathleen would be frantic. And Evelyn had promised Harriet they might practice the minuet on the morrow. The poor girl would think Evelyn had abandoned her like her mother so often did, and that distressed Evelyn to no end.

And Pierce! She'd been on her way to meet him— what must he have thought when she didn't come?

Surely he believed she'd been detained by Mary, but how long would it be before he sought her out? What would he think when he heard she'd been taken away by her husband? Oh, she had no doubt he'd hear of it— it would be all over London in a matter of hours, spread about like a winter plague.

She'd write him, that's what she'd do, and explain everything, tell him that as soon as she could escape her deranged husband, she would return to London. Looking out at the countryside, she ignored the niggling thought that returning to London seemed impossible.

She sighed and glanced at the boy, who was watching her warily from the corner of the coach. Evelyn smiled, trying to put him at ease. "Frances Brady, is it?"

He nodded uncertainly.

Her smile brightened. "I'm not as bad as all that, Master Brady. Lord Lindsey and I had a small disagreement, that's all."

He nodded again, but one leg started to swing, nervously kicking a box beneath the bench on which he sat.

"Sometimes adults disagree."

"I've never seen his lordship disagree with other ladies," he said.

Evelyn's smile faltered. "Haven't you, indeed?" she said. "Well." She forced another smile. "Perhaps other ladies don't know his lordship quite as well as I do." Honestly, even the *boy* knew of Nathan's predilections? She reached for her reticule, hoping to find a handkerchief within. But when she pulled the strings to open it, she found something else.

A letter from Pierce.

The sight of his familiar handwriting confused her

until she remembered she had put it in the reticule for safekeeping.

Ode to Evelyn Grey, it read, *the beauty of Buckingham, the angel of England, the lark to my soul. How I dream of you, think of you, wait anxiously for a mere glimpse of you . . .*

She lowered the letter and stared out the window a moment. Pierce had a way of making her feel wanted and admired. She hadn't realized how much she needed that.

It occurred to her that Nathan might see the letter— or Frances would tell him of it—so she folded the letter, returned it to the reticule, and drew the reticule shut.

She wondered what time it was. The realization that she'd likely lost Pierce saddened her as much as it exhausted her, but she couldn't sleep in this infernal contraption of a coach, at least not more than a bit. The constant jostling didn't seem to bother Frances, she was pleased to see after a time. He was slumped in the corner of the squabs, his mouth slightly open.

Evelyn was at last able to drift off, but was awakened by a rude jolt that bounced her head against the wall.

"Ouch," she muttered, pushing herself up and pressing a hand to the side of her head. The coach had come to a dead stop. She leaned toward the window to look out, and saw nothing but barren trees and gathering clouds. Her feet were cold, too. The coals in the warmer beneath the seat had gone out. She folded her arms around her for warmth and looked at Frances.

He was sleeping in a ball, his coat pulled tightly about him. Evelyn reached carefully to the box below him and withdrew a lap rug, which she proceeded to lay over him, tucking it around his body.

When she'd finished, she held herself as tightly as she could and looked out the window again.

The door was suddenly flung open and cold, gray light streamed inside. The coach dipped to one side with Nathan's weight as he climbed aboard and settled across from Evelyn, next to the sleeping boy, his long legs touching hers. He brushed his hat from his head, tossed it onto the bench beside Evelyn. She looked at the hat, then at Nathan.

"It's rather cold in here, is it not?" he said, glancing around at the silk-covered walls and the velvet squabs. He glanced at Frances and smiled warmly as he tucked the lap rug a little tighter about him. When he was satisfied that Frances was properly covered, he looked at Evelyn. "You're cold."

"I'm perfectly fine," she lied, and gestured toward the door. "Ride your horse, sir—there is not enough room within for all of us."

Nathan flashed a roguish grin that had always made her weak in the knees, and rapped on the ceiling, signaling the driver on.

"You cannot think to join us!" she whispered loudly. Her response was the lurch of the coach as it suddenly moved forward. *"Lord,"* she muttered, sagging against the squabs. *"Must* you?"

"I must. I've not seen you in three years, Evie."

That small endearment—his pet name for her—had a surprisingly strong effect on her. "Don't call me that," she said.

Nathan shrugged, propped one foot against the bench next to her. "Very well, my Lady Lindsey. Your wish is my command."

"If my wish were your command, I would be in

London and not on some country lane hurtling along to my fate."

He laughed softly.

She yanked her cloak away from his boot and scooted closer to the window.

Nathan's gaze drifted upward. He cocked his head to one side and peered curiously at her head.

"What?" she asked self-consciously, and put a hand to her head. Her bonnet, she realized, was askew. She yanked it off and tossed it down on top of his hat, then once more folded her arms across her body and looked out the window. She'd forgotten how much the temperature could vary between London and the country. It was downright frigid in the interior of the coach.

"You are cold," Nathan said again.

"I am *fine*."

"I can plainly see you are shivering."

"Yes. Yes, I am. But from fury. Not the cold."

"That is quite a case of fury."

"You have no idea," she muttered beneath her breath, and glanced out the window again.

Nathan reached across the coach and removed the two hats. In one graceful movement, he switched places with the hats, settling in beside her.

"No!" she whispered loudly, moving away from him. "Go back!" she demanded, pointing to the empty seat beside Frances.

"*Sssh,*" Nathan said. He put his arm around her shoulders, drawing her in close.

"Stop that!" She slapped at his hand and his leg, but it was no use. Had he always been so solid and immovable?

"You may as well enjoy the ride," Nathan said, and

pulled his cloak across her body, tucking her in beneath it and next to his long, firm body. "I've no intention of going anywhere."

It *was* warmer beneath his heavy cloak. If she hadn't been so furious with him, she might have actually appreciated the warmth. She was reminded of their first Christmas together. They had traveled four miles to dine at the home of the closest gentry, Mr. and Mrs. DuPaul—the same Alexandra DuPaul who Evelyn had considered a friend and who would later betray Evelyn—but on that particular night, on the drive home it had begun to snow, and Nathan had taken off his cloak, arranged it around them, and held her in his arms. They'd laughed at the plumes of their breath. *"It is just as I always suspected. You are all wind, sir,"* she'd teased him. *"You didn't think I was all wind last night,"* he'd said, nuzzling her neck.

If there was one place where she and Nathan were in perfect harmony, it was his bed. His big, soft, bed . . .

The memory of it gave her a deeper sort of chill, and Nathan's arm tightened around her. "Why must you make this so difficult?" she groaned.

"I don't believe I am the one who is making this so difficult. You are being unduly peevish."

He said it so congenially that Evelyn wanted to punch him. *"Peevish*? I have been abducted from my home and hied halfway across the country!"

"Now, now," he said, as if she were a child. "You were abducted from the street, not your home, which, I might also point out, is Eastchurch Abbey and *not* the queen's house, as you seem to believe. And neither are you being hied halfway across England—we are within a day's drive to London."

"You know very well what I mean!"

"You are hardly bound for Perdition, Evelyn, at least not today. You are bound for home."

"For what *was* my home," she said petulantly. "I have not resided there in three years. It is nothing to me now but a place of wretched memories."

"Ah, how that warms my heart. If they are all truly wretched, then we must make an effort to create some pleasant memories," he said with a wink.

"Please," she muttered, and looked down at her lap. "There is nothing about that house that can ever be a pleasant memory."

He said nothing for a moment, but when he did speak, his voice was low and soothing. "You are not the only one who misses him, Evie. I miss him, too."

He was referring to their son, their beautiful son, who died at the age of fifteen months. He'd been a sickly baby, and the last fever had come upon him so quickly that he was, for all intents and purposes, lost to them before the doctor arrived. They could do nothing but wait four agonizing days for his death. Frankly, they had waited fifteen months for his death—but he'd been a beautiful boy, and she—*they*—had loved him dearly.

Evelyn swallowed down an unexpected whimper of grief. Not a day passed that she didn't think of Robbie. But the raw grief, the grief that had once clawed at her throat every waking hour, had subsided with time. In its place was a distant and dull pain, an ache that pulsed weakly but persistently at the bottom of her heart.

She feared Eastchurch Abbey would bring that excruciating pain back to her. Not just the death of her son, but the implosion of their fragile marriage under the weight of his death as well. Their marriage, which was based on the compatibility of fortune and privilege, had strengthened with Robbie. But with his death had come a cold distance that only deepened with time to the point that Evelyn's resentments and fears and hurts had nailed her heart firmly closed.

"You can't avoid Eastchurch forever," Nathan said a bit curtly.

"You obviously don't understand, Nathan. This isn't merely about *missing* him," she said bitterly. "It's about you, too. You are a *roué*. You'd rather hunt and . . . and cat about. We were never really meant for one another."

She could feel him stiffen. "And you would rather carp, is that it?"

No, that wasn't it at all, but her inability to explain herself clearly had always been her failure with Nathan. She wouldn't try now, and turned her head and bit her lower lip against the tears that burned the back of her eyelids.

"Perhaps," he said shortly, "your journey to Perdition might be hastened along to its conclusion if you tell me why you might be involved in the scandal surrounding the prince."

"I've *told* you, I don't know why."

"When was the last time you were in the prince's company?" Nathan pressed.

"Several times of late," Evelyn said irritably. "But what does it matter? You know as well as I that the prince surrounds himself with dozens of people. The last time I was in his company, a pageant was performed in his apartments," she admitted. "It was really awful, about a large woman who made love to a variety of men, and then . . ." Evelyn frowned as she recalled the vulgarity of that pageant.

"And then?"

"And then she . . . the woman produced a doll as if she'd just given birth. It was very distasteful, but the prince laughed."

Nathan seemed not to think much of it. "Did you overhear any talk? Did you speak to him?"

She shook her head. "I conversed with Mrs. Fitzherbert most of the night, actually about nothing more exciting than a new modiste in London. I rarely spoke to the prince directly, and even then, only in passing."

"I see," Nathan said, but Evelyn could tell from the timbre of his voice he didn't see at all. He didn't believe her. That pricked at her, and she tried to move away, but Nathan held her close. "Stay warm. You'll catch your death of cold—"

The sudden shouts startled them both; the coach rumbled to an awkward halt. "What is it?" Evelyn asked.

Nathan leaned up and glanced out the window.

"Highwaymen, my lord!" the driver called down.

"Damnation," Nathan uttered. "We're being robbed."

"What?" Evelyn cried, rousing Frances from his sleep.

The coach suddenly began to rock; there was quite a lot of shouting, and then the coach was still. "Everyone step out!" someone outside shouted.

Evelyn's first thought was Frances, who was scrambling to sit up and look out the window.

"Stand back, Frances," Nathan said sternly as he lifted his trouser leg and withdrew a pistol from his boot.

"Nathan!" Evelyn exclaimed as she moved to sit next to Frances and gather him in her arms. "What are you about to do?"

He responded by taking aim at the door, then leaning back and kicking the door open with his foot at almost the same moment he fired. The next moment, he had vaulted out the door.

Evelyn's basic instinct to survive propelled her to the floor of the coach with Frances, her body on top of his. Men were shouting and several more shots were fired from what sounded like a variety of guns. Frances twisted out from beneath her and peered out the open door, but Evelyn pulled him back from the opening.

Within moments, it was over. The robbers had fled into the woods, one of them clinging to the pommel of his saddle, shot in the side, as eagerly reported by Frances.

Frances escaped Evelyn and leapt from the coach when one of the coachmen called "*all clear.*" Evelyn reluctantly followed him.

The Lindsey men seemed all accounted for, milling about, clapping one another on the shoulder. Frances was squatting next to several dark drops of blood. "Milord! You shot one of them!" he said excitedly.

"It would seem that I did," Nathan said soberly, and pulled the boy up and away from the blood. "Jenks!" he called to the driver. Evelyn looked at Jenks, noticed his arm hung strangely at his side, and realized he'd been shot, too.

"How bad is it?" Nathan asked, bending a little to see the wound.

"I'll be all right, milord," Jenks said, a little uncertainly.

Evelyn looked about for something to bandage his arm, and remembered a clean handkerchief in her reticule. It was a gift from Princess Mary, embroidered by her own hand. Evelyn returned to the coach to fetch it, then marched to where Jenks was sitting, determined to be of use.

"Feels a bit strange, but I'll be no worse for the wear," Jenks said unconvincingly. He was growing pale.

Evelyn reached for his arm. "I'm going to bind it tightly, Mr. Jenkins, to stop the flow of blood."

"Ah, mu'um," he said, shaking his head. "You don't need to do that."

"Do as she says, Jenks," Nathan said sternly, and helped Jenks remove his coat.

Evelyn wrapped the handkerchief around his arm and bound it tightly. When she was convinced there was nothing more she could do for him, they managed to get his coat back on him.

"Fred, you'll handle the ribbons and ride postilion, will you?" Nathan said to a coachman, and helped Jenks to his feet. "You, sir, will ride on the bench. We'll have you properly tended when we reach the abbey," he promised. "All right then, lads, let's have everything in order and continue on, and be quick about it for Jenks's sake." He gestured for Frances to return to the coach.

"May I ride with Jenks, milord?" Frances asked eagerly. "I'll mind him properly, I will."

"I'd not mind the help, milord," Jenks said when Nathan looked at him.

Nathan nodded, and as Frances scrambled up ahead of Jenks, Nathan cupped Evelyn's elbow and steered her into the coach. He followed her inside, settling in beside her on the bench and pulling his cloak over them once more before rapping on the ceiling to send them on.

"Highwaymen!" Evelyn exclaimed, still in a bit of shock.

"They are a scourge in these parts," Nathan said.

"They are as thick as grass and strike with alarming regularity."

"Will they come back for us?"

"They are halfway to France now, you may trust me." He smiled reassuringly and put his arm around her shoulders, drawing her into his side again.

She did not fight it. "I'm allowing you to do that only because you saved my life," she warned him.

"Aha, a small victory," he said, and leaned his head back and closed his eyes.

As they bobbed and swayed down that awful road, Evelyn didn't mean to fall asleep, but in the safety of Nathan's arms, when she felt herself sliding into it, she didn't have the strength to stop herself.

He knew she was sleeping when her body sagged into his. The feel of her body against his reminded him of the nights he'd spent in her bed and the passion they'd shared. As he rearranged his cloak around her, he could picture her holding herself above him, her hands braced against his bare chest, her breasts hanging like ripe fruit, and her gold, wavy hair spilling around her shoulders as she rode him.

The highwaymen were forgotten, replaced by her voice echoing in his head. *We were never meant for one another, you and I . . .*

Those words resounded ridiculously in his mind. It was passing strange, actually—the Lord knew they had said worse to each other at one time, but then, her words had bounced off him.

Today, her words made him feel hollow and old.

Her head lolled onto his chest with a delicate snore;

lashes fanned out against her cheeks and her lips parted slightly. She was exhausted.

Unfortunately, the roads had been pitted with the autumn rains, making the ride quite rough. He thought of poor Jenks above and realized he was a fool for believing Wilkes when he said this road through Cricklade was the quickest. He tried to keep Evelyn from bouncing by holding her tight, but his efforts were useless. Yet nothing could wake her, and for that, he couldn't help but smile.

That was another thing he knew about his wife—she could sleep through a cyclone. Worse, she was a horrible thief of the bed linens and covers. How many times had he awakened, shivering and naked, while she slept soundly in the cocoon she'd made?

Eventually, the coach turned into the three thousand acres that made up the estate of Eastchurch Abbey. It was quite late, but Nathan knew when they passed by the ruins of the old Cistercian abbey for which the estate was named and continued down a tree-lined road. As they neared the iron gates that marked the main house—a redbrick, ivy-covered mansion—they passed the church and the churchyard where their son was buried.

As was his habit, Nathan looked in the opposite direction. He would give all if he could take that pain from Evelyn. He would have given his own life if it might have saved his son.

Alas, nothing he could have done would have saved Robert or Evelyn. He couldn't have stopped it, and Robert's death and Evelyn's despair had broken him into pieces. He'd been so broken he'd not had the strength to wrestle cherub angels, and his fear and sadness and inability to surmount emotions that he *knew* were surmountable had humiliated him. It had taken months, years, to rid himself of that helpless, useless feeling.

He couldn't fix the damage done then, but as he looked down at the top of Evelyn's golden head on his chest, he dared to hope that perhaps he could fix it now.

chapter seven

E velyn had a visceral reaction when she walked
across the threshold of her home for the first time
in three years. It was one o'clock in the morning, but in
spite of the late hour, Benton was instantly on hand, still
a model of decorum with his clean-shaven face and pris-
tine clothing. He hardly seemed surprised to see her, but
then again, the earth could spin away from the sun and
Benton would remain stolid. "It is my great pleasure to
welcome you home, my lady."

"Thank you, Benton. It's good to see you."

"Shall I show you to your suite?"

Her suite was directly adjacent to Nathan's through
a pair of sitting rooms, and Evelyn's heart ticked up a
notch at the suggestion. "No, no," she said hastily. "Is
there another suite, perhaps?"

"She would sooner be hanged than be so near to me,
Benton. Put her in the suite next to the nursery—"

That suggestion stabbed her heart. Her son had died
in the nursery. "No!" she said hastily. She couldn't go

near it. She could never see that room again. She could feel her hands start to shake as Benton and Nathan looked at her. "M-my suite will be fine, Benton."

"Very good, madam." He pivoted and began walking.

With a glare for Nathan, Evelyn reluctantly followed the butler.

They moved through the main corridor and public rooms by the light of a candelabra Benton held high. But even in that light, Evelyn could see bits and pieces of furnishings were missing, and some things looked a bit drab. There were two pairs of boots in the corridor, which she thought odd, and on one table, the sort of basket one might take fishing to hold the catch, a pair of fishing poles, and a stack of curling, yellowed newsprint.

The house, the beautiful, grand mansion, had been turned into a hunting lodge!

Fortunately, Evelyn's suite was exactly as she'd left it: pale blue walls, heavy floral drapes. The canopied bed with the intricately embroidered bedcovering, a wedding gift from her aunt. It seemed almost as if no one had entered the room since the day she'd left it.

The moment Benton left her alone, Evelyn collapsed onto the chaise and covered her face, trying to catch her breath, trying not to see her son in every corner of this room. Trying not to think of the horrible, wretched argument she and Nathan had had in this very room the night she told him she wanted to go to London.

"*I don't understand—you sit in the dark and stare out the window, or make a spectacle of yourself, and suddenly, you want to go to London?*" he'd railed at her. "*I have tried and tried to reach you, Evie, but you have shut me out! You move as a ghost through these halls, you shirk your duty as mistress and wife, and yet you want me to understand that now you must suddenly be in London!"*

"I should rather sit in the dark than spend my days gambling and hunting and carrying on like a libertine! We may as well admit it—we are irretrievably broken down!"

"No, not we, Evelyn. You. Go. Go to London! I'll be glad to see you gone."

Memories came rushing at her, one after the other, all of them overwhelming. Evelyn stood and walked to the middle of the room, hugging herself. She really didn't know what to do. She was too restless to sleep, too tired to think.

She moved again, sitting heavily on the edge of her bed. She was shivering again—nothing overt or anything a casual observer could detect, but from some place deep inside. Apprehension churned in her belly, along with desire, confusion, loathing, and fear, all of it mixing in one toxic brew.

The history that lived within these walls surrounded her, suffocating her. She could feel it, seeping in under the doors and through the windows, spreading like a bloodstain across her path.

Robbie, beautiful Robbie. She could almost hear his laugh. She could picture him running to her as fast as he could manage on his chubby little legs, his arms held out for balance, his toes pointed in so that he rocked from side to side in his haste.

And his cough, a cough that had plagued him from birth.

Evelyn dropped her head and closed her eyes, trying to recall his face. It was slowly but surely fading from her memory. He had the blue eyes of his father,

her gold hair. But she couldn't remember his smile—hard as she tried, it was as if she was looking through a veil. *What did his smile look like?* How was it that she could forget something as cherished as his smile, but remember with such stinging clarity that early spring day when the weather held after days of cold rain and weak sunshine had allowed them in the garden? The gamekeeper had brought round a pair of puppies that would be trained as hunting dogs. Robbie had squatted, holding his hands out for their lapping tongues. He'd laughed, and the rattle in his chest had made Evelyn turn.

Robbie turned around. *"Mam-ma!"* he'd said happily, but all she had seen was the bright glow of fever shining in his eyes, turning his cheeks rosy.

She couldn't say how she'd known—call it a mother's instinct or perhaps a nudge from the heavens above—but she'd dropped the basket into which she was putting cuttings and run to her son. She could never forget the way his skin felt when she touched her mouth to his forehead. He'd been burning with fever. *Burning, burning.*

Evelyn squeezed her eyes shut. Would she ever stop reliving that moment? Would she ever stop dreaming about his bright, fevered eyes? In this house, how could she? Robbie was everywhere. Her failed marriage was everywhere. And perhaps the cruelest curse of all—when she looked at Nathan, she saw Robbie.

There was only one way she might survive until she could return to London. Avoid all the places—and people—in this house that reminded her of Robbie. Don her blinders, never look back, only forward. She could endure this indeterminate exile only if she could avoid her past. And by God, if she could survive the death of her child, she could surely survive Nathan.

Donnelly and Lambourne, two of Nathan's three perennial house guests, were surprised to see Nathan when he strolled into the billiards room with whiskey in hand, judging by their twin expressions. Perhaps because they'd expected him to be away longer. Or perhaps because they were in the presence of two attractive young women, sisters from Eastchurch, the daughters of the village cobbler. Nathan's phaeton had been dispatched frequently of late to retrieve them to the abbey.

"Lindsey! Good evening, lad!" Lambourne, slightly taller than Donnelly, with coal-black hair and vivid gray eyes, cheerfully clapped Nathan's shoulder. "Did London no' appeal to you, then?"

"At least as much as having a broken bone set," Nathan drawled, and sipped from his glass. It was his third whiskey, following the two he'd had in the privacy of his study after Evelyn had balked at having her old suite of rooms connected to his.

He'd watched her following Benton like a doomed prisoner, and he, in turn, had retreated to numb the headache that resulted from a very long day in which he'd abducted his wife, fought highwaymen, and then experienced the feel of a woman's body next to his.

It had felt so damn right, so bloody natural.

And now, the whiskey had gone to his head, that was all. Contrary to his reputation as a libertine—which he'd certainly once been—he'd long since lost his desire for drink to numb himself completely.

Even a long, hot bath had done nothing to relax him. He felt like his old broken self, just arms and limbs moving disjointedly through space with no cohesive thought.

He smiled at the two young women. "Good evening, Miss Franklin. Miss Sarah," he said, slurring the latter's name a little.

The two sisters curtsied in perfect unison.

"And what have you done with Wilkes?" Donnelly asked as he extended his hand. His golden brown hair and brown eyes were unusual for an Irishman. "Left him aside of the road, I'd suspect, ogling a wench in a public house."

"He remained in London," Nathan said. "He had unfinished business."

"Unfinished," Lambourne scoffed. "A game he could no' pass up, aye? No man enjoys a wager quite as much as he, especially at the prince's table."

"One man's vice is another man's curse, Jack," Donnelly said. "He gambles. He's not got the gift of strutting about like a bloody peacock to win the charms of ladies like you, has he?"

"*Ach*, Declan," Lambourne laughed. "There's a persistent twinge of jealousy in your voice, lad."

Donnelly snorted and retrieved a billiard cue from the wall rack and held it out to Nathan. "Will you join us?"

Anything to shut them up. Nathan shrugged and caught the cue Donnelly tossed him. He put aside his whiskey, ran the cue between his fingers. "Stand aside, lads," he said, and winked at the Franklin sisters, who both giggled in response.

Unfortunately, Nathan wasn't much of a billiard player this evening—Donnelly took the first match and

Nathan finished his whiskey. Donnelly took the second match and Nathan poured an uncharacteristic fourth whiskey as he flirted shamelessly with the youngest Franklin sister. How old was she, he wondered as she prattled on about some church social. Seventeen years? Perhaps eighteen? *Eighteen* . . . the age Evelyn had been when he'd married her.

"How did you find London?" the young woman asked.

He didn't want to be reminded of London. "I found it ridiculously close," he said, moving away from her to take his turn. "The entire city is caught in the grip of the scandal—one is either firmly in the camp of the prince, or firmly in the camp of the princess, and everyone eagerly awaits the next bit of titillating gossip like vultures at a hunt."

"Gossip?" one of the girls asked.

"Who is bedding who, love," Donnelly offered helpfully.

The two young women exchanged a wide-eyed look, but were obviously enthralled with the prospect of royal gossip, and turned eagerly to Nathan.

Nathan focused on the older one. Specifically, her bosom. Small, he thought. He preferred a woman with some curves. Evelyn had curves. "Seems like there is hardly a soul in London who isn't caught in the vice of adultery," he said, surprising himself. "It is my impression that everyone in the company of the royal family has the morals of a bloody snake," he said, and punctuated that remark with a horrible shot. He studied the table a moment, his thoughts wandering to Evelyn.

It took him a moment to realize no one was responding, and that in fact, Donnelly had cleared his throat twice now. Nathan glanced up; all heads were turned toward the door.

He knew instinctively what they saw and felt like a boy caught looking up a woman's dress. "*Bloody hell*," he muttered, and turned around to face his wife.

Evelyn was standing framed in the doorway, wearing her traveling gown of russet gold and red. He noticed a few spots of blood near the hem of the gown. Her expression was impassive as she calmly surveyed the room. She had a regal bearing now, a stark contrast to the young bride who used to fly into the room and kiss him, whether it was appropriate or not.

Nathan was vaguely aware that Donnelly and Lambourne were bowing, that the Franklin sisters were curtsying. "My lady, please forgive our ill manners," Lambourne said. "His lordship had no' mentioned you'd come home."

"How surprising," she said as she took in the Franklin sisters, her hazel gaze now glistening with ire. "I should think he'd be about the business of bragging how he abducted me from the streets of London." At the gentlemen's looks of surprise she smiled coolly. "No? Then certainly he mentioned how he thwarted a robbery?"

"Aye?" Lambourne asked, looking at Nathan.

"He likewise failed to mention we had guests," Evelyn continued, "or I would have been down to greet you sooner." She smiled then, a pretty, warm smile. "How good to see you again, my lords Donnelly and Lambourne. And look at you, Miss Franklin, Sarah, all grown up."

"Thank you, my lady," the elder sister murmured.

Evelyn walked into the room, still smiling, but her eyes were trained on the Franklins. "Shall I have a car-

riage brought round for you?" she politely asked Miss
Franklin. "The hour has grown so late. I am certain your
mother is frantic for your safe return."

"Oh no, mu'um—"

The older stopped the younger from saying more with
a sly hand to her arm. "Thank you, my lady, that is most
kind." With a sharp look for her younger sister, Miss
Franklin curtsied. "Good night." She took her sister in
hand and moved to the door. Her sister reluctantly allowed herself to be pulled along.

"I'll call for a carriage, then," Lambourne said quickly.

Donnelly must have thought to help him do it, because he moved to offer his arm to the older sister. The
four of them went out, dancing around Evelyn, who
smiled and nodded as they left. When they were gone,
only Nathan, Evelyn, and a footman who looked positively dumbstruck by her presence remained.

Evelyn glanced at the poor man.

Nathan gestured lamely. "Wilson, meet your mistress,
Lady Lindsey. She is home for a time."

"Oh, I am certain the news has already traveled
downstairs, my lord," Evelyn said cheerfully. "How do
you do, Mr. Wilson?"

"Ah . . . very well, mu'um."

"That will be all, Wilson," Nathan said.

Wilson bowed and hurried from the room, stealing a
glimpse of Evelyn from the corner of his eye as he went.

When he'd departed, Evelyn picked up a billiard
cue. Nathan was reminded of the time he'd taught her
to play. *"It won't do for a lady to play billiards,"* he'd said,
standing behind her, his hands on her waist. *"This must
be our secret."*

"I adore our secrets," Evelyn had said, and giggled as

he'd cupped her breasts when she bent over to try her hand.

She leaned over the table now, put the cue between her fingers, and expertly struck a ball. It glided into a pocket.

"Well," Nathan said with some surprise. "It would seem you have honed your skill at Buckingham."

"Not at Buckingham. The queen would never abide such a game."

"Then at Carlton House," he remarked as she moved around the table and examined the choice of billiard shots. "I rather doubt the prince has such lofty notions of propriety."

"It might surprise you to know that the atmosphere at Carlton House is often quite subdued," she said. "The Prince of Wales admires his sisters and is on his best behavior when they are about."

"He allows them to play billiards?"

She made another shot that landed squarely in the pocket. "Certainly not his *sisters*," she said pointedly, and smiled devilishly.

A variety of images of when and how Evelyn might have played billiards instantly sprang to Nathan's mind, the most prominent of them involving a host of gentlemen offering her their expertise in billiards—and other things—while the prince entertained the princesses.

Evelyn moved around the table and leaned over for another shot, revealing the line of a graceful arm, the curve of her breast, her slender back. An unwelcome ribbon of desire uncurled in Nathan. He did not want to desire her. He did not want to think of coupling with her. *Cue ball*, he thought. *Cue ball, cue ball, think of cue balls*. "It hardly seems proper for a lady of an exalted royal bedchamber to indulge in billiards, either," he said.

"Oh?" Evelyn said lightly. "I suppose Londoners aren't as provincial as the queen or country gentry." She glanced at him sidelong. "In London, a bit of sport between ladies and gentlemen is expected. I would think you'd know that."

His pulse leaped with resentment. "I know that a bit more circumspection should be expected."

Evelyn laughed and moved again, this time passing so close to him that her skirts brushed his trousers. "That's a rather amusing sentiment coming from the Libertine of Lindsey." She paused and looked thoughtfully at him. "Correct me if I am wrong, my lord, but it *was* you, was it not, who hosted the infamous grouse shoot that ended with one gentleman shot in the foot, and the only game bagged a prized bantam rooster and his proverbial farmer's daughter? I seem to recall that delightful tale circulating about London more than once."

Nathan gave her a withering look. "That is not precisely what happened, if it matters. Surely you do not expect me to control everything that happens in the shire."

"No . . . but I would hope as the earl, you could control at least a *bit* of it. Really, Nathan, the *Franklin* sisters?" She leaned over, made another shot. The ball just missed the pocket and rolled to the middle of the table.

"Did you come down here to persecute me?" he asked irritably—and, if he'd admit it, a little guiltily. It was true—there had been some rather raucous affairs at the abbey. But he'd been numb, so numb, drinking in order not to think or care—

"My, my," Evelyn said with a laugh. "*You're* rather cross. I didn't come to persecute you, Nathan. I came to ask if a trunk of my clothes might be found, as I was abducted without my things, and to inquire what happened to the French secretary that was in my suite. I should like it returned along with vellum and ink, if you please."

Nathan eyed her skeptically. "Vellum and ink?"

"Is that a problem?" she asked sweetly, turning to face him.

He abruptly put down his cue and walked around the table to where she stood, pausing directly before her, so close that Evelyn was compelled to back up against the billiards table. But she lifted her chin, her eyes glittering, and Nathan had the distinct impression that she relished a challenge.

"Not in the least," he said as his gaze drifted down the long, smooth column of her neck. "As has always been the case in our marriage, you may have whatever you need or desire. I suppose you intend to correspond with Princess Mary?"

"Of course. We are friends, as you know."

He admired her luscious décolletage and asked, "Is there anyone *else* with whom you intend to correspond?"

Evelyn smiled impishly and fingered the small locket at the hollow of her throat that contained a lock of Robert's hair. That was something else Nathan knew about his wife. She would fidget with her necklace or earring when she was nervous or on the verge of dissembling.

"I have other acquaintances in London. I might write to them as well," she said with a shrug.

"Ah," he said, and stepped so close to her that he had to straddle the skirt of her gown. He leaned forward; Evelyn leaned back. Nathan smiled, placed his hands on the edge of the billiard table on either side of

her, and forced her back even more. She caught herself
with a hand braced against the table and held tightly to
the cue.

"Who else, Evelyn?" he asked, his gaze on her mouth.

"Why? Do you intend to censor my letters?"

"Should I?" he asked as his gaze drifted down again
to the swell of her breasts, rising so delectably with her
breath.

"It is none of your concern with whom I correspond."

"Perhaps. But if I discover you are corresponding
recklessly, or adding to the scandal into which you've already put us—" He looked up. "In *any* way . . ." He lifted
his hand, stroked a bit of hair from her temple. "I shall
have your pretty head on a platter. Do you quite understand me?"

Instead of the anger or indignation he fully expected,
his very alluring wife smiled seductively. Her gaze
drifted to his mouth, stirring up the ribbon of desire in
him again. "Just so that we are perfectly clear," she asked
politely, "are you *threatening* me?"

"No threat, my love," he said, caressing her neck and
the curve of her shoulder. "Just the most sincere approx-
imation of what will happen should I discover the *slightest* bit of duplicity in you. You may think this national
scandal is some sort of jest, but I assure you, it is very
serious. I won't allow you to harm the Lindsey name or
holdings any more than you may have, no matter what
you say or want."

She chuckled low, obviously relishing his challenge.

He relished her, damn it.

With his knuckle, he traced a light line across her
collarbone. He could feel her tense beneath his touch.

"And while you hold me hostage here, I suppose you

will continue to host your billiard parties with girls from the village?"

He could hardly guess what he might expect now that she was under his roof again. He carelessly flicked the gold locket with his finger. "If I do, you shall be the consummate hostess. You are home now, and you will behave as a countess. God knows your father paid for that right."

Evelyn cocked a brow. "Oh, how very charming. By the bye, you never had rules before."

"Perhaps I never appreciated my responsibilities as much as I do now." He spoke to her mouth, to her perfect lips that when curved into a smile, ended in a single dimple in her right cheek. He mindlessly stroked her skin from the hollow of her throat to her cleavage. "Mind yourself, Evelyn," he said low, and palmed the top of her breast. Her smooth skin was warm; he could feel the breast begin to swell, and the ribbon of desire turned into a serpent, striking at his groin.

"Are you attempting to seduce me?" she asked softly.

"Don't tempt me, darling. I am foxed, and I've missed my wife dreadfully."

He thought he might have imagined the little shiver in her—he would never be entirely certain, for Evelyn suddenly brought the cue up perpendicular between them, holding it in both hands, and pushed hard against him, knocking him off balance.

"What's wrong, Evie? Do you fear you might *be* seduced?"

"Not surprisingly, your estimation of your allure is quite large and grand."

"There was a time you thought so. There was a time I could have brought you to me and made you purr like a kitten with a single caress," he said, and caressed the rise of her breast, then cupped it in his hand.

"I was but a naïve girl then. Now, I am a woman who knows men like you."

"Indeed?" he asked, moving his hand to the other breast. "You had that many lovers in London?"

"You'll never know, for unlike you, I am very discreet." She shoved hard, but Nathan merely smiled.

"Do you honestly believe you can keep me from your bed?"

"Oh," she said, smiling dangerously, "I *know* I can." She shoved him again, hard enough that he took a step backward. She tossed the cue onto the billiards table and glided to the door, where she paused. Her gaze swept the length of him and she smiled saucily. "Good night, Nathan." She went out before he had an opportunity to speak again.

Nathan bent over the billiard table a moment, then straightened up and looked down at the hand that had touched her skin, her breast. He stared at it, closing his fingers tightly, opening them, and closing them tightly again.

With the same hand, he suddenly picked up the cue she'd left and hurled it at the wall, bringing some of the game's accoutrements crashing down.

chapter eight

Her first night at home was a long and restless one, but Evelyn was determined to put the best face on her predicament. She was not the same meek little flower she'd been when she last lived there. She was stronger. She knew how to care for herself.

But now, having seen Nathan in the billiard room—his dark hair mussed, his neckcloth undone, and that look in his blue eyes—that *look*—Evelyn had no place to escape.

She was, she had to admit, disappointingly ill-prepared for guarding herself against him. How alarming to discover that after all this time, he could still tantalize her so completely!

How was it possible that after all these years, Nathan's touch could have such a reverberating effect on her?

The events of the last twenty-four hours had befuddled her to the point she could not sleep.

Evelyn was up and dressed in an old gown still hanging in the wardrobe, and had startled the young woman—Maude, Evelyn remembered—who had entered her room with a cup of hot chocolate in hand.

"Good morning, Maude," Evelyn said, taking the cup from her before the poor thing dropped it.

Maude dipped a curtsy.

Evelyn could hardly fault the maid's surprise—they all knew her to be a heavy sleeper and one who was seldom up at dawn, if ever. Not to mention she'd appeared from what must seem like nowhere after three years.

Maude seemed nervous. She cast her gaze to the carpet as she spoke. "His lordship said I am to dress your hair or help you as I can until your ladies' maid arrives from London."

"Did he?" Evelyn asked cheerfully. "Then I suppose you might help me make myself presentable to his lordship and his guests for breakfast." She would carry on as expected—she'd never allow Nathan to see how he had affected her. She would never allow him to believe he had somehow gained the upper hand.

"Oh, but his lordship has gone away for the day," Maude said.

He'd *gone*? "Pardon?"

"Aye. He and Lord Lambourne. Lord Donnelly—" Maude smiled a little. "Lord Donnelly will sleep until luncheon if he's allowed by the others."

"Where has Lindsey gone?" Evelyn demanded, feeling a bit slighted on her first day back in Eastchurch. She would have thought such a momentous occasion would require some . . . some *notice*.

"I wouldn't rightly know, mu'um," Maude said as she picked up a hairbrush.

"That's Lindsey for you," Evelyn muttered angrily. "He hasn't changed at all!"

Maude looked startled. "But . . . but he has changed, mu'um," she said as Evelyn took a seat at the vanity. When Evelyn didn't respond, Maude relaxed a bit. "Not outwardly," she amended, "but in the little things. He's not the same as he was." She blushed and smiled sheepishly. "Listen to me, prattling on, mu'um. I surely don't need to tell *you.*"

Yes, *yes*, she did need to tell her—tell her everything! Who *was* Nathan now? Evelyn smiled at Maude's reflection. "I've not seen my husband in three years, Maude, so please do tell me. I am curious, how has he changed?"

The maid blinked with surprise. "Oh I mean naught by it, mu'um," she quickly backtracked. "Just that his lordship and his friends, they don't hunt as they used to, and Mr. Brady—that's the gamekeeper—he says the boars are so thick on the lower acreage they are devouring the crops."

That was hard to imagine. Nathan was an avid hunter, perhaps one of the best in all of England.

"And he's been away quite a lot," Maude continued. "I suppose that's why he let some things like the orangery go to seed."

Evelyn yelped with surprise. "The *orangery*? My pride and joy?" It was beautiful, full of miniature topiary orange trees from France, with a cozy sitting area on the terrace just outside the French doors. She'd often used the setting for garden tea parties in the spring. "But what of the orange trees? What happened to them?"

"All gone," Maude said, her eyes wide. "Sold, I think."

He'd *sold* her orange trees? She'd bought that group of topiaries shortly after Robbie died. Frankly, she'd gone through a period where she'd spent quite a lot of money—furnishings, clothing, the orangery—but at the time, she told herself it was a needed diversion, something to take her mind from the death of her son. Looking back on it, it seemed more like an obsession, as if she were trying to fill some invisible hole.

Nevertheless, the orangery had turned out beautifully, and the day the orange trees had arrived, Nathan had stood in the drive, his feet braced apart, his face darkening as each tree was unloaded from the wagon.

"You said I could have whatever I wanted," she'd reminded him sharply, anticipating his protest. He'd told her that in the course of a heated argument they'd had when she'd complained of his constant absences. *"You are always gone from here, and I know with whom!"* she'd shouted at him.

"Anywhere is far better than being here with you," he'd snapped. *"You are never happy, Evelyn!"*

It was true, she was never happy, but Lord God, she'd tried. *"I am trying! What am I to do?"* she'd demanded angrily.

"For heaven's sake, I know not! Get out! Visit friends! Go to Bath with your sister and take the waters, I hardly care, just do something!"

"And listen to you scold me for spending—"

"In exchange for your silence, Evelyn, you may have whatever you want."

"In exchange for your freedom is what you mean, isn't it?"

It had gone on from there, the endless arguing.

But of all the meaningless things she'd tried to console herself with, things and activities and vices that could not fill the weeping gash across her heart, the orangery had been her haven.

Evelyn looked at Maude's reflection in the mirror as she wound her hair into a chignon on the back of Evelyn's head. "He's away quite a lot, you say?"

Maude paused in the winding of Evelyn's hair and removed the pins from her mouth in a manner that suggested she enjoyed having information to impart. "Mr. Benton says his lordship doesn't like to be about when there is no one in residence, for he finds the place far too empty. It's as if he cannot bear to be alone here. He's had guests nigh on three months this time." She stuffed the pins back into her mouth.

Evelyn frowned. "And the Franklin sisters? Do they come around often?"

Maude removed the pins again. "Mary and Sarah Franklin?" She shook her head. "No, mu'um, I wouldn't know of the Franklin girls."

But as Evelyn's hair went up, Maude told her of the night Nathan and his friends had frightened a new chambermaid near unto death by playing a game of ghost, and that Mrs. Gillette, the housekeeper, had stumbled on Wilkes and a scullery maid in a rather compromising position. The scullery maid, Maude said, was no longer employed at Eastchurch Abbey, but in the home of the earl's sister in Birmingham, a ten-hour carriage ride from here.

That hardly surprised Evelyn. It fit with the many tales of debauchery at Eastchurch. Someone at court always delighted in telling her of the latest gambling debt or bawdy gathering.

When Maude had finished putting up her hair, Evelyn's head was spinning.

She had a solitary breakfast in the east dining room, staring out over the landscape as she dined. Benton was in attendance, stalwart butler that he was, and informed Evelyn that Nathan had gone into the village, but planned to return in time for the evening meal.

So he'd left her here, alone in this house of memories. He had no more regard for her feelings now than he did then.

"I need a secretary or a writing desk, Benton. I should like to post some letters."

"Yes, mu'um, his lordship so instructed me."

"And I should like a horse saddled."

"Yes, my lady."

Evelyn finished breakfast. With her shawl gathered tightly around her, she left the dining room. She walked carefully through the east wing, her gaze on the carpet runner in the hallway, refusing to look right or left. This was dangerous territory—there was the parlor, where she'd kept some of her son's favorite toys, and during afternoon tea, she would sit on the floor and play with him. There was the salon, where he'd gotten underfoot of one of the footmen and had sent the poor man tumbling to his bum. The family study, where he'd gotten into Papa's ink and marked the wall. It had taken two days and a bit of lye to get the ink off his fingers, but the marks, as far as she knew, remained on the wall.

That was enough. She couldn't allow herself to feel. She'd spent the last three years pushing down all those feelings just so she could bear the pain. If she began to feel again, she'd feel the ache again . . . *don't feel*, she chanted in her head as she walked along. *Don't feel*.

When Evelyn eventually reached her suite of rooms, her heart was palpitating. But she had survived it.

She changed into an old riding habit that she found in one of two trunks that had been brought up from storage. It was tight, but it would do. She made her way out onto the drive where a horse was indeed waiting for her. The air was crisp and cool, perfect for riding.

She used to love to ride the grounds. The estate was so large she would find a new trail every day. She struck out across the parkland, to where the river carved through valleys and the tenants farmed. It was late autumn, and the fields were mostly fallow, but she rode past tenants who were baling hay, others turning the dull brown top-soil over into the black, damp earth that would support new crops come the spring.

She admired the countryside, filled her lungs with the clean air. She gave her horse her head, letting her run freely up and down the sloping terrain. But she was careless—she didn't recognize some of the markers she'd once known as well as the back of her hand, and found herself on a crest overlooking the neighboring estate.

Evelyn reined the horse to a halt on the rise and looked down at the mansion where the DuPauls lived. She felt a prick of deep hurt that she'd thought was long gone. Alexandra DuPaul had been her friend, but when Robbie died, Evelyn could not find space in a heart overflowing with grief and rage for friends or family. It had been her great surprise, then, to ride up on this crest one morning and find her husband walking arm in arm with Alexandra, their heads bent together, so lost in one another that they barely noticed her on the path ahead.

Alexandra had tried to pretend they were merely walking and had invited Evelyn to join them. But Evelyn had seen the look in Nathan's eyes and knew she was intruding. She'd seen them together many times after that, always huddled together like lovers . . .

Part of her wanted to ride down there and announce that she had returned. But another part of her was too cowardly—she turned her horse around and headed back to the abbey.

Unfortunately, at the abbey, there was nothing to occupy her thoughts or her hands. She paced in her rooms a bit, feeling that thing, that restlessness in her chest. When she thought of her things arriving on the morrow as Benton said they would, she thought of how final that seemed. How would she return to London? When she thought of London and of Princess Mary, and Harriet, poor, sweet Harriet, and everyone between Buckingham and St. James's, she thought of Pierce.

Oh, but it was useless thinking of him now! No matter how high his regard for her, he'd not challenge Nathan openly for her! The moment Nathan had carried her off like a bag of seed, he'd destroyed her flirtation with Pierce. There was nothing she could do to change that. She was in her husband's house now, here in the bed that she'd made when she'd married Nathan ten years ago. *Don't feel.* She couldn't return to her marriage, it was impossible! She didn't *love* Nathan anymore.

She just wanted out.

There was no escape from her thoughts—until it suddenly occurred to her.

Evelyn looked up and smiled. "Benton!" she called, knowing full well he was out of earshot. Never mind that. She knew what she would do. The house looked like a young buck's hunting lodge. She would restore it to its glory.

With pencil and paper, Benton accompanied Evelyn from room to room in the main corridor, the part of the house most frequented by guests and visitors, and distinct from the wing where the family rooms were situated.

Evelyn dictated notes: they would remove the draperies and have them cleaned, and if the stench of tobacco was not removed, she would have new draperies made. They determined that the carpet in the petite salon just off the foyer would need to be replaced, as mud had been tracked onto it once too often.

They had moved into the green salon—a less formal but larger receiving salon—when a pair of footmen carried in a rickety old secretary for Evelyn's perusal.

She stood with her hands on her hips, gaping at the thing.

"There you are, madam," Benton said with a thin smile. "A place to pen your letters."

"Yes . . . but the secretary I had before was made of cherrywood. And it had these lovely gold inlaid scrolls," she said, painting a scroll with her hand in the air. "Where is *that* secretary, Benton?"

"That secretary has been sent up to the Marchioness of Sudley."

"To the marchioness?" Her mother-in-law had quite a lot of secretaries, as Evelyn recalled. Why on earth would she need another? But Nathan was solicitous of his mother, and three years ago, Evelyn had been intimidated by that. Three years ago, she would have smiled when he'd sent the secretary and pretended not to care at all.

Well. She was hardly *that* mealymouthed, naïve, cake-headed woman any longer. She was not the young mother they all believed had gone mad with grief and should be tucked away so they could all forget about the tragedy.

"His lordship remembered this piece in the attic," Benton continued. "Mrs. Gillette oiled it."

"Mrs. Gillette should have burned it." How was she supposed to write on that thing? It looked as if it was barely nailed together. "But you must thank her for me," she added.

"There is foolscap and ink in the drawer," Benton continued.

"*Foolscap?*" She shot a look at the butler, who actually blinked. "Haven't we any vellum?"

"We do, my lady. But his lordship specifically suggested foolscap. He said the economy of it would be greater, as he suspected you intended to write quite a lot of letters to London."

"Well, he is right about that. I intend to write a lot of letters. A *lot*. So many letters that he'll need a carriage to carry them all! I will need more foolscap, Benton! Boxes of it, if you please! And a carriage to carry them all to London!"

Benton's lip twitched.

"Mr. Benton, Cook says she must speak with you," one of the footmen said.

"If I may?" he asked.

"Yes, yes," Evelyn said, waving at him, still staring at the secretary. "I can finish here."

She gave the secretary a push with her hand as Benton and the footman went out. It swayed on its wobbly legs. "Oh for heaven's sake!" she muttered. She kicked at one of the legs; it moved an inch or two inward. She kicked it harder. The leg gave way.

A quarter of an hour later, she had the old secretary completely dismantled, and had marched into the foyer, determined to clear her lungs of the dust the thing had kicked up.

Outside, she was hit with a brisk western wind, and pulled her cloak tightly around her. She took the long way around the house—she could not see the churchyard where Robbie was buried, even at a distance.

But she passed by the small ornamental rose garden just outside the morning room, where she had recognized the first signs of the illness that would take Robbie's life. Evelyn couldn't help herself—she peeked through the gate. The garden was wildly overgrown. Decaying petals littered the ground and blooms hung sorrowfully from long, spindly branches.

Why had it been neglected? Where was the bloody gardener?

She moved on.

At the orangery, Evelyn found similar conditions. The bushes in front of the large French windows were overgrown and the grass too high. In addition, the door was locked, bolted with a rusty old lock that, try as she might, she could not budge. "*Blast* it all," she muttered irritably. She looked down the row of windows and the bramble bushes that grew untended, picked up her skirts and cloak, and stepped behind a bush. The edge of her cloak caught; she yanked it clear as she inched her way behind the bushes until she reached the first window.

Cupping her hands around her eyes, she pressed her face to the windows and peered in. The window was so grimy she couldn't see a thing. So she moved farther down, peering into each window until she finally found one through which she could almost see.

Was she seeing things? Was the orangery truly empty? Were her miniature orange trees and the furniture she had selected so carefully and the beautiful landscape paintings that had hung on the wall all gone?

Evelyn stepped back, looked around, and stooped down to pick up a rock. She backed up, took aim, and threw the rock with all her might. The pane shattered. Using her sleeve, she banged the shards of glass away and then carefully leaned forward, peering through.

chapter nine

Jack Haines, the fourth earl of Lambourne, was in a jolly good frame of mind, having divested Aaron Major, an officer of the Royal Regiment of Dragoons, of two hundred pounds.

Lindsey had not been as fortunate, although he'd had the hand to win. But he'd seemed distracted, as if something was weighing heavily on his mind. Jack could very well guess what that might be. No one had been more surprised than he to see the countess at the abbey. Frankly, he'd thought the marriage doomed.

He'd have the story from Wilkes when he returned, Jack supposed, but in the meantime, Lindsey had, in uncharacteristic fashion, quit the game early by tossing in his hand and downing his ale. "Forgive me, gentlemen. I am not much for sport today."

Jack almost fell out of his chair. If there was ever a man who was ready for sport—at any time, day or night—it was Nathan, and thank heavens for it. Jack might have perished in the dreadfully boring English countryside had it not been for his good friend's lust for life.

"I beg your pardon!" Major exclaimed. "There is an unpaid debt, my lord!"

"Yes, yes," Lindsey said, and patted the pockets of his waistcoat. "I thought I had brought along a bank draft," he said, his brow burrowing in thought. "I suppose I forgot it, Major. I'll have my man bring it round. Good day."

And out he'd stalked from the private room, his cloak snapping at his ankles, his hat pulled low over his brow.

"He bloody well owes me a hundred pounds," Major said angrily.

"*Ach* now, lad," Jack said congenially as he raked in his earnings. "You know very well that Lindsey is good for it." He stood, smiled at the man. "Seems as if the game is done, aye?"

He left a loudly complaining Major and paid a call to Lucy Wren, a favorite of his in the back of the public house. Lucy had generous hips and a beaming smile, and she was always happy to see him. He was a man who had a strong appetite and enjoyed variety—in life and in love. In the country, however, women were too concerned about their virtue. Bloody virtue. It was really given far too much importance to his way of thinking. Ah, but there was Lucy, and he showed her a rousing time, if her flushed round cheeks were any indication.

Two hours later, feeling rather warm and benevolent given the two hundred pounds in his pocket and the romp between the sheets, Jack rode back to Eastchurch Abbey. He had in mind rousing Donnelly and paying a call to the Franklin sisters. He liked to tease Donnelly that he'd end up on the wrong side of a church altar if he didn't curb his efforts to seduce the older sister. She was no match for Donnelly's ability to seduce—neither were half the chambermaids at Eastchurch—but Miss Franklin nearly swooned each time he so much as smiled. Aye, it was a wonderful diversion.

But as Jack walked into the main hall, tossing his hat and cloak to a footman, he heard voices and followed them to the red drawing room.

He found Lindsey inside with his neighbor, Mrs. DuPaul. She turned and greeted him warmly. Jack liked her. She was small and pale, and had a little oval face. She was very friendly and her husband seemed a good man.

"I beg your pardon, my lord, I was just leaving," she explained to Lambourne.

"No' on my account?"

She laughed. "Of course not! My husband is waiting. But I'd heard in the village that Lindsey was back from London."

"It is good to see you, Alexandra," Lindsey said. It was apparent to Jack that Lindsey had affection for Mrs. DuPaul, much like he had for Jack's sister, Fiona.

Mrs. DuPaul put her hand on Lindsey's arm and smiled up at him. "Shall I invite your parents to a weekend? I know they'd very much enjoy seeing Evelyn."

"If I were you, I'd—what is it, Benton?" Lindsey asked, looking over Jack's shoulder.

The three of them turned toward the door as Benton walked in, his arms outstretched, holding the debris of what looked like a piece of furniture.

Lindsey frowned. "What is that?" he asked as Benton put the pieces on the floor at his feet.

"It is the secretary you sent to her ladyship returned, my lord."

Lindsey's expression darkened, and in it, Jack saw the same befuddlement he'd noted earlier today at the card table. It struck him as odd—Nathan Grey was one of the strongest, most assured, and accomplished men he knew. He could not imagine that anything might rattle him—but he was clearly rattled.

"I don't understand," Lindsey said dumbly.

"The countess asked that I inform you the secretary did not hold up to her writing, and requests you ask if the Marchioness of Sudley might possibly return *her* secretary."

Mrs. DuPaul bit back a smile and looked at the ground.

"I see," Lindsey said low, his gaze darkening.

"In addition, the countess has requested more foolscap, for she intends to write quite a lot of correspondence to London."

That brought Lindsey's head up, and he glared at Benton. "Is there anything *else* the countess wants?"

"Indeed there is, my lord. The countess would like a carriage to convey all the correspondence she intends to post," Benton responded calmly.

They all looked down at the debris.

Jack edged one piece with his toe. "It looks as if this piece was broken over a knee."

"She didn't break it over her knee, Jack," Nathan said irritably. "But perhaps *she* ought to be put over a knee."

The delicate cough behind them prompted the four of them to turn. The countess was standing at the threshold, her brows knit in a vee of displeasure.

"Evelyn!" Mrs. DuPaul cried, and hurried around the debris to greet Lady Lindsey. She took Lady Lindsey's hands in hers and kissed her cheeks. "I can't tell you how wonderful it is to see you home!"

"Thank you," Lady Lindsey said a little stiffly. "I . . . I didn't know you were expected, or I—"

"Oh no! No, I wasn't expected at all. I just stopped by because I'd heard Nathan had returned from London."

The countess gave Lindsey quite a look at that.

"We must have you over for tea soon," Mrs. DuPaul continued. "I want to hear all about London and waiting on the queen!"

"Yes," Lady Lindsey said, glancing at the floor now. It seemed to Jack as if she forced her smile. "Yes, of course."

"Now I really must go," Mrs. DuPaul said.

Lindsey moved to escort her out, but Mrs. DuPaul stopped him with a gentle laugh. "Please, Nathan—you too, Mr. Benton. Stay right where you are. I know my way out. Good day, everyone."

"Good day, madam," Jack said.

An awkward silence followed Mrs. DuPaul's departure. None of them spoke. Jack was uncertain *what* to say. But then the countess suddenly moved, marching into the room, deliberately stepping over the broken furniture. Jack noticed that her windblown hair had come loose from its coif, and in places, thick strands of hair hung down, one curving over a cheek. Her skin was flushed, and her eyes bright.

Frankly, Jack did not remember her being such a deliciously handsome woman.

"Good afternoon, my lady," Benton said crisply, for he was, if nothing else, England's finest butler. "Shall I pour tea?"

"Thank you, Benton," she said cheerily. "Two lumps of sugar if you please."

Lindsey squinted at her. "Are you quite all right?"

"Oh, I am *very* well, sir!" she exclaimed. "I've had a rather vigorous walkabout this afternoon!"

"Through the forest?" Jack asked, eyeing the wet hem of her gown.

"Why, no. To the *orangery*," she said, looking pointedly at Lindsey.

He raised a quizzical brow. "The orangery is empty."

"Yes! I discovered that!" she said with a wave of her hand that almost hit the teacup Benton held before her. "Imagine my surprise—the orangery *empty*! It was so lovely there! Benton, didn't you think it was lovely?" she asked, her eyes locked on Lindsey.

"I did indeed, madam."

"Did you know it was empty, Benton?"

He calmly put her tea beside a chair near the hearth. "Yes, madam."

"It is empty because it has gone unused for some time," Lindsey curtly interjected.

"Ah. Of course," she said, and smiled sweetly at Lindsey as she passed by them and took a seat next to the tea. "It's really a pity," she said as she picked up the cup. "I put quite a lot of effort into it. *Quite* a lot."

"Indeed you did," Lindsey agreed, his voice tight, as if he was refraining from speaking too loudly. "But as it has gone unused for nigh on three years, the fruit was rotting, the furniture mildewing, and I saw no reason to keep it up."

"Oh, I *see*." The countess daintily sipped her tea. "Benton? Have you seen the small rose garden?"

"Yes, madam."

"Do you think it has gone unused and that is why it has not been properly maintained?"

"I would wager that is a fair guess."

"And the house, as well? The worn carpets, the fishing accoutrements in every room?"

"I could not say," Benton said, and with a bow of his head, he stepped away and put his back to the wall. Jack wished to do the same and exchanged a helpless look with the butler.

"What is the matter, Evelyn?" Lindsey asked, his voice cooler.

"I beg your pardon," Jack said. "I should . . . be about the, ah . . ."

"No, sit, sit!" Lindsey snapped. "My wife is distressed about the bloody orangery, but I assure you, she will recover! Benton, pour whiskey all around!"

Jack expected the countess to swoon with indignation, but she turned a charming smile to him. "My husband is right . . . for once," she said sweetly. "I *shall* recover. In fact, I have recovered completely already. Please do sit, my lord. How is your sister? I scarcely saw her at all in London."

Jack looked uneasily at Lindsey.

The countess stood. "*Please*, sir," she said again, and smiled in a way that could make a man lose his head. The woman possessed a feminine charm Jack had never seen in her, and of a sudden, he was filled with pity for his good friend Lindsey.

"I beg your pardon if I have made you uncomfortable," she continued. "It's just that I loved the orangery so. And the little rose garden. And my cherrywood secretary. Alas, they have fallen into such disrepair—or disappeared altogether—and I don't know if any of them can be reclaimed."

"Bloody hell," Lindsey muttered irritably.

The countess resumed her seat and took a sip of her tea, set the cup and saucer down, and abruptly stood again. "What am I thinking? I have intruded and run off your guests. I will leave you to your whiskey, gentlemen—I know how much you enjoy sitting and drinking . . . and sitting. Besides, I have some correspondence to attend to."

She started for the door, but paused when she saw the remains of the furniture. She looked up, smiling mischievously. "I am certain Benton told you that my old and brittle secretary fell apart. I shall have to avail myself of the library, my lord."

"That secretary belonged to my grandfather," Lindsey said, pointing at the debris.

"Oh!" she said, and looked wide-eyed at the pieces of wood. "That must have had great sentimental value."

"Evelyn—"

"I suppose it went unused for some time and fell into a state of disrepair." With a nonchalant shrug, she smiled again. "Good afternoon," she said, and deliberately stepped over the remains of the secretary and walked impertinently out of the room.

The three men stared after her.

Jack couldn't help but notice the look on Lindsey's face. It was a mixture of excruciating pain and powerful lust. He could hardly blame the poor man, but oh, how he pitied him.

Lindsey whirled away from the door and pinned Benton with a look.

"Yes, my lord?" Benton asked.

"Whiskey," he said gruffly, and stepped over the broken secretary and stalked to the hearth, where he stood with his hands clasped tightly behind his back, staring into the flames.

On a hill above Eastchurch Abbey, the lone rider stared down at the massive neoclassical mansion. Smoke curled out of ten of the fourteen chimneys, and the river that ran behind the house was rushing. A phaeton was speeding away from the house, and a pair of horses stood tethered in the drive. A coach, still stained with the mud and grime of the road, was parked outside the stables. The door was open, and a lad emerged with a pail and a handful of rags.

The rider watched a few moments longer before adjusting his hat and turning his horse around, toward the main road.

chapter ten

Evelyn did not dine with them that evening, which was undoubtedly a good thing, for Nathan could not be certain what he would do or say.

He'd stood at the windows of the green salon late that afternoon, watching her ride away from the house on one of his best horses, her speed reckless, her golden hair spilling out behind her.

He was disturbed by the sight of it. He sensed there was something more than anger that filled her by the reckless way she rode. He knew that sort of rash carelessness, for it was the same way he reacted when he felt the world crashing down around him.

Was it Dunhill? Did she yearn for him? Had she loved him?

Lambourne began to regale them with tales of the soirées he'd attended at Montague House in an area of London known as Blackheath, where the Princess of Wales resided. He seemed to be particularly amused by a night of Egyptian dancing.

"What do you mean, Egyptian dancing?" Donnelly asked, staring at Lambourne intently. Donnelly was as randy as the rest of them, but his primary interest in life was horses, and as a result, he sometimes missed the adventures with women that Lambourne seemed to find almost routinely.

"Sounds quite erotic, aye?" Lambourne teased him. "Imagine if you will," he said, painting a picture in the air with his hands, "a lovely abdomen, bared but for a thin layer of silk above the soft sway of her hips . . ."

"If you will excuse me, I've an early meeting with my solicitor," Nathan announced.

Neither of his guests took much notice. "Good night, Lindsey," Donnelly said, then looked at Lambourne again. "How was she moving her hips?" he demanded.

"Declan, lad," Lambourne said with a laugh. "Have you no' seen a woman move her hips?"

Nathan walked out of the dining room.

He *did* have an appointment with his solicitor on the morrow, but it was neither early nor particularly important. In truth, he had something else entirely on his mind, the only thing, really, that had been on his mind since Christy had explained he must go to London: his wife.

This afternoon had rendered him incapable of thinking of anything else. She'd appeared looking so windblown and alluringly fresh. Alexandra, his good friend, had all but disappeared beside Evelyn. *Evelyn*—Lord God, the woman was *exasperating*! He didn't know how it had happened, but his wife had grown into a beautiful, independent, and infuriatingly bold woman. That was an explosive combination for any man.

She was not the least bit intimidated by him as she'd

once been. In fact, she was trying to goad him—into what, he hadn't a clue.

He took the grand staircase that curved up toward a celestial painting on the domed ceiling and turned right into the corridor where the family rooms were located.

He rapped on the door of the sitting room between his suite and hers, and strode inside.

Evelyn was not within.

He moved on, entering a bare dressing room. There had been a time when wardrobes and trunks would be open, gowns and undergarments spilling out and pooling on the floor between beaded slippers, boots, and evening shoes.

Nathan had forgotten what it was like to live with a woman, how their things could creep into every corner of every room, crawl up under your skin, and wrap around your heart. Evelyn's stockings would hang on a rack used for towels and linens in the bathing room, and jars of face creams and vials of perfume would litter every surface of her dressing room. Somehow, those things even made it into *his* dressing room and *his* bedroom.

But he'd never minded it. He'd rather liked it.

He strode through the dressing room and opened the door leading into her bedroom.

With a shriek of surprise, Evelyn, seated at her vanity in a dressing gown, jumped up and caught the edge of the vanity. "I beg your pardon!"

Nathan likewise was a bit taken aback. The dressing gown she wore was made of silk and was belted loosely at her waist. It skimmed every curve of the luscious body beneath.

Evelyn backed away from him as he moved deeper into the room, gathering her gown and wrapping it more tightly around her. But her modest gesture did not have the effect she desired—it only accentuated her curves and made him hungrier.

He clasped his hands tightly behind his back, eyeing her, admiring her. She returned his gaze with one full of distrust. Clever woman—she should distrust him, for the thoughts running through his mind were anything but chaste. He'd forgotten the secretary, the orangery, her impudence before his friends. He had but one thought on his mind.

"Please stop looking at me in that manner!"

Nathan did not stop. "In what manner?" he asked. "In the manner a man looks at his wife? A wife as lovely, as beautiful as mine?"

"*Stop*, Nathan," she said sternly.

He wouldn't stop, he would never stop. He was a man, and he had a man's thirst, a thirst that had gone unslaked for longer than he cared to admit. She was a delectable, desirable woman—and she was *his* woman. He instinctively reached for her.

Evelyn darted out of his way, scurrying around the end of the bed.

Nathan was not the least deterred; if anything, he was spurred by it. The more she denied him, the more he felt an almost primal need to reclaim his rightful role as her husband.

"What's the matter, darling? Afraid you will enjoy it?"

She tried to run around the bed for the door, but Nathan easily bounded over the bed and caught her from behind, anchoring her to him with an arm around her waist.

She clawed at his arm. "I suppose now you intend to

take me as you took me from the streets of London?" she asked breathlessly as she struggled against him.

He forced her around to face him. "You once craved my touch."

Something flickered in her eyes. Oh yes, she remembered, too. "That was long ago. I certainly don't crave it now," she said, and shoved hard against him.

But Nathan was impervious. He leaned forward; she tried to lean back, but he simply slipped his hand behind her head and pulled it closer to his. In the golden light of the hearth, he admired the furious flush of her cheeks, the slender column of her neck, and the rapid rise of her chest. There was a look in her eyes that he felt very deeply inside him—it was an odd mix of the familiar and the unknown.

"I *mean* it, Nathan! If you do not unhand me, I shall scream and bring the house down around your ears."

One hand drifted down her back. "If you scream, I rather suspect they will assume I am pleasuring you as I would very much like to do."

"Ha! What makes you believe you *ever* gave me pleasure?"

"I was there, love, remember?"

She managed to get one hand on his ear. She grabbed it, twisting.

"*Ouch!*" he cried, and let go of her.

Evelyn twisted around and leapt over the chaise, putting it between them. Nathan straightened and looked at her. The color in her cheeks was high, her eyes were glittering. He rubbed his ear with one hand and pointed at her with the other. "You are *enjoying* this little game of cat and mouse. Admit it."

"You flatter yourself."

"Come now, Evie. You remember as well as I do that if there was one place you and I were at peace, it was in that bed."

She frantically looked around and grabbed up the fire poker. "If there was one time you and I were at peace, it was when I was in London and you were here! If you touch me again, sir, I shall feel not the slightest bit of remorse for defending myself." She raised the poker high, revealing the curve of her breast.

He laughed. "Don't be so pugnacious, Evie. It doesn't suit you."

"Don't be so aggressive, Nathan. It gives you an air of desperation."

That wasn't very far from the truth. "I like to think of it as unmitigated desire for my wife. And I recall a woman who was always rather desperate with desire herself."

"You are a bloody scoundrel."

He grinned. "At your service, madam," he said, and lunged toward her. With a shriek, Evelyn tried to leap out of his reach, but Nathan caught her and landed with her on the chaise. The poker clattered to the floor, and without so much as a word, a breath, Nathan touched his lips to hers.

Evelyn made a sound of protest against his mouth and grabbed his lapels, trying to shake him loose, but Nathan was lost in her lips. Soft, wet, and plush, they were everything he remembered. His hand slipped to her neck, his thumb on the velvet curve of her ear. She wore the scent of lilacs in her hair and on her neck, fueling many deep and intimate memories. His anger, his uncertainty about who or what she had become, about who or what *they* had become, was swallowed whole by his desire.

Evelyn pushed hard against his chest, but when he slipped his tongue into her mouth, he felt a change in her. She still pushed against him, but at the same time, she curved into him. He kissed her madly, his tongue in her mouth, his teeth on her lips, his hand drifting to the swell of her lovely bottom, grasping it and holding her against him.

She made another sound, but it was different—it was a small cry of desire, one he recognized and knew well. Her hands loosened on his lapel; one slid up, to his neck, to his jaw. The other went around his neck as she pressed her breasts against his chest, her pelvis against his erection.

He kissed her reverently, and with remorse, too, for all the years they'd lost, for the chasm they'd created and could not seem to cross.

She plunged her hand into his hair, and dug her fingers into his shoulder, digging through fabric to bone. Nathan slipped his hand into her dressing gown, covering her breast, kneading it. Evelyn responded with a moan and moved seductively, sliding against him, driving him wild.

His body flared with excitement; there had never been a woman who affected him, who *moved* him quite the way she did now and always had. Familiar feelings of wanting her, needing her, roared to the surface of his mind.

He couldn't wait another moment. He held her head with one hand and dipped down, intent on picking her up and carrying her to her bed—but Evelyn suddenly gasped and shoved against him with all her might.

All her might was not enough to move him, but it was enough to give him pause.

She shoved him again and jerked back, out of his grasp. Her eyes were blazing with passion and anger as she dragged the back of her hand across her mouth and glared at him. "How *dare* you!" she cried, and scrambled off the chaise, pushing him so hard with her foot that he lost his hold and had to stop his fall with a hand to the floor.

"How dare *I*?" he demanded as he pushed himself up.

She pressed her hands to her abdomen as if she were going to be ill and turned from him. "Surely you do not expect me to just . . . just fall into your arms!"

Nathan's vexation turned to white-hot anger. Honestly, he didn't know what he expected, but the sound of revulsion in her voice angered him. "You seemed to be falling quite readily, Evelyn," he snapped, and leapt to his feet.

"Only because you seduced me!" She jumped out of his reach again. "I must be mad—this house makes me *mad!*"

"What in heaven's name are you talking about?" he demanded.

"Is it not as obvious to you as it is to me that we are not the same people we were three years ago? Six years ago? Ten years ago? We've changed, we've grown apart!"

"Who's to say we can't grow together still—"

"*No,*" she said, adamantly shaking her head. "No, no, *no,* Nathan! I will *never* go back to the way we were!"

"I'm not asking you to go back!" he said angrily. "Do you honestly believe that *I* want to go back to that wretched time? But Evelyn, it has been more than three years since Robert died—"

"*Please!*" she cried, throwing up a hand.

The pain in her eyes was so real that Nathan checked himself. He caught her by the shoulders; she pushed against him, but weakly. He looked at the delicate beauty of her features, the depth of color in her eyes, and felt sorrow for her. How she had loved that boy! "It's been more than three years since Robert died," he said again.

Evelyn pressed her lips together and closed her eyes.

Nathan shook her. "But we have mourned, Evelyn! God knows we have *mourned* him, and mourned him deeply. It has long been time for us to put it behind us."

She gasped and pushed his hands from her shoulders. "I can never put him behind me! How can you expect me to put my child, dead or alive, behind me?" she cried, pressing her hands to her heart. "But lest you think I have not moved forward, I have. I have gone forward from the worst moment of my life and now . . . now I want a divorce."

The very word, so unexpected, sent him reeling. He stilled, gaping at her. "What in the bloody hell did you just say?"

Evelyn defiantly lifted her chin. "I want a divorce. What more is there for us?" she cried, throwing her arms out wide. "We were never suited, we've not seen each other in three years, we scarcely speak, we are not husband and wife—"

"*No*," he said sharply. "Never utter that word to me again, do you hear me?"

"You won't even listen to me?" she cried. "Having endured this . . . this sham of a marriage for three years, you won't even listen to what I would say?"

"This *sham* of a marriage, as you put it, was not a sham until Robert died and you went to London. I agreed to that only to help you, Evelyn! I gave you precisely what you wanted—to leave Eastchurch and all that had happened here," he cried, sweeping his arm wide. "I did it to make you happy because God knew everything else I tried failed! I wanted to take the sorrow from you in any way that I could, and that seemed the only way. So I let you go—for *you!*"

"Oh dear heavens!" she cried, throwing up her hands. "You wanted to make *me* happy? You never thought of me at all, Nathan! You were constantly gone, constantly in the company of your friends, *constantly* in the company of Alexandra DuPaul! You left me alone to suffer through the greatest tragedy of my life!"

"Because you would not let me in!" he roared to the ceiling. "As God is my witness, you sat in that chair," he said, pointing angrily to the chair before the hearth. "You would not eat, you would not sleep, and you would not talk to me, Evelyn! And on those occasions you did deign to speak to me, it was to complain."

"What did you want me to do? Gladly accept your affair?"

"There was no affair!" he shouted. "She was my friend, Evelyn. She was my friend because God knows I found none here!"

Evelyn blinked. And turned away from him. "Please do not make this so difficult," she pleaded with him. "I cannot return to the life we had. I want to make a *new* life. I want a divorce."

He gaped at her. It felt almost like a dream, so odd, as if he were standing outside his body. How did one respond to such an outrageous request? Divorce was impossible. Impossible! Even if he were so inclined, and assuming they—*she*—could survive the scandal, for society would be much harsher on her, no one would marry her after it was all said and done, she would be ruined. There were few options open to them to even attempt a divorce. Any legal divorce, short of an act of Parliament, which would be a costly and public affair, would render their dead son a bastard.

Surely he did not need to tell her so. Divorce was unthinkable, unconscionable. "Was it truly so wretched?" he asked low. "Was I so unkind? Did I raise my voice to you? Did I deny you anything?"

"Nathan—"

"What is it, Evie?" he asked, meaning the question quite sincerely.

A tear slid down her cheek. "Isn't it obvious?"

"Nothing is obvious—nothing makes any sense. What do you think is so damn obvious?"

"I don't love you anymore," she said, and quickly put a hand to her mouth to stifle a sob.

The words cut right through him and released the wind from his lungs. He supposed he had known it deep inside, but hearing her say the words aloud—he clenched one hand at his side, tried to find his bearings. "Did you ever?" he asked tightly.

Two more tears slid silently down her cheek. "How could you possibly ask me?"

"Because I need to know." For some insane reason, he desperately needed to know. "It seems a logical question," he said numbly. "Did you?"

"Of course I did," she said, her eyes rimmed with anguish.

Nathan felt another slice of pain and looked down at the carpet in something of a fog.

"Did . . . did you love me?" she asked with a hollow voice.

Nathan slowly looked up. He was surprised to see how hopeful, how uncertain she looked. If he were brutally honest, he'd tell her that he hadn't loved her in the beginning, and now . . . Now? At that particular moment, he couldn't say what he felt, other than a cold pain.

Evelyn gave a soft sob and turned away from him, gripping the back of the chair as if she was feeling unsteady.

"The scaffolding of our marriage was rather complicated, Evie. It was weak in some places, stronger in others. Perhaps it was too weak to survive Robert's death. But . . . but that doesn't mean we can't build anew."

"No," she said with a somber shake of her head. "You weren't there, Nathan." She hugged herself tightly and glanced helplessly at the window. "There were days I thought I would collapse under the weight of it all, and I didn't know what to do, and you were gone."

"I was there, Evie," he said quickly. "If you had collapsed, I would have picked you up and carried you. I was there."

She looked at him skeptically—she did not believe him. She did not believe he would have been there for her if she had called out to him. And really, why would she? His grief had been just as great if not greater—he'd lived every day of Robert's short and sickly life wondering if his debauchery had made his son weak. Perhaps he'd drunk too much ale in his life, or the recklessness of various sports had weakened him somehow, and he passed that along to his son. He'd tried to understand why Robert had been so sickly, and nothing made sense.

When his son had died, he'd not been able to bear it any better than Evelyn. At least Alexandra had offered a shoulder to lean on when all the world expected him to be strong. For that, he would be eternally grateful to her.

But there was nothing else between him and Alexandra as Evelyn believed. In truth, Nathan had never looked at another woman until she'd gone, and even then, only here and there when he could deny the physical need no more.

Nathan turned away, pushed his hand through his hair, confused and angry.

"I would prefer to be in London," Evelyn said quietly.

He felt depleted, empty, emptier than he'd felt in a very long time. He was broken into pieces all over again. He looked back at Evelyn, saw that she was trembling slightly. He reached out, touched his fingers to her cheek, then her jaw. "I will not divorce you, Evelyn. And you will not return to London." He removed his hand.

"Nathan—"

"Never speak of it again," he said, and turned away from those tearful eyes and the invisible wounds that still oozed after three years.

He walked out without thinking, his path old but familiar, his feet moving almost of their own accord. He walked down the corridor, not noticing the chambermaid who stepped back to allow him to pass, or the footman who hastily swung the pail of coals for a brazier out of his path.

Nathan walked, stretching the palm that had touched her.

It burned.

It burned with his own private pain, his own conflicting, churning emotions that the touch of her skin, the smell of her hair, the feel of her in his arms had caused to erupt in him. He walked down the main staircase, nodded at the footman in the grand foyer, strode to the back of the foyer, took a candle from the wall, and opened a door to stairs leading to the lower floors.

The corridor below was dark, but Nathan knew his way under the east wing. Using his burning hand as a guide, he groped his way to the very last door, the room that had once served as a grain store, and pushed it open. The room was empty now, and he walked in, carefully shut the door behind him, and placed the candle in a holder on the wall.

He turned and looked at one stone wall, dimly lit by the flickering light of the candle.

He'd first come to this room the night his son had died. He'd been here so many times since then that he could no longer count them. The wall was scarred and stained, bearing the marks of his rages these last few years. Very calmly, almost by rote, he raised his arm and crushed his fist against the wall.

He continued to hit his fist or palm against the wall until he could no longer feel the burn in it, until he'd beaten his overwhelming desire and suffocating disappointment into submission.

Panting, and perspiring in spite of the bone-chilling dampness of the room, Nathan finally stopped and braced himself against the wall with both hands, gulping air and swallowing down a pain that ached so deep, it felt like a mortal wound.

chapter eleven

Evelyn went about the business of methodically sealing the letters she'd written this morning: to her mother, her sister, Princess Mary, and Harriet. She wrote to Claire, too, and asked her—in vain, she knew—to continue Harriet's dancing lessons.

She did not write to Pierce.

She had intended to. She'd thought carefully of what she would say, of perhaps even asking him to help her. But after last night, after sharing that fiery, searing kiss with Nathan, she didn't know what she thought anymore. Everything felt different somehow. She didn't know where exactly she fit in her own life any longer.

There were some things she needed to work out, things that had kept her awake until the early morning hours. *"The scaffolding of our marriage was rather complicated, Evie. It was weak in some places, stronger in others . . ."*

She folded the foolscap, melted the wax, pressed the Lindsey seal into the warm wax, and stacked the letters neatly on the edge of the small dining table she was using as a writing table.

The scaffolding of their marriage, as Nathan had so eloquently put it, had been built on too many lofty expectations and assumptions about what marriage truly entailed. Evelyn had been naïve when she'd agreed to marry for money and position. She'd been so young, and she believed that was what she was supposed to do—it was an expectation her parents had put on her even in her earliest memories.

A knock at the door roused her from her thoughts. "Come!" she called.

Benton opened the door. "Kathleen Maguire, madam."

Kathleen, her friend, companion, and ladies' maid, entered behind him. She barely reached Benton's shoulder, but what she lacked in height she made up in girth. She grinned at Evelyn but stepped aside so the footman could carry in the trunks and place them in the dressing room. "There you are, lads," she said cheerfully. "Leave them be, I'll tend to them as needed."

Evelyn leapt up from her seat and threw her arms around Kathleen. "Never have my eyes seen such a welcome—*Harriet!*" she cried, spotting the girl over Kathleen's shoulder.

Harriet wandered in behind Kathleen, looking a little lost.

"Harriet, darling, what are you doing here?"

"My mother left me," she said. "She said she needed the waters at Bath."

Evelyn blinked, but Kathleen said cheerfully, "There'll be time to chat after we've fed this girl, eh, milady?" She gave Evelyn a look that suggested they talk privately.

"Of course!" Evelyn grabbed Harriet and hugged her tightly. "I am so pleased to see you! This is the best surprise I might have hoped for."

Harriet smiled a little. "I *am* hungry," she said. "I've been wanting oatcakes."

"Benton! *Benton!*" Evelyn called. She put her hands on Harriet's shoulders, turning her about as Benton appeared from the dressing room. "This is my dear, dear friend, Lady Harriet French. She desperately needs a hot chocolate and some oatcakes."

"At once, my lady," Benton said, clicking his heels and bowing low before Harriet.

Evelyn leaned down and whispered, "Go with Benton now. I'll finish up here and meet you when you've had your fill."

The girl nodded and allowed Benton to lead her out. Kathleen shut the door behind them and turned to Evelyn.

"Did you hear what happened?" Evelyn asked anxiously.

"Did I hear? All of London has heard it, mu'um!"

"Oh *no!*"

"Lady Balfour put it out that you'd gone off with Dunhill," Kathleen continued, her face pinched with displeasure.

"She didn't!"

"Aye, she did indeed, and it had Her Highness quite distraught. But then word came from Sir Wilkes that you'd gone home with your husband and Her Highness was at peace again. Naturally, everyone speculated it was because of that awful to-do between the Prince and Princess of Wales and that you and Lord Dunhill knew something about the prince that you oughtn't."

"I don't!" Evelyn insisted.

Kathleen's expression was skeptical. "Her Highness thinks you are protecting her brother and bids you stay here lest you be questioned. They are rounding up people, you know, especially gentlemen Princess Caroline is suspected of . . ." Kathleen colored. "You know very well what I mean."

"Yes," Evelyn said. "But what of Harriet?"

"Oh, that woman!" Kathleen said, pulling a face. "For the life of me, I don't know why you call her a friend! She went off to Bath for the weekend and said Lord Balfour would come for the girl. Just left the poor thing behind as if she were a hat. Well, Lord Balfour *didn't* come, and Lady Balfour didn't return as she said she would, and when I was sent for, the queen said it wasn't proper for the girl to be there at Buckingham as if she were an orphan, that Princess Caroline might take her in and call her her own, so I sent word to Lady Balfour that the girl had come with me. Lady Balfour is to come for her when she returns from her holiday."

"Oh my. You did the right thing, Kathleen."

Kathleen nodded curtly and began to tidy the room.

"W-what of Dunhill . . . did he come for me?" Evelyn asked meekly.

Kathleen did not look at her as she straightened the bedcovers. "No . . . but it wouldn't do to give rise to more rumors," she said. "It was thoughtful of him not to come."

It didn't feel very thoughtful, Evelyn thought morosely.

"Oh, 'tis good to be back! I'll just put these things away," Kathleen said, and picking up a small portmanteau, she walked into the adjoining dressing room.

The news from London made Evelyn feel restive and unsettled again. "I'm going to take Harriet for a walk," she announced, and followed Kathleen into the dressing room to find a muffler in one of the trunks. As she dug through one, her hand touched something hard and cool. She pushed aside several articles of clothing and accessories and withdrew the Limoges music box. She opened the hand-painted lid; the dancing couple popped up and instantly began twirling in one another's arms to a Handel tune.

It had been an extravagant and dangerous gift from Pierce and she ought not to have kept it . . . but she had. Kathleen had always believed it came from Mary. Evelyn had never disabused her of the notion.

When she'd found her muffler, she told Kathleen she'd be back after Harriet had a chance to stretch her legs. She put the music box on the mantel of her bed-chamber and quit the room.

By the time Evelyn and Harriet made it outside, a wind was kicking up, and a thin covering of clouds was approaching from the north.

With her arm around Harriet for warmth, Evelyn showed her the grounds. They were immaculate, particularly the parterres in the back of the house, where flowers bloomed so gloriously in the spring. And of course, there was the small, overgrown, and mostly moribund rose garden, which had once been renowned. Evelyn did not show Harriet that small space.

Instead, she pointed out a row of beech trees along the service road. "See the trees?" Evelyn said. "His lordship and I planted them many years ago. They were only half the size they are now."

She could remember standing next to Nathan, watching men plant them, one after another. *"We shall watch them grow like children,"* she'd said laughingly, but Nathan had given her a startled look. *"I suppose,"* he'd said.

He'd gone off with his friends that afternoon.

"They're very nice," Harriet admitted. "But I prefer flowering trees. My grandfather grows flowering trees. Where does that lead?" she asked, pointing to the path that led down to the river.

"That is a lovely walk along the river. If you're not too cold, we could take it."

Harriet said that she wasn't the slightest bit cold, so Evelyn took her down the path to where it narrowed along the river's banks. It was narrower than Evelyn remembered—extremely so—there was scarcely enough room for a wagon to pass. The slightest mistake and a wagon would topple right into the river. Nevertheless, Evelyn had always loved this path. It was rustic and picturesque and removed from everything. In a moment of abandon, she glanced over her shoulder, and determining that no one was about, she took Harriet by the hand and said, "Let's run!"

Harriet's eyes lit with delight. The two of them ran, just for the sake of it, because they were free to do so, because there was no one there to tell them that ladies did not run.

They ran until the path curved, where Evelyn had to slow her step and press a hand to the stitch in her side. With the river rushing below her, she laughed at herself. When she'd caught her breath, she shouted, "Harriet! Where are you, halfway to the sea?"

There was no answer.

Evelyn began walking briskly, her muffler swinging at her side, looking up through the bare branches of the trees at the pale blue sky. She found Harriet ahead, at a fence railing, gazing upon a thatched-roof cottage. Evelyn knew the cottage and believed it belonged to the gamekeeper. Someone was about; smoke was rising from its single chimney.

"It's lovely," Harriet said. "I should like to live there."

Evelyn laughed. Beneath the boughs of a pair of old elm trees, on the banks of the river, it was an idyllic setting, but Harriet was destined for a far grander house, and Evelyn said so.

But Harriet shook her head. "I should like to live in a cottage. People who live in cottages are quite happy, I think."

Evelyn didn't say anything to that, but she rather supposed anywhere Harriet might live would be happier than her current circumstance.

They stood silently, admiring the cottage. Having been in London all these years, with the crowds and noises and the perpetual haze that seemed to hang over the city, Evelyn had forgotten how beautiful the grounds at Eastchurch were. It was little wonder there were so many landscape portraits hanging on the walls—the earls of Lindsey had wanted to preserve it for all eternity.

The door suddenly swung open, startling them. Evelyn grabbed Harriet and pushed her behind her as an elderly man wearing a leather apron emerged carrying a wooden bucket. He had a three- or four-day shadow of gray beard and a tuft of gray hair that stood up from the crown of his head. He paused when he saw them, and bobbed his head. "Afternoon."

"I beg your pardon, sir—"

"I'd heard tell you returned to the abbey," he said, and tossed the contents of his bucket—a rust-colored liquid—onto the ground. Two hens appeared from nowhere and began pecking the spill, looking for food.

Did she *know* him? "I . . . I beg your pardon again, sir. I'm afraid I don't recall—"

"Oh, I've not had the pleasure of making your acquaintance," he said matter-of-factly, and eyed her closely. "But I know who you are."

The way he looked at her made Evelyn a little nervous. She glanced at the path behind her, looking for a quick escape.

"I live just over the hill there," he continued, drawing Evelyn's attention again. Harriet stepped out of her shadow, staring curiously at the man. "I come round each day to help his lordship with the plants." He shook the bucket to ensure it was empty, then at Evelyn. "I've long had an interest in his work."

She had no idea what he meant. "His *work*," she repeated, trying to imagine what that might be. *Gambling? Hunting?*

"The botany."

The word did not quite register with her. She must have looked a little dumbfounded, because Harriet said, "I think that means science."

The old man chuckled, put the bucket aside, and squinted at them. "Don't know of his lordship's work, eh?" When Evelyn slowly shook her head, he gestured for them to come in through the gate.

Harriet followed him instantly, and therefore, so did Evelyn.

"I've been working here for nigh on fifteen years," the

man said to Evelyn. "The lad is just inside. Come, then, and I'll show you a bit of it."

Her curiosity won over her suspicions.

"Milburn is me name," he said as he opened the door and held it open. "I was a tenant on these lands for thirty years until me back gave out. His lordship took pity on me, he did, and I've been tending to his work since."

"I don't understand," Evelyn said.

Milburn gestured for them to precede him. Harriet disappeared into the darkened interior. Evelyn had to bat some of the roof's thatching that had come loose away from her face as she stepped across the threshold. A cheerful fire was burning at the hearth where a small kettle hung. The air was filled with the sweet smell of lavender. As her eyes adjusted to the dark interior, she noticed the boy who quickly doffed his hat and held it nervously in his hands. "Frances!" she exclaimed happily.

He looked at her with his big, brown eyes, and his hair stood up every which way.

"I've not seen you since our drive from London! Is this where you've been keeping yourself?"

Frances looked at Harriet.

"Oh, forgive me. This is Lady Harriet French. Harriet, may I introduce you to Master Frances Brady?"

They eyed one another until Frances announced proudly, "I am his lordship's helper."

"I am her ladyship's *friend*," Harriet instantly responded.

"The lad helps with this," Milburn said, indicating a long, wooden table that stretched almost the entire length of the room. On that table were plants in various stages of growth. Some of them were tall, reaching almost to the ceiling. Some of them were so small she could barely see them over the tops of the little clay pots. On the walls were shelves full of beakers and vials and cups, some of them containing liquids, some of them empty.

Evelyn stepped deeper inside and untied the strings of her bonnet. "I smell lavender."

"His lordship is working to graft various lavender plants to create a more potent oil."

Evelyn looked at him curiously.

"For medicinal purposes," Milburn said. He picked up a small clay pot and carefully fingered the plant. "It is the oils," he said. "The plants his lordship have produced have greater medicinal properties than the lavender that grows wild."

Evelyn looked at the table with the plants, at the vials and the leather-bound ledgers neatly stacked on the table. Harriet picked one up and opened it. A little cloud of dust rose up—it had obviously been there for some time. "Are we speaking of my husband? The Earl of Lindsey?"

Milburn's grin was missing a couple of teeth. "Lord Lindsey has done some very fine work in the botanical sciences, mu'um. I grant you, it's not a well-known fact among the gentry, but in the science, his work is quite well respected."

Evelyn gaped at him incredulously. "*What?* How? When might he have done these things? In the last three years?" she asked as she tried to comprehend how he could have gone from a libertine to a . . . a *scientist*.

"Oh no, much longer than that. On and off since he was a lad, really." Milburn put the little pot aside. "He's taken a keener interest in the last few years, aye."

He proceeded to show her the plants in various stages of growth, with Frances's help, of course, who chimed in with what he'd done to assist Lord Lindsey. His comments, Evelyn couldn't help notice, were directed at Harriet, who countered with the things she and Evelyn had done. Frances did not seem to be terribly impressed with dancing, however.

There were notebooks that contained Nathan's familiar scrawl and meticulous notes, dating back twelve years. There were gaps, she noted as she ran her fingers over the leather-bound notebooks; the year they had married, for example. The two years in which Robbie was born and died. He'd not resumed his notes until three years ago, but there were several notebooks containing his work since then.

Frankly, Evelyn didn't know if she felt betrayed or strangely proud. How was it she did not know this about him? Why had he never mentioned his work in this small cottage?

"May she try the oil, Mr. Milburn?" Frances asked.

He opened a small brown vial; a very fragrant scent of lavender filled the room. Evelyn and Harriet held out their fingers, onto which Milburn dabbed a drop so small Evelyn could barely feel it. "Only a drop is needed," he said.

Evelyn quickly dabbed it behind her ears and onto her wrists. Her nose filled with the sweet scent, prompting a host of memories, such as walking to church on Sunday mornings. Or taking tea in her mother's garden.

And another, far more distant morning, shortly after they were married, when Nathan had awakened her with his hands and mouth and she had experienced true carnal pleasure for the first time in her life on bed linens scented with lavender.

The memory caused her to blush, and she picked

up her muffler, stuffed her hands into it. "Thank you,
Mr. Milburn and Master Brady, for showing us," she
said, nodding to the table. "I had not . . . that is to say,
my husband never . . ." She did not finish her sentence.
Why he'd kept this from her, why he'd failed to mention it, confounded her. Did he think she would criticize
him? That she would not understand? That she would
not care?

"I suppose he thought not to bother you with it,
mu'um, what with all you've endured," Milburn offered
matter-of-factly.

"Are you still sad?" Frances asked.

"For the love of Christ, lad!" Milburn exclaimed.

Harriet's eyes grew wide, but Evelyn merely smiled
and tucked the tiny vial of lavender oil Mr. Milburn had
given her into her pocket. When Robbie had died, it had
felt as if the whole world was watching and waiting for her
to be crushed by the weight of her grief, and she'd come
dangerously close to that fate. She gave Frances a tight
smile as she ushered Harriet to the door. "I will always be
sad, Frances, but I am not as sad as I was." She opened
the door. "Thank you again, Mr. Milburn. Frances."

"Good day, mu'um," Milburn said.

Walking back to the house, Evelyn was oblivious to the
cold, in spite of the temperature having dropped dramatically since they'd gone into the cottage. Harriet was
skipping alongside her, chattering about Frances, and
how he didn't *really* know as much about plants as his
lordship, and asking questions about Frances that Evelyn could not answer. She was too wrapped up in her
own thoughts.

The interest in botany and the work he'd done was a side to Nathan she'd never seen. What else did she not know about him?

A curl of uncertainty crept into her thoughts, winding around other, persistent thoughts. Some of the things he'd said last night would not leave her. It seemed impossible that he was the same angry man who had, several years earlier, told her to go to London and leave him be.

She was so lost in thought that she hadn't realized she'd followed Harriet onto the main path leading to the house, the one that crossed in front of the church and alongside the church graveyard where decades of Greys had been buried. They stumbled upon it before she realized it, and her eyes were instantly drawn to the stone cherub in the corner that marked the place where her son was buried.

Her belly tightened painfully. She came to a halt, rooted to the path, her gaze glued to the cherub. Her instinct was to flee, but there was another, stronger instinct—the instinct of a mother—that prompted her forward.

"Lady Lindsey?" Harriet asked uncertainly.

Don't be afraid. Don't feel, don't feel. The cherub held his tiny hands under his chin as he looked up beseechingly at the sky. Her father-in-law had had the sculpture made. Evelyn hated it. It seemed to imply that Robbie had been whisked away by little angels, and in her heart, he'd been snatched by the devil.

"Is something wrong?" Harriet asked.

Evelyn couldn't answer straightaway. She was remembering the day they buried him, the memory as fresh as if she were reliving that awful morning. It was cold and gray, and sleet fell, stinging their faces as they gathered in the churchyard. She supposed they had all huddled together for warmth, but she'd been heedless of rain or cold. She'd been unaware that her father stood steadfastly behind her, matching her movements with the umbrella he held over her head—Kathleen told her that later. Nor did she feel Nathan's grip on her elbow. It wasn't until she'd felt her knees begin to buckle that she'd realized he held her so firmly.

The only thing she could remember feeling—other than the bottomless pit of despair—was the small wooden pony she clutched in her hand, its head stained dark with a baby's saliva and scarred by the imprints of his few tiny teeth.

She remembered staring into the bleak, black hole of his grave, trying hard not to imagine her son there. She remembered thinking, in the inebriation of her grief, that Robbie would be frightened in that hole. That he would want his mother, and she wouldn't be there.

She'd lost her head then. She'd said aloud, "He should have his pony," and the people around her had started to move, trying to shield her from the hole that would swallow her son.

"Evie," Nathan had said in her ear, and had slipped his arm around her waist, pulling her into his side, holding her securely.

"He should have his pony," she'd pleaded with him.

"Oh my darling, don't do this," her mother had whispered beside her, caressing her arm, as if she thought Evelyn might drop the wooden pony if she caressed it hard enough.

But Evelyn could not be appeased. In moments, the earth would swallow her son. She'd cried out—what she said, she could no longer remember, but she was suddenly frantic that her son have his pony before they put him in that hole. She'd wailed at the pastor, begging him to open the casket, holding out the wooden pony.

A cold shudder of memory ran through her, and she glanced at the tree at the side of his grave. She'd stood under that tree, and Nathan had grabbed her up, caught her face in his hands, and made her look at him.

"He needs his pony," she'd begged him. "Please, Nathan."

Nathan's eyes were etched with pain and grief, but he'd looked her squarely in the eye and said soothingly, "He shall have his pony, Evie. He shall have his pony." And then he'd wrapped his arms around her, pressed her face into the lapel of his coat, and Evelyn had dissolved into a torrent of tears from a bottomless well. She'd had no strength to hold herself up and had let go, sinking into Nathan's warmth, allowing him to shore her up.

To this day, she did not know if Robbie had his pony.

"Lady Lindsey?" Harriet said again. "Are you all right?"

Evelyn remembered the girl and smiled. "I am very well, Harriet. I just . . ." She looked at the cherub again and glumly noted the bit of mold growing in the grooves of his wings. "M-my son is buried just there," she said, amazed she was able to say it aloud.

"Is that why Frances asked if you were sad?"

"Yes," Evelyn said, and smiled down at Harriet. "It was a long time ago. I'm freezing, darling! Let's run and see if Benton will bring us tea," she said, and took Harriet's hand in hers.

At the edge of the forest behind the church, the man chewed on the end of a sodden cheroot, watching the

Countess of Lindsey and the girl. He wondered if the earl was close at hand, or if he had gone off as he was wont to do. If only he could lure the earl away from Eastchurch, he might find a way to complete his task.

He tossed the cheroot to the ground and turned, walking away from the church and deeper into the forest, where he'd tethered his horse.

chapter twelve

After a night of heavy drinking and gambling, Nathan left Lambourne and Donnelly sleeping off their drink and rode into the village to meet with his solicitor.

Except that riding was not a very apt description. It was more as if he'd hurled himself at the village, forcing Cedric to run at breakneck speed. He could feel the horse straining beneath him, his enormous hooves chewing up the earth in great chunks of turf. But even with Cedric's champion bloodlines, he could not run fast or hard enough to suit Nathan that morning. Nothing was fast or hard enough to remove the dull ache from his head brought on by too much whiskey . . . and Evelyn's request for a divorce.

Divorce! What a ridiculous, preposterous, *imbecilic* thing to ask of him! Was she so oblivious to the mood of the nation? Was she so callous that she could disregard the sanctity of their vows? Had she no care for the scandal that would create for both of them?

Did she truly despise him so completely?

When he'd left that bleak room in the basement—his body still suffering from the madly passionate kiss they'd shared—he'd drunk his fill of whiskey, and his anger had ebbed into familiar feelings: Remorse. Guilt. Emptiness.

It was those old companions that had him by the throat when he left his solicitor's modest offices and turned right on High Street toward the stables.

He *had* allowed the orangery to fall into disrepair, and if he were truthful with himself, he would admit that he'd done it out of anger. He'd been so angry when she'd gone to London, so furious that he could not reach her or bridge that gap that had widened between them after Robert's death.

He'd let the small rose garden waste away, too, in spite of the protests of his head gardener. He'd left her rooms to rot as well. Benton, however, had blatantly disregarded his wishes and kept them up. *Bloody butler.* One would think *he* was the lord of the estate.

After stabling his horse, Nathan stalked up the street, nodding curtly to those who passed him, and entered Williams and Son, Purveyor of Fine Goods, by throwing open the door a little harder than was necessary.

Mr. Williams the elder or Mr. Williams the junior—Nathan hardly cared—jumped a good foot off the ground at his rather noisy entrance. "My lord!" he exclaimed, and dropped the quizzing glass he was using to examine some jewelry. "Welcome, welcome!" he said, coming around from behind his counter. "Please, sir, how may I help you?"

"Can you arrange for . . ." He could scarcely bring himself to say it without feeling like an utter fool.

"Yes?" Mr. Williams asked eagerly.

"Orange trees," he said brusquely.

"*Orange* trees?"

"Miniature orange trees. From France, I believe. A dozen of them. No—two dozen."

Mr. Williams opened his mouth . . . but being an ambitious merchant, he quickly shut it. He reached for a pencil and paper and began to write. "It is not the season for trees, my lord, but I might be able to find the hothouse variety."

"*Make* it the season for trees," Nathan said irritably. "They are for an orangery."

"Ah. Two dozen, as you wish. What else may I assist you with, my lord?"

"Ah . . ." Nathan slapped his gloves against his thigh. "A divan and a pair of chairs that one might sit in to read. With . . . with a flowery fabric." Or was it birds? He tried to remember, but could think of nothing more specific than something frilly. "Or birds," he said uncertainly. "Flowers or birds, I hardly care! Just have them upholstered in something that would suit a woman's . . . *very* particular tastes."

Mr. Williams nodded and made a few notes. As he did, Nathan pictured Evelyn's cheeks, stained pink with desire last night.

She'd looked absolutely delectable, damn her! Dressed in hardly anything at all, her hair down around her shoulders—he clenched his hand, and winced inwardly at the shot of pain that gave him. He stole a glimpse of his bruised knuckles, scraped and varying shades of purple.

He wanted her. By God, he wanted her with a strength that surprised and confounded him. She was infuriating, but that made him want her even more. It was ironic—there had been a time he could not bring himself to look at her, much less touch her. He wanted to touch her now. He wanted to touch every inch of her flesh—

"My lord?"

Nathan started.

"Is there naught else?"

"No. No, just what you have there," he said, waving his gloves at the paper.

"Yes, my lord," Mr. Williams said, and quickly scratched something out on the paper. When he'd finished, he looked up with a beaming smile that told Nathan he would pay dearly for this.

His instructions complete, Nathan wished the man a good day, and walked outside—and collided with Wilkes.

"Lindsey!" Wilkes said cheerfully.

Nathan was hardly in the mood to chat and scarcely glanced at Wilkes as he started in the direction of the stables. "Back from London so soon? I thought you'd be a fortnight."

"My business was unavoidably interrupted and the lady was not inclined to a fortnight," Wilkes said with a laugh.

"Lost your charm, have you?" Nathan goaded him as Wilkes fell in beside him.

"Once I lost the desire to pay for expensive rooms and bills from a dressmaker, she was less than enthralled with my considerable charms," he said, and laughed again. "I take it the trunks arrived?"

Nathan's jaw tightened; he did owe Wilkes a debt of gratitude for helping him abduct his wife—he'd seen that her things were collected and sent to Eastchurch. "They did. Thank you."

"Think nothing of it," Wilkes said cheerfully. "I should mention, however, that in the course of paying the call to Buckingham, I discovered you acted without a moment to spare."

Nathan looked up. "Oh?"

Wilkes glanced around, then said low, "Rumor among certain ladies in waiting is that Dunhill has booked passage for two to France."

Nathan blinked, the words slowly sinking into his brain.

"He clearly meant to escape with her," Wilkes continued blithely as they reached the stable. "It seems to have been a rather open and bold friendship."

Nathan gestured for his mount.

"I tell you this only as a friend, naturally," Wilkes added.

"Naturally." Nathan handed a coin to the stable boy who brought Cedric.

"The roan there," Wilkes said to the lad. To Nathan, he said, "There is more."

"Bloody hell, I don't think I can take more without the aid of at least a pint," Nathan said, and swung up on his horse.

"Ah, but this will delight you. Were I Lambourne, I'd purchase one of Donnelly's fastest mounts and ride for bonny Scotland posthaste."

"Why?" Nathan demanded, not the least bit amused. "What's he done?"

Wilkes grinned wolfishly, glanced around him, and stepped closer. "Has he ever mentioned a tryst with the Princess of Wales to you?"

Nathan very nearly choked. "No!" he exclaimed, disgusted. There was not a more unappealing woman in the kingdom than the Princess of Wales, Nathan thought, and he could scarcely imagine the dashing Lord Lambourne would find her any less so. Jack Haines was very particular about his bed partners, unlike Wilkes, who would bed any chit that would accept his coin, or Donnelly, who tended to become infatuated very easily.

"It's true," Wilkes said as the boy led the roan out. He was clearly enjoying the role of bearer of news. "It seems that during the investigation into Caroline's misdeeds, Jack was named as one of her many lovers."

"I would sooner believe that Benton had bedded the princess before I'd believe it of Lambourne," Nathan said gruffly, but a small smile curved his lips. "Yet it certainly bears investigation, does it not? Come on, then, let us bring the news to Lambourne together, shall we?"

Benton met them in the foyer at Eastchurch. "Shall I have tea brought up, my lord?" he asked as he took the cloaks, hats, and gloves from the two men and sent a footman up to a guest room with Wilkes's bag.

"Tea?" Wilkes scoffed. "A pint or a whiskey, Benton, something that will truly warm us. It's bloody cold out."

"Very good, sir," Benton said with a bow of his head. "You may wish to join lords Lambourne and Donnelly in the billiard room."

Nathan could hear their laughter echoing down the hall. "Have the ale sent there," he said, and looked at Wilkes. "I should see to the post before joining you."

"It is in the family study, my lord, awaiting your attention," Benton said perfunctorily.

"We'll keep a pint warm for you, Lindsey," Wilkes said as he headed in the opposite direction. "And I'll save the news for Lambourne until you can join us."

Nathan was really in no mood for his guests now, and frankly, he wondered if they ever intended to leave the abbey or if he should designate spots in the family grave-yard for each of them.

A footman reached the study door before Nathan and opened it, but the action hardly registered on Nathan. He strode across the threshold, looked toward his desk, and faltered.

Evelyn was sitting at the Louis XIV cherrywood desk. She made a sound of surprise at his sudden entrance and dropped the pen she was holding.

Nathan instantly felt ill at ease and mentally stumbled—he was unaccustomed to rejection, unaccus-tomed to being looked at as if he were a monster. He was accustomed to feeling like one, perhaps, but not being per-ceived as one.

Evelyn scrambled to her feet and tried to gather the papers on which she was writing, almost frantic to es-cape him.

"Leave them!" he said roughly.

She clutched the papers to her chest and stepped around the desk. "I will not."

"And just who are you writing, madam, that you must take it from my sight?" he snapped.

Evelyn's brows dipped into a dangerous vee. "Not that it's any of *your* concern, sir, but I am writing my sis-ter." She thrust the letter forward.

Nathan strode across the room and took it. He read the first sentence. *My dearest Clarissa*, it read.

He thrust the letter back at her and brushed past her as he stepped around to his desk. He caught the fragrant scent of lavender, and it slowed him a step or two; but with a quick look at her face, he continued on and took his seat behind his desk.

She had spilled ink on the blotter and the point of his pen was flattened.

"Why are you here?" he asked brusquely as he examined the pen. "I made paper and pen available to you."

"You made foolscap available to me. Not vellum. And the pen was old and brittle. The tip of it broke."

It broke because she wrote long and passionate letters. He remembered that about her, too.

"And I didn't realize I required your permission to use the study."

"You do not require my permission," he said, glancing up, "but given your utter loathing of me, I rather thought you'd want to keep a safe distance."

She sighed irritably. "Really, Nathan, I do not *loathe* you."

"No? When a woman asks her husband to grant her a divorce, what else might he assume?"

Evelyn opened her mouth. Then closed it again. He could almost hear the wheels turning in her head as she worked out her response.

"Don't fret, darling," he drawled. "I won't force you to reveal the reason why. I think your little secret is apparent to both of us."

"*My* secret?"

He rolled his eyes. "France?"

"*France?* What are you talking about?"

He was in no mood for her prevaricating. "You and Dunhill! He bought passage for two to France."

She at least had the grace to feign astonishment. "I have no idea what you are talking about," she said curtly.

"Honestly, Evelyn."

"I don't! And how would you know if he had? Do you have spies in London?"

"Spies!" he scoffed. "No, Evelyn, I don't have spies. It's precisely what I warned you about—*everyone* is talking. Everyone watches everyone else. There are no secrets, and if you were fool enough to believe there were, then heaven help you."

"I never claimed to have any secrets!" she snapped. "On my honor, I know nothing of France. And before you accuse me of having secrets, what of your secrets, Lindsey? *You* seem perfectly willing to keep them."

He leaned back in his chair and cast his arms wide. "I'm no saint, love, but my life is an open book."

Her eyes went wide with surprise. And then she laughed. "I beg your pardon, but you are perhaps the most taciturn man I have ever known!"

"Taciturn! I am most certainly not!"

"Indeed you are!" she said, as if she found it all very amusing—which he did not. "I cannot begin to recount the many times I would attempt to engage you in conversation, and you would answer, 'yes, darling,' 'no, darling,' and little else!"

"You make no sense," he said gruffly.

Evelyn suddenly braced her hands against the desk and leaned forward. "There are things you should have told me and did not, such as your deep and abiding friendship with Mrs. DuPaul," she said irritably. "On the anniversary of our son's death, you never told me you and Mrs. DuPaul would . . . would . . ." She made a gesture with her hand.

Nathan knew very well to what she referred. "Hold a private memorial?" he said. "Only because you were in no state to mark the date of our son's death. However, I *needed* to mark it."

"With Mrs. DuPaul?"

His eyes narrowed. "You and I were hardly speaking at the time," he reminded her. "Can you honestly stand there and pretend you might have humored me that day? No, Evelyn, you would not have done so, and I could not cope with your anger on a day I very much needed to cope with my grief."

Something like confusion passed over her eyes, and she suddenly reared back, folding her arms. "You might have coped with your grief without your ever-present friend. Nevertheless, you said you were an open book, Nathan, yet that is surely at least one occasion when you neglected to tell me what you were thinking or planning. Did you consider it from my viewpoint? I was *very* distressed by the anniversary, and to add to my grief was the knowledge that my husband was at the church where we buried our son with another woman!"

Praying for us, Nathan thought, and gained his feet. This time, it was he who leaned across the desk. "I *did* tell you what I was thinking, Evie," he said calmly. "I told you I was thinking we should memorialize our son, but you flatly refused. You said you could not bear to think of it, remember? You could not *bear* much of anything. I beg your forgiveness if I did not feel the tragedy of your loss as sharply as I felt my own."

She blinked her big hazel eyes. "You . . . you are willfully misunderstanding me."

"I assure you I am not. And lest you think you are so forthcoming, you never gave me the slightest hint you would ask for a divorce."

"What did you think would come of our estrangement?"

"Not that," he snapped.

"All right, then," she said, nodding. "What about your botanical interests, hmm?" At his puzzled look, she exclaimed wildly, "You are an open book, Nathan! Yet I have never heard of your interest in *botany*! I should think that the medicinal properties of lavender oil might be worth at least a brief mention."

He couldn't imagine why she might be interested in his little hobby. Frankly, he'd worked at it on and off for years—more off than on, really. He'd only picked it up again in the last two years as something he might share with Frances.

Evelyn was glaring at him, munching on the canary she obviously thought she'd captured and stuffed into her mouth.

"Why?" he asked simply.

Evelyn gaped at him. "*Why?* It seems rather significant to me, sir! Your work is renowned among the scientists!"

He scoffed at that with a flick of his wrist. "That sort of work is *always* renowned among certain scientists. They have such a small body of work on which to rely."

"Nathan, this is precisely what I have tried to convey!" she exclaimed, flinging her hand at him. "I scarcely know you any longer!"

"You don't *know* me?" he shot back, coming around the desk to stand before her, towering over her.

Unfazed, Evelyn tilted her head back. "Oh, I may have guessed at certain things, but I am beginning to suspect I never really *knew* you. I certainly never knew about your work in botany!"

"This has become a favorite theme of yours, this silly notion that we do not know each other!"

"You have just proven it is so!"

"If I failed to tell you about a bloody hobby—again, my apologies. But you *know* me, Evie. We shared a bed! We conceived a child! There are certain things one gleans from the other in such intimate circumstances."

She could not argue with that, and in fact, she blushed like a girl. She pressed her lips together and looked down at the carpet. "Why didn't you tell me about the botany?" she asked softly.

"Evelyn!" he said, flustered. "It didn't bear mentioning!"

She looked up again, and the tears in her eyes startled him. "One can only wonder what else you thought didn't bear mentioning through the years that might have made a difference to me."

She started for the door. Nathan went after her, catching her with a hand to her shoulder, forcing her to turn around. She tried to resist him, but he caught her by the waist, put his hand to the side of her face. "Do not," he said low, "use your pique as some foolish excuse to dissolve this marriage."

"Marriage? *What* marriage?" She pushed out of his clutch and marched from the room.

chapter thirteen

Evelyn knew her husband was right, of course. She *was* looking for an excuse to bolster her request for a divorce . . . instead of congratulating him on his botanical work as she ought to have done.

Frankly, as she sat next to the hearth in her rooms now, watching the flames dance against the brick, it seemed unreal that the word *divorce* had ever passed her lips. Perhaps she'd *thought* it many times . . . but to say it aloud now seemed unfathomable, even to her.

Damn him! He'd confused her last night with his kiss and his hands! Her pulse had been racing, her skin tingling, and she'd scarcely been able to draw a breath into her lungs! All she could think was that she had to *do* something, for when the glow of pleasure abated, she would still be trapped in this marriage from which she had detached herself years ago.

Detached. Severed, disengaged, dismembered. In the aftermath of Robbie's death, something inside her had fundamentally changed . . . hadn't it?

Heaven help her, she was suddenly uncertain what was truly changed and what had perhaps just lain dormant. But her view of life was forever altered, and for so long now she'd felt unsettled and restive, always seeking . . .

But there was a certain steadiness to her here, she realized. At first, she'd believed it was her determination not to feel again, but now . . . now she could not help but wonder if it was something much deeper than that. This was the place she'd become a woman, a wife, a mother. Nathan had made her all those things. Despite their differences, they were inexorably bound to one another. She didn't hate him. She wasn't really even angry anymore. But she was done with that part of her life.

And Nathan *did* care for her, or believed he did. She could see it in his expression today. She'd seen it in the fierce way he'd protected her when the highwaymen had attacked them. And she'd definitely seen it in the look in his eyes last night, that intoxicating mix of desire and affection and bewilderment shimmering in them. Perhaps their separation had dimmed his memory. Familiarity would inevitably rekindle the proverbial contempt after a time, she'd wager.

It was best to somehow end the marriage before the contempt crept in. They simply couldn't go back.

Yet while she was ready to end their marriage, she did not want to play games with Nathan. Tonight, she wanted nothing more than to make amends for having been so peevish about his accomplishments. His botanical interests were something to be admired, not brought down by his failure to tell her about them.

"Therefore," she said, rising from her seat at the hearth, "you must resolve to be the lady you were bred to be, Evelyn." She resolved to approach her delicate situation with more decorum and grace than perhaps she had shown him thus far.

Evelyn called for Harriet, who helped her dress for supper. She dressed in a pale blue gown with soft pleats that bled into a dark green.

"Oh my," Kathleen said approvingly as she admired Evelyn after arranging her hair. "You look like a princess, mu'um."

Evelyn laughed. "I assure you, I am no princess." She leaned over, pinched her cheeks in the mirror to bring some color to them. Kathleen had outdone herself— her hair was swept up in an artful chignon, held in place with tiny crystal pins that caught the candlelight.

Satisfied with her appearance, she put out her hand to Harriet. "Shall we make your presence known to my husband?"

Evelyn took the wrap Kathleen offered her and wore it loosely around her arms. With Harriet in tow, she made her way to the main dining room, careful not to look left or right, careful not to see those places that would spark a memory of her son, careful not to think or feel. She smiled at the servants she passed and pretended not to see the looks of obvious curiosity directed at her or Harriet.

A footman stood at the entrance to the dining room and opened the door for them. Evelyn took a deep breath, lifted her chin, and walked across the threshold.

Into an *empty* dining room, save the two footmen standing next to the sideboard. Two place settings graced one end of the mahogany table that had been a wedding gift from Lord Donnelly, handcrafted in Ireland and brought over in large pieces to England.

Evelyn glanced apprehensively at the two footmen as she walked to the end of the table, her fingers trailing along the backs of the chairs pushed up to the table and perfectly spaced. As she reached the end of the table, Benton came through an adjoining door as if he'd been waiting for her, and quickly moved to hold out her chair as a footman seated Harriet.

"Where is everyone?" she said as she took her chair.

"The others have already dined, madam."

Already *dined*? Evelyn glanced at the clock on the buffet. It was a quarter to eight. In all the time she'd been married, supper was served at precisely eight o'clock. "I don't understand," she said as one footman poured wine and the other ladled soup into their bowls.

"It was not a meal, per se," Benton said as he presented her lap with a linen napkin. "They chose to dine on nuts."

"On *nuts*?"

"Yes, madam. Nuts."

She looked up at Benton. "Pray tell, sir, where are they now?"

"In his lordship's private drawing room, engaged in a game of cards."

"You don't say," she said, her eyes narrowing. She glanced again at the two footmen. "Benton? Would you please ask Kathleen to prepare to receive Lady Harriet after supper?" She smiled at Harriet. "And please tell Kathleen that my lady is an avid fan of the game of chess."

"Don't fret," Harriet said sagely. "I dine alone quite a lot. It's really rather easy, for no one is making you mind your manners."

Evelyn's heart went out to the girl, but she laughed.

"I won't make you mind your manners if you won't make me mind mine."

She and Harriet chatted about Princess Amelia as they dined—she'd lost a pin, which, Harriet reported, had caused quite an uproar, for they believed a chambermaid had taken it. Harriet seemed relieved that it was found and the chambermaid was exonerated. "Mamma said she ought to have been tossed out. Mamma is always tossing out servants," Harriet said, as if she were speaking of rubbish. "I will never toss out a servant, for they are always very kind to me. Would you?"

Evelyn smiled. "I certainly hope not."

Harriet dipped her spoon in her soup. "I'll be a better mistress than Mamma," she opined. "My servants shall never want to leave my house, for we shall have parties and be gay as often as we like."

"I know that I would never want to leave your house!" Evelyn exclaimed. "May I come, too?"

"Of course," Harriet said solemnly. "But you cannot bring Mamma, for she might go about tossing the servants."

Evelyn laughed.

When they'd finished the meal, Evelyn said good night to Harriet and promised to meet her at breakfast. She watched Harriet walking away in the company of a footman, and then turned in the opposite direction, bound for the green salon.

She continued on to Nathan's private drawing room, debating with each step whether or not she should . . . but then she heard their laughter and smelled their tobacco.

To think only hours earlier, she'd felt a bit sorry for him! The bloody lot of them hadn't changed as much

as an inch—she could just picture them, well into their
cups. Carousing had been a source of friction between
her and Nathan in the past, and now he would have her
believe he'd changed?

Evelyn put her hand on the crystal knob and turned
it. The door swung open, catching on the thick Aubus-
son carpet. She peeked around it—the four of them
were seated at a card table, slumped ungraciously in
their chairs, cheroots clamped between their teeth,
whiskey tots at their elbows.

Evelyn pushed the door open further and walked in.

The moment the men saw her, they scrambled to
their feet—Donnelly managing to knock over his whiskey in the process without noticing, while Evelyn
watched, horrified, as it soaked into the carpet.

"Madam?" Nathan said, squinting as he braced himself with one hand against the card table.

"I beg your pardon—I came down for supper and
found the dining room quite empty."

Nathan glanced at Lambourne. "Supper. Yes, supper.
I, ah . . ."

She clasped her hands behind her back and walked
deeper into the room. "I understand you fortified yourself for a night of cards with some nuts. What delicious
fare."

Nathan suddenly smiled; a warm and exceedingly
charming smile. She knew that smile. There was a time
in her life when it had made her feel as if she was made
of nothing but air. "The nuts were indeed delicious."

"Oh dear," Donnelly said. He'd only just noticed his
spilled whiskey. The other three, noticing it, too, began
to laugh.

"Lord," Evelyn muttered, and moved to the hearth,

which was, she noted, going cold. She passed closely by the card table, her eyes on Nathan.

"Ah, lavender," Wilkes said. "Not a lovelier scent on a woman, if you don't mind me saying, madam."

"So you've been to Lindsey's little laboratory, aye?" Lambourne said. "I've no' known a man to be so enamored of lavender as he."

Evelyn blinked with surprise, then looked at Nathan. "*They* know of it?" she asked, sweeping her hand to indicate his friends.

Nathan swayed a bit. "They discovered it on their own," he said, casting a murderous look at Lambourne.

"Aye, that we did," Lambourne added hastily. "Quite by accident. Hunting," he said, gesturing vaguely with his hand. He cleared his throat. "Just . . . stumbled upon it, we did."

Apparently, Nathan's friends thought she was a little fool. "I am amazed you were able to *walk*, much less stumble on it," Evelyn said dryly, and shifted her gaze to Nathan. "It may interest you to know, my lord, that you are not the only one with a hobby. I intend to restore the abbey and the orangery to its former beauty."

"Well. There you are," Nathan said, and looked at the cards he still held in his hand, as if he was surprised to find them there.

"I shall spare *no* expense, of course."

"Of course," Nathan drawled, glancing up again as the men looked anxiously at the floor, the table . . . any place but her.

"Well," she said pertly. "I will leave you to your nuts and your cards, sirs."

"Good night, Lady Lindsey," Donnelly tried.

Evelyn rolled her eyes and strode to the door. Before

she could reach the door, however, her eye was drawn to the marks on the wall Robbie had made with ink. They were big swaths of lines, scribbled back and forth. Her gut clenched a little but she was, she was relieved to discover, more resilient than she'd feared.

When the door closed behind Evelyn, Nathan thought, in his drunken state, that his wife looked a bit like an angel from on high. He poured himself into his chair and tried to focus on his cards. "Bloody *hell*," he muttered.

"What is it, Lindsey?" Wilkes asked congenially. "Have you not yet brought her to heel?"

"She's not a dog, sir," Donnelly said as he picked up his cards.

"'Tis a figure of speech, Declan," Wilkes said with exasperation. "She is obviously *not* a dog."

"Have a care, gents," Nathan muttered.

"Consider the source," Lambourne said with a look at Wilkes. "Wilkes has a way of saying the wrong thing."

That was met with howls of laughter. "It was not *I* who said you diddled Caroline," Wilkes said, laughing loudly, as Nathan attempted to pour more whiskey into his glass.

"*Ach!* I've no' touched the woman!" Lambourne objected. "On my poor father's grave, may he rest in peace, I have no', lads!"

"Best have more than your word," Donnelly said, "given the charge of high treason that could be leveled against you."

"Did I tell you? They've begun questioning men," Wilkes added.

"Aye, aye, you told me! I've naugh' to fear," Lambourne boasted unconvincingly to no one, and began to recount the many ways he was innocent.

Nathan scarcely heard him. He'd long since had his fill of whiskey, but when Donnelly handed him another tot, he continued to drink, hoping against hope it would ease the ache he'd not been able to rid himself of since laying eyes on Evelyn at Carlton House. Then, it had been dull and distant, but it was suddenly pounding through him.

Nathan never knew when he slipped into oblivion; he only knew that the ache was still with him and in his mind's eye, the vision of an angel in blue.

chapter fourteen

Dressed and ready for bed, Evelyn spent two hours calming her anger and her anxiety by methodically making a list of all the things she would purchase in the village on the morrow that were necessary to begin reviving the public rooms. The hunting and fishing gear would be gone, carpets and draperies cleaned or replaced, and beeswax candles ordered to supply every room.

She had just put the finishing touches on her list when she heard a loud commotion outside her door. The noise frightened her—it sounded like an invasion of some sort—and she jumped up from the vanity, gripping the hairbrush like a weapon.

She shrieked when someone pounded on her door.

"Lady Lindsey, I beg of you, open the door!" she heard Donnelly shout.

"Why?" she called back. "What's happened?"

Her question was met with what sounded like a

physical confrontation in the corridor. Evelyn moved back from the door, still gripping her brush.

"Lady Lindsey, if you please! We've nowhere to leave him, but we canna leave him in the salon!" Lambourne exclaimed on the other side of the door.

She took a tentative step closer. "Leave *who*? Lindsey?"

"Aye, madam!"

Oh, of all the infuriating, *ridiculous*—she marched to the door, throwing it open. Her lord husband was being held aloft by his three constant companions, his legs and arms tucked up under their arms.

"Dear God! Can't you just put him in his bed?"

"We could, aye, we could . . ." Lambourne said with a wince, "but you know Benton very well. He'd be up all night with him, he would. We canna have that on our conscience."

"Oh no, of course not," she said, shaking her head. "But having *me* up all night will not rile your conscience, will it?"

The three of them exchanged a sheepish look.

With a sigh, Evelyn stepped aside and gestured impatiently with her hairbrush for them to carry him to her bed. They made quite a commotion coming in, bumping up against the doorjamb and knocking Nathan's head against a chair as they passed. They deposited him like a bag of coal onto Evelyn's bed; Donnelly tried to remove Nathan's boot, but he was too inebriated to manage it.

"Out!" Evelyn said sternly to all of them as they tromped around her bed. "All of you! *Out!*" She ushered them out, ignoring their slurred apologies and thank-yous. She slammed the door shut behind them, locked it, then whirled around, put her back to the door, and stared at her slumbering husband. He groaned and rolled onto his side.

His friends had divested him of his coat and waistcoat, as well as his neckcloth. His shirt had been pulled from his trousers, and through the open neck of his shirt, she could see the dark hair on his chest. His hips and thighs, strong and powerful, took up more space on her bed than she recalled.

He groaned again, rolled onto his back, and flung one arm over his eyes.

"And to think I wanted to give you the benefit of my doubt," Evelyn muttered. She pushed away from the door and walked to the foot of the bed, watching him. "You haven't changed at all, Nathan."

"I'm sorry, Evie," he said, startling her.

"You're *awake*?" she cried.

He didn't answer.

She moved around to the side of the bed and poked him with her hand. He didn't move. "Nathan, are you awake? If you are awake, sir, you may take yourself to *your* bed and leave me in peace!"

His response was a loud snore.

She frowned down at him, but when he didn't move, she returned to the end of the bed and grabbed his foot. "I remember the last time this happened," she said aloud, just in case he was practicing his theatrics on her. "It was the night after he died. You disappeared for more than a day and I thought . . . I thought . . ."

She bit her lower lip and yanked the boot from his foot, put it aside, then reached for the other. "Then at midnight," she continued, "Benton and a pair of footmen brought you up and laid you on this very bed." She gave the second boot a yank, laid it at the foot of the bed alongside the other. With hands on her hips, she stared at him. "I thought I'd lost you both," she said softly.

She pulled the counterpane out from beneath his feet and pulled it up over him, around his shoulders. He snored softly as she completed her toilette, stealing glimpses of him from time to time to assure herself he was still breathing, and that he was, indeed, asleep. When she had finished that, she puttered about the room, stoking the fire, putting away a few things. Nathan did not move.

At last, she snuffed the two candles that had lit her room, and stretched out on the chaise. Her feet dangled off the end and her head was propped against the back at an odd angle. It was really meant for sitting and not sleeping. Nevertheless, Evelyn was determined to make herself comfortable—she curled up on her side and closed her eyes.

An hour later, she sat up, pushed her hair from her face—it had come loose from the braid with all her twisting and turning—and glared at the bed. Nathan was sleeping like a baby, sprawled beneath her beautiful silk counterpane. She put her feet on the ground and carefully—reluctantly—walked around to the other side of the bed.

She sat on the edge a moment, questioning the wisdom of what she was doing. With a glance at him over her shoulder, she carefully peeled back the counterpane and lay on the very edge of the bed. The bed curtains moved slightly, and through the diaphanous panes she saw the long shadows the low light of the fire cast across the room. It reminded her of another time she had lain here and had seen the form of a nurse moving quietly about the room.

She rolled onto her back and stared up at the embroidered canopy above her head. His weight made the bed feel different. He was like a rock, anchoring her in this little sea of a bed. The mattress beneath her dipped toward him, a familiar sensation—and a lovely feeling of security.

She listened to the sound of his breathing, steady and deep. She used to love those nights he slept in her bed, his body providing warmth against the winter's chill, his breathing the assuring sound that she was safe.

Evelyn relaxed and shifted a little closer to him, stretching out beside him. She pulled the counterpane up beneath her chin and settled onto her side.

A moment later, Nathan grunted and rolled onto his side, directly at her back. His arm snaked around her midriff, and he pulled her closer to him with a soft grunt. His breath ruffled the top of her head. She froze until his breathing grew steady again, then slowly, she released her breath.

He was warm. And hard-bodied. *And she liked it.*

Evelyn closed her eyes and drifted to a warm and peaceful sleep for the first time since her husband had appeared before her like a ghost at Carlton House.

Nathan had a dream.

In his dream, he was in the stables, lying on a bed of hay in an empty stall, with Evelyn. It was raining out, and the horses were . . . were gone, he didn't know where, but they were alone in the stables.

He lay on the hay beside her, his lips on the nape of her neck. He slipped his hand into the open neck of Evelyn's nightgown and cupped her breast, squeezing it gently, feeling it swell and warm in his hand, rolling the peak between his fingers. Evelyn sighed, then drew a slow breath and pushed her breast against his hand. He realized he could feel her breath in him—when she breathed, he felt the draw in his own lungs. When she sighed, he felt the breath leave his body.

Nathan moved his hand down the smooth plane of her belly, his fingers sliding into the soft curls at the apex of her legs. He kissed her neck, catching a bit of her hair at the corner of his mouth as his fingers slipped between her legs and into petal-soft folds slick with desire. He stroked her, his fingers dipping deep inside her, then out again, swirling around her tiny peak, faster and faster until Evelyn began to gasp softly and press her hips into his cock.

The heat in her body was swirling in his. He could feel her in his blood, could feel her heart pulsing in his veins. He took her ear between his teeth, pressed his cock into her hips, moving against her, sliding up and down as his fingers danced at the very core of her.

In his dream, she whimpered and closed her legs around his hand, squeezing. She arched her back, her breath coming in ecstatic little gasps that swept through him, thrumming in all his nerves. With one last moan, her body slackened, and she slowly drifted away from him, disappearing into the ether of his dreams.

Nathan lay in the hay, his body aching for release . . . until he thought of the horses. He began to wonder where they had gone. *Where had the horses gone? Donnelly would be frantic . . .*

He tried to get up and find them, but his limbs felt dead. The door was suddenly thrown open, and a rude and blinding light filled the stables . . .

Stables.

Nathan groaned. He wasn't in a stable at all, but in his bed. "What in the devil are you about, Benton?" he snapped. "You must harbor a secret desire to shovel coal, sir!"

"Not Benton. Me."

Evelyn's voice startled him. In the ravaged corners of his mind, he worked to understand what she was doing in his room and tried to bolt upright. But only one arm would move. The other arm, and one leg, for that matter, felt oddly restricted. He opened his eyes.

His gaze landed on Evelyn at the foot of the bed. *Her* bed. She was dressed, but her hair hung loose around her shoulders. She had her arms folded and was drumming the fingers of one hand against her arm. "You owe me an apology," she said simply.

Nathan glanced around him. He could not begin to imagine how he'd ended up here, in her bedchamber— good God, what had he done? The last thing he remembered was losing fifty pounds to Lambourne.

"Well?"

She was smiling wickedly, one brow cocked high above the other. He glanced up; his wrist was bound with a silk stocking to the poster of the bed. A tidy little slip knot was tied high up the post, out of his reach. His leg, he noticed further, was bound at the ankle to the post diagonally across from his bound arm.

"May I ask why I am bound to your bed?" he asked hoarsely, wincing at the pain in his head.

"Because you owe me an apology."

"All right, I apologize." He tugged at the restraint on his arm. "Perhaps you might tell me how I came to be here."

"You may ask your companions why they thought to bring you here."

Lord. His head was throbbing. He needed his own bed. "All right then, you've made your point, Evelyn. Let me up."

"Not until you apologize," she said.

He closed his eyes, rubbed his fingers in them. "I apologize. Profusely. Completely. With all that I am, I apologize," he said, and opened his eyes.

"For what?"

He couldn't begin to name all his transgressions, but he was aware the list was quite long. "For . . . everything," he tried lamely.

She shook her head, sending a curtain of golden hair spilling over her shoulder. "That's not quite good enough, Nathan."

All right, then—she was going to make him pay dearly for this. "I beg you, madam, my head feels as if it might explode at any moment and all over your lovely and expensive linens. I feel like a bloody fool for having somehow ended up in your bed trussed up like a Christmas goose. I apologize. Now please let me up."

Evelyn chuckled in a way that sent a little shiver of fear up Nathan's spine. "Do you honestly believe that is apology enough?"

"No," he admitted. "But I hoped." He tried to kick free of his restraint. It was useless—she'd apparently been very studious when he'd taught her how to tie a slip knot.

Evelyn laughed at his efforts. She walked around to the side of the bed and peered down at him.

Nathan smiled, too. Charm was the only defense left to him. Perhaps she would take pity on him.

But when Evelyn smiled back, it was the smile of a woman who held all the cards. She surprised him by picking up her skirts, stepping up onto the bed, and straddling him, sitting on his abdomen. With her knees squeezing his ribs, she put her hands on his shoulders, holding him down, and then leaned over him so close that her hair spilled onto his chest, and her face was only inches from his. "You owe me an apology, Nathan," she said silkily.

Her lips were so wet, so plump and enticing, and so close to his. In spite of his predicament, all he could think of was kissing her.

"Apologize."

"I apologize," he said, and he meant it. "Whatever it is, I apologize."

"Apologize for abducting me. And drinking to excess."

"My sincerest apologies for it all—especially drinking to excess." He caught her hair in his free hand and lifted his head, tried to kiss her, but she laughed lightly and moved her head just enough that he couldn't reach her.

"Now apologize for leaving me to face my demons alone."

"I didn't know you were coming down to supper," he muttered, and tried to nip her lips again, but again, she moved just out of his reach; her hair brushed across his mouth. He smelled lavender, and his body went hard with want. "I didn't know, love. On my word, I didn't know. Kiss me, Evie," he growled. "Untie me and kiss me."

"I scarcely mean for leaving me to face my *supper* alone, Nathan. For leaving me to face my grief alone."

She was serious. *Bloody hell,* she was serious. "I didn't leave you alone, Evie," he said earnestly. "You wouldn't let me help you—or I didn't know how to help you. But I did not leave you alone, I swear it."

She slowly sat back, considering him, her eyes searching his face as she moved ever so subtly upon him. Up and down. Up and down. "Then please do explain how we could have drifted so far apart when we needed to be so close?"

Not only was she serious, but she expected him, in this miserable state, to explain how the scaffolding of their marriage had collapsed. He shook his head. "I can't rightly say. I have often questioned it myself."

Her eyes dipped to his mouth, to his shoulders, and to his eyes again. "You owe me another apology."

"I can't possibly guess what else—"

"For your chums bringing you round," she said, her eyes narrowing dangerously. "And being *constantly* underfoot."

One corner of his mouth tipped up, and he caressed her shoulder, her arm. "They are rather underfoot, aren't they? I apologize, darling. Sincerely, deeply, I apologize."

"Oh, Nathan," she sighed, and bent forward, brushed her lips so close to his that he could have sworn she touched him. He strained to rise up and meet her, but she kept just a hairsbreadth of distance between them. She did it again, and then glided down his body, feathering his chest and abdomen with tiny little kisses. His body reacted; his blood began to rush. "Oh Nathan . . . poor Nathan . . ." she whispered.

She was driving him mad. He struggled beneath her, one hand on her head, the other one straining to come free of its ties.

"Poor, dear, Nathan," she said as she reached the waist of his trousers. She nipped at the buttons with her teeth, then suddenly rose up and climbed off him. "But the apology for your friends wasn't good enough," she said with mock sadness, and twirled around, walking away from him.

"Evelyn—"

"I am going down to breakfast, my lord," she said breezily, and stepped before the mirror at her vanity to check her appearance.

"Evelyn!" he said gruffly. "You will not walk out that door! Untie me!"

She laughed as she sailed out of the room, leaving him trussed to her bed with silk stockings. *"Evelyn!"* he shouted. Her response was the unmistakable sound of a door closing. "Ah hell," he moaned, letting his head drop back. "Bloody, *bloody* hell."

Nathan came to a rather heartfelt conclusion after Kathleen, her face as round and red as an apple, untied him. He stood up, thanked her, and walked out of the room, his thoughts clear and focused in spite of the ringing in his ears. He was sick unto death of apologizing. He was weary of treading lightly around his wife. But he was beginning to understand her needs, and he'd made a decision: he would court her. He would court her, woo her, seduce her back to him, and by God, he was going to return to her bed whether she liked it or not.

chapter fifteen

Evelyn needed a place where she could think. What had happened in the middle of the night had been . . . *extraordinary*. From the moment he touched her she couldn't—*wouldn't*—stop him. She wanted to feel his arms around her, his lips on her skin. She had wanted him inside her—moving, caressing, breathing inside her.

She'd never felt desire as sharply as that.

There was no place she could go to quiet her mind, no room without a memory to confuse her even more. So she walked, her head down, her eyes on the carpet, thinking. How long she walked, she had no notion.

She pressed her cool hands to her warm face as she recalled the way he'd stroked her body, so reverently, so provocatively. The memory of it stirred her again, snatching a small gasp of breath. One small touch, a single touch, and her body had raged with thirst for him.

Yes, but when the sun rose, she was still furious with him for falling into her bed swimming in his cups.

She was still furious that they lived like this—he and his friends, she in her rooms. How many times had his friends come to Eastchurch in the years they were married and diverted him, keeping him out, keeping him away in pursuit of tawdry sports?

She was furious that he'd forced her from London, furious that she'd ever felt as if she had to escape there.

And she was livid with the world at large that things hadn't gone differently for them, that they hadn't borne a healthy son, or that they couldn't seem to navigate the sea of emotions after Robbie's death.

She was furious, and she was only beginning to realize she'd been furious for a very long time.

As she pondered that, her eye caught sight of a stain on the carpet.

Evelyn drew up. She knew that stain—it had been made by a little hand who couldn't stay out of the ink-well.

She knew precisely where she was and drew a steadying breath. She'd managed to avoid it, but she'd been lost in thought and suddenly found herself in the one place she promised herself she would never ever lay eyes on again.

How could she have been so careless?

Staring at the nursery's green door with pale cream trim, her breath shortened. She almost expected Robbie to come toddling out, that look of joyous wonder on his upturned face. She could see him in the room beyond that door, sitting at the little table and chairs, his feet just scraping the floor, or sleeping in his tiny bed. She could see him standing on the stool before the basin, happily splashing the palm of his hand in the ice-cold water. She could see the wooden blocks stacked neatly in the corner alongside his wooden animals. A cow. A dog. His pony.

Her heart was beating rapidly, pounding the breath from her lungs. Evelyn pressed a hand to her breast, turned her back to the door, and walked quickly in the other direction, fleeing the room that held so many vivid memories.

She didn't slow her step until she reached the foyer. Benton was there, laying out hats and gloves for the gentlemen.

"Good morning, Lady Lindsey," he said congenially. "If you've not yet broken your fast, a light repast is served in the family dining room. Lady Harriet has taken her breakfast with Kathleen."

"Thank you," Evelyn said.

Lord Donnelly was the only other person in the dining room besides a footman. He sat with his head hanging over a cup of tea. When Evelyn slammed the door behind her, he winced painfully and laboriously pushed himself to his feet. "Good morning."

"Good morning, sir!" Evelyn smiled brightly as the footman went about laying a place for her at the table directly across from Donnelly, who rubbed his forehead as if it pained him.

Evelyn took her seat, calmly lifted her heavy silver fork, and let it drop onto the very fine china plate. The resulting clatter made Donnelly jump a good foot in the air. "How clumsy of me," she said sweetly when he gaped at her. "I beg your pardon, you don't look well, sir. Late night?"

"All right then, you have every right to be angry," he said, sparing them both the need to pretend. "But what were we to do with him?"

"Oh, you must think nothing of it, my lord," Evelyn said with an airy wave of her hand. "I've grown quite accustomed to it. It's certainly not the first time someone has carried that old dog to a bed."

"It is the first time *I* have done so, madam," Donnelly said, bristling a little. "It is unlike Lindsey to fall so far into his cups."

"It's *quite* like him, actually," Evelyn disagreed as the footman poured tea. She hardly needed Donnelly to tell her about the many nights of Nathan's drinking, or gambling, or hunting parties that ended only God knew where.

"I assure you, it is not," Donnelly argued. "Granted, there was a time . . . but he doesn't care for drink as he once did."

Evelyn raised a brow.

Donnelly frowned. "Yes, all right, as of late he's had a bit of a thirst. But I assure you he—"

The door suddenly opened, and speak of the devil, Nathan strode through. He looked, Evelyn thought, rather remarkably virile, particularly given his condition last night. So virile, in fact, that she had to look down at her tea . . . she couldn't help the small smile that curved her lips at the memory of him trussed up in her bed.

"Please, don't let me interrupt," he said, noticing her smile.

"Not at all," she said, trying to bite back her smile without much success.

He walked to the sideboard, waved the footman away, and poured himself a cup of tea. "I owe you a debt of thanks, Declan."

"You owe me two hundred pounds," Donnelly said. "That's twice in one week."

Evelyn rolled her eyes heavenward and sipped from her teacup.

"Breakfast, my lord?" a footman asked.

"Thank you, but no. I dined earlier in my rooms."

Evelyn choked on her tea. She could just imagine it: *"Thank you, Kathleen, for untying me. Now be a love and have breakfast sent up . . ."*

"For the sake of Lady Lindsey, I would that I had followed your lead, sir," Donnelly said, and pushed away from the table. "If you will excuse me, madam, I shall leave you to your breakfast."

"My lord! You've hardly touched your porridge!" Evelyn protested sweetly as he strode to the door.

"Good morning, all," Donnelly said as he quit the room.

Nathan settled into a seat next to Donnelly's vacated one and leveled a gaze on Evelyn . . . a very darkly sultry gaze. In fact, Evelyn slowly realized, she was squirming a bit.

"Enjoying yourself?" he drawled.

"I am sure I don't know what you mean," she said pertly. "Oh dear, Nathan, you look so fatigued! Did you not sleep well?"

Nathan ignored her cheeky smile and looked her directly in the eye, his gaze piercing hers. "I slept better than I have in years, darling, complete with one very vivid and *very* sweet dream."

She could feel the color bleeding into her cheeks. "Indeed? I am astonished! One would think that given your condition, breathing might have been impossible, much less dreaming."

If anything, his gaze turned even more sensual; she could feel it trickling down her body. The memory of him last night, his hands and mouth on her bare skin—

"Quite the contrary. Mine was an extraordinarily potent dream. I'm not entirely certain it wasn't real."

Evelyn had to look away. "Marvelous! I, on the other hand, hardly slept at all." She abruptly stood. She felt hot in her gown; the fire was too bright in here, too high for such a close room. "If you will excuse me," she said without looking at him, "I believe I shall start the refurbishment of your little hunting lodge today."

"Evelyn—"

"Do not trouble yourself," she said hastily, and glanced sidelong at him. He was watching her closely. He knew the truth about last night. She could tell by the way his gaze devoured her. Her feet were moving ahead of her mind. She was at the door before she realized it, her hand on the knob.

"Darling?" he drawled.

She reluctantly turned back.

He was smiling, a lustful, cocksure smile. "Thank you for taking such exquisite care of me last night."

All right then, she had to be as red as the drapes now. Evelyn nodded curtly and strode from the room.

A hearty breakfast, a cup of medicinal tea, and Nathan felt renewed. He and Frances had the morning planned: They would ride down the east valley to see that the cattle had enough fodder, and then on to the cottage to check on some of their grafting. Milburn kept a close eye on the plants, but Frances had taken his responsibility for a pair of cuttings quite to heart.

Frances wore the buckskins Nathan had purchased

for him in London. His father had given him a new game bag that Nathan attached to his saddle. They wouldn't bag any game today, but Nathan finally convinced Frances that the bag could hold other important things as well, such as interesting rocks.

Frances was quite chatty and told Nathan about Evelyn's visit to the cottage. He also spoke of a girl—Nathan supposed he meant a maid of some sort—but Frances seemed more impressed with the fact the girl knew nothing of botany, and that he had to teach her about the plants and grafts.

Frankly, Nathan didn't hear much of what Frances said. He was thinking of Evelyn, of her body on his, the scent of lavender on her skin that made him feel almost desperate to have her.

Milburn was not about when Nathan and Frances entered the cottage, but it was obvious he'd been round today, as Nathan knew he would be. A fire at the hearth was reduced to coals, but the small cottage was quite warm. A pot still hung over the hearth, and the scent of rabbit stew lingered.

Nathan and Frances puttered about the table, examining the new grafting, noting in the ledger, Nathan with his bold strokes, Frances with his rough scrawl, the various changes in the cuttings and grafts they observed. After they'd finished checking on all the plants, and had put away the ledgers, Nathan ruffled Frances's hair. "These will keep for a time, eh?"

Frances nodded.

Nathan looked at the boy, put his hand beneath his chin, and tilted his head back. "I need your help, Frances."

"Aye, milord."

"You must be patient for a time," Nathan said. "I've quite a lot to keep me very well occupied."

"What of the plants?" Frances asked earnestly.

"Milburn will keep a watchful eye on them and will notify us if there is the slightest cause for concern. But of course, you must check your plants as often as your father can spare you."

The boy fingered one of the graftings. "But . . . what of the baby's grave?"

"We'll go by today and have a look. And then . . ." Nathan squatted down before him and put a hand on his shoulder. "And then I must rely on you, Frances. You are the only one I can depend upon to keep it tidy."

Frances rubbed his hand under his nose as he studied Nathan.

"I can depend on you, can I not?" Nathan asked.

"Aye, milord," Frances nodded solemnly. "Are you going away?"

"No, I'll be here at Eastchurch Abbey."

Frances's expression was one of confusion. "Then why will you not come to work in the cottage?"

With a hand to the boy's back to usher him to the door, Nathan pondered how to explain to an eight-year-old boy the sorts of things that only grown men knew. "It's rather complicated, but the countess needs me just now."

Frances seemed to accept that explanation. He pulled his hat down around his ears and shoved his hands in his pockets. "She's still sad, isn't she?"

Surprised, Nathan nodded.

"Then I'll look after her baby's grave," he vowed.

"There's a good lad," Nathan said, and put his arm around the boy's slender shoulders as they walked outside. "Would that I had a son just like you."

chapter sixteen

The cold air that had blown through the day before disappeared almost as quickly as it had come; the afternoon was pleasantly cool as Evelyn and Harriet visited the merchants in Eastchurch, ordering fabrics for draperies and carpets to replace those that could not be properly cleaned.

In the village green, a small monkey in a red coat hopped about with an upturned hat as a pair of musicians played a lute and a fiddle. Harriet was delighted; Evelyn gave her a few shillings and laughed as Harriet came nose to nose with the little monkey. To the delight of the crowd, he tried to snatch the ribbon from her hair—the green ribbon Evelyn had given her, she noted—and Harriet yelped with surprise, and laughed and laughed.

Several people gathered to watch the monkey; Evelyn stepped back to let them in. She was standing at the back of the small crowd when she heard someone call her name. She turned slightly and saw Alexandra DuPaul hurrying toward her.

Instinctively, Evelyn looked around for a polite escape, but of course there was none, unless she thought to cut her directly. She reluctantly turned to greet Alexandra.

She could see in Alexandra's confused expression that she had detected her desire to escape. "Good afternoon, Alexandra," Evelyn said as cheerfully as she could manage.

"Evelyn, I am so happy to see you in the village! I hope that means you are settling into life at the abbey."

Settling into life at the abbey . . . Those words kicked up emotions like a cloud of dust inside her.

"I would be so honored if you could come for tea," she added, a little too earnestly. "I should very much like to hear about your time in London."

"Oh!" No, no, she couldn't sit across from Alexandra and pretend all was well. Evelyn glanced at Harriet as she tried to think. The monkey was now sitting on Harriet's shoulder. She tilted her head back to see if Evelyn was watching. Evelyn waved at her. "That . . . that is very kind of you," she stammered, "but I . . . I have begun to refurbish the abbey, and that has me terribly occupied at the moment."

Alexandra's hopeful smile faded. "Yes, of course. Perhaps, then, when you've finished with the refurbishment?"

Evelyn nodded.

That seemed to appease her. "Oh, by the way, I have taken the liberty of inviting your parents—and the marquis and marchioness, of course—to a small supper party. I hope you won't mind, but when I spoke to Nathan about it, he thought it a capital idea."

Evelyn blinked.

"I have often hosted them while you've been away, you know—your mother was so good to mine before she passed—and I thought that you might enjoy seeing them. But you've just come home, and I realize you might not be prepared as yet to entertain, so I would be delighted to host. I told Nathan I'd send the details around to Benton. Does that suit?"

"I . . . I suppose," Evelyn said uncertainly as her mind swirled around the astounding notion that Alexandra had invited *her* parents, and Nathan's as well. Her mother had never mentioned dining with the DuPauls!

"Lady Lindsey!" Harriet called. Evelyn turned and waved again.

Alexandra looked at Harriet, then at Evelyn. "I won't keep you."

"It's good to see you, Alexandra," Evelyn said.

"And you, Evelyn. You look so . . . beautiful," she said with a warm smile. She waved her fingers and began to walk away.

But Evelyn suddenly and strongly felt the need to know the truth—cold, hard, unaltered truth—and said, "No, what I said is not true."

"Pardon?"

"It's not good to see you, it is actually rather painful to see you," Evelyn said.

Alexandra gasped.

"Alexandra . . ." How did she verbalize thoughts she'd had for years? "When Robbie died, I . . . I needed my husband, but he . . . he was with you," she said, her voice shaking. "He was with *you.*"

"What? *No*, Evelyn!" Alexandra exclaimed. "Oh no, you have it all wrong."

"Do I?" she asked sincerely. "I should very much like

to know if I have it all wrong, because I *saw* you, both of you, walking arm in arm, or sitting in the garden so closely together, as if you were whispering poetry to one another. And sitting at the church chapel, just the two of you with heads bowed on . . . on the anniversary of my son's death," she managed to choke out.

"But I—"

"It's all right," Evelyn said, holding up a hand. "I wouldn't begrudge anyone that, but the point I am trying to make is that I saw the way Nathan looked at you when I was near, as if I were intruding, and yet I could never understand how I could be intruding upon the two of you, time and again, unless . . . unless . . ."

"Evelyn, no!" Alexandra cried. "Oh my dear, my poor dear—"

"It was the worst time of my life, Alexandra, and I needed my husband. I *needed* him." She caught a sob in her throat. "*I* needed him," she said again, pressing her fist to her heart as a tear slipped from the corner of her eye.

"Evelyn. Oh Evelyn, you could not be more wrong," Alexandra said solemnly, and put her hand on Evelyn's arm.

"Don't," Evelyn said shakily.

"You must hear me, Evelyn. You are right—I spent quite a lot of time with Nathan after your son died. He is my dear friend and he was lost."

Evelyn couldn't bear to hear Alexandra describe her husband's grief to her, and tried to turn away, but Alexandra gripped her arm, forcing her to hear what she would say.

"He was completely despondent. He'd not only

lost his precious son, he'd lost his precious wife. He'd lost *you*. *You* were all he ever spoke of. *You* were the only thing on his mind when in my company. He worried about you ceaselessly, he felt inadequate to help you, and he didn't know how to reach you. No one did."

Evelyn could not have been more stunned if Alexandra had confessed to a torrid, passionate affair with Nathan. She was unable to believe what she was hearing. But Alexandra would not let go of her arm.

"It was always only you, Evelyn," Alexandra continued. "I did nothing but lend an ear to him, and I would have done the same for you, but you . . . you never spoke at all."

She couldn't speak. It was true—God had taken everything from her but an indescribable pain when Robbie died. She looked heavenward and tried to blink back tears. "Alexandra, if you are lying to me now—"

"I would *never* lie," she said heatedly, "and certainly not about something so terribly important as that. Oh, Evelyn, your husband *loves* you."

"Stop," she whispered as Harriet handed the monkey to a boy and started toward them. "Please stop."

Alexandra saw Harriet approaching, too. She let her hand drop from Evelyn's arm as Evelyn quickly dabbed her eyes. "Good day," she said quietly, and walked on before Harriet could reach them.

Harriet watched Alexandra hurry away, then looked up at Evelyn.

"A friend," Evelyn said with a thin smile, and wanted desperately to believe that was true. "Do you like hasty pudding?" she asked brightly. "I know a delightful little inn where the best hasty pudding in all of England may be had," she said, and shakily wiped a tear from beneath her eye.

When Frances mentioned a girl in his recounting of Evelyn's visit to the cottage, Nathan had believed it was a maid, but when he saw the girl emerge from the Ivy Inn with Evelyn, he was confused as to who she was.

He started toward them, but something gave him pause. If he didn't know Evelyn, he'd think they were mother and daughter. They looked very close to one another, strolling along, engrossed in conversation. And laughing.

Nathan looked at the girl's hand in Evelyn's, and his heart did a funny little flip.

He'd forgotten what a good mother Evelyn was, how naturally it came to her.

"That's her," Frances said.

"Pardon?"

"She doesn't know the least bit about plants, milord," Frances added with disdain. "But she tries to pretend that she does."

Nathan laughed. "Have a care for your pride, lad. There are very few of us in the world who know about plants." He playfully cuffed the boy's ear. "Let us greet the ladies properly, shall we?"

Frances groaned, but began walking before Nathan.

Evelyn didn't notice Nathan until she was almost upon him. When she at last looked up, Nathan saw something warm in her eyes, but it was quickly shuttered. "My lord," she said. "And Master Brady!"

"My lady," Nathan said with an incline of his head. He glanced at the girl.

"Lady Harriet, may I introduce my husband, the Earl of Lindsey?" Evelyn said, and to Nathan, "Lady Harriet French. She is the daughter of Lord and Lady Balfour."

"Lady Harriet, how do you do."

The girl sank into a perfect curtsy.

"She came with Kathleen for a visit," Evelyn said.

"You are most welcome."

"We were just on our way to the abbey," Evelyn continued. "We are eager to begin work refurbishing the public rooms." She moved as if she were so eager, she intended to step around him and carry on.

"We'll accompany you," Nathan quickly interjected before she could escape.

Evelyn smiled and put her hands on Harriet's shoulders. "We came in a curricle. I'm afraid there is no room."

"How fortuitous we came on horseback. We may ride alongside."

Evelyn continued to smile, but her eyes narrowed. "You'll find it tiresome. The curricle is rather slow."

"We'll find it delightful," Nathan said. "It's a lovely autumn afternoon." He clamped a hand on Frances's shoulder before he could utter a protest. "Shall we?" he asked, motioning toward the stables.

Evelyn sighed. So did Frances. Nathan ushered them all along to the stable, where the curricle stood just outside. The back of it, Nathan noticed, was piled high with wrapped packages. The team harnessed to the curricle was two of his oldest horses. The only thing that would put them into a gallop was the promise of their oat bag. "Frances, would you like a turn at driving the curricle?" Nathan asked.

Frances's eyes lit at the same moment Evelyn gaped. "Truly?" Frances asked.

"But . . . but there isn't room for three of us," Evelyn reminded Nathan. "And Frances is quite small."

"Perhaps he might ride with the packages," the girl suggested.

"There is room if you ride with me, madam. Frances is a hearty lad—he can handle the ribbons, I assure you."

"No," Evelyn insisted. "I am hardly dressed for riding, and I can't imagine Frances has an appropriate saddle, nor can I allow Lady Harriet to be left to the experience of a small boy."

"I'm nine years!" Frances said.

"I'm *ten* years," Harriet responded.

"Lady Harriet may ride with Frances," Nathan said, to the girl's obvious delight. "And you, my darling, will have to ride with me."

She knew what he was about, judging by the way her eyes suddenly sparkled with ire. "I cannot agree to this, sir. They are children. They cannot be expected to *drive* a curricle."

"I can drive, Lady Lindsey!" Harriet said eagerly.

"You can't! You're only a girl!" Frances cried.

"I think they are both capable," Nathan said easily, as if he handed over carriages to children all the time.

"You'd be as wrong about that as most other things."

Nathan chuckled and nodded toward the carriage. Both children were already seated, arguing over the reins. "Rest easy, madam," Nathan said, signaling the stable boy. "Those old horses know their way to their oats, and no boy at the reins will convince them to alter their course. We'll ride alongside to ensure no one drives off the road."

A frustrated Evelyn looked at the curricle where the two children had settled in. Frances was telling Harriet the horses' names.

When the stable boy brought the mounts, Nathan smiled at Evelyn, and patted the saddle on Cedric's back. Resigned, Evelyn walked slowly to where he stood.

Nathan put his hands on her waist, bent his head, and whispered, "A pity you cannot ride astride this afternoon in that gown. With my hands free, I might show you a thing or two."

Before she could respond, he lifted her up and settled her on the saddle.

Evelyn caught the pommel and settled herself, then looked down at him with a saucy smile. "Do you really believe such talk will titillate me?"

Nathan grinned. He tethered the smaller mount to his horse, then swung up behind her. He slipped his hand around her abdomen and pulled her tightly against his chest. "I think such talk already has titillated you."

She laughed. "You continue to believe you have some hold over me." She glanced at him sidelong. "But I think we discovered this morning that it's quite the opposite. You cannot titillate me . . . but I *can* titillate you."

He smiled wolfishly. "If the steady rhythm of the horse's gait will not titillate you, love, then I know another rhythm that shall," he said, and nuzzled her neck.

Evelyn gasped and twisted away from him. But she was smiling.

So was Nathan. In fact, Nathan smiled for three-quarters of an hour because he held his wife's body pressed against his. He felt every curve, every flex of her muscle, every jiggle of her bottom. And he felt no less a sense of elation when she finally relaxed and allowed herself to lean against him.

A deep longing was pounding through him with every beat of the horse's hooves. Perhaps she was right, he mused. Perhaps she did hold all the cards. But by the time they turned into the drive at Eastchurch, Nathan was more determined than ever to win her back.

chapter seventeen

There was a coach in the drive at Eastchurch that Frances almost hit—or rather, the team of horses ran recklessly near, so eager were they to get to their oats. Fortunately, a groomsman was on hand to bring the horses to a halt.

Nathan helped Evelyn down from his horse; they both looked at the coach. It was emblazoned with the seal of the Duke of Kent, a brother to the Prince of Wales. They exchanged a wary look—Evelyn couldn't begin to guess what Nathan was thinking, and as an exuberant Harriet was at her side, she did not ask him, but she couldn't imagine it could possibly be good news.

She sent Harriet up to Kathleen. A footman directed her and Nathan to the green salon, where Benton had taken the caller.

As it turned out, the caller in the duke's coach was Lady Balfour, who was waiting impatiently in the green salon. "There you are!" she said, sinking into a curtsy when Evelyn and Nathan entered.

Evelyn quickly made introductions; in characteristic fashion, Claire eyed Nathan as if he were a sweetmeat. In contrast, Nathan eyed Claire as if she were a mortal enemy. Evelyn could hardly blame him—Claire had a brazen air about her. Nathan made stilted small talk until Benton appeared with the post. "I beg your pardon, my lord, but there is a note that requires your immediate attention."

Nathan picked up the foolscap from the stack of letters and scanned it. He frowned and looked at Evelyn, then at Claire. "I do beg your pardon, Lady Balfour. I have a tenant dispute that requires my attention."

"Yes, of course," Claire purred. "I do not mean to keep you—I must be on my way as soon as I collect my daughter."

"So soon?" Evelyn asked after Nathan had taken his leave.

"I shouldn't want to be a bother, and frankly, I'm in something of a rush to reach a hunting lodge at Freegate by day's end."

"In the duke's coach," Evelyn said suspiciously.

Claire smiled mysteriously. "That was very generous of him, don't you agree?"

"Claire, you're going to meet the duke with Harriet in tow?" Evelyn couldn't help herself from asking.

"Don't look so disapproving," Claire said laughingly. "Harriet is far more aware of the world than you realize. She quite understands it, really, and besides, there shall be quite a lot to divert her. She loves horses and that sort of thing and I think there should be lots of them at Freegate. It's a hunting lodge, after all."

Evelyn didn't think Harriet understood her mother's world as well as Claire wanted to believe.

"Oh! I've scarcely been able to contain myself with the news!" Claire suddenly whispered. "*Dunhill* called for you." She glanced at Benton over her shoulder and hurried forward to link her arm with Evelyn's. "Do you know, he took my suggestion quite to heart and promised me that he would purchase passage for two to France! If you can only return to London—"

"So *that* is where the awful rumor started," Evelyn said irritably. "What did you tell him?"

"I didn't tell him anything! I had no idea where you were, how could I possibly tell him anything?" she asked innocently. "But I suggested that if he were truly as caring of you as I believed him to be, he should help you flee your wretched situation."

"And then you proceeded to tell everyone that was what he'd done?"

"I told no one!" she insisted. "Just one or two very good friends." At Evelyn's look, Claire feigned hurt. "I didn't want anyone to fret about you! Why? Have you had a change of heart? I shouldn't blame you—your husband is quite . . . *desirable*."

"Claire!"

"I had the opportunity to meet a friend of his earlier," Claire blithely continued. "Lord Lambourne? Oh, Evelyn, darling, there are ladies who *dream* of being as well situated as you appear to be."

"*Lord*, Claire, please do stop! Lambourne is like . . ." Evelyn wasn't entirely certain what he was like, but he was not *that*. "A brother," she said unconvincingly, but quickly changed the subject. "Really, the Duke of *Kent*?"

Claire shrugged. "He's not so awful, is he?"

"He's had almost as many mistresses as George," Evelyn reminded her.

"Has he? Oh, look at the time, Evelyn! I really must collect Harriet and be on my way. I don't want to keep the duke waiting."

It was with a surprisingly heavy heart that Evelyn saw Harriet off. The day was sliding into dusk when the girl boarded the duke's coach behind her mother, looking quite forlorn. Evelyn had tried very hard to convince Claire to let Harriet stay at Eastchurch, but Claire wouldn't hear of it. "Her father doesn't like me to leave her behind," she'd said, as if she found that vexing.

So Evelyn promised Harriet she could come back to Eastchurch whenever she wanted—she had an open invitation. Harriet was hardly consoled by that, and as the coach pulled away, she pressed her face to the window, waving at Evelyn until Claire pulled her away.

Evelyn stood on the drive until she could no longer see the coach. Life could be so dreadfully unfair at times.

She slowly turned and walked back into the house.

On a hill above her, in the shadows of twilight, a man watched the duke's coach rumble away from the house, and the countess walk back into the house. *Patience*, he told himself.

Even though Harriet's visit had been brief, Evelyn missed the girl's company. Refurbishing the abbey wasn't quite as much fun without her bright suggestions and constant chatter. Nevertheless, Evelyn had to keep herself occupied to steer her thoughts away from the sadness of the past, and busied herself with the changes she wanted to make to the abbey.

The first thing she did the morning after Harriet left was to meet with Mr. Gibbs, the head groundskeeper, in the orangery. He was a short, round man, and doffed his hat, crumbling it in his hands as Evelyn explained what she wanted. "Essentially, it should be cleaned top to bottom, and the window repaired," she finished, and looked at him.

Mr. Gibbs nodded.

"Shall I ask Benton to send someone to help you?"

"No, mu'um. Me two boys will assist me."

Evelyn left him and returned to the green salon, where she spent the morning overseeing the removal of draperies. She worked alone with a pair of footmen. She had no idea where Nathan was or what he was about, until he appeared quite unexpectedly when the two footmen struggled to remove a stag's head from the wall of the library.

She instantly suspected Benton of having informed him.

"Wait!" Nathan cried with horror just as the two men managed to dislodge the enormous head from the wall. "What are you doing? Leave it, leave it!" he said sternly.

The two footmen looked at one another and began the laborious process of putting it up on the wall once again.

"Take it down, sirs," Evelyn said calmly, and stood between them and her husband. The two footmen stood uncertainly with the thing suspended between them.

"You have no right, madam," Nathan started.

"We shall turn one of the outbuildings into your hunting lodge, my lord, but a library is no place for . . . *that*."

Still, he looked very distressed. "You've no idea what I had to do to kill that stag. I stalked him for *weeks*. He was crafty, he held me at bay, and it was only through my wits and expert hunting skills that I was able to catch him at all."

Evelyn shook her head.

"Evie," he said, pleading now, "it was an epochal battle of man versus beast."

"I am not burning it, Nathan, I am moving it."

He obviously smelled his defeat because he looked at the stag's head as if he were on the verge of weeping. "I cannot bear to watch it," he said, and left them, muttering under his breath about a woman's lack of understanding of a man's world.

Shortly after luncheon, Mr. Gibbs came in search of Evelyn. They'd finished cleaning the orangery, he said, but there was a stain that he could not seem to remove and he did not want to risk ruining the slate floor without her having a look.

Evelyn joined him in the orangery. It was empty and swept clean, save a round stain near the north windows. It was cold in the orangery, and Evelyn noticed the hearth was not lit, nor did she see a brazier. "Aren't you cold, Mr. Gibbs?" she asked, shivering a little.

"No, mu'um. The room had the western light to warm us," he said, although it seemed rather dim to Evelyn. In fact, Mr. Gibbs had to light a candle to better show her the stain.

Evelyn squatted down to have a look at the stain. "Rust, I think."

"Aye, mu'um. If I take it up, it will leech the color from the slate . . . unless . . ."

"Unless?"

"I've got a solvent that might work," Mr. Gibbs said. "Might I have your leave, mu'um? I'll be back straightaway."

"Of course," she said, and took the candle he offered her.

Mr. Gibbs started for the east door, then paused and said sheepishly, "Locked." He turned and hurried diagonally across the room and out the open western door, through which they had entered.

Evelyn held up the candle, looking around at the empty orangery. She would make it a lovely place to be once more, and just in time for winter. She did not allow herself to dwell on the idea that she might be here in the future.

She was startled to hear the western door close and looked over her shoulder. No one had entered, but the door was definitely shut. Evelyn started toward the door when she heard someone behind her and paused, turning partially to look back.

"I'd have sworn the door was locked," Mr. Gibbs said with a shrug as he walked into the orangery, carrying a small jar.

Confused, Evelyn looked back at the western door.

She felt the explosion before she heard it. The force was so great that it knocked her off her feet and sent the candle flying. Evelyn fell hard, hitting her head on the slate-tiled floor. The blow made her head spin; she pushed herself up and saw flames quickly engulfing the southern end of the orangery.

She screamed with terror and rolled onto her knees as smoke began to fill the room. "Mr. Gibbs!" she shouted, and picked up the hem of her gown, holding it over her face as she desperately crawled toward Mr.

Gibbs. She could feel the heat at her back and knew the fire was spreading quickly. "Mr. Gibbs!" she shouted again.

He was on his knees, crawling toward her. Evelyn changed course, for the door. When she reached it, she rose up and grabbed the levered handle, but it would not open. She dropped her gown and tried with both hands—but the door would not budge. "*No!*" she shrieked. She and Mr. Gibbs would die in this inferno. She tried again, yanking with all her might.

Nathan and Frances heard the explosion as they raked Robert's grave. Nathan jerked upright at the sound, turning in the direction from which it had come. He could see the smoke billowing, and for a moment, he tried to understand where it was. It was too far to the east to be part of the house, and too close to him to be the stables. It could only be the orangery.

The orangery . . . *Evelyn!*

Something almost preternatural came over him. He dropped the rake and started running, oblivious to Frances's shouts, or those that were now coming from the house. He ran, vaulting over the iron fence that surrounded the graveyard, hurling himself into the trees and vegetation that grew between the graveyard and the orangery, his legs powered by the strength of his fear.

When he reached the orangery, it looked almost completely engulfed. Evelyn was on the outside, wildly pounding on a window. Her gown was streaked with ash and her hair had come partially undone. Nathan quickly shrugged out of his coat. "*Evelyn!*" he shouted as he reached her, and tried to pull her away, but she fought him.

"Mr. Gibbs is inside!"

Nathan pulled her back, all but tossing her into Declan's hands, who had rushed to help him. He wrapped the coat around his arm and took a swing at the window. The glass shattered, cutting his skin as a rush of hot air and smoke blasted his face. Using his arm as a battering ram, he knocked glass away and climbed in through the window.

Thick, black smoke made it almost impossible to see. The fire had covered the walls and the ceiling. But somehow, by some miracle, he saw Mr. Gibbs's crumpled figure near the door. Nathan fell to his knees and rolled the man onto his back, saw that Gibbs's nose and mouth were smudged with smoke, his eyes closed.

Terror rose up in him. *"Gibbs!"* he shouted, and slapped his face.

Gibbs coughed. Thank God, he was alive. Using his coat, Nathan felt for the door handle. With one mighty tug, he opened it.

"What the devil!" he heard Lambourne shout, and then there were hands on Nathan, hands on Gibbs, pulling them out.

The servants had gathered and were queuing to form a bucket brigade under Benton's quick thinking. Every other free hand was beating the embers that flew from the building onto the grass around them, or digging a fire line between the orangery and the other outbuildings. As men carted Mr. Gibbs away, Nathan spotted Evelyn sitting on the rise, and groped for one of the blankets someone had tossed to him.

He hurried to put the blanket around her shoulders.

She looked stunned. "Dear God, Evie, are you all right?" he asked desperately as he ran his hands over her body and limbs looking for any blood or broken bones. "Are you hurt?"

Evelyn responded by coughing.

"Water!" he shouted at a groomsman running by. He cupped Evelyn's face in his hands. "Can you speak? Can you tell me what happened?"

She shook her head, grabbed his wrist, and coughed again. The groomsman appeared with water. "Mr. Gibbs," she said hoarsely.

"He's all right and out of the orangery."

Nathan held the tin cup to Evelyn's lips. She coughed, drank thirstily, but pushed the cup away when he tried to give her more, shaking her head.

"Fetch a doctor quickly!" Nathan ordered the groomsman, and turned back to Evelyn, stroking her head. "What happened, Evie?"

"I don't know," she said hoarsely, and rubbed the back of her hand across her forehead, smearing more ash. "Mr. Gibbs asked me to look at a stain, but he went out to fetch a solvent, and the door closed, but no one was there, and I couldn't see very well by the light of a single candle, but then everything exploded—"

Another coughing spell came over her, and she clutched his arm. When at last she could breathe, she looked at him with hazel eyes filled with terror. "Nathan, I think it was intentional."

"No, no, darling, I am sure it was an accident," he said reassuringly, and honestly believed that was true. He stood up, pulled her to her feet. "We must get you inside."

chapter eighteen

Wilkes met them at the door in a cloak, on his way out. "What has happened?" he asked anxiously.

"The orangery is burning," Nathan said.

"Dear God. No one was hurt?" Wilkes asked, casting a worried gaze at Evelyn.

"By the grace of God," Nathan said gruffly, and pushed past Wilkes, who shouted after him that he'd go lend a hand.

In spite of Evelyn's hoarse protests, Nathan carried her up the winding staircase to her rooms. He kicked open the door to her dressing room and marched through, stepping over and around her things where he could, but earning a cry of alarm from her when he managed to walk across the silk train of a gown that was draped over a chair.

He walked through the adjoining door into her bedroom and deposited her on the bed. "Don't move," he ordered her. "Not as much as an inch."

She groaned and rolled onto her side, overcome again with a painful cough.

Nathan found a linen handkerchief and soaked it in the basin, then returned to the bed to clean the ash from her face. He'd scarcely touched her when the door from the corridor swung open with a bang, startling Nathan.

"My lady!" Kathleen shrieked. "Lord help us!"

"For heaven's sake, woman, she is not dead," Nathan said sternly, and wiped Evelyn's face.

"Oh my lord, I shall do it, shan't I?" Kathleen asked anxiously, reaching for the handkerchief. "You're apt to scrub her skin right off the bone."

The thought horrified him—and in the moment of his hesitation, Kathleen took the handkerchief from his hand. It was just as well—he was needed outside. He backed away from the bed. "You're not to leave her. Mind you keep her here until a doctor comes," he said, and hurried out.

The orangery was completely engulfed in flames. The staff—joined by some of the tenants now—were all working to keep the fire from spreading by digging ditches and beating back the flames with whatever they had available. Nathan took a shovel from one of the groundsmen and began to work.

They worked for hours. A wind picked up late in the day, and they didn't dare slow their efforts, lest the embers spread. It was late into the evening before Nathan felt the fire was suitably contained; the groundsmen would keep vigil through the night with the help of some tenants.

The weary residents of Eastchurch Abbey began to fade into the night. Nathan was still stomping out small embers that scattered with the wind when Benton appeared at his side. In all the many years Benton had served at Eastchurch Abbey, Nathan had never seen as much as a single hair on Benton's head out of place, but tonight, ashes blackened his face and his suit was in complete disarray. "The doctor has come," he said. "He awaits you in the salon. Mr. Gibbs has been put in a guest room and is resting comfortably, as is Lady Lindsey."

Nathan nodded, relieved. "See to it everyone is fed."

"It has been arranged, my lord," Benton said, as if they were standing in the foyer on any given day.

Nathan blinked, then shook his head. He clapped a hand on Benton's shoulder. "You do amaze me, sir. Thank you." He walked on, anxious to have a word with the doctor.

Dr. Bell met him with his hand extended, in spite of Nathan's sorry appearance. "My lord," he said, nodding his head. "It has been quite some time since we have had opportunity to meet."

"That is the good news, sir."

"Shall I have a look?" he asked, nodding at Nathan's arm.

He glanced down—it was the first he'd noticed his shirt was torn and he'd been bleeding. "I'm fine, I'm— what of Mr. Gibbs?"

"His throat is inflamed, as would be expected. I have given him a tincture and instructed his wife to leave all the windows open through the night. He needs fresh air to heal his throat and lungs quickly, but I believe he will recover fully with proper rest for several days."

Thank God for that. "And my wife?"

"Ah yes," the doctor said with a smile. "I hadn't heard that Lady Lindsey was returned to the abbey."

Bloody hell if he hadn't. Nathan rather imagined the entire shire was completely tantalized by her return.

"I am certain she will recover completely as well. In fact, she should be recovered by morning, save a bit of discomfort in her throat. She wasn't exposed as long as poor Mr. Gibbs. I have given her some laudanum to help her sleep, and she should have fresh air as well."

Nathan shoved a hand through his hair. "Thank you."

"The fire is contained?" Dr. Bell asked as he started toward the door. When Nathan confirmed that it was, the doctor sighed. "What a tragedy. What do you suppose started it?"

"Carelessness, I'd wager. I'll see you out." Nathan said no more, convinced Evelyn's candle had somehow touched a solvent.

"Let me have a look at your arm," Dr. Bell said.

Nathan had forgotten about his injury. "Yes," he said, and held it out for the doctor.

When Dr. Bell had finished bandaging him up, and Nathan had seen him out, he returned to Evelyn's suite. He was too impatient to wait to be invited within; he opened the door and stuck his head through. Kathleen was busily gathering up clothing and linens; Evelyn was washed and sitting on the bed, propped up against what looked like a dozen pillows, her golden hair—made dull by the ash—spilling around her shoulders.

"Am I intruding?" Nathan asked as he entered the room.

"No, my lord," Kathleen answered. She gathered up the mound of clothing and linens and walked to the door. "I was just on my way out to take these soiled garments to Fran. I suspect she'll have her hands full in the laundry this week."

"I suspect you are right," he said, and stepped out of the woman's way, holding the door so that she might quit the room. When she'd gone, he quietly closed the door and turned round.

Evelyn was watching him, her arms folded across her body, her lids heavy. "I'm quite all right," she said hoarsely.

"I would see for myself," he said, walking to her bedside.

"Here you are, then," she said, gesturing to herself.

She looked so small; the pillows seemed to swallow her almost whole. So small, so fragile . . . he remembered thinking the very same of her after Robert died. Then, she'd seemed almost childlike, curled up in the chair she had pulled up to the window, staring out into a bleak landscape.

"What of the orangery?" she asked behind a yawn.

"Lost."

She winced. "Everything?"

He nodded solemnly.

She sighed and leaned her head back against the pillows, her eyes closed. "I cannot imagine how it might have happened."

"Perhaps an ember from the fire."

"But the hearth was cold," she said, opening her eyes and looking at him. "I didn't see even a brazier."

He frowned and took a seat on the edge of her bed. "Then a candle, perhaps."

She adamantly shook her head. "I had the only candle. I . . ."

Nathan's frown deepened. "What is it, Evie?"

"I heard something odd before it happened," Evelyn said. "Someone closed the western door. It was open, I know it was open, for Mr. Gibbs went through it. But he came back through the east door and said he thought it had been locked, and then there was the explosion."

He did not see the significance and shrugged. "A breeze must have shut it." Evelyn shook her head. "Evie," he said patiently, "I suspect a breeze caught the door and the flame of your candle, and perhaps you didn't realize it, but the flame may have touched a solvent."

"No," she said stubbornly. "It happened just as I told you, Nathan."

"I believe you, but I think you must have missed a detail or not seen the solvent. Perhaps Mr. Gibbs was careless with it, but it is the only logical explanation," he tried patiently.

"It is not the only logical explanation. Have you considered that perhaps it has something to do with *you?*"

"*Me?*"

"Just consider it—we were set upon by highwaymen on a rarely traveled road only days ago."

"I don't see what that possibly has to do with this."

Evelyn sank deeper into her pillows. "You are known about England as the Libertine of Lindsey—I would imagine that in earning your name, you attracted an enemy or two along the way."

He reared back, surprised. "Do you honestly believe that a bit of gambling and hard hunting would lead to the sort of enemy who might try and burn my house?"

She shrugged and rolled onto her side. "I don't rightly know, Nathan. I am merely suggesting you consider the possibility before blaming me or an innocent groundskeeper. You are so quick to assign blame for tragedies."

It seemed there was no end to the wounds between them. "I never blamed you or Mr. Gibbs."

"Really, I am desperately weary," she said, and pillowed her hands beneath her cheek and closed her eyes.

Nathan stood up, doused the candle at her bedside. He walked to her door, but remembered what Dr. Bell had said—she needed fresh air. He changed direction and walked to the dressing room, opening that door, and then moving through, to open the door onto the corridor and the one that adjoined her sitting room. When he was satisfied that the circulation was adequate, he walked quietly through again. But as he entered her bedroom once more, and trod lightly across the carpet to the door, he heard a sound.

He paused, mid-step, and turned his head toward the bed. There it was again—the unmistakable sound of weeping.

He hesitated—he could not bear to hear her cry another tear, not after what they'd endured. But neither could he bear to leave her. He moved through the dark, put his hand on her shoulder.

"Go away," she muttered. "Please just leave me be. *Please.*"

Nathan slowly removed his hand. He backed away from the bed, then turned and silently left the room.

He didn't return.

Not for two hours, anyway, after he'd visited the room below stairs, releasing his anger and frustration and fear in the only way he knew how. And not until after he'd eaten something and bathed the soot and grime from his body.

Only then did he return to Evelyn, crawling into bed beside her, hushing her weak protests. He was intent on keeping her warm through the night and wrapped his arms around her.

The tincture had done its work—she slipped into a

deep sleep again. Her breath was slow and deep. The dead couldn't wake her now, he knew from experience.

He closed his eyes.

He would keep her warm. He would keep her safe. He would discover on the morrow who had tried to harm him by harming his wife, and tear him limb from limb.

chapter nineteen

Jack Haines would not admit it to a bloody soul, but he was more than a fair bit concerned about the allegations against him.

Having announced to one and all that Jack had been accused of bedding the Princess of Wales—much to the delight of his oldest friends, Jack noted wryly—Wilkes had confided that the authorities were rounding up the men rumored to have committed treason by bedding her. When the Duke of Kent's coach had arrived yesterday, Jack had thought himself doomed. That the caller had been for Lady Lindsey felt a bit like a hangman's reprieve.

That was the moment Jack decided to return to Scotland until the situation between the Prince and Princess of Wales was resolved. He did not relish the thought of being put on trial before a room full of Englishmen. Historically, that had not gone well for the Scotsman, and he had no reason to believe it would go any better for him.

He'd wanted to be gone as soon as was humanly possible, but unfortunately, the fire had kept him. After a long day of helping to battle the blaze, he'd returned to his rooms and packed his bags. The next morning he was just about to send for a footman when, by happy coincidence, one appeared, asking for him to please repair to the study, where the earl was waiting to receive him.

"Of course. I wanted a word with him myself, I did. Be a good lad and bring down the bags, aye? And have my horse saddled." He held up a crown between two fingers, then tossed it to the young man.

The footman deftly caught it in his left hand. "Yes, sir."

Donnelly was in the study when Jack arrived, looking as if he'd just been roused from bed. Wilkes was nowhere to be seen—but then again, Wilkes was often catting about the village until the morning hours.

"Lambourne, you look quite refreshed," Lindsey said, eyeing Jack thoughtfully. Lindsey, on the other hand, did not look the least bit rested.

"I owe it all to Scottish whiskey," Jack said with a wink for Donnelly, with whom he had a running argument as to the quality of Irish whiskey compared to Scots whiskey. "I had a tot or two after battling that bloody fire."

"As to that . . . I can't thank either of you enough for your help yesterday," Lindsey said, and shoved his hand through his hair. "It could have been quite disastrous had we not had as many hands, or if the winds had picked up earlier in the day."

"Fortunately, only the orangery was lost," Jack said.

"Yes. Fortunately," Lindsey said, and frowned a little as he looked at his hands, which Jack could see were cut and bruised. Lindsey studied them as if he didn't quite know what to do with them. "Tell me something, will you?" he asked. "Can you think of a reason someone might want to harm me in such a manner?"

"*Harm* you?" Donnelly echoed incredulously. "It was an accident, Nathan—not arson."

Lindsey shrugged, still looking at his hands. He suddenly put them down and smiled thinly at the two of them. "What the devil is taking Wilkes so long, do you suppose?"

"I'm here!" Wilkes called from the hall just as he strode through the door. "Bloody hell, Lindsey, you had them *wake* me?" he asked as he dropped into a chair.

Lindsey clasped his hands behind his back and looked at the three of them. Jack had known him a very long time, and through all the trials of Lindsey's life he'd never seen him look quite as awkward as he did now. "I regret that I . . . I must ask you all to, ah . . . well, to leave," he said.

"I beg your pardon?" Donnelly asked with a laugh.

"I have just discovered there is no polite way to ask this," he said. "You have all been my good friends for as long as I can remember. But I must ask that you leave Eastchurch for a time. Evelyn and I . . . we . . ."

"You need no' say more," Jack said abruptly. He could not bear to hear his friend attempt to speak about something that was obviously very painful to him. "We've been guests in your home far longer than a body has a right." He clapped Donnelly on the shoulder. "I am for Scotland, lads. If the king's men come looking, you'll no' tell them, aye?"

"Scotland?" Donnelly laughed. "How long has it been since you claimed to be a Scotsman?"

"A day too long, it would seem," Jack responded with a grin.

"I should be to London," Wilkes added as he stood and stretched his back. "There is a lass I've a hankering to see," he added with a wink. "I'll be gone by day's end."

"Thank you," Nathan said.

"You don't possibly mean to make us leave today?" Donnelly asked.

"Donnelly's fallen in love again," Wilkes said congenially, "and he is loath to leave her."

Donnelly laughed as he gained his feet. "I wouldn't call it *love*," he said with a wink. "But she is a bonny lass, as Lambourne would say."

"Come to London with me," Wilkes said. "There are more bonny lasses than one man can possibly handle."

"All right, then. Take me to the land of bonny lasses," Donnelly said. "Let's gather our things and be gone, eh?"

"I'll see you all before you're off," Lindsey said, his gratitude evident.

As Wilkes and Donnelly walked out, the Irishman suddenly grinned at Jack. "Running off to Scotland, are you? Have a care who you bed there, my friend. I've heard tell the Scots are rather ruthless when their women are ruined."

Jack laughed. "No one would know it better than I, my lord."

The day was cold and damply gray, but the work on cleaning up the debris of the fire continued. As all free hands were thus engaged, it was midday before hot water could be brought to Evelyn's rooms for a soaking bath. The thorough washing she'd done at the basin the night before had helped, but nothing would soothe the feeling of having come so close to death as a hot bath.

In her bathing room, heated by two coal-burning braziers, Evelyn rested her head against the rim of the tub, her eyes closed, and thought of Robbie.

He was tottering ahead of her, dragging a stick that was longer than him. It was an unusually warm March day that year, and the scarf she typically kept wrapped about his throat was in her basket. Robbie stopped at the trunk of a sycamore tree and laid his chubby little hand against it. *"Tree!"* he cried with delight, having only recently learned the word.

"Tree!" she'd cried with him, just as delighted. He was such a smart boy! *"Brilliant, darling!"*

"I beg your pardon."

Evelyn gasped and came up with a start. Lost in memory, she'd not heard him enter. Water splashed over the side of the tub as she groped for a towel, but it was just beyond her reach, and she quickly sank back into the water and covered her body with her arms. "I would like some privacy, please!"

Not only did her husband not leave, his gaze openly and hungrily drifted down her body, prompting a shiver inside her. Evelyn sank lower into the water, almost up to her chin. "Please, Nathan," she said again.

He ignored her request and slowly lifted his gaze to her eyes. "How are you today?"

"Improved, obviously." She felt entirely exposed, but he was looking at her with such unabashed desire that she also felt oddly alluring. "You're gaping at me as if I were one of your doxies."

He smiled a little. "I assure you, I know of no doxy as enchanting as you."

Evelyn smiled and absently moved one arm, trailing her fingers across the surface of the water. "And now you think you can seduce me like one of your doxies. Whatever it is you want, I would prefer that you say it and go. The water is cooling."

His gaze drifted to her breasts, just visible at the surface of the soapy water. "I have sent our guests home," he announced as his gaze moved over her legs and her knees, protruding from the water.

Astonished, she was speechless for a moment. "You did *what?*"

"Sent them home," he repeated as he admired the bit of her thigh he could see.

Evelyn could not remember a time when one or more of Nathan's friends weren't about. "Why?" she asked.

"*Why?*" Nathan smiled a little lopsidedly as he shifted his gaze to her face. "I thought you'd be inordinately happy they are on their way."

"I'm astonished. You're rarely without them."

"The time has come to put away childish things," he said as he moved to the side of the tub.

She couldn't agree more. "How did they respond?"

"They cheerfully went on their way," he said, and went down on one knee beside her, propping his arms on the edge of the tub. He poked the fingers of one bruised and cut hand into the water, swishing them idly about as his eyes roamed her face. "I think it is best if you and I start at the beginning . . . without them."

His gaze was so intent on her that Evelyn felt almost bewitched by it. His eyes were so blue, yet ocean deep. When they made love, his eyes filled with light and desire and sheer lust.

Thinking about it gave her another, stronger shiver. "The beginning of what?" she asked softly.

Nathan touched his finger casually to the tip of her breast. "Of us."

She could feel the desire draw again, pooling in her belly.

"You deserve a new beginning at Eastchurch," he murmured, and slipped his hand into the water, cupping her breast.

Evelyn drew another abrupt breath.

"And I intend to give it to you."

Her body reacted with alarming prurience. She tried to shift away from his hand, but the tub was too small—there was nowhere to go. "I don't want a new beginning at Eastchurch."

"Yes, so you've said, but I aim to change your mind." He palmed her breast as he watched her eyes, tweaking the tip between his fingers and sending another wave of desire through her. His touch was ruining her, weakening her. She wanted to protest, but she was powerless to do so.

"There are only the two of us now," he said low. "We are alone in this house. There is nothing and no one to distract us." His gaze unwavering, he moved his hand, sliding to the other breast. "It is you, and me, and what is left of our marriage. We may either tear it down completely . . . or build it up again."

She looked at his mouth and remembered how he had once trailed a moist path down her belly. She wanted to tell him no, to beg him to leave her be, but she couldn't seem to find the words or her voice. She was aware of nothing but his blue eyes and his hand on her body, stroking her, caressing her, arousing her.

His expression suggested that he knew what he was doing to her . . . but then again, he always did. "Imagine, just the two of us, completely and utterly alone with nothing but our imaginations to occupy us."

Heaven above. "I am imagining peace and quiet," she insisted.

Nathan chuckled low and lifted his hand from the water, brushed his knuckles across her cheek. "I will see you at supper," he said, and leaned across the tub, touched his mouth to hers, so lightly, but so sensually, that her body felt as if it had been lit up like a candelabra. He lifted his head and looked at her. "Don't be late."

He stood. He smiled roguishly. With one last look at her body beneath the water, he casually strolled out.

The moment the door shut, Evelyn slid down, submerging herself completely in the water, rubbing her hands on her arms, trying to rid herself of that powerful feeling of yearning.

Kathleen was practically levitating with excitement at the news that the gentlemen had left Eastchurch. She had gathered quite a bit of intelligence surrounding their departures from the staff and was dutifully reporting it as she dressed Evelyn's hair.

"What a ruckus it's caused!" she exclaimed as she dressed Evelyn's hair for the evening. "Maude is beside herself, for she'd been rather cozy with Lord Donnelly, don't you know, and the rogue promised he'd take her from here. They always say such things, those randy lords, but then he was on his horse and away pretty as you please, without more than a fare thee well to Maude!"

"Are you certain?" Evelyn asked. She could hardly imagine Donnelly would have said such a thing. She knew his type—very careful not to promise anything but just precisely what was needed to get him between the bed linens.

"I have it from Deschell—you know him, do you not?" Kathleen breathlessly continued. "The tall red-headed footman, he's the one. Deschell told me that Lambourne left this morning just after an interview with his lordship. They had an awful falling-out. Supposedly you could hear the shouting in the kitchen. Imagine that, a falling-out! And those two thick as thieves!"

Such wild gossip that circulated below stairs! Evelyn cringed inwardly, imagining what sort of wild gossip about her circulated among the staff, now and then. Especially then.

"It's just as well, if you ask me," Kathleen said as she wound a string of seed pearls through Evelyn's hair. "Now that you've come home, mu'um, Eastchurch should return to a proper place befitting a grand lady, as it was meant to be."

Evelyn merely smiled at her reflection in the mirror. She wasn't certain Eastchurch could return to being a "proper place," or if she was capable of transforming it.

Kathleen continued to prattle on with household gossip, but Evelyn's thoughts wandered. The fluttering in her belly was the nerves of anticipation. She'd debated going down to supper at all—what purpose would it serve? She knew precisely what her husband wanted—his conjugal rights—but that unbridled desire only muddied the waters even more.

Yet the memory of the way he'd looked at her in her bath kept shocking her with tiny little tremors of deep, deep desire.

In the end, it was that unearthly yearning that propelled her down to supper. She convinced herself that it wouldn't hurt to hear what her husband had to say. Or that after years of pain and heartache, there was no reason the end of their marriage had to be acrimonious.

She was dressed in her best gown. The top skirt was made of raw silk the color of new grass, over a skirt of royal fuchsia that matched the embroidery on the sleeves and the train. It was beautiful. It made her feel strong.

As she fingered the locket that hung at her throat, she idly wondered what had happened to the eager young woman who had come into this house ten years ago, the naïve young woman whose head was filled with fantastic ideas of marriage.

In actuality, marriage had been much harder than she ever imagined, and in many ways, *too* hard. The woman going down to supper now—the one who had spent years in London watching couples who were joined in marriage by law but not in heart—wondered if it was even possible to have the sort of fantasy marriage she'd once dreamed of having.

No. This marriage had been based on the need to maintain rank and privilege. The sort of marriage she had dreamed about was based on the need for love. She had loved Nathan, and perhaps he had loved her in his way, but their marriage had crumbled into sand when the strength of it was tested.

A strange sense of sadness drifted over her as she walked down the stairs, destined to dine with the man she had lost in what he called the scaffolding of a fragile marriage.

chapter twenty

Benton was waiting in the foyer for Evelyn at a quarter to seven. "Good evening, madam," he said, and gestured to the corridor to the right. "His lordship requested that you meet him in the morning room."

"The *morning* room?"

"If you please," he said, and walked briskly in that direction, pausing by the corridor's entrance to await her.

Evelyn paused, too, and peered down the long hall. "Why?"

"His lordship has requested it," was all Benton would say.

Eyeing him suspiciously, Evelyn started for the morning room, Benton at her side. "What is *in* the morning room?" she tried again.

"I am not at liberty to say."

"Benton!" she said with a smile. "We've known each other for quite a long time. You might at least tell me if I should draw my sword."

Benton allowed her a ghost of a smile. "I cannot,

madam. I have been threatened with my position if I as much as breathe a word of what is in the morning room, or do not replace the paraffin candles in the upper floors with beeswax."

"What has that to do with the morning room?"

"Not a thing. But it is likewise a condition of my continued employment."

Evelyn smiled. She'd long admired Benton's unflappable dedication to the earl.

"Here we are," Benton said, and put his hand on the door's handle. "Good evening, Lady Lindsey."

"What . . . you're leaving?" Evelyn asked, confused.

His expression unreadable, Benton opened the door to the morning room and stepped aside.

The scent of lavender wafted out. Evelyn looked into the room and gasped with delight—it was filled with flowers and greenery. Giant palms and ornamental elm and ash trees had been brought up from the sun room and scattered about the room. Vases of hothouse flowers were interspersed in between the trees, covering most of the floor. A birdcage hung in the corner of the room, and a trio of twittering canaries hopped from one swing to another. At the far end of the room was the hearth, where a fire was burning.

Evelyn walked into the room. Before the hearth, a green cloth covered the carpet. Big, thick pillows were scattered in a semicircle around the cloth. In the middle of the green cloth was a large basket covered with a gingham cloth. Perhaps the most amazing thing of all was the large canopy umbrella, the sort servants dragged out to hilltops to shade ladies who picnicked.

Evelyn realized it was precisely that. "A *picnic?*" she said aloud to no one.

"Yes. A picnic."

She turned about—Nathan was leaning against a sideboard across the room from the hearth, his arms folded and one ankle crossed over the other. He was watching her reaction closely.

"I don't understand," Evelyn said.

"You once professed a liking for picnics. The time of year prevents me from giving you a proper one, but madam, here is your picnic nonetheless."

She couldn't help but feel delighted. "Nathan, this is . . ." She couldn't think of the correct word. *Insanity? Charming?*

"Is what?" he asked, pushing away from the sideboard and walking toward her.

Her pulse fluttered. "Madness." She unthinkingly took a step backward. "This is not a picnic."

"By whose definition?"

"By *mine*."

He paused and looked around. "What is lacking?"

"The sun, for one," she said, folding her arms.

Nathan arched one dark brow and pointed heavenward. Evelyn looked up; the ceiling was painted sky blue with white puffy clouds floating across it. "That's new," she said wryly.

"Benton's idea," he said with a flick of his wrist. "There are trees," he continued, gesturing to the palms and the ornamental potted trees. "And a lovely lawn," he added, nodding to the green cloth that had been laid over the carpet. "All the makings of a picnic are here."

He'd gone to quite a lot of trouble. It reminded her of the occasion of her twenty-second birthday, when he'd awakened her with a trumpeter outside her window. When she'd opened the drapes and looked down, she'd laughed with delight—he was dressed in the costume of a king. He'd swept a bow low over one extended leg, then motioned to the white horse behind him—borrowed, as it turned out, from the DuPauls. *"Come down, my love, so that I might whisk you away and ravage you properly on this important occasion."* Inside, Kathleen had appeared, holding a gold dress with long tapering sleeves and a hat in the style worn hundreds of years ago.

Evelyn had been more than happy to go off with her husband and be properly ravished, but Nathan had taken her up to the abbey ruins where her family and many friends from around the shire were waiting to surprise her, all of them dressed in the clothing of a medieval court. It had been a magnificent day; they'd feasted on turkey and ale, and musicians from the village had played country dances. They'd danced in what was once the common room of the old abbey.

That night, when they lay in bed, Evelyn had twined her fingers in his. *"You went to much trouble and expense,"* she'd said.

"Did you enjoy yourself?"

Oh, she'd enjoyed it. It was one of the best days of her life. *"It was marvelous, Nathan! However shall I repay you?"*

He'd gathered her up in a strong embrace, pulling her on top of him. *"I can think of one or two ways, indeed . . ."*

He had disappeared the next morning, of course, off with his friends. But the memory of that birthday made her smile nonetheless.

Tonight, Nathan strode to the sideboard and poured two glasses of wine. He returned, handing her one.

"This is all very creative," she said as she took the wine and sampled it.

"Try not to look so astonished," he said with a lop-sided smile. "I thought that after yesterday's high drama, you deserved it."

She didn't know if she deserved it or not—for all she knew, Nathan was right and she'd somehow, accidentally, burned down the orangery—but this room was so cheerful on what had been a cold and drab day, she was beginning to feel a bit jolly. "Does this picnic include food, or do we just sit on our make-believe hill and look down at our make-believe village?"

"Is there food?" he repeated with feigned shock. "Madam, you may think I do not know you well, but you must at *least* grant that I know you have an appetite so healthy that it belies your tiny waist."

Evelyn laughed. "I shall consider that remark a compliment."

Nathan's smile deepened, and he held out his hand, palm up. "Then come to my picnic, Evie."

Out of habit or desire—she didn't know which—Evelyn slipped her hand into his.

He led her to the green cloth and helped her down onto her knees. He crouched down beside her and removed the cloth from the basket. She gasped with surprise when she saw the feast within. Grapes, cheeses, cold chicken, a fresh loaf of bread. There were other items wrapped in cloth at the bottom of the basket, too, but Evelyn was more interested in the fare that Nathan heaped onto a Sèvres china plate for her.

She picked up a grape and popped it in her mouth. "Did you grow these in your botanical cottage?"

Nathan laughed as he bit into the chicken. "No, I

grow lavender in my 'botanical cottage.' Not grapes. These come to us courtesy of Mr. Roberts's hothouse. You recall him, do you not?"

"I recall his wife," Evelyn said with a snort. "She was quite awful to the servants' children. On rainy days, they would walk through her hedgerow on their way to the schoolhouse, and she would chase them with a broom. It frightened Mary Stern's son so badly, he refused to go to school for a time."

"Mary Stern died a year ago," Nathan informed her.

"Died?" Evelyn exclaimed, wide-eyed. "But she was so young!"

"Yes, she was," he said, and proceeded to tell her about the woman's illness and subsequent death. That led to questions about other residents in the shire, and as they ate, Nathan told her the news she had missed over the last three years.

He did not speak of London, or remark on her long absence. He spoke to her as if she'd been gone a fortnight—not a lifetime.

Evelyn was struck by their easy companionship, and how relaxed she felt dining at their make-believe picnic. It was almost as if they were two old friends who had not seen each other in a while—not an estranged couple. He made her laugh with ease, just as he'd done in the early days of their marriage.

For the space of an hour or so, there was no past between them, no questions about the future. There was just the two of them in that moment, two people content in one another's company, and Evelyn enjoyed herself as she had not done in a long time.

Nathan had just poured them a second glass of wine when Evelyn discovered the pudding cakes. She cried out with delight when she saw them. "My favorite!" she exclaimed. "Cook remembered!"

"*Cook*," he scoffed. "While I suspect the entire sovereign nation knows of your love of pudding cakes, it was *I* who requested them."

"You did?" she asked, and beamed at him as she bit into the cake. She closed her eyes and sighed. "Oh, they are heavenly."

Nathan chuckled and propped himself beside her, his back against the pillows, stretching his long legs toward the fire. With his finger, he swiped a crumb of cake from her lip and put it in his mouth.

Evelyn smiled.

"Do you recall that wretched winter, and a particularly cold and snowy night?"

Evelyn playfully rolled her eyes. "Yes," she said with a smile. "How could I possibly forget?"

"We were snowed in," he said. "No one could come or go, and we were filled to the rafters with guests."

"The vicar and his mother," Evelyn giggled.

"Your parents," Nathan reminded her. "Lambourne, Donnelly, and Wilkes."

"Naturally," Evelyn said, nudging him with her shoulder.

"New snow was falling on old snow, and it looked as if it would never end."

"I feared it would end with us eating the draperies," Evelyn said with a laugh. "How is it possible we ran out of meat? We were sick to death of carrots—raw carrots, stewed carrots, mashed carrots . . ."

"Then Cook found the sack of flour," Nathan said with a chuckle, "and made pudding cakes."

"Oh, what a relief it was!" Evelyn exclaimed. "We ate

pudding cakes until I thought I could never bear to see another one," she said, and took another bite from the one she held.

"I am happy to see you are wholly recovered." Nathan laughed, and closed his hand around her wrist, pulled the pudding cake she held to his mouth, and took a healthy bite.

"Completely," she assured him, and took another bite, savoring it. "I've not seen pudding cakes in London."

"I remember you wore a dark red dress that night. The décolletage was rather spectacular."

Evelyn gave him a coy smile.

Nathan looked at her décolletage now. "I remember licking the crumbs from your breast," he said, and brushed his knuckles across her collarbone.

A flutter of desire rose up in her again. Evelyn lowered the pudding cake. "Are you attempting to seduce me?"

The look in his eye sparked the memory of his body that strange dark night only days ago, and it quite literally snatched her breath away.

"I am not attempting," he said low, as his eyes languidly took in the swell of her breasts above her bodice. "I am determined."

"You are remarkably arrogant."

"Arrogant?" He grinned wolfishly. "I think you mistake an eagerness to please for arrogance." He touched the hollow of her throat, tracing a line down into her cleavage. "Yet I confess I can't help myself. I see a certain light in your eyes, Evie, and I know it well. I see the flush of your skin and the set of your mouth . . ." He brushed his thumb across her bottom lip. "And I am reminded that I am your husband. I want to make love to you."

He'd always held a seductive power over her—there was a time he could seduce her with a look or a tender touch. But Evelyn was not so impressionable any longer. She knew a man's game, and as much as her body heated at his touch, as hard as her pulse beat at his suggestion, there was too much beyond the bed that weighed on her.

She leaned forward and put the last bite of pudding cake in the basket and carefully wiped her hands. Nathan put his hand to her nape and caressed a long, slow path down her spine.

"I cannot forget how much you enjoyed our marriage bed," he murmured. "I think about it often."

Evelyn shifted onto her knees and glanced over her shoulder at him. The longing in his expression was almost her undoing. She felt beautiful, desirable . . . and a bit afraid. Perhaps because she felt that desire within herself, right alongside her misgivings.

"Is that what you recall?" she asked, her voice intentionally breathless.

He smiled a little. "That," he said, caressing her back again, "and how it feels to be inside you. How you look when you find fulfillment—"

She moved abruptly, pouncing on him, knocking him deep into the pillows and onto his back, pinning his arms to his sides. "Do you recall anything other than your lust, Nathan?"

Nathan suddenly surged up. He recklessly twisted them both around, toppling the basket as he put her on her back on the green cloth. He braced himself and stared down at her. "Don't you recall yours, my love?"

"The pleasure from a marriage bed should not be the measure of a marriage!" she said adamantly.

"In your eyes it seems every bump, every cross word, is the measure. Do you want to know what else I remember, Evelyn? Not every cross word. Not every bump. I remember how you look in the morning when you first awake. I remember the sound of your laughter. I remember how your hair catches the candlelight and seems at times to be spun with gold," he said, roughly caressing her head. "I remember the wreath of flowers you wore in your hair and how beautiful you were the day I married you. I remember the brilliant glow of happiness in your eyes when you told me you carried our child. I remember how much you love pudding cake and lavender perfume and how it delighted you to participate in an archery match."

Evelyn couldn't breathe, could not draw a breath. She was mesmerized by him—he was passionate and angry at once, his eyes blazing yet full of yearning.

"And I remember," he said, his eyes tracing a burning path down her body, "what it feels like to make love to my wife. There is no feeling on this earth quite like it, and I refuse to apologize for wanting it again."

Oh, but she wanted it, too. Now, in this make-believe picnic. Yet her fears, all the things she had tamped down, locked away, were beating at the door. "Physical desire colors your opinion of our true situation, Nathan," she said. "But it won't change the reality of all the pain between us. What of our past and everything that's happened between us?" she asked, trying to move, trying to escape those eyes.

Nathan held her firmly. "More than bad things have happened between us. *Good* things have happened between us! But Evie, if you don't want to remember, we'll make new memories. Starting now," he said, and slipped his arm beneath her neck, pulling her up to him at the same moment he lowered his head to kiss her.

She gasped at the sensation of his passionate kiss. She tasted the wine on his lips, felt the stubble of his beard on her chin, the strength of his embrace. She had always loved to be in his arms. When he held her, nothing could touch her, nothing could hurt her. But tonight she was frozen, uncertain of what to do, unsure of how to proceed. Part of her wanted to stop, for herself, for her sanity—but her heart and her body, starved for a man's touch, was urging her on.

Evelyn dipped her tongue into his mouth, touching the tip of his. He groaned, and Evelyn felt as if a part of her were falling, drifting down into the woman she'd once been, the woman who had craved this man with every fiber of her being.

Nathan rolled them onto their side, and then onto his back, dragging Evelyn on top of him. He cradled her head in his hands as his lips moved across hers, feeling them, tasting them, nipping at them. His tongue swirled inside her mouth as desire swirled inside of her. He caressed the column of her neck, his knuckles grazing her earring, then moving again, rolling her onto her back once more, his lips never leaving hers. His hand drifted down to her bosom, and he cupped her breast, massaging it.

Evelyn was lost, entirely captive to his hands and mouth. She was heedless of anything but him, his body, and the evidence of his longing pressed against her thigh. His mouth was so enticing, and as he kissed her, she imagined those lips on her breasts, between her legs. When he touched his mouth to her neck, she shuddered with uncontrollable desire. *"Nathan . . ."*

"Whatever you want, Evie," he whispered in her ear. "Whatever you need, I will give it to you."

She was without reason or thought, filled with physical and emotional longing that surprised her. Her gown felt heavy. She wanted to feel his skin on her skin, his body hard and lean against her softness. She pushed her fingers through his hair, felt his ears, his shoulders, his back. He lifted her breast from her gown and bent his head to it, laving the tip, sucking it in between his teeth, while she gasped with the prurient sensation.

But when Nathan grabbed a fistful of her gown and began pushing it up her body, her heart skipped. She put her hand on his, pushing it down. "No, please wait," she said weakly, trying to swim out of the fog of her desire.

"What?" he said roughly, his hand on her thigh. "Do I displease you? Tell me what you want me to do," he said, and gazed at her with dark eyes. "Do you want me to touch you here?" he asked, touching her between her legs.

Evelyn sucked in her breath.

"Or here?" he asked softly, slipping a finger inside her.

"You . . . you let passion cloud the truth of our marriage," she whispered breathlessly. "What will come on the morrow when your lust is satisfied?"

"I will work to satisfy yours," he said roughly, and rolled her over onto her belly. With his hands on her bottom, he leaned over her, his breath in her hair as he caressed her. His thumbs slid between her legs, parting her and reaching the center of her pleasure. "You are wet for me, darling. *That* is the truth. You want me as I want you," he breathed into her hair. "The question is, do you want me here?" he said, pressing against her as his thumbs teased her. "Or here?" he asked, and rolled her onto her side. He lifted her leg with his hand and slid against her, rubbing his hard body against hers.

"I am human, Nathan," she said, closing her eyes to the pleasure he was giving her. "I can be tempted, just as you can—but you are willfully misunderstanding me."

"I understand that your body wants me inside you," he said roughly, and fumbled with his trousers, freeing his erection, then pressing it against her, sliding it between her legs, rubbing her swollen peak. "It was always good between us, Evie," he said breathlessly. "I think you have missed it as much as I have. Tell me you have missed this," he said, and slid deep inside her.

She had missed it. "No, *no* . . ." She pushed away from him.

"Don't do that, Evie. Please don't do that," Nathan said through gritted teeth. But it was too late. Evelyn had almost succumbed, but now she was pushing and scrambling to move away from him. Nathan wouldn't let go of her at first—he seemed stung by her sudden rejection. He was panting, restraining himself. Evelyn pushed again, and he finally let go of her, rolled onto his back, and slung one arm across his eyes.

His erection was clearly evident; his chest was rising and falling rapidly. She felt the need to explain, to smooth it over. "There is too much that cannot be repaired, and we cannot . . . we cannot—"

"We *can*," he said gruffly, and sat up. Evelyn couldn't look at him. She busied herself straightening her clothing, then put a hand to her hair. One thick strand had come undone and hung over her shoulder.

Nathan watched her for a moment, then said tightly, "For God's sake, tell me what it is that you believe is so irretrievably broken. Tell me so that I might repair it."

"It is difficult to explain," she said. *All the hopes and disappointments*, and the fear, that ever-present fear that she would be forced to relive the most excruciating pain a woman could possibly endure. "I can't do this again, Nathan. I can't rightly explain other than to say I am a different person now. I am no longer willing to be married for the sake of rank and privilege."

"What?" he said incredulously, and leapt to his feet, buttoning his trousers and turning to face her, hands on hips. "What in God's name do you mean by that?"

"Don't pretend we were married for any other reason," she said, leaning down to smooth her skirts.

"I *won't* pretend it," he said curtly. "But it went beyond that, and you know it well, Evie." He startled her by catching her chin in his hand and forcing her to look at him. "You *know* it did."

She wrapped her fingers around his wrist and calmly pulled his hand from her face. "Whatever we had fell apart when Robbie died."

"Lord *God*, what is it you want?" he cried.

"I want love, Nathan! I want to know that there is nothing that can come between us, that it—I mean, *we*—will be forever!"

"That's it?" he said incredulously. "That is what you need?"

She hadn't really managed to put her deepest desire into words until this very moment, but she did mean it, quite sincerely. She wanted him, but she didn't want him without that at the very least. She nodded.

Nathan groaned. "I *love* you, Evelyn," he said, his eyes now glittering with anger. "I love you, I love you!

How many times must I say it? I have *always* loved you!"

"Don't, Nathan," she said, shaking her head. "You cannot repaint the past—"

He cupped her face with his hands, forcing her to look at him. "*Listen* to me, Evie. I loved you then, and I love you still. I may not have always loved you in the way you wanted to be loved, but as God is my witness I loved you the best way I knew how. If I never told you it would be forever, then I beg your forgiveness, but I never saw it any other way."

"You . . . you wanted your friends and diversions more than you wanted me—"

"There are many things I did that I wish I hadn't done, and many things I didn't say," he said, his eyes searching her face. "You are not the only one who has changed, Evie."

She felt a piece of the invisible guard around her heart break off and fall away. She tried to avoid his gaze, but Nathan turned her face up, forcing her to look at him.

What she saw was heartbreaking. She saw an old and familiar pain she understood better than he could possibly know. It was the pain of being set adrift with no anchor.

"Do not doubt it will be forever, Evie. *Forever*. It will be until we can no longer draw a breath."

He left her completely breathless.

His fingers splayed across her cheek. He gazed deep in her eyes a moment, then leaned down, kissing her gently. "*Forever*," he whispered, and kissed her again. "*Forever*."

She was falling. She sank into his body, her arms

going around his neck. The sound of someone knocking on the door seemed a distant noise, a different door. But she heard it again. And again.

Nathan lifted his head. He didn't move; his gaze locked with hers. "Go away!" he bellowed.

"My lord, I beg your pardon, but it is a matter of some urgency!" Benton called through the door.

"*Go away!*"

"My lord! It is urgent!" Benton called.

"Bloody hell," Nathan muttered, and shook his head in disbelief. "Bloody, *bloody* hell!" His hands fell away from Evelyn's face and the warmth of them dissipated quickly.

Nathan turned around and looked at the door, almost hidden behind the ornamental trees. "It had better be urgent, sir, or you will be shodding horses at the smithy on the morrow! Come!" he shouted.

The door opened a crack, and Benton slipped through. His eyes, Evelyn noticed, were respectfully on the carpet. "Guests have arrived, my lord," he announced.

"*That's* your urgent matter? *Guests?* Bring me a gun, Benton, for I must shoot you. Who is it—Wilkes? Donnelly? Tell them to sleep in the stables!"

"I beg your pardon; it is not Lord Donnelly or Sir Wilkes. It is the Marquis and Marchioness of Sudley, and the Baron and Baroness of Wainwright. There seems to have been a misunderstanding. They believe they are expected for supper this evening."

Evelyn gasped and looked at Nathan. A current of understanding flowed between them: their parents had come calling. Together. *A misunderstanding.*

"Good *Lord*," Nathan said with a sigh, and waved at

Benton. "Put them somewhere. Find something to feed them—I hardly care what. But for the love of all that is holy, do please give us a moment!"

"Yes sir," Benton said, and quickly stepped out, shutting the door.

Nathan looked at Evelyn, his eyes narrowed suspiciously. "I am cursed. I must be cursed. Nothing else explains our parents *here*, tonight of all nights," he said irritably.

chapter twenty-one

The misunderstanding, it seemed, was a note from Alexandra DuPaul that was lost in all the commotion of the fire. Alexandra had expected to host the supper at her house this evening, but the marquis—Nathan's father—had asked her to change those plans so that they might dine at Eastchurch. The DuPauls had respectfully decided not to attend what seemed an intimate family reunion.

Unfortunately, the note went unread.

Nevertheless, their parents had made themselves at home in the blue drawing room; Nathan's mother, petite but sturdy, seated next to Evelyn's mother, who was a little younger and bigger, and with the same hazel eyes as Evelyn. Nathan's father, the marquis, had silver hair now, but still possessed an athletic build. Evelyn's father, however, had relaxed in the last years—he'd grown rather portly since Nathan last saw him.

"The Greys and the Brantleys," Nathan said as he entered the room and strode across the carpet. "What a pleasant surprise." He greeted them each, and explained that the note had been lost, which, fortunately, they laughed about.

"Benton, some wine," Nathan said, gesturing to the sideboard. "Evelyn will be down shortly. She and I are very happy that you have come," he said, before noting that Benton had already served wine before Nathan had even entered the room.

"Darling, we must celebrate Evelyn's return to East-church Abbey!" his mother exclaimed. "On my word, I've not heard happier news all year!"

"It's been what . . . four or five years since she was last here?" his father inquired.

"Three."

"Well! It is good she has come home at last!" he said awkwardly, and lifted his glass in toast to Nathan.

"Good evening, one and all," Evelyn called from the door, sweeping into the room.

"Darling!" her mother cried, rising up, her arms held wide.

"Mamma," Evelyn said, walking into her mother's embrace. Her father was instantly at their side, taking her in his arms the moment her mother let go of her. When they at last let her go, she curtsied to Nathan's parents.

Her skin was flushed as if she'd run from her rooms. She was beautiful, Nathan thought, her gown exquisite, her bearing elegant and gracious. He was proud, he realized. Quite proud.

"Benton, when . . . ?"

"Supper is served, madam," Benton said, bowing low.

Evelyn gave Nathan a look of surprise, but then quickly suggested they all repair to the dining room.

In the dining room, Nathan could hardly contain his surprise. He knew Benton's capabilities, but this was incredible. The table had been exquisitely set, and there was, much to Nathan's shock, a roasted bird, as well as bread and, presumably, soup in a large tureen.

"We'd like to welcome you home, Evelyn," the marquis said as he took a seat at the table. "We are each of us happy to see you where you belong." The four of them beamed at her.

"Thank you."

"How *are* you, dear?" Nathan's mother asked.

"Very well, thank you," she said politely.

"Good. Very good," the marchioness said, and the four of them exchanged little smiles with one another.

Nathan did not like how they were looking at Evelyn. It was beginning to dawn on him that this was not a social call. "Benton, wine," he said, although the glasses brought from the blue drawing room were still quite full. "Darling?" he said to Evelyn, and helped her into her chair. She sat, folding her hands in her lap, gripping them so tightly that he could see the whites of her knuckles.

If it weren't such a maidenly thing to do, he might have joined her. He took his seat at the head of the table.

Evelyn asked after their parents' journey as footmen began ladling soup. The four responded in a lively manner, claiming not to have seen each other in a pair of months and expressing their delight at receiving the invitation from Mrs. DuPaul.

Nathan watched them talking and laughing. The four of them had been fast friends for as long as he could remember—it was their idea to marry their two children, an arrangement that was sealed when he was in short pants and Evelyn in the nursery.

Nathan had never objected to it. He'd rarely seen Evelyn until it came time for him to marry and assume the responsibilities of his title, but what he knew of her, he liked. She was freshly pretty then, her eyes bright and eager. He had courted her a few times to assure himself and his parents of their compatibility. He'd seen what he needed to see—that she would make a good countess and a marchioness one day. Evelyn had been eager to marry as well, he recalled, and therefore the deed was done, just as it had been done countless times before them.

He realized, as he watched Evelyn squirm a little at the questioning from her mother about life in London, that he never really thought of how his life would change once he married. He'd been a young man and had thought of marriage only when his father impressed on him that he must marry. The day he and Evelyn stood before God, their parents, the king and queen, and half of London, he did not think what his vows truly meant.

He'd thought of them since, but he wasn't yet entirely certain that he understood how to live up to them.

Evelyn laughed politely at something silly his father said, nodding along as his father told her some terribly tiresome tale, and Nathan wondered how a man could crawl out of a hole as deep as the one into which he'd fallen with his wife.

After the meal was consumed, Benton whispered something to Evelyn, and she suggested they retire to games in the blue drawing room.

In the blue drawing room, they sat around one round table as the footman returned their wineglasses to them.

Nathan dealt the first hand of Loo. They played one or two rounds before the marquis gestured to the four of them and said, "We all thank God you've returned to your rightful place, Evelyn. Now that you have, you won't leave again, will you?"

"Father—" Nathan started, but his father threw up a hand.

"I really must ask, son," he said. "The nation is gripped with scandal so foul that it threatens the existence of the monarchy. Our two fine families cannot be part of it. I mean by that, no behavior that will cause talk. No gambling debts. No mysterious fires."

"How did you know of that?" Nathan asked.

"We could smell the burn in the air at the DuPauls', Nathan. There is quite a lot of speculation about the fire, I am sure you know, which only strengthens my point—the two of you must have a care. You *must* patch up this spat between you and behave properly, as befitting your names and titles!"

Nathan looked at Evelyn; he could see the spark in her eyes and gave her a slight shake of his head. He knew his father too well—to engage him on this matter would be fruitless. "Thank you, Father," he said tightly. "Shall we play on?"

Evelyn looked at her cards. The baroness dealt a round and glanced at Evelyn. "Are you feeling well, darling?"

Startled, Evelyn looked up. "I am very well, Mamma."

"She will be very well indeed as long as Nathan treats her tenderly as he ought," his mother added.

"Ah, for the love of God," Nathan sighed.

"What?" his mother asked innocently. "Nature dealt her a harsh blow, Nathan, and naturally, it can take a bit of time for one to pick one's self up and go on. But it is important that one do so," she said, gesturing in a pick-yourself-up sort of way.

"Mother, really—several years have passed."

"But she's been in London all that time nursing her wounds."

"That is really quite enough," Nathan said, and looked at Evelyn. She was staring at her cards, her skin pale.

The table fell silent for several moments.

"What will you do with the orangery?" Wainwright asked after a time.

"Clear it," Nathan said, at the very same moment Evelyn said, "Rebuild it." She said it rather firmly for a woman who had only a few days ago requested a divorce, and who only hours ago insisted there was too much damage between them to go on. He cocked a curious brow in her direction.

"I very much enjoyed the orangery," she said to him.

"You must rebuild it, sir," Lady Wainwright said as she peered at her cards. "It will help Evelyn to have it restored."

"Help me?" Evelyn echoed, and shifted her gaze to her mother. "Help me what?"

The four parents looked at one another. Lady Wainwright looked at Evelyn. "It will help you to heal, darling. You must heal so that you can be a good wife. Nathan needs you to be his countess."

Evelyn looked helplessly at Nathan.

He felt just as helpless.

"I do beg your pardon," Evelyn said, as she carefully laid her cards aside. She rose to her feet, looking around at the four of them. "I had not realized I'd failed you all."

"No one said you'd *failed*, Evelyn," Lady Wainwright said. "Just that we are concerned for you."

"Concerned about your reputations, I think you mean," she said calmly.

"Now see here!" Nathan's father snapped.

"Excuse me," Nathan said loudly, and abruptly stood. He walked around the table, put his arm around Evelyn. "Thank you all for your concern," he said. "I understand that your intentions are good, but this is a matter between my wife and me. If you don't mind, we'll retire for the evening. Benton, please show them to their rooms when they are ready," he said, and led Evelyn away from the room and the unsolicited judgments on their marriage.

chapter twenty-two

"*D*ivorce, Evelyn?" her mother exclaimed angrily the next morning as Evelyn sat at her vanity, her face in her hands.

It was bad enough Evelyn had spent such a wretched night. She'd paced the floor for half of it, tossed and turned the other half, trying to reconcile the extraordinary events of the last few days with feelings that had been ingrained in her for several years now.

There was the picnic, such a lovely effort, and of course the things Nathan had said that *still* reverberated in her heart. His words had made her heart swell, and she'd felt something fundamental shift inside her.

But then their parents had come.

This morning, Evelyn had only tried to be honest with her mother when she told her what she was thinking. It was obvious her mother thought it was insanity to even *think* of divorce. And if she wasn't clear on that point, the Baroness of Wainwright would not rest until she'd made it perfectly clear.

Her mother angrily paced the floor as Evelyn stared at the hot chocolate Kathleen had brought her before she was summarily dismissed by her mother.

"It was no small feat to keep the worst of it from the marchioness," her mother continued irritably. "She has heard the rumors from London about you and that scoundrel Dunhill, Evelyn, not to mention some complicity in the awful scandal between the Prince and Princess of Wales?"

"That is not true—"

"The *point*, daughter, is that she knows what is said about you! It's nothing short of a miracle that she hasn't heard of your desire to bring scandal to us all with this ridiculous notion of divorce!"

"It is not a *ridiculous* notion—"

"*Hush*, Evelyn!" her mother snapped. "Of all the foolishness we have endured on your account, this is the most egregious! And to think of all the effort we put into bringing you and Lindsey together again!"

Yes, there had been letters and general gnashing of teeth, and many, many tedious calls to Eastchurch. Evelyn sighed with resignation and picked up the cup of chocolate and sipped.

"When I think of the heartache we were forced to endure as a result of your madness, only to be rewarded with *this!*"

With a groan, Evelyn sank down, laying her cheek on the surface of the vanity.

"I should like to ask *why*," her mother demanded crossly, whirling around, "you would dare to dishonor us all so completely!"

"I didn't want to dishonor anyone," Evelyn said wearily. "But we have lived apart these years and—"

"That was *your* choice. Not his," her mother angrily interjected.

"It was indeed," Evelyn said evenly. "But he agreed. In fact, you *all* agreed. Everyone seemed to think it was best for me to leave the abbey . . . and *you*, Mamma, would have put me in an asylum, but Nathan wouldn't allow it."

"I most certainly did not want that! How can you possibly believe such a thing! I wanted to *help* you, Evelyn! Do you not recall how I worried, or the doctors your father and I brought to you? I wanted you to loosen your unnatural grip on your grief!"

All of the doctors had advised the same thing—stop grieving for her son. "Yes, you've mentioned my unnatural grief several times now," Evelyn said. She stood up, finished with the interview, and walked into her dressing room.

Her mother was close on her heels. "That is all in the past and neither here nor there," she said crisply. "I cannot understand this notion of divorce."

"Is it not obvious?" Evelyn asked irritably as she threw open the doors of her wardrobe. "Nathan and I tried, Mamma, and we failed. We've lived apart, and it seems impossible to repair the years of rift between us."

"There would be no rift," her mother said as she reached over Evelyn's shoulder and withdrew a plain, brown day gown and thrust it at her daughter, "if you could put the tragedy behind you. It was clear that child was sickly at birth, and we all warned you to keep your distance from him. Nature can be very harsh, and you did not gird yourself properly against the inevitable."

"We could no more have *distanced* ourselves from

that child than we could from each of you. To suggest we somehow erred in loving our son is insupportable!"

The baroness glared at her. "On my word, you make life difficult for us all! What good does it do to dwell on it?"

"I don't dwell on it! Not when I'm in London, anyway," Evelyn said, and shoved the brown gown into the wardrobe and withdrew a golden yellow instead. "But when I am here, at Eastchurch, how can I possibly avoid it? There are so many things to remind me! And I can't forget it, I can't stop picturing Robbie's face or hearing his laugh, or *seeing* him, like a ghost in every room!" She abruptly pushed past her mother, returning to the bedroom.

Tears were welling again—how was it possible that three years after his death she was still defending her grief? Why couldn't she make anyone understand how it felt to see his marks on the wall, or the path in the rose garden where he pushed the little wooden horse Nathan had put on wheels for him? Or how a horrible, empty ache descended on her heart by merely walking past the closed door of the nursery?

"I held my child in my arms as he drew his last breath, and when his breath was gone, so was mine. For *weeks*, Mamma, I was completely breathless, entirely incapable of *breathing*, much less picking myself up and tending to Nathan's needs!" She sat heavily at her vanity and rubbed her forehead against a sudden and fierce pain.

"Darling!" Her mother sank to her knees at Evelyn's side and took her hand. "I say these things because I love you, angel. Do you think you are the only woman to have ever lost a child?"

Of course she didn't. Evelyn shook her head.

"It is a tragic fact of life that women sometimes lose their children," her mother continued. "Some babies live, and some do not. Do you remember Mrs. Wells, our housekeeper? She buried all four of her children before their fifth year. We buried her among them when she died."

Evelyn's heart sank. How did one woman bury four children? How could Mrs. Wells possibly bear another child after losing one?

"It *is* tragic," her mother said, patting her knee, "but just as God takes those we love, He helps us to bear it. You must open your heart to that, Evelyn. Allow Him to help you bear it."

"I have *borne* it, Mamma," Evelyn insisted.

"No, you have not," her mother said firmly. "If you cannot bear to set foot in Eastchurch yet, you have not borne it as you ought and put it in its proper perspective. You are allowing your grief to rule you."

"It's not as easy as that," Evelyn said morosely. "There is a huge hole in my heart that I cannot fill," she said, pressing a fist to her chest. "Lord knows I've tried."

"Oh, Evelyn, you can never fill that hole—but you can face it headlong and cope with it in the bounds of your marriage. And really, what choice have you? You can't honestly expect that anyone will entertain this foolish notion of divorce."

Evelyn hadn't thought of anyone else entertaining it other than Nathan, and even then, she supposed she knew he'd never allow it.

Her mother squeezed her knee and stood. "I think the first order of business is to make amends with your husband."

"*Please*, Mamma!" Evelyn groaned. "Do not attempt to advise me—"

"He deserves your esteem," she continued. "He has suffered greatly in your absence."

Evelyn laughed with surprise. "If the rumors of *my* life have reached you, then surely you have heard of the Libertine of Lindsey!"

"Yes, I have," her mother said, frowning with displeasure. "But you cannot deny his loss was very great. He not only lost his son, he lost his heir."

Evelyn sighed. "Thank you, Mamma, for explaining my husband's grief to me." She stood, picking up her gown. "For what it is worth, you should know that only days after we buried Robbie, Nathan was gone with his friends, playing the tomcat. He came and he went, flitting in and out of the blackest days of my life. He did not appear to me to be a man grieving the loss of a bloody heir!"

"Evelyn!"

"I am sorry, Mamma, but you have made me the villain since the earth was spilled into my son's grave!" She shrugged out of her dressing gown and stepped into the day gown.

"Only because you were out of your mind!" her mother retorted. "I'd never seen such grief, and I feared for you! I believed you were making an impossibly wretched situation even worse."

"That's the difference between us, I suppose," Evelyn said crossly as her mother began to button her gown. "I cannot pick and choose my emotions. I gladly would have died to ease the pain. But you mustn't worry. I have picked myself up. I no longer want to die, I just miss him terribly." She walked toward the door.

"I beg your pardon, where are you going?" her mother demanded.

"Away from this interminable interview!" she called over her shoulder, and walked out of her suite, her eyes straight ahead, looking neither left nor right.

She sailed down the curving staircase, her feet flying down the marble steps. She scarcely stopped in the foyer, grabbing a cloak from the coatrack and throwing it around her shoulders before sweeping out of the main doors and running down the steps into the drive. The gloom of yesterday had lifted; the day was cool and breezy, but filled with bright sunlight. Her spirits rose instantly, and she began walking with no particular destination in mind. She wanted to be away from the orangery, the smell of which still hung in the air. She wanted to be away from the little rose garden, where she had seen the illness in the eyes of her son. She wanted to be away from the house itself, where the nursery was ever looming and her parents were overbearingly present.

She might have walked away from it all, kept walking all the way to London, had it not been for a single thought in her head: *Nathan*.

Nathan, who'd told her in no uncertain terms that he loved her. Last night, she had begun to believe that perhaps she had misjudged him, but then her parents had ruined everything by reminding her of the worst time of her life, a time when Nathan hadn't loved her, but more likely, had despised her. She remembered how angry they'd been with one another. He was frustrated with her inability to stop moping about. She was frustrated that he didn't understand it. He would come to her bed, and she was lifeless.

He took her lack of response to heart. And he'd sought comfort with Alexandra.

How long might it be before his memories began to revive and he despised her again? The question worried her, and lost in her private thoughts, Evelyn didn't realize she'd walked as far as the graveyard until she happened to see the cherub looking up to heaven above her son's grave.

She followed the cherub's gaze up to a cloudless blue sky. When she looked down again, she saw a patch of red behind the cherub. She squinted; the patch of red moved.

It was a boy. It was *Frances*. She watched as he walked around the back of the cherub and bent down. He carried a shovel.

A *shovel*?

Her mind racing through all the things he could possibly be doing with that shovel, she moved quickly. The iron gate to the graveyard was open, and she strode through.

He was nowhere to be seen at first, but then she caught sight of him again through the obelisks and grave markers. He went down on his knees at Robbie's grave and seemed to be digging.

With a gasp, Evelyn ran forward, reaching him just as he stood and picked up a bucket. Her sudden appearance startled him; he cried out and dropped the bucket, spilling leaves and dirt and plants of some sort.

Evelyn caught him by the shoulder. "What do you think you are doing?"

"Nothing!" he cried fearfully. "Only what his lordship told me!"

"*What?* What did he tell you?"

He tried to back away from her, but she held tight, leaning over to see his face. "To keep it tidy, mu'um!"

Evelyn blinked. She turned her head and looked at the headstone and the cherub, then slowly straightened, dropping her hand from Frances's shoulder. *The Lord giveth, and the Lord taketh away* . . .

She looked up to the cherub's angelic face and waited for something to wash over her—overwhelming grief, a sadness that would drive her to her knees.

Nothing came but a dull ache.

"He said he would depend on me," Frances said nervously.

Evelyn looked at him. He was frightened of her, and she felt wretched for it. She smiled. "Please forgive me, Frances. I did not realize my husband had entrusted the care of our son's grave to you."

But Frances firmly shook his head. "'Tis his lordship that tends to it, mu'um. But he said I was to look after it for a time because you needed him. And I've come every day, I have," he said, and nervously dragged the back of his hand under his nose.

Her smile grew. She didn't know which of them touched her more—Nathan or Frances. "You've come every day?"

"His lordship, he came every day, too. Until you came home, that is."

He came every day . . . She looked at the grave again. It was clean of debris, save that which had scattered when she'd caused Frances to drop his bucket. The grass was trimmed, the weeds were pulled, and she could see now that the shovel had been used to clean a trough around the headstone.

Slowly, Evelyn sank down onto her knees at the foot

of her son's grave. She picked up a pair of leaves and handed them to Frances for the bucket. He looked at her curiously, but then placed the bucket next to Evelyn and went down on his knees to pick up leaves, too.

"My papa says your baby would be almost six years now."

"Yes, that's true," Evelyn said.

"What was he like?" Frances asked blithely.

Evelyn grew still.

"His lordship, he doesn't like to talk about it. But he said your baby was a good boy. Sometimes, I wonder what he was like."

"Well, he was only a baby when he died, but he was a very smart little boy," she said, smiling at the memory. "He began to walk when he was only eleven months old, and he'd hold his arms out straight, like this," she said, holding her arms perpendicular to her body, "and waddle about the nursery. Then he began to talk."

"What did he say?"

"Just a few words. He said Mamma, and Papa. And words like shoe, or door, or pony. He loved strawberries but he hated peas." She slanted Frances a look. "He took after me in that. I despise peas," she said, wrinkling her nose.

Frances wrinkled his nose, too.

"He loved ponies," she said with a sigh. "He loved them very much. He had one that was on wheels, and he'd pull it everywhere he went." She picked up more leaves. "Sometimes, his father would take him riding. He'd sit in front of the earl, and he'd shout, *hossy, hossy!* He'd grip the pommel so tightly that we'd have to pry his fingers from it." She laughed, recalling how she and Nathan could scarcely get him off the horse. "He was a good boy," she said, looking thoughtfully at the cherub. "A very good boy."

Frances grinned. "My papa says he died of a wasting fever," he remarked as he scooped up a handful of dirt and debris and placed it in the bucket.

"Something like that," Evelyn acknowledged. "He was sick when he was born, you know—something wasn't right with his little heart, and fevers weakened him. He had one too many," she said, and glanced down at her son's grave.

God in heaven, she was doing it—she was talking about him, thinking about him, looking at his grave . . . and she wasn't fainting from grief. That she could even breathe so close to his grave was nothing short of a miracle—she was so enthralled with the realization that she didn't see Nathan standing against the fence, watching her, until Frances called out, "My lord!"

She sat back on her heels and shielded her eyes from the sun with one hand. Nathan pushed away from the fence and walked to where they were, his eyes on Evelyn.

Frances held up the bucket to Nathan. "I've tidied up, milord, just as you asked."

"You've done a fine job of it," he said. "You always do, lad. Perhaps you should return the bucket and the shovel to Mr. Gibbs. He's probably missing them by now."

"Aye, milord," Frances said cheerfully, and stood up, grabbing the bucket and the shovel. He paused, propped the shovel against his chest, and tipped his hat to Evelyn. "Good day, mu'um."

"Good day, Frances. And thank you for tending to my son's grave so carefully."

Frances ran off, the bucket banging against his legs.

Evelyn glanced up at Nathan, who came down on his haunches next to her, his eyes full of concern. "Stop looking at me like that," she said with a hint of a smile. "I am not going to fall to pieces. Frankly, I'm feeling remarkably strong at the moment."

He smiled, rose up, and offered his hand to her. Evelyn took it and let him pull her to her feet. She paused to dust the dirt and leaves from her cloak, then looked again at the grave marker.

She felt Nathan's hand slide around her waist, and he drew her in close. "The inscription," she said, folding her hands over his. "*'The Lord giveth, and the Lord taketh away.'* How did it come to pass?"

"You don't recall?"

There were so many blank spots in her memory and she sheepishly shook her head.

"The vicar suggested it."

Evelyn nodded. They stood there together, staring at the cherub, his hopeful face turned to the sky.

"D-did you . . ." She paused and swallowed down a sudden lump of grief that had risen up in her throat.

Nathan bent his head close to hers, as if he couldn't hear her, in the same way he used to whisper intimate little things to her when they were first married.

Evelyn cleared her throat. "I have often w-wondered," she said shakily. "Does he have his pony?"

Nathan tenderly caressed her arm. "Yes."

Her relief and gratitude was almost overwhelming. She sagged against him, resting her head against his shoulder. Nathan curved his arm around her waist, holding her.

They stood silently together, looking at the cherub until the cold seeped into Evelyn's consciousness.

The man stood deep in the woods, his horse tethered to a tree just off the river path. He held a small brass telescope to his eye and watched Lindsey and his wife standing at the grave of their son. A very touching picture.

Pity the fire hadn't done the trick.

He lowered the telescope and withdrew the pistol from his waist. He pointed it at the couple, closing one eye to better sight them.

He was at too great a distance, of course. He'd need a flintlock musket to have any hope of succeeding from here.

He lowered the pistol and smiled a little. He'd not fail a second time. He turned away from the parents of the dead boy and untethered his horse. He heaved himself up and calmly turned in the direction of the river, in the opposite direction of the graveyard.

chapter twenty-three

Predictably, the marquis was perturbed when Nathan informed him that he'd arranged for the Greys and the Brantleys to dine at the DuPauls'—without him or Evelyn. The marquis was a clever man and saw the ploy for what it was and promptly upbraided his son for it. "It is the height of inhospitality!" he snapped.

Nathan stood calmly, his hands clasped behind his back, listening attentively as he knew he ought, having just gained the upper hand.

When his father had finished, he glared at his son, waiting for a response that would not come. "Have you nothing to say for yourself?" he demanded at last.

"No," Nathan said calmly.

"You show an incredible lack of decorum!"

"I believe the lack of decorum was in your declining the DuPauls' hospitality at the last moment and arriving here uninvited."

"Are you saying that I must have an *invitation* to call on my son?"

"If you intend to scold me like a wayward child . . . yes."

His father's face turned red. He abruptly pivoted and marched to the sideboard in Nathan's private study, helping himself to a generous tot of Donnelly's whiskey. Nathan thought to warn him against it, but decided that would infuriate his father further.

The marquis tossed it down his throat and quickly poured another one as a harsh cough rattled his lungs. "This is the thanks I am to have," he said hoarsely before tossing back the second tot. "I have only come to help you, Nathan. But if you won't accept it—"

"I fail to see what help you have offered," Nathan said, "other than to cause both Evelyn and me to feel like a pair of wretches."

"Don't think for one moment that I am blind," the marquis said. "I know about you and your ways, and all of London knows of hers. It's a disgrace, what she has put us through, but your carousing is as much a source of discord as her mental weaknesses."

"She is not *weak*," Nathan said angrily. "Stop making her sound like an invalid."

"You'll have a rather hard time convincing anyone in this shire that she's not," his father shot back. "But I fear *your* weakness is far more harmful than hers."

"*My* weakness?"

His father scoffed at him, then pointed at the window. "Have you asked yourself how that fire in the orangery was started, or are you so immersed in your wife's homecoming that you have failed to consider it?"

"Of course I have considered it! Yet I cannot believe someone would willfully set fire to the orangery— particularly with Evelyn inside—to harm me."

"I would think again, were I you."

"Why?" Nathan asked, looking at his father curiously.

"*Why?* You have a notorious reputation, son. You rack up gambling debts as if they are scraps of paper instead of banknotes! You and your friends have kept the company of rude women—there is no end to who might want to see you harmed."

Nathan knew he'd had his share of encounters with men who were unsavory. He'd had his debts, yes, but he'd *paid* his debts and could not understand why any of his so-called enemies would set fire to the orangery. What would be gained from it?

"Your expression suggests that you see the validity of my concern," the marquis scoffed.

"Your opinion of me is alarming, sir," Nathan said wryly.

"Were I you, I'd have the sheriff look into it," his father continued, ignoring Nathan's remark. "And furthermore, I would keep your wife in this house for her own safety. The more she is about, the more people begin to speculate."

"Speculate as to *what*?"

"Your marriage," his father said curtly.

Something in Nathan snapped. There was little wonder Evelyn could not stand to be at Eastchurch. Not only had she suffered the greatest of tragedies here, but the entire world seemed to have an opinion on how she had shouldered the death of her child.

"Thank you," Nathan said curtly. "I am doing my best, Father, to mend my marriage. I appreciate your concern, but I think that only Evelyn and I can know best how to proceed with our life together."

"I cannot impress on you enough how such scandals

appear to those who would tear down the monarchy. And if the monarchy goes, you may be certain that families like ours shall be right behind it."

"How I wish," Nathan said tightly, "that you desired my marriage to be repaired for my sake as opposed to the monarchy. Please excuse me, Father," Nathan said, and walked out of the study before he said something he truly regretted.

When Evelyn appeared for supper wearing a gown the color of autumn leaves and trimmed in dark green, she walked into the blue drawing room as if she were walking into the Inquisition. The emeralds that dangled from her ears and throat twinkled in the light of the candles as she glanced around the room, looking for the Inquisitors.

When she didn't see them, she looked curiously at Nathan.

"The DuPauls have graciously invited our parents again to dine," he said simply.

That clearly confused her. "To dine . . . without us?"

He smiled. "No. The invitation was extended to us as well. But I declined on our behalf."

Her brow furrowed. He nodded. A light dawned in her eyes, and she smiled so brilliantly that he felt the force of it down to his toes. "*Nathan!* You're a scoundrel!" she exclaimed. "A brilliant, wonderful scoundrel!"

"Thank you," he said, and held out a glass of wine to her.

Evelyn didn't hesitate; she glided forward, took the glass from his hand, and put it to her lips. She sipped, then lowered the glass and smiled saucily. "I owe you a debt of gratitude, my lord. I could not possibly have endured another evening." She laughed and held her wineglass out from her body, and pushed air into her cheeks. "*Evelyn, you must buck up,*" she said, mimicking her father. "*Men do not care for weepy women.*"

Nathan chuckled and touched his glass to hers.

"*Nathan, my darling,*" she said, affecting the gravelly voice of his mother, "*surely you know ladies do not care for gentlemen who smoke. The smell weakens their constitution.*" She laughed.

"Very good," he said with a grin.

Evelyn snorted into her wineglass. She took another sip, smiling coyly. "So what have you planned for tonight? Another picnic?"

He shook his head.

"No?" She actually sounded disappointed.

"A quiet supper," Nathan said. "I hope you don't mind—I had quite enough to do to arrange the evening with the DuPauls after my father's abuse of their hospitality."

Evelyn laughed, the sound of it sweet to his ears, and his smile deepened. His wife seemed relaxed, more at home than he'd seen her yet.

A brisk rap on the door and Benton entered. Evelyn moved away from Nathan as Benton busied himself with stoking the fire. She stood directly behind Benton, one hand extended toward the warmth of the fire. Her hair was tied up in bandeaux, the same green as her gown, leaving her neck bare.

Nathan wanted to kiss her neck, just at the base.

"I hope Cook has made venison stew," she said wistfully. "I've never had venison stew quite like she makes it, and I confess, I've missed it terribly."

"Benton, you'd best tell Lady Lindsey that she will dine on venison stew tonight, or surrender your position and repair to the stables to pitch hay at once," Nathan ordered without taking his gaze from Evelyn.

"I beg your pardon, my lady, but Cook has prepared the quail his lordship specifically requested," Benton said with a bow of his head.

Evelyn giggled.

"To the stables, then, Benton," Nathan ordered.

"As you wish, my lord." Benton went out.

"You're horrible!" Evelyn laughingly exclaimed. "You've always been entirely wretched to the poor man."

"The threat of losing his position keeps him keenly attentive to my needs," Nathan said with a lopsided smile as he moved closer to her. "It makes for a better butler."

Evelyn rolled her eyes. "*You* would lose your position here before Benton, and well he knows it."

"Oh? I could have sworn he trembles at the sound of my voice," Nathan argued playfully, and reached up, catching one of her earrings with his fingers. "May I remark that you look stunning tonight, Lady Lindsey?"

She smiled and tilted her head back. "You may."

He looked into her eyes—fell into them, really. "You *are* stunning tonight. You have grown more beautiful with time."

She laughed lightly and poked him in the chest. "You never thought I was beautiful."

"I did indeed!"

"No," she said, shaking her head. "You once told me I was pleasing . . . but never beautiful."

"Then I am a bigger fool than I thought," he said,

smiling at her lips. "To me, you are the most beautiful woman in all of England."

She laughed a little as he toyed with her earring. "Such flattery! Another attempt to lure me into your bed."

He smiled. "Am I so obvious?"

"No," she said lightly, "but I am a lot wiser."

He touched his finger to her ear lobe. "I have noticed. Perhaps a more direct approach is in order. Will you come to my bed?"

Evelyn went up on her toes, lifting her face just inches below his. With her head tilted back, her eyes half closed, she was incredibly alluring, and Nathan's pulse leapt with hopeful anticipation.

"I am ravenous," she said silkily, easing back down. "Might we have that quail sooner rather than later?" With another impudent smile, she moved away from him and toward the door of the salon.

Dear God. At that moment, he feared he could give the woman whatever her heart desired, her affair, their separation, all of it notwithstanding. Jewels, wealth— honestly, he'd follow her to hell and back if that was what she wanted. Evelyn astounded him. She was as seductive and captivating as any woman could ever hope to be, and he was completely besotted.

She paused gracefully at the door, waiting for him to open it. He could imagine how many times she'd done that in London, how many ways she had intrigued the men who followed her about like rabid dogs. He could not allow himself to think of those things—he had to push them from his mind, for it made him outrageously jealous.

He calmly opened the door and offered her his arm.

She placed her hand on it lightly and allowed him to lead her down the hall.

As they neared the dining room, Evelyn slowed. But Nathan kept walking, leading her past the dining room.

She smiled up at him. "I thought you said there were no surprises this evening."

"I said no picnic," he said with a wink, and watched Evelyn's face light with pleasure when he paused at the door to the sun room. "One of my favorite rooms!" she exclaimed.

Nathan opened the door and ushered her through.

He had to hand it to Benton—he'd outdone himself again. The reflection in the glass windows and ceiling of a dozen beeswax candles made it seem like dozens more. On either end, fires burned in the small hearths of the supporting brick walls. For a cold November night, the room seemed cozy and warm.

In the middle of the room was a small table, set for two. A five-pronged candelabra and vase of floating hot-house flowers graced the middle. Wine had already been poured, which could only mean that Benton was lurking somewhere nearby, ready to serve at a moment's notice.

"Oh my," Evelyn said as she walked in and twirled around, turning her face up to the ceiling. "It's remarkable!" She smiled brilliantly at Nathan. "I don't know what I have done to deserve such extraordinary attention."

"Survived our parents," Nathan said.

She grinned and twirled around again. "It's lovely, Nathan."

"Shall I serve, my lord?"

The sound of Benton's voice startled Nathan and he

sighed irritably. The man had a knack for interrupting at the wrong moments.

"Please, Benton. I am starved," Evelyn said politely.

With Benton off to bring the supper, Nathan helped Evelyn into one of the two chairs at the table, then took a seat across from her. Her eyes shimmered in the light of the candles and Nathan could not help picturing those eyes as she lay beneath him. He shifted uncomfortably; he couldn't say when it happened, but somehow, Evelyn had gone from being his fragile, grief-stricken wife to this self-possessed beauty.

"Do you recall the summer of the kitchen fire when we lived with your parents at Sudley House?"

"Of course. It was the longest summer of my life," Nathan quipped.

"At least you were free to come and go." Evelyn laughed. "I spent most of the summer in the company of your mother and aunt."

"Ah," he said with a grimace.

"It was a very sedate summer with quite a lot of reading and embroidery work," she continued. "I very much liked to ride, but your father would only permit me an old horse, as he was fearful I would fall. I very much liked to walk the grounds, too, but I had to do it early in the morning before your mother was about, for she believes too much walking can be harmful to a lady."

"Mother has many such opinions," Nathan agreed. "When I was a lad, she didn't like for me to run, as she thought it would harm my lungs."

Evelyn smiled. So did Nathan.

"I found the conservatory one morning," she continued. "It was my haven. I went there in the afternoons to read or to paint. Or to sing if I liked, for no one was about. Just the old groundskeeper." She laughed. "He would pause just beyond the walls and peer in as if he were seeing an animal at a zoo."

Nathan's belly did a queer little flip. He scarcely remembered that summer. He was gone for most of it, off to London with Donnelly for a time, and then the two of them up to Edinburgh to fetch Lambourne.

Her reminiscing was interrupted by the arrival of a pair of footmen, who carried in twin platters covered with silver domes, Benton just behind them. They uncovered the platters and placed plates with roasted quail, barley, and asparagus before Evelyn and Nathan.

"Oh, it smells delicious, Benton!" Evelyn exclaimed, clasping her hands before her. "You must give my compliments to Cook."

"I shall indeed, madam." He removed Evelyn's linen from the table, snapped it open with a flourish, and laid it carefully in her lap.

If Benton and his band of merry footmen didn't leave at once, Nathan was going to plant a boot up his arse and help him out the door. When Benton moved for Nathan's linen, he batted his hand away. "All right, all right, you've served," he said. "Be gone with you, all of you. Can't a man dine with his wife without everyone hovering about?"

"Very good, my lord," Benton said, and gestured for the two footmen to quit the room.

As they went out, Nathan sighed and leaned back in his chair.

Evelyn smiled as she took a bite of quail. "It's divine," she said, and gestured with her fork to his plate. "You should try it."

He picked up his fork. She was right—it was delicious.

"I certainly never had quail in the conservatory," she added with a laugh.

"I wonder if you have any good memories of our marriage," Nathan asked bluntly.

Her brows rose as she daintily cut another piece of quail. "Of course I do. Several, in fact."

"Such as?"

"Such as the day of our wedding, for one," she said. "And the birth of our child."

She said it, he noticed, without flinching.

"I remember the county horse races we attended and how much we both enjoyed them. We always seemed happy with one another there."

"We were happy with one another most places," he said.

She shrugged and smiled a little. "Would you like to know when I was happiest?" she asked as she ate another forkful of quail.

"I wonder," he drawled, "if it could possibly be the same moment I was happiest."

"Oh, no, I'm certain it was not," she said instantly.

Her answer disappointed him. He was feeling ridiculously sentimental and wanted to believe they'd been happy. "Tell me," he said, taking a generous bite of the quail himself.

"When I bested you so handily at archery."

His head came up at that; she was smiling, and it made him feel infinitely lighter. "*Bested* me?" he echoed incredulously. "You did not *best* me, Evie!"

Evelyn burst out laughing, the sound of it as light as air. "I most certainly did! How could you have forgotten, Nathan? You are positively horrible with a bow and arrow, and I have a very steady arm."

"Your memory has served only to elevate your prowess." He laughed. "I'd wager you could no more beat me in the game of archery than you could pick me up."

Her eyes narrowed slightly. "Is that a challenge?"

"It most certainly is," he said, and picked up his wineglass. "To the winner go the spoils of their choosing."

"*Ooh*," she said, clinking her glass to his. "That should make it quite interesting, *mmm*?"

He fervently hoped so.

As they continued their meal, Evelyn continued her litany of things she remembered. Sledding down the hill near the lake one very snowy day. Watching the fireworks he'd brought to Eastchurch to commemorate Guy Fawkes Day. The New Year's gathering at the home of Lord Montclair.

In the midst of it, Benton returned and cleared their plates, and placed ice sorbets before them with a dessert wine. As Evelyn was recounting the day they'd been chased by an angry goose along the river's banks—at great length, Nathan noticed, which, coupled with the rosy glow of her cheeks, he suspected was a bit of the wine's doing—Benton went out, closing the door quietly behind him.

Nathan remembered the day as clearly as if it had happened yesterday. He had been teaching her how to fish, and she'd managed to toss her line too close to the goslings. The mother goose began to chase after her; Evelyn panicked and threw down her pole. Screaming, she ran to him, her arms outstretched. But Nathan was laughing so hard he could not help her. Evelyn had flung herself into his arms, and down they'd gone, rolling into a patch of reeds, Nathan's arm the only thing between them and the angry goose.

Just thinking of it made Nathan laugh again.

"Must you laugh at my misfortune still?" Evelyn demanded playfully.

"I beg your pardon, madam," he said with a broad grin. "But I've never seen a sight quite like it."

Evelyn smiled. "Now I've spent the entire evening talking of my memories of Eastchurch. What of yours?"

He gave her a wolfish smile. "My memories are much simpler . . . the moments we shared when there was nothing or no one but you and me, and of course later, the days we had with Robert . . . those are the memories I hold most dear."

"Oh yes, Robbie." She glanced off. She was seeing their son now, Nathan guessed, as was he. But she suddenly looked at him with a mischievous look in her eye. "Is that all?"

"All?" He smiled. "I remember everything you remember—save the outcome of the archery match." He shifted forward, pinning her with a look. "But what I remember *most* vividly is you lying naked in my bed, your skin moist and your lips," he said softly, his gaze dropping to her mouth, "slightly swollen. Do you recall?"

A slow, sultry smile curved Evelyn's lips. "I do," she said sweetly as she fingered the small cluster of emeralds at her throat. "I remember it perhaps as keenly as you."

Hope rose up like a phoenix in him. "Do you, by chance, recall what my hands feel like on your body? Because I cannot seem to think of anything else."

One corner of her mouth tipped up in a smile. "*Another* attempt to seduce me."

"Evie . . . I won't seduce you unless you want to be seduced."

Her smile broadened and she leaned forward, too, so far that he could see into her bodice. "And how will you know if I want to be seduced?"

He could scarcely bear to look at her across the table without wanting to sweep the candles and flowers and sorbet to the floor and take her here. He let his gaze wander over her face, her bosom, her hair. The desire in him was building, pulsing, breathing inside of him. "I think—I *hope*—that you will let me know," he said, hoping desperately that she would do so—*now*.

Evelyn smiled and put her hands against the table. With her eyes on his, she pushed herself up. The linen fell from her lap, but she didn't heed it as she walked around the table. Nathan leaned back in his chair, and Evelyn did something he never thought his proper young wife would do. She picked up her skirts, revealing her shapely legs, and very gracefully straddled his lap.

Nathan was almost too shocked to speak. He gripped the arms of his chair, watching her as she slid her arms around his neck and whispered, *"I want you to seduce me."*

She could not have possibly aroused him any more than that. He put his hands on her ribs, holding her there on his lap. The heat of her body on his made him hard instantly. "Don't toy with me, Evie," he said roughly, his humor gone.

She pushed her hand through his hair.

"No regrets," he said far too anxiously, but his body was raging with the promise of holding the only woman who had ever mattered to him. "If you come to regret it, then you'd best lie to me."

She cupped his face in her hands and tenderly

touched her lips to his. She slid off his lap, straightened out her skirts, and walked to the door. Nathan was powerless to move, he could do nothing but watch her.

When she reached the door, she glanced over her shoulder. "Are you coming?"

chapter twenty-four

Nathan surged to his feet so suddenly that Evelyn unthinkingly stepped back. He strode forward, catching her around the waist. He kissed her, bending her over backward so far that Evelyn was compelled to grab his arms and hold on.

He lifted her up; his blue eyes searched her face as if he were seeing her anew. "Come," he said, grabbing her hand. He kicked the door open, almost hitting Benton on the other side. The butler quickly moved out of the way as Nathan strode past, pulling Evelyn with him. "That will be all, Benton!" he called out as he and Evelyn hurried past.

At the end of the corridor, he started up the servant stairs, but Evelyn pulled back.

"What, what, what is it," he asked a bit frantically, his eyes roaming over her face, her neck and bosom.

"Not this way," she said. "The main staircase."

Nathan scarcely looked at the servants' stairs, then at

her. "It's a shortcut, darling. Past the nursery and directly to your rooms—"

"No!" she cried, stepping back, pulling his arm with both hands. "The main staircase."

Thankfully, he did not argue, but put his arm around her waist and drew her into his side, and hurried her along as if every moment counted against them.

When they reached the door to her suite, Nathan ushered her in first, then closed the door behind him, locking it.

When he turned, Evelyn was standing in the middle of the room, breathless from their eagerness to get here. A million things ran through her mind—such as why she'd suddenly changed her mind. Why now? Why today? Had it been the good memories? The kindness and hope in his eyes? Or simply that he was a handsome, virile man, and she could not seem to look away from the breadth of his shoulders or the size of his hands, or his mouth, *his mouth* . . .

That handsome, virile man was moving toward her now, his head down, the look in his eyes so full of desire for her that it stirred her deeply. He caught her hand in his, tangling his fingers with hers as he slowly drew her to him. Evelyn walked into the circle of his arms. He touched his lips to her hair, then trailed his mouth down, glancing over her temple, her cheek, and pushing her hair aside to kiss her neck.

The touch of his lips glinted through her, seeping into her blood, spreading into every vein, soaking into every muscle. He tasted her lips, and his kiss felt different than before, raw and deep, the sort of kiss that went beyond mere pleasure.

She drew a shallow breath and gripped his shoulder, holding herself up to the deliberate caress of her body.

Nathan splayed one hand across her cheek, his fingers soft and warm, and Evelyn began to gulp for breath. Something had shifted in her heart; she suddenly wanted him as she'd never wanted another man. She'd never yearned to feel him thick and deep inside her as she did now.

"Evelyn," he said, his voice rough and dark. "This is where you belong, with me. Always." He abruptly cupped her face and turned it up toward him. "I love you. God knows I do. Words seem too small to describe it, but know this—you belong with me. Nowhere else."

How odd that a few simple words could turn her thoughts and her life upside down. She felt as if she'd been waiting for him to say those precise words for ten years. The restlessness that had plagued her for so long seemed to leave her body. She felt beautiful. She felt at peace.

Her eyes locked on his, she stepped back and reached across her body, to the buttons that ran up the side of her gown, and began to undo them.

His gaze followed her hands, and he drew a long, slow breath into his lungs as she unbuttoned her gown. She slipped her arms out of the cap sleeves, held the gown to her bosom a moment, then let it slide down her body.

Nathan drew another breath through clenched teeth and shook his head. "I don't understand how you have changed, Evie," he muttered. "But you have enchanted me in a way I did not believe was possible."

Her heart leapt. She pushed her chemise off one shoulder.

Nathan's gaze heated; he licked his bottom lip as she pushed the garment from the other shoulder and let it slide from her body. She stood before her husband brazenly and completely bare, fired by his admission of love and his obvious, glaring desire for her.

He lifted his hand, filling his palm with one breast. His breath hissed. "You are more beautiful than I dared recall," he said, his eyes darkening. He ran his hand down the side of her body, and without warning, he swept her up into his arms. His eyes on hers, he carried her to the bed and lay her there. He quickly shed his coat and waistcoat, his neckcloth and shirt as his gaze devoured her.

She had forgotten his beauty, too. His shoulders were thick, his arms muscular. His chest broad and strong, his abdomen flat and hard.

Nathan came over her and caught her head between his hands. He looked at her for a long moment before his lips touched her mouth. The moment he did, she felt the heat of his blood surge through her veins.

He rolled her over, putting her on her stomach, and began to kiss a line down her back, to her hips, nibbling at her flesh there before rising up again to her shoulders.

His kiss was enough to push Evelyn toward the edge of fulfillment—she'd been stranded in a woman's wasteland for years now, longing deeply for a man's touch. And after last night, her husband's ardor—powerful and potent—was swelling around them, opening up deep, sensual wells inside her that filled with every touch of his lips.

With a groan of desire, Nathan rolled her over again, his hands spanning the breadth of her body. Evelyn stroked his face. "You give me hope."

He stilled and looked down at her. "Hope? You can't know the meaning of hope, Evie." He kissed her madly, his lips leaving an indelible sensation that sank into her marrow. He feverishly caressed her body: her neck and the curve of her shoulder, and the swell of her breasts and the flat of her belly, the dip of her waist, the span of her hip.

He moved down her body, caressing, licking and biting, tasting her, taking her scent and her taste inside him.

She closed her eyes and caressed his body, feeling the corded muscles in his arms and his back, the firmness of his hips and thighs. She fumbled with his trousers and pushed them as far down his hips as she could manage. She was aware of nothing but him and the intense passion building in her, and the strong sensation of knowing that this was where she belonged, this was where she was anchored. *This was right.*

She was not the only one experiencing such remarkable feelings. Nathan was driven to an unthinkable passion. Yet his desire was more than the monstrous sexual urge he was feeling, much more primal than that. It was possession, a comprehension that she belonged to him, that she was his alone to protect and cherish and devote himself to.

He would push the earth from the sky for her. In this moment, with the feel and scent of her skin driving him mad, the dampness between her legs beckoning him, he could not imagine ever being without her. Their problems seemed to melt away from them—with every stroke of his hands and his tongue against her warm skin, he was sent a little closer to the edge of his control. Every place she touched him inflamed him. Every press of her lips engorged him. He was ravenous—the need to be inside her and bring her back to where she belonged had created a force of love in him he'd felt only a handful of times before.

That force gripped him by the throat. As his hands and mouth covered her body, she caught his head and claimed his mouth with hers, filling his body with her breath.

"I've needed you, Nathan," she said. "I hadn't realized how much I've needed you."

He hungrily returned her kiss; she pressed against his aching erection as he dragged his mouth to the flesh of her breasts and their swollen tips. As he took them into his mouth, teasing them with his teeth and his tongue, she pushed her hands through his hair and arched into him, gasping with delight.

When he slipped a hand between her legs, he found her hot and slick and moved down her body, between her legs to dip his tongue between the folds of her sex. Above him, Evelyn cried out. She clutched desperately at his head and his hands, but Nathan gripped her thighs, keeping her open to him. She began to pant and move against him, pressing herself against his mouth, then falling away, as if the pleasure was too great.

Nathan lifted his head and climbed over her. She opened her hazel eyes, full of desire and satisfaction, and he was lost. He shoved out of his shoes and trousers, then carefully pressed his flesh against hers. Holding her gaze, he laced his fingers with hers. "You are beautiful," he said, his voice hoarse with raw emotion. "Too beautiful. I am hopelessly enchanted."

Her hand closed around his hard cock.

He sucked in a sharp breath and summoned what little control he possessed. He kissed her again, greedily and hard as he slid into her, into that wet, hot place that was his. Evelyn gasped and began to move against him, angling her legs and drawing him in deeper still, moaning with pleasure as her body opened to him.

Nathan moved fluidly, withdrawing to the tip, then sliding in deep again, watching her eyelids flutter with each stroke. Evelyn's hands were on his body, flitting everywhere: over his ears, his shoulders, down his chest, tweaking his nipples. But as he began to stroke her faster and harder, she arched her neck and swallowed hard, panting for air. Her body moved in perfect time with his, rising up to meet each thrust, sinking again as he withdrew.

Nathan's release raged in his veins, feeling impossible to control. Evelyn suddenly arched her back and opened her eyes, crying out as she reached her peak.

The rage inside Nathan exploded then. He roared with his orgasm, throwing his head back and crashing into the pool of longing they had created as he spilled hot and long inside her.

He collapsed to her side as the waves of desire began to slow and recede.

He tenderly kissed the space between her shoulder and collarbone. Evelyn's fingers curled around his wrist; her eyes were closed, her breath still coming in short little bursts. Her skin was moist and warm as he traced a line from the hollow of her throat to her navel.

She sighed like a satisfied woman and rolled into him, burying her face in the curve of his shoulder.

Nathan propped a pillow behind his head and

caressed her arm as he looked into the fire. He'd never felt so sure of anything in his life. This was right between them. This was where Evelyn belonged—there was no question in his mind.

He did not ruin that extraordinary moment by asking if there was a question in hers.

chapter twenty-five

When Evelyn awoke the following morning, she was in the middle of the bed and tangled in the bedclothes. Nathan was nowhere to be seen, but on his pillow he'd left a flower he'd taken from a vase at her wash basin. She smiled and picked it up, touching it to her nose.

The door opened; she looked up with a smile, hoping it was Nathan.

It was only Kathleen with a cup of hot chocolate, and the condition of the room stopped her abruptly. "My goodness!" she exclaimed, her eyes falling on Evelyn's clothing on the floor. "Oh my!" She blushed. "*Well*," she said pertly, and marched on to Evelyn's vanity.

"I want the green silk today, Kathleen," Evelyn said as she stretched her arms high above her head.

"Oh, that's lovely, mu'um, and a good day for it, too. The sky is sunny and the air warmer than one might expect this time of year. The marchioness and the baroness had a walkabout in the east rose garden."

They could have walked all the way to India for all Evelyn cared. "Have you seen his lordship this morning?"

"Aye, indeed I have. He and his father have gone into the village, but said they'd return by luncheon." She turned her back to Evelyn to pick up discarded clothing. "He was quite jovial, actually. *Quite*."

Evelyn grinned. She could scarcely wait to see him— she felt as giddily happy as a girl. She'd been married to the man for ten years, but it felt as if she'd only just become his wife.

When Evelyn descended the stairs at the lunch hour dressed in her best day gown, Benton was waiting to meet her. "The marchioness and baroness should like an audience in the morning room," he said.

Even the prospect of another interview with her mother and mother-in-law could not dampen her spirits.

The two women had the doors open onto the terrace. The air was still, the sunlight bright. Her mother stood and the marchioness put down the embroidery she'd been working when Evelyn entered.

"Good morning, Mamma," Evelyn said brightly, kissing her mother's cheek. "Lady Sudley, how do you fare today?"

The marchioness peered closely at her. "Very well, Evelyn. And you?"

"Oh, I am well. *Very* well," Evelyn said with a beaming smile.

"Darling, Annette and I have been talking," her mother began. "We think that perhaps you are missing a proper activity to occupy your time. A proper activity will help you keep your thoughts from wandering too far afield."

"We can't have that, can we, thoughts wandering so far afield that they could not be called home again, eh?" Evelyn asked laughingly, and picked up a vase of flowers to admire them. "The hothouse flowers are extraordinary this time of year, are they not?"

Her mother looked at the flowers, then at her daughter. "Yes. Evelyn—"

"It's a lovely day for a walk, isn't it?" Evelyn interjected. "We so rarely have weather as fine as this in late autumn."

"Are you even listening, Evelyn?"

Evelyn never had a chance to respond, for at that moment, the door swung open and Nathan strode in, a smile on his face.

Her husband looked more robust than Evelyn had ever seen him—he was tall and strong and his blue eyes were clear and shining with delight. "Good morning, ladies," he said with a very gallant bow, then unabashedly swept Evelyn up with one arm and kissed her mouth.

"Nathan!" his mother chided him.

He let go of Evelyn with a wink and turned to his mother. "Mother, I hope you enjoy your luncheon," he said, stooping to kiss her cheek. "After luncheon, I've something planned for us all: a game," he said with a grin.

"A game," the marchioness repeated, her distaste evident. "What sort of game?"

"Archery," Nathan said, and glanced at Evelyn. "My wife believes she can best me with a bow and arrow."

"Evelyn, you shouldn't boast," her mother chided her.

"I didn't boast, Mamma," Evelyn said sweetly. "I merely stated a fact, and Nathan took umbrage at it."

"And we're to play this game out of doors?" the marchioness demanded of her son.

"You forbade me from using bows and arrows indoors many years ago, Mother. Therefore, we will be on the west lawn."

"I didn't even know that Evelyn engaged in archery," the baroness sniffed.

"Oh, Mamma! You are unaware of many activities in which I engage," Evelyn said with a wink. Nathan laughed. The baroness, however, glowered at her.

But nothing could dampen Evelyn's spirit. Something had changed in her over the last two days, something not unlike the turning of a ship in the ocean. The turning had been hardly noticeable at all, but once the ship was facing a new direction, it was full bore ahead.

Evelyn was that ship. She'd righted herself, changed her course, and now it was open seas before her, a whole new horizon.

She could scarcely wait to see what she might discover on this new course.

That afternoon, while their mothers complained that it was too cold, and their fathers called out advice, Evelyn and Nathan engaged in a game of archery. Evelyn won by two points, although there was quite a row between the marquis and the baron as to whether one of her shots, which landed on the line between the gold and the red circles, should be counted at the higher points value.

In the end, it didn't matter—she won with the lower

value, although she suspected that when Nathan's last shot went horribly astray and landed beyond the target, he'd done it to give her the advantage.

Later, after supper, Nathan insisted they all engage in a game of charades. Their parents looked horrified, to a person. Evelyn's father tried to beg off, citing fatigue, but Nathan insisted. They played well into the early morning hours until Nathan's mother begged to be let out of the game.

Their parents retired, their fatigue evident. Nathan saw his parents up to their rooms, and Evelyn escorted hers.

"It's good to see you come round to reason," her father said, hugging her tightly to him. "We've worried about you so."

She smiled at her father. "On the morrow, Nathan and I thought it would be diverting if we all took a long walk through the forest."

Upon hearing that news, her father looked anxiously at her mother. Her mother said, "Let us not be too hasty, dear. The weather may turn."

"Oh, I think it will be lovely on the morrow, Mamma. Shall we say half past seven? We want to get an early start."

"Ah. Well. Perhaps. Good night, dear," her mother said, and closed the door.

Evelyn smiled devilishly at the closed door before moving on to her suite.

Thinking of Nathan, she dreamily dressed for bed, then crawled beneath the coverlet. She lay on her side, looking at the starry night through the window. She'd just begun to drift to sleep when she heard the door open.

It was Nathan. He was wearing a dressing gown and his feet were bare. He climbed into bed with her and kissed her shoulder. "I don't mean to disturb you, but I have the most fortuitous news," he murmured.

"Oh?" she asked, shifting around to face him.

"When I suggested that we all go boating on the morrow, Father informed me they will be taking their leave."

Evelyn gasped with delight. "Oh no! I told my parents we would trek through the forest!"

Nathan laughed with her. "I suspect the Brantleys will join the Greys in an early departure."

"Are you certain? All of them?"

"*All* of them. It would seem we have put their fears to rest." He lightly bit her shoulder. "Father advises we are to continue working to patch things up."

"Ah." She touched his face, her fingers trailing over his mouth. "Did he also advise how we are to do that?"

"Oh, indeed he did," Nathan said. "But I've a better idea," he added with a wolfish grin, and slipped his hand inside her gown, cupping her breast.

They made love, slow and easy, taking time to enjoy one another, finding fulfillment together. When Evelyn was at last lulled to sleep by the soothing sound of Nathan's steady breathing, she felt as secure as she could remember ever feeling in his arms.

Shortly after luncheon the next day, Evelyn and Nathan stood on the drive, holding hands and waving at the departing coach as their parents drove away from Eastchurch Abbey, leaving their children to fend for themselves.

When the coach had turned a bend, Evelyn looked at Nathan sidelong; he smiled down at her. "It's only you and me now, Evie," he said.

"Thank you, Lord!"

He grinned. "Are you certain you can go it alone with me?"

She smiled. "Are *you*?"

"Oh," he said, as he lifted her hand to his mouth and kissed her knuckles, "I am quite certain. Come. I want to show you something. Would you like to ride?"

"You would ask me that after last night?" she asked with a saucy smile.

"And might I add that the lesson was one of indescribable joy. Come, then," he said, taking her hand. "Benton!" he called over his shoulder. "Where the devil are you, Benton? Lady Lindsey needs her cloak!"

The place to which Nathan took Evelyn was the old abbey ruins. They tethered the horses, picked their way through the rubble, and climbed ancient stone steps up to the top of the lone remaining tower. Part of the retaining wall had given away up top, and one could see all of Eastchurch—the abbey grounds, the village, and the earl's estate.

It was a beautiful view, one that Evelyn had forgotten. She thought of the years she'd spent in London. The town's luster was dull in comparison to the raw nature of the countryside. Here, the colors of the sky were brighter, the greens and browns of the earth more vibrant. Evelyn realized that Robbie's death had dulled the world around her. For so long, everything had seemed the same shade of gray.

"Look there," Nathan said, pointing. "You can see where they run the horses in the summer."

"Oh, do they still?" she asked excitedly. "I always enjoyed the racing!"

"Then you shall have your racing," he said, kissing her neck. "We shall have My Lady's cup this summer, and to the winner will go whatever prize you choose."

They wandered around the abbey a while longer, recalling her birthday spent playing at medieval court, and the ancient Christian relics the local chap who dabbled in antiquities had discovered one cool autumn morning. Those relics were now displayed at a museum in London.

But when the sky began to cloud, Nathan suggested they return to the main house. "It looks like rain," he said, squinting up at the sky.

He helped Evelyn onto her horse, then mounted his. He turned back to speak to her, Evelyn presumed, but the only thing she remembered before hearing the shot fired was the warm smile on his face.

Everything after that was a blur.

chapter twenty-six

Nathan felt the sting of the bullet in his arm at the same moment he heard the report of a musket, so loud that it startled Evelyn's young mount. The horse reared and bolted.

Evelyn shrieked, but she managed to hold on. Nathan quickly started after her; he could see her frantically trying to rein her mount, but the horse was too excited to heed her, and raced for the forest.

She would lose her seat when a limb snared her, or God forbid, an entire tree, if the skittish mare went crashing into the trees. Nathan spurred Cedric hard, forcing the steed to run faster. Fortunately, he'd invested in some of the finest horseflesh money could buy and Cedric easily caught up to the younger horse.

Nathan reined him close to the mare at the same time he grabbed for the mare's bridle. His fingers wrapped around it and he flung himself off Cedric's back, pulling back with all his might on the mare's bridle, bracing with his feet, and by some miracle, forcing the horse to turn her head. She neighed, bared her teeth, and bucked once, then twice, but Nathan held on, and more important, so did Evelyn.

In a few moments the mare had calmed, yanking only halfheartedly at Nathan's hold on her bridle.

He let go and caught the reins Evelyn held in a death grip and eased them, letting the mare relax. "Are you all right?" he asked quickly, putting his hand to her leg. "Are you hurt?"

"Nathan, you're bleeding!" she cried.

He looked down, saw the blood oozing from his arm. He hardly felt it and believed the bullet had only grazed his arm. "I'm all right, I'm fine," he said. "Now listen to me," he said, taking her hands in his, "you must ride to the house. Tell Benton to send some men up to the ruins at once."

"What?" she cried, panicking. "No! No, no, *no*, Nathan, you must come with me—"

"Whoever has done this is running now," he said, reaching for Cedric's reins. "I can still catch him. Go home, Evelyn! Ride as quick as you can!" He threw himself up onto Cedric's back. *"Go!"* he ordered her again, and dug his spurs into the horse's sides.

The bastard who shot at him had had a few minutes' head start, but Nathan knew a deer path through the forest that might gain him ground. He gave Cedric his head, sent him crashing into the tree line. He rode low over his mount's neck, one arm raised slightly to protect his head from low-hanging limbs.

Cedric leapt over brush and small streams without fear, dodging and running recklessly through the woods. When at last they did emerge on the path along the river, Nathan caught sight of the gunman as his horse rode over a crest, just ahead of him. He slowed and turned, pointed the musket at Nathan, and fired wildly.

He missed.

Nathan kicked Cedric hard and sent him flying down the path. As he suspected, the man's horse was no match for Cedric, and when Nathan caught up to him, he sent Cedric alongside the other horse on that narrow path, causing the smaller horse to draw up for fear of being run into the river. It was enough that Nathan was able to launch himself at the bastard, catching his leg and pulling him off his saddle.

The two men fell to the ground behind the horses, rolling partially down the embankment. The bastard struck first, catching Nathan in the jaw. But he'd underestimated Nathan's rage—he grabbed the cretin by the lapels and slammed his head into the earth. The man cried out.

"Who are you?" Nathan roared. When the man did not immediately answer, Nathan slammed his head against the ground again.

Still, the man would not respond. He squeezed his eyes shut and locked his jaw, and tried to buck Nathan off of him. Nathan straddled him and sat up, holding him tightly with his legs and his hands. "By God, if you want to escape with your life this day, you will bloody well tell me who you are!"

The man's response was to try to reach for his waist. Nathan struck him hard across the jaw. He went slack, his head lolling to one side. "Take a shot at me, will you?" he breathed angrily as he unwound his neckcloth. "You're lucky I don't skin you here and now," he said. He stood up, kicked the man over onto his belly, then knelt down, put a knee to his back, and proceeded to bind his hands with his neckcloth. "As it is, I will settle for see-ing you hanged."

He'd managed to get the man up and prop him against a tree when help arrived in the form of three groundsmen. They were quick off their mounts, each of them noticing the blood on Nathan's arm—an arm that was beginning to ache like the devil, Nathan vaguely no-ticed. They stood at Nathan's back, glaring down at the culprit. He was a small man, at least a decade older than Nathan. He looked as if he'd lived a hard life, judging by the lines around his mouth and between his brows.

"Who are you?" Nathan asked.

The man bowed his head.

"Very well then. Pick him up, lads, and deposit him in the river," Nathan said casually as he inspected his bruised knuckles.

His men instantly moved to do just that.

The bastard's head jerked up and he gaped at Nathan wide-eyed. "What? *No, milord!*" he cried frantically as they hauled him to his feet.

"All right," Nathan said, looking up. "Then tell me your bloody name."

The man glanced nervously at those who held him. "John."

"How helpful. *John who?*"

John pressed his lips together and shook his head.

Nathan took a step closer. "What quarrel have you with me?"

"No quarrel, milord. But the man offered me fifty pounds—"

"*What* man?" Nathan demanded.

John clenched his jaw.

Nathan sighed. "Into the drink with him, then,"

he said with a shrug, and watched insouciantly as his groundsmen dragged the bellowing man to the river's edge. They held him up, his feet dangling over the rushing water.

"For the love of God, don't do it, sir!" John cried.

"You'd have me save your bloody neck when you just tried to put a bullet through mine, is that it?"

"Please, milord, please!" he begged. "Don't kill me!"

Nathan walked down to the river's edge and looked the man square in the eye. "If you think I won't put you in that river and watch you drown, you are a fool. If you want me to spare your life, you will tell me who sent you."

"Rhys!" the man cried. "Rhys Sinclair, that's the name he give me."

Nathan nodded at his two footmen, who eased back from the edge, putting John's feet on muddy terra firma. He sagged with relief.

"From Eastchurch?" Nathan asked him, trying desperately to think who he could be.

"London, milord."

"*London?* A lord's man?"

John seemed confused by that, but shook his head.

"If you won't tell me more than that, then to hell with you, man," Nathan said with a flick of his wrist, and turned away.

"I don't know more than that, milord, I swear I don't! I was in London looking for a bit of work and he give me fifty pounds!"

Nathan slowly turned, peering closely at him, trying to detect any sign that he was lying. If John truly had been hired in London, then Nathan could rest assured it was a man of import who wanted Nathan's hide. "And what did this man Sinclair tell you to do, precisely, for fifty pounds? Kill me?"

The color bled from John's face; he shook his head rather violently. "I won't say," he said tightly.

"Bloody stupid of you," Nathan said, and nodded at the groundsmen to lift him up again. But as they held him over the rushing water, John leaned his head back and looked up to the sky, apparently resigned to drown.

Nathan let him hang there a moment, and with a sigh, gestured for the groundsmen to set him down again. The man's knees gave way and he fell to the ground, landing face-first.

"Take him to the stables and hold him there until the sheriff arrives," Nathan said. "Do not let him out of your sight."

"Aye, milord," the tallest of the three said. "Have a care for your arm, milord. The doctor should have a look at it."

Nathan glanced down again, noticing that the sleeve of his coat was drenched in blood. The bullet must have taken quite a lot of his hide. He nodded and gestured for them to go on. He watched them drag John up the embankment, then put him on a horse. One of his men swung up behind him. Another picked up what appeared to be a rather old musket, and they rode on.

Nathan followed them, accompanied by the third and youngest groundsman. When he reached the house, people from the village had already begun to arrive, having heard of the attack on the earl's life when a stable hand rode to the village in search of the doctor and the sheriff.

Nathan called out to them all that he was all right, and sent Cedric off with a lad who stared with wide-eyed terror at his blood-soaked coat.

"Did you find him, my lord?" one of the men from the village called out to him.

"That I did!" he said. "He's in the stables, where he'll keep until the sheriff arrives."

"He's on his way!" another man called out to him.

Nathan nodded and turned toward the house. The door opened as he walked up the steps, but Nathan waved off Benton as he entered. "It looks rather bad, but it is only a superficial wound."

"The doctor is away from the village, my lord," Benton said, frowning a little at his arm.

"Nathan!" Evelyn hurried down the staircase and threw her arms around his neck. For a moment. She quickly reared back and looked at his arm. "Oh no. Oh dear God."

"It is nothing," he assured her. "It seems much worse than it is."

She frowned and exchanged a look with Benton. "Did you find him? Who was it?" she asked as she began to tug him into a corridor. "Did you know him? Why would he try to shoot you?"

"Never saw the bastard before in my life," Nathan said.

"Nathan, you are bleeding badly. We have to clean it—we cannot wait for a doctor. Benton, we need hot water and some bandages!" she said over her shoulder as she pulled Nathan along. "And . . . and . . ." She looked at Nathan's arm. "Lord, but I've never dressed a gunshot wound."

"A bit of whiskey on the wound ought to do the trick," Nathan said.

Surprised, Evelyn blinked up at him.

"I've not dressed a *lot* of gunshot wounds, if that is what you think," he groused.

She pulled him again, dragging him along until they reached a sitting room near the servants' stairwell. She sat him in a chair and helped him remove his coat. The sleeve of his shirt was soaked completely with blood, and Evelyn, finding a letter opener, ripped the cuff. Using both hands, she tore the sleeve up to the shoulder.

"Very well done," Nathan said with a grimace. He'd never had a bullet graze him before and was surprised at how bloody painful it was. "If I didn't know better, I'd suspect you were a nurse."

"Hush," she said, frowning at his arm. "It looks as if the bullet went through."

"No," Nathan said with a disbelieving snort. "It just grazed me, Evie."

She shook her head. "There is a hole."

Nathan looked down, saw dark red blood oozing from a hole in his arm, and suddenly everything in the room began to swim. "Oh hell," he said, leaning his head back against the chair and closing his eyes. "Oh *hell*."

"There now," Evelyn said soothingly, and caressed his brow the way she used to caress Robert's brow when he was ill. Nathan had no choice but to let her, for seeing his blood pumping so starkly from his body had compounded the situation by making him quite ill.

He heard the door open, heard Benton's familiar footfall across the room.

"You will have to help me, Benton," Evelyn said. "I think the bullet is lodged in his flesh." She touched the backside of his arm, but her finger felt like fire, and Nathan jerked at the excruciating pain.

"I gathered as much," Benton said, his manner as unflappable as always. "I took the liberty of bringing a few things. Tell me what you would have me do, madam."

Nathan opened one eye and saw the silver tray that held a knife and a small pair of forceps that he believed was used in the kitchen. "No," he said, instantly shaking his head. He glared at his butler. "I'd advise against it, Benton!" he said loudly. "If you value your employment—no, your *life*—you will not touch me."

"The bullet is protruding from the wound. If you hold his arm, I think I can pull it out," Evelyn said. "And then Nathan thinks we should pour whiskey on it."

"I didn't mean to pour whiskey into a bullet hole!" Nathan exclaimed.

"We've some just here," Benton said, holding up a decanter with the amber liquid.

"Yes, that should do." Evelyn studied his arm. "All right then, Benton, if you will take him in hand?"

Benton walked behind Nathan and locked his arms around his chest with surprising strength.

"*No—*" Nathan started, but Evelyn had already caught the tip of the bullet in the forceps. She gave it a yank, pulling it free of his flesh with what felt like a torch. Nathan hissed at the pain, felt the decanter pressed to his lips, and opened his mouth. Benton poured whiskey into his mouth as Evelyn pressed a cloth of hot water to the wound in his arm.

Nathan pushed the decanter from his mouth. "By God, that's it," he said hoarsely as she worked to clean the wound. He clutched the armchair against the pain. "You should remove that undertaker suit of clothing you wear and pass it on, Benton, for you are no longer the butler here! You may stay on as a chambermaid if you like, but you'll not be opening my doors any longer!"

"Very good, sir," Benton said, and held his arm tighter as Evelyn continued to clean it.

"This might sting a bit," she said, and poured whiskey on the wound.

Nathan came out of his chair.

"There," she said, after his arm had gone quite numb. "I should think that will serve until a doctor arrives, don't you, Benton?"

"Indeed. Shall I wrap it?" he asked, as if he were asking if he might arrange flowers for her or something equally sedate.

"Please."

She sat back on her heels and looked at Nathan as she dipped her hands into the basin Benton had brought. "Dr. Bell will examine it as soon as he arrives. In the meantime, what should we do?" she asked simply.

"About Benton?" he asked crossly. "Hang him."

"The man who shot you," she said patiently as she dried her hands. "Who is he? Who would do this? Who would want to shoot you?"

"According to my father, any number of people," Nathan said gruffly. "This man would give me no more than the name of the man who'd hired him. A Londoner. Rhys Sinclair is his name—do you know him?" he asked as Benton began to wrap his wound.

"Rhys Sinclair," she repeated, and shook her head. "I've never heard of him. Have you?"

"No," he said. "But I intend to go to London and find him."

"I'll go with you—"

"No," he said, and sat up, caught her chin in his hand. "You will stay here, Evelyn. There is still the . . . the scandal," he bit out. Funny how he'd managed to allow himself to forget that. He'd been too caught up in the promise of having his life back to allow it to cloud things. Funny how quickly the mention of London brought it back to loom over them. Frankly, it made Nathan feel a little sick.

Maybe Evelyn was right. Maybe they couldn't escape reality after all.

"I don't know what I will find," he said shortly, and tried to smile. "I would rest easier knowing you were here, safe with the chambermaid," he said, indicating Benton. "I don't intend to be gone more than a few days. A week at most."

"No, Nathan," she said sternly. "Since I've come back to Eastchurch, we've been attacked by highwaymen, the orangery has burned, someone tried to shoot you—"

"Strange coincidence," he said abruptly. "This *shooting* is a coward's attempt to make a point with me, nothing more. You are safe here, Evelyn. You mustn't worry."

"I don't want to stay here!" she insisted.

"Evelyn," he said calmly as Benton finished bandaging his arm. "You must. I'll send for your sister if you like, but you must remain here."

Her hazel eyes filled with helplessness. "But . . . what of your arm?"

"There are doctors in London." He leaned forward to kiss her. "There is no time to waste, Evie," he said, and stood, holding out his hand to help her to her feet. "Come help me gather a few things in a bag," he said, and put his good arm around her, forcing her to come along, trying very hard not to think of all he might discover in London.

chapter twenty-seven

Nathan had left before dawn the following morning in a cold rain and with an aching arm. The sheriff and his men had come last night and had interrogated the man who'd tried to kill Nathan—but he'd revealed nothing more than what he'd already told Nathan.

The sudden turn of events left Evelyn no choice but to face her last few demons.

She thought she'd been well on her way to doing it, but with Nathan gone, the house seemed big and empty and full of ghosts. Evelyn could almost hear the ghosts of her past echoing in the halls.

Benton sent a messenger to Evelyn's sister, and Evelyn tried to occupy her thoughts and hands as she waited for a response by continuing to work on the public rooms. The next day, however, Clarissa sent word back through a note:

My dearest Evelyn . . . I had hoped to find another way to tell you my good fortune rather than in this letter. We have come home from Bath on the advice of a physician. I

*cannot come to you, even though I am only eight hours by
coach, as I am with child. You will understand that travel
is not advised . . .*

The news stunned Evelyn. She sank onto her chaise
and read the sentence over again. A *baby*. She was happy
for her sister, she was, but . . . but how would it feel to
hold her niece or nephew in her arms?

How would it feel to bear another child?

Her belly clenched at the mere thought, and she
closed her eyes. It was certainly a possibility now that
she had resumed her marriage, but she'd ignored the little voice in her head telling her to take precautions. It
had been so difficult to conceive Robert; it had taken
years. The times she'd been with Nathan in the last few
days, she'd been so caught up in the moment and the
wonder and the intense desire, that she'd allowed herself to tuck her fear away.

Now, without him here, she could scarcely bear to
think of it. She could not bring another sick child into
this world. She could not lose another child, or she
would lose herself, and this time, forever. She was certain of it.

What had she begun?

She worked in the green salon in the first days of Nathan's absence. On the morning that someone from the
village was due to help her determine the sort of drapery the room required, a footman met her at the salon
and announced Mr. Williams. "He's come with the orange trees."

"Pardon?" she asked, confused.

"Orange trees, mu'um."

In the foyer, Evelyn extended her hand to the man,
which he took nervously, bobbing over it. "Lady Lindsey,

it is a true pleasure to see you again," he said, balling up his hat. "I had heard you'd returned to the abbey."

"Yes," Evelyn said, peering at him curiously.

"I had a bit of good news for his lordship," he said brightly. "I rather suspect he believed it would be a month or two before the orange trees arrived, but as luck would have it, I've just returned from Devonshire, where I found some in a hothouse, the exact variety he'd requested."

"Orange trees?"

Mr. Williams nodded. "Two dozen of them."

Evelyn frowned.

"He said something about the orangery?" Mr. Williams said.

Evelyn gasped with surprise. "When did he do so?"

Mr. Williams blinked. "It has been a week or so. Is . . . is there an issue?"

"Oh no," she said quickly. "I, ah . . ." *He'd ordered the trees for the orangery. He'd meant to restore it for her.* Her heart was swelling; she couldn't think for a moment. "Well!" she said brightly. "I suppose we should do something with them."

"I could put them in the orangery, if you'd like."

"Yes, well, that poses a bit of a problem, Mr. Williams. Unfortunately, the orangery has burned."

"Burned!"

"To the ground," she said with a firm nod. "But we shall rebuild it! Until then, we must find a place for the trees."

"The morning room, mu'um?" the footman suggested.

Evelyn shook her head. The pots were heavy and the floors in the morning room were made of cherry. She did not want them marked. Besides, furniture filled most of that room.

"Is there a room below stairs we might use until Mr. Gibbs might find a place for them?"

The footman thought about it a moment, then nodded. "There is a room at the end of the corridor with the stores, mu'um. It's been empty for some time."

She smiled at Mr. Williams. "If you'd be so kind as to wait in the salon," she said, gesturing in that direction, "I'll have a look to ensure it is suitable for a time." To the footman, she said, "Please send Benton to me once you've seen Mr. Williams to the salon."

He nodded and gestured for Mr. Williams to come with him. Mr. Williams followed slowly, his head craning to take in the grandeur of her home.

Evelyn slipped down the servants' stairs to the ground floor and made her way to the stores. It had been many years since she'd been down in this dark, musty corridor. She walked to the end. There were two doors on either side. She opened the first and found crates—of what, she couldn't guess.

She shut that door and opened the one across from it. It was empty.

The room was illuminated by the bright sunlight streaming through a small, single window. She stepped inside and looked at the floor. The room would do for now, she thought, and turned to go, but something on the wall caught her eye.

It was a stone wall, but it looked as if it had been gouged and scored. It was stained, too, and as Evelyn moved closer she gasped—the stains looked like blood.

The sound of someone behind her scared her out of her wits; with a cry of alarm, she whirled around.

"I beg your pardon, madam," Benton said. "I did not mean to startle you."

Her heart pounding, Evelyn nodded and looked at the wall again. "Benton, what happened to this wall?" she asked, peering closely at it. "This looks like blood. Did they hang meat here?"

Benton cleared his throat. "No, madam."

When he did not elaborate, Evelyn turned to look at him.

For once, Benton looked positively flustered—she'd never seen him look so disconcerted. "Benton?"

He glanced at the wall and swallowed hard. "The room has sat empty for several years, madam. It is . . ." He was having difficulty speaking.

"It is what?" she prompted him.

Benton looked her directly in the eye. "This is where his lordship comes to . . . to release his grief, so to speak."

"I don't understand."

"After we lost Master Robert, his lordship would come here and release his grief . . . physically."

"Physically?"

Benton clasped his arms behind his back and stood stiffly. "There are times, madam, when circumstances are so far beyond a man's control that he can do nothing but strike out."

Understanding began to dawn. Evelyn slowly turned and looked at the wall again. "How do you know?"

"I . . . I inadvertently discovered him here a week after Master Robert's passing. He'd broken his hand."

She vaguely remembered seeing a bandaged hand. At the time, she'd assumed some sort of drunken brawl. She'd been too incapacitated to even care. She reached out, running her finger along one scar. "Dear Lord, what did you do?"

"He refused to see a doctor, as he is wont to do, so I set the broken bones. My father was a surgeon, and I knew a little about it."

"And then?"

"Then?" Benton gave a hint of a fond smile. "He dismissed me from service."

"He did all this to the wall with his hand?" Evelyn asked incredulously.

"Hands. Feet. I can hardly say what all. He . . . he has come many times."

"*Oh my God*," she whispered. "I never knew."

"No, my lady, he prefers that no one knows. He believes it is a weakness in him. I don't believe anyone has ever known the depth of his grief."

"No one but you," she said softly. "Not even me."

"No, madam. I have only guessed at it."

It was more than she'd done. She knew Nathan grieved, but she'd been so consumed with her own grief. She'd assumed, given his absences, that he had done what their parents had suggested and prepared himself for Robbie's death. But *this* sort of grief, the pain behind these marks made her knees weak. She could feel the pain of each and every scar.

She'd never known. She wasn't there to help him. She was guilty of the very thing she accused him of.

"We need a place to put the orange trees until the orangery is rebuilt, Benton," she said absently as she stared at the wall. "I will leave that in your capable hands. I should . . ." *Apologize. Forgive. Forget.* "I should see about . . . things."

"Of course, madam," he said.

Evelyn touched her hand to the wall again. "That will be all for now. I'll be along shortly."

"Yes, madam," he said, and quietly went out, leaving Evelyn at the wall, her mind completely consumed with the image of her husband striking out at his grief in this barren room, all alone, because she could not comfort him.

Nathan's inquiries about a man named Rhys Sinclair were not yielding any information. Donnelly and Wilkes had departed for places unknown, and none of Nathan's friends or acquaintances had heard of this Sinclair.

Nathan remained convinced that the person who wanted him dead was a lord or a lord's man—fifty pounds for his head was not an insignificant sum.

If anyone would know where he might begin to look, it was Grayson Christopher, the Duke of Darlington. Unfortunately, Christy was away and not expected to return to London for a day or two. Nathan chafed at having to wait, and spent his idle time in the gentlemen's clubs he'd not frequented in years.

He intended only to drink enough to keep himself company, but as it happened, more than one vague acquaintance was eager to speak of the growing scandal invoked by the Delicate Investigation.

Since his last visit, even more rumors circulated as to who was involved in the debauchery in the royal couple's separate households. Rumors were rife that the Prince of Wales, angry with his father for favoring the Princess of Wales in their dispute and not agreeing to seek the parliamentary divorce the prince craved, conspired to have his father removed from the throne on the basis of his bouts of madness. If he succeeded, the Whigs would be in power—in direct opposition to the king.

Everyone knew that "the book" the princess threatened to make public would broaden the scandal. Speculation as to who would be accused of high treason and other nefarious acts was rampant. It seemed to Nathan that the entire aristocracy was on tenterhooks, waiting for the scandal to bring the monarchy crashing down around their ears.

He could not help but imagine Evelyn in that mêlée.

On his third day in London—God, but he'd never meant to be away so long, and how he worried about Evelyn, *longed* for Evelyn and what they'd begun again—Darlington returned.

The man had hardly settled in when Nathan called.

"Lindsey," Darlington drawled when the butler showed him into the study. "I see time has put you upright again."

"Very amusing," Nathan said. "Welcome home, Christy—I was beginning to despair you'd ever return."

"Heavens, that sounds so maidenly. Have you come alone, or have the cohorts come with you?" Darlington asked pleasantly.

"No. Lambourne has fled to Scotland to save his hide from prosecution. Donnelly and Wilkes were to London, but neither of them are about now."

"A hunting party somewhere, no doubt," Darlington said with a smile. "I confess there are times I miss it." He was referring to the days he'd been one of them. But his responsibilities to his family and duties in London had put some distance between him and the rest of them over the years. "Whiskey?" he offered Nathan.

"No, thank you," Nathan said, missing the look of surprise from his old friend. "Tell me, Christy," he said as his friend poured a tot of whiskey for himself, "who would want to see me dead?"

Darlington laughed. "I'd wager any number of fathers, husbands, or gamblers."

"I am quite serious," Nathan said. "Someone tried to shoot me at the abbey."

The statement obviously startled Darlington; Nathan indicated his arm, where the outline of the bandages was evident in the sleeve of his coat.

"When?" Darlington asked, frowning at his arm.

"A few days ago. Evelyn and I had ridden to the ruins, and were starting back when someone fired a musket at me. It narrowly missed Evelyn and struck me in the arm."

Darlington put his glass down.

"I caught the bastard," Nathan continued. "The only thing he would tell me was that his name is John and a man in London named Rhys Sinclair had given him fifty pounds to shoot."

"*Why?*" Darlington demanded.

Nathan chuckled derisively. "That is what I'd like to know. The sheriff has him now. Perhaps when I return he will have inspired John to say more, but I could not sit idly by knowing someone desires to see me dead. For fifty pounds, I assume a lord . . . yet no one seems to recognize the name. I was hoping you might."

"Good Lord," Darlington said. He folded his arms and stared at the floor a moment.

"What is it?" Nathan pressed him. "Do you know something?"

"No, nothing," Darlington said quickly, shaking his head. "I've never heard the name. Nor do I know anyone who would want to see you dead, Nathan. But there is something that occurs to me . . ." He paused, obviously thinking.

"What?"

"I am a fool to suggest the two are linked, but . . ." He looked at Nathan.

"For God's sake, speak!"

Darlington sighed. "I beg you forgive me for what I will say. I'd no more say a word against your wife than I would my own sisters, but I must tell you this."

Nathan's heart skipped. "Tell me *what?*"

"As you know, she . . . she was widely believed to be engaged in an affair with Lord Dunhill."

Nathan's heart began to pound. It was all he could do to stand while Darlington reminded him of what all London believed—he was a cuckold. "I am aware," he snapped. "What of it?"

"Dunhill is openly a Whig sympathizer and a confidant of the Prince of Wales. That makes her, in essence, a confidant by way of talk between the sheets."

"*Yes?*" Nathan demanded angrily. "Several of my friends are confidants of the prince."

"Yes . . . but not all of your friends take the political cause to heart quite as deeply as perhaps a few of them do. Look here, the king has suffered from bouts of madness, and the prince chafes to sit on the throne and control his own purse strings. There are some very powerful men around him who would stand to gain if that should happen."

"I don't understand," Nathan said. "What might that possibly have to do with me?"

"Someone wants Dunhill dead. An attempt was made on his life about a week ago," Darlington continued. "A mysterious shot fired, the same as happened to you."

"A bloody shame it didn't find its mark," Nathan snapped, "yet I still do not see what that possibly has to do with me."

"Good Lord, you are obtuse," Darlington said. "What I am trying to suggest, Nathan, is that perhaps the shot was not intended for *you* at all."

"Then . . ." Something exploded in Nathan's chest as he understood what Darlington was saying. He stood abruptly and began striding across the carpet.

"Lindsey! What in the devil are you going to do?" Darlington shouted after him.

Nathan didn't respond; he didn't need to. Darlington knew very well he was on his way to have a word with his wife's lover—the one man in all of England who might shed some light on who would see Evelyn dead.

chapter twenty-eight

The driver Nathan had hired deposited him on the street outside Dunhill's London town home because the bloody gates to the property were locked. Nathan clambered out of the carriage, walked up to the gates, and kicked them.

Through them, he could see a carriage was being loaded. "You there!" he shouted at a footman. "Open these goddam gates!"

Another, smaller man wearing the clothes of a butler appeared from behind the carriage and hurried forward. "I beg your pardon, sir," he said breathlessly, looking nervously up and down the street, "but we are not to open the gates. His lordship is departing within the hour."

"I would be too, if I were him, the bloody rogue!" Nathan slammed his fist against the lock on the gate. "Open them! I would have a word with Dunhill!"

"Sir! I am under *strict* instructions—"

"Unless you want my second and a witness to come calling, sir, you will open these gates!"

The butler paled. "Who shall I say is calling?"

"*Lindsey*," he breathed furiously.

The butler swallowed and turned, hurrying up the drive, leaving Nathan to pace before the gate, his anger and impatience growing with each step. His heart was racing, his breath coming in furious bursts. He hoped he would at least have the presence of mind to extract the information as to *who* would harm his wife before he choked the life from Dunhill with his bare hands.

A few moments later, the butler hurried down the drive again, but this time, he had a key in hand. He unlocked the gate; Nathan shoved the gate aside, almost knocking the man on his arse as he strode through and up the drive.

"My lord! Please wait!" the butler called after him, and hastened to catch up to him.

He managed to do so just as Nathan reached the front door, and quickly pushed it open, running in ahead of Nathan and pivoting about. The man's chest was heaving as he pointed to a door. "His lordship . . ." He paused to take a breath, but Nathan was not inclined to wait.

With both hands, he shoved against the door the butler had pointed to and strode across the threshold.

He was met by the barrel of a gun pointed directly at him. "I don't want to shoot you, Lindsey!" Dunhill bellowed behind it. "But I will defend myself!"

Nathan clenched his hands at his side and forced himself to take a breath. Standing in this room—this room where he imagined Evelyn might have lounged with this bastard—infuriated him. And picturing Dunhill's hands on her body, which he could not seem to help, blinded him with rage.

Dunhill seemed to sense the precarious ground on which he stood; he took a step backward but kept the gun trained on Nathan.

"I understand that someone shot at you," Nathan said, his voice surprisingly even.

"Was it you?" Dunhill asked suspiciously.

"I would prefer to kill you with my bare hands," Nathan snapped.

"It was not I who failed your marriage, sir," Dunhill responded icily.

Oh dear God—it was all Nathan could do to keep his hands from the man's throat. He moved forward, causing Dunhill to cock the trigger. "You may go to hell," Nathan said low, "but first, you will tell me who would want to harm Evelyn."

At least the blackguard had the good sense to look startled by the question. The tip of his gun lowered a moment. "Harm her?"

"*Kill* her, actually, had his aim been any better. As it was, he managed only to nick me."

"What makes you think he was trying to shoot Evelyn?"

Nathan's anger soared. "Do me the courtesy," he bit out, "of not using my wife's given name. Someone tried to kill her, Dunhill, and someone tried to kill *you*. Now what is it that has you running from London like a cur with his tail between his legs?"

Dunhill lowered the gun. "That is no concern of yours," he said coldly. "But heed me, my lord. Take your wife as far from London or Eastchurch as you might possibly get her until this entire debacle of the Delicate Investigation is at its blessed end!"

"You know something," Nathan said, and angrily pushed a chair from his path.

Dunhill brought the gun up once more. "You only exacerbate the danger she is in with your foolishness!" he warned. "Just know this, Lindsey—there are men around the prince who might do anything to see the prince put on the throne. Protect your wife! Take me at my word and remove her from harm's way before it is too late!"

"It was *you* who put her in harm's way!" Nathan roared.

"Will you debate it while she is in danger?" Dunhill asked smugly.

It was more than he could endure; Nathan lunged at him. His movement startled Dunhill, and he fired the gun, shooting over Nathan's head. Plaster fell to the carpet where the bullet entered the ceiling, and beyond the door, Nathan heard a high-pitched cry of alarm.

Dunhill managed to cock the gun again and level it at Nathan's chest. "Get out of my house," he said shakily.

Nathan stepped back. He glared at Dunhill. "We are not done, you and I," he said, pointing at him. "Not by the wildest stretch of imagination are we done." He pivoted and walked out of the room before Dunhill could respond, pushing past the butler and the pair of footmen who had come to their lord's defense.

He walked blindly, the need to protect his wife mixing badly with the need to know what had happened between her and Dunhill.

Since stumbling on Nathan's private room, Evelyn had found new resolve to face the past. She did the best she could—visiting her son's grave each day to help Frances tidy it up, looking at her house again and seeing the impressions her son had made—but she had not visited, *could* not visit the nursery.

Frankly, it had taken her two days to find the courage to step into the small rose garden once more. Many of the bushes had died from neglect, but it was several moments before she could even focus on the bushes. Her eyes were on the spot where Robbie had been standing when he had turned to her, a puppy in his arms.

She could see him as clearly as if he'd only just been in this garden, as if he'd only just run through, his eyes full of the fever she knew would take him.

She deliberately walked to that spot in the garden and stood awkwardly, her arms wrapped tightly around her, her mind's eye full of the scenes of that day. He hadn't wanted to go inside, he'd wanted to play with the puppies.

A lone tear slipped from the corner of her eye—she was rarely able to think of that moment without tearing up—but surprisingly, the tears didn't fall as fast or as thickly as she had supposed they would. She felt sorrow—but not for herself. She felt sorrow for a happy baby boy who had not had the privilege of living his life.

She knelt down on the very mark where he'd stood and ran her fingers over the ground. A tiny speck of color caught her eyes and she turned her head, peering into the bushes. Just beyond the path, partially buried by the decay of roses, was the red tip of a toy. Evelyn instantly reached for it, digging the decay away and dislodging the toy from the dirt and debris.

She sat back on her knees, holding it up. It was a small boat. It had once been red, but only the tip of it was red now, the rest of the paint having faded away to the raw wood beneath where it had been buried. Evelyn turned it over in her hand. She thought she remembered every detail of that day, but she hadn't remembered the boat until this moment. Robbie had been toddling, pigeon-toed, beside his nurse. He was wearing a child's gown and the boots Nathan had specially made from kidskin for him. She remembered that he was holding his nurse's hand, and in his free hand, he held the boat.

She remembered it now! He'd dropped the boat when he'd seen the puppies. "Oh my God," she said to herself, and stood up, studying the little boat.

"Evelyn!"

Nathan! At the sight of him, she broke into a broad smile and scrambled to her feet. "Nathan! I am so happy you are home!"

He didn't speak—he marched forward, his stride long and determined.

"You won't believe what I—"

He caught her up in his arms, lifting her off her feet and holding her so tightly she gasped for breath. He buried his face in her neck before setting her down and holding her at arm's length, studying her face.

"I was beginning to wonder if you'd come back," she said with a nervous laugh.

"I never meant to be away so long," he said earnestly. "There were matters that . . ." He looked into her eyes and shook his head. "Never mind that now. How do you fare? Are you all right? Has anyone called here? The sheriff?"

"I am quite well!" she said with a bit of a laugh. "And no one has called," she said. "I've not heard as much as a peep from the sheriff."

Nathan didn't seem to hear her—he was staring at her, his thoughts obviously elsewhere.

"Look what I discovered, Nathan," she said anxiously. "It belonged to Robbie. He carried it the last day we were in the garden."

That caught his attention—he looked down at the boat she held up in the palm of her hand. He frowned, as if trying to recall it, and slowly released his grip of her arm to take it from her hand.

"He must have dropped it," Evelyn said. "I remember he was carrying it. He must have dropped it to pick up the puppy. I suppose it has lain beneath that rosebush since then."

Nathan's jaw clenched. He studied the boat a long moment, then glanced up at Evelyn. He put his arm around her shoulders, drawing her closer, and leaned down to give her a warmly tender kiss on her mouth. "Come," he said, lifting his head and slipping his hand around hers. "There are many things we should discuss."

"Oh my," she said, smiling. "That sounds rather ominous."

Nathan's only response was to lead her out of the garden.

He took her to the library and rang the bell for Benton. The butler appeared almost instantly, nodding quickly when Nathan asked for tea. As they waited for the service to be brought, Evelyn watched her husband pace at the pair of windows that looked out over the lake.

"What is it?" she asked him, clutching the boat. "You seem so anxious, Nathan. What did you learn?"

Nathan flashed a thin smile and continued his pacing. "We'll talk over tea." He seemed oddly distracted. When he wasn't looking at her as if he wasn't quite certain if she was here or not, he was looking at the bank of windows, as if he was trying to see something there.

By the time tea arrived, Evelyn's stomach was a knot of nerves, and she could scarcely stomach the first sip.

Nathan never took a sip; he stared into the cup.

"I cannot bear it another moment, Nathan," Evelyn said, putting down the teacup. "What has made you so pensive?"

"I beg your pardon, I didn't mean to be so sinister. I have much on my mind, Evelyn. So many unanswered questions—"

"Such as? Who tried to shoot you?"

He studied her a moment, then put down his cup and leaned forward. She could see the worry in his eyes. "Evelyn . . . can you think of any reason someone might want to see *you* harmed?"

That stunned her. "*Me?*"

He watched her closely as the implication of what he was asking began to sink in. "You must be joking."

"Please think—what might you have heard in London about Prince George or Princess Caroline? It might have been something that seemed quite innocent at the time, but perhaps was more important than you realized."

"Nathan!" she cried, coming to her feet. "I cannot believe what you are implying! Who would want to kill *me*? I don't know anything!"

"Listen to me, Evie," he said, slowly rising to his feet, too. "I did not believe it myself initially, but it would seem that perhaps you were privy to some information that has put you in danger. What that information is, I cannot begin to guess, but it is imperative that you help me discover it. Until we know precisely what it is you heard, I cannot find the man behind it. Your . . . your life could be in danger."

She made a sound of alarm, put her hand to her throat. It couldn't be true—what could she possibly know? "That's ridiculous, Nathan! I don't know who has put this notion in your head, but that man shot at *you*! Not me!"

Nathan winced a little. "He was a poor shot at that distance."

"That's madness," she said low. "I don't *know anything*! Who has made you believe that I have? Is it Lady Balfour, back from Freegate so soon? She delights in stirring gossip and innuendo. But she is lying, Nathan!"

"It wasn't Lady Balfour," he said, his eyes going a bit cold. "It was Dunhill."

Pierce's name knocked Evelyn flat. She hadn't thought of him for days and she certainly didn't want to think of him now. Her breath seemed to be lodged in her throat; she didn't know where to look. Not at Nathan, who was watching her closely. Not at the floor, for she would see Pierce's face there. She didn't want to see his face, she didn't want to think of him at all— everything was different now!

"Evelyn?"

She turned away from Nathan's probing gaze, her hand at her throat. So many conflicting emotions were staggering through her mind—Pierce seemed no better to her than a stranger. She couldn't even imagine Nathan in the same room with him.

Perhaps he hadn't said it to Nathan. Perhaps Nathan had heard it from someone else. She looked at Nathan sidelong. "You *spoke* to him?"

Her question clearly aggravated him—his face darkened. "Yes," he said tightly. "I *spoke* to him."

Evelyn felt ill. She sank onto the chair again, her hands pressed against her knees. She didn't want to ask him, but she had to know. "W-what did he say?"

"What do you think he said?" Nathan asked coolly.

She could scarcely begin to imagine the things he might have said—things that would ruin the fragile truce and reconciliation she and Nathan had begun. "It would seem that he said I know something I do not know. Did he say what it is I supposedly know?"

"No," Nathan said, surprising her. She looked up. "He urged me to take you as far from London and Eastchurch as I possibly can until the royal scandal has passed."

Evelyn's mouth dropped open. "But . . . but *why?*"

"That, he wouldn't say," Nathan said, his gaze piercing hers. "So I must rely on you, Evelyn. *Think*. Think what you might know," he said, and looked at her as if he expected her to dissemble. "I find it hard to believe that you don't suspect *something*."

Her belly was churning acidly. "On my honor, I don't know what I could possibly know, Nathan. There were rumors, always rumors—but everyone gossiped. I can't begin to recount it all."

"Rumors and gossip. Such as?"

She gripped her knees even harder. "Awful rumors. Such as incest between a royal brother and sister. Or murder. A-affairs, and children born out of wedlock," she said, letting her eyes drop to the floor. "But I never heard anything about the Prince or Princess of Wales that wasn't reported in the morning newspapers."

"You're entirely certain?" he asked, his voice a little softer.

She nodded as she searched her memory. "I am certain I heard nothing that would cause anyone to want to shoot me."

Nathan sighed; Evelyn looked up as he dragged both hands through his hair. "Very well," he said softly. "I won't press you further. But for the time being, you are not to leave this house without escort."

"Oh, Nathan—"

"No," he said curtly. "You will do as I say, Evelyn. The risk is too great."

Funny, but she already felt constricted.

An awkward moment passed between them; Nathan put his hands on his waist and looked at the carpet. "I must see to the estate's correspondence," he said.

"Of course," she said weakly. Was it her imagination, or was their fragile relationship beginning to crumble so soon? He began to walk from the room. Devastation seeped into Evelyn's veins, and she picked up Robbie's boat and ran her finger over the tiny helm.

"Evelyn."

She turned—he was standing at the door, his hand on the knob. His gaze swept over her, lingering on Robbie's boat. "Did you have an affair with him?"

Her heart climbed to her throat, choking her a moment.

"I would know," he said, letting go the door and turning back toward her. "I have a *right* to know, although frankly, I don't know why I even ask. It seems I am the only man in all of England who had not heard of it, for now I hear it from every corner. I have seen the bloody music box in your suite. Yet I have this . . . this thing eating at me," he said, gesturing to his chest, "that demands I hear it from you."

He looked so dark, so cold, that Evelyn put down the boat and slowly stood. "This is madness, Nathan. What good does it do—"

"Did he take you to his bed?" Nathan abruptly interjected.

Evelyn could feel herself coloring hotly. His blue eyes seemed cold as ice as he considered her. She instinctively looked about the room for an escape. Of course there was none, unless she wanted to leap from a second-floor window.

She didn't hear Nathan move; she was startled by the strong hands that suddenly clamped on her arms, yanking her around. "Did he?" Nathan asked roughly, and pushed her up against the wall, planting both hands on either side of her head. "Did you *lie* with him? You are my *wife*, Evelyn! I am asking what I should have asked the moment I saw you with him at Carlton House—*did he take you to his bed?*"

Her heart was pounding in her throat now, but Evelyn lifted her chin. "*No*," she said quietly, and could see the doubt in his eyes. "But had you not come when you did, my lord, I most certainly would have."

Her honesty took him aback; he shoved away from the wall and turned his back to her. He stood a moment, then took an angry swipe at the tea service. It clattered to the carpet; one cup bounced and skidded several feet, crashing into the leg of a chair.

Evelyn looked down at the debris and bent down to pick up the boat. She rose up, looked at her husband's back. "I suppose you were a paragon of husbandly virtue while I was gone?" she asked calmly.

"I am no saint, Evelyn," he said gruffly.

She walked to where he stood and put her hand on his arm, forcing him to look her in the eye. "Neither am I," she said quietly, and turned away, walking from the room. Let him judge her. Let him judge her if he dared.

chapter twenty-nine

The day after he returned to Eastchurch Abbey, Nathan walked along the riverbank wishing to hell he'd never asked Evelyn about Dunhill. He wished to hell he'd let well enough alone. But what sort of man would remain silent with the question eating away at him, making him second-guess everything that had occurred between them in the days before he'd left for London?

Ah, but he had his truth now, didn't he?

He was, he realized, astoundingly and surprisingly hurt by her truthful admission. He berated himself for that, too—she had been gone three years, and God knew he'd been glad to see her go at the time. She was right—he hadn't exactly waited chastely for her return, had he?

Nevertheless, this seemed different somehow, and it tasted bitter in his mouth.

He marched along to the cottage—the one place that didn't contain any signs of her presence, the one place he might find some relief from his raging imagination.

In the cottage, he walked directly to the end of the table and picked up his current journal. He flipped it open, studied his most recent notes—once, twice, thrice, until the words registered in his brain.

Fortunately, his attention to his work proved to be a respite from thinking about her. He'd slept poorly last night, his thoughts churning. He worried for her safety first and foremost, of course he did, but he believed she was safe under his roof, and he had put two armed footmen to the task of staying with her every moment she was away from the house.

But it was images of her with Dunhill that made his nights excruciating. He couldn't seem to shake them, and now he feared they would mar any hope of true reconciliation with his wife. He wanted to forget it, but he was having a devil of a time understanding how precisely he might do that.

When he'd finished his work—including the recording of some meticulous notes and drawings he intended to send to a friend at the University of St. Andrews for his thoughts—Nathan returned to the main house under an increasingly cloudy sky. More rain was coming.

He'd retired to his study when he heard a commotion in the foyer—specifically, a woman's raised voice. It sounded as if an army had trooped in behind her. He was about to go and have a look when someone rapped sharply on his door and then pushed it open.

"Come," he said wryly as Evelyn sailed across the threshold with two footmen in her wake.

"My lord," Evelyn said, folding her arms crossly, "would you *please* tell these two that keeping an eye on me does not mean shadowing my every move! They've made it quite impossible to do any sort of browsing in the shops!"

"Have they?"

"Yes!" Evelyn exclaimed as the two footmen exchanged a look. "They accompanied me to the village, which I thought entirely unnecessary, what with the driver and the coachman, but I acquiesced, given your wishes. Yet they insisted on following me into every shop! I expressly told them they could wait at the shop's door and they refused to heed me!"

Nathan looked at the two footmen. So did Evelyn, her expression triumphant as she waited for Nathan to deliver what she obviously thought would be a sharp reprimand. "Thank you, gentlemen," Nathan said. "You have performed admirably in what seem to have been difficult circumstances."

Evelyn gasped and jerked her gaze to him. "Nathan! They accompanied me into a ladies' dress shop to peruse undergarments!"

The two footmen looked at the floor; one of them turned crimson.

"If Lady Lindsey does not appreciate your loyal service, please know that I do," Nathan said to the men. "You are relieved from your afternoon's duty . . . in more ways than one, I suspect."

"Thank you, milord," one of them said hastily. They both bobbed their heads at Evelyn as they went out, but she never saw it—she was glaring at Nathan, her hazel eyes shimmering with her wrath. "When you said I should be escorted, I didn't think that you could possibly mean into every little shop in Eastchurch!"

"I meant for you to stay here, but if you did not, I did indeed mean every little shop," Nathan said as he turned back to his desk. "Every room, every carriage, every step. You are not to be alone except in the privacy of your suite of rooms, Evelyn. And even then, I'd feel better if Kathleen remained with you at all times."

"No! Nathan, there is no real proof that the bullet was meant for me, nothing but the remark of one man!"

"I can and I *do* mean it," he said firmly. "Do not argue—I am inflexible on this subject."

"For how long?" she cried.

"As long as is necessary," he said, and insanely, pictured her dancing with Dunhill. "If there is nothing else, I have some work I really must be about." He turned toward his desk and picked up a piece of correspondence, staring blindly at it.

But Evelyn didn't move. *Damn it, why didn't she leave him?* Nathan waited for her to speak, to leave the room, but she didn't move as much as a finger. He glanced at her sidelong and winced inwardly at her wounded expression. "I have quite a lot of work to do," he said again.

She suddenly put her palms to her cheeks. "I don't understand what has happened," she said, dropping her hands again. "You've come back from London and now you seem a stranger to me. You won't dine with me, you won't come to me—I've scarcely seen you since you returned."

"I beg your pardon for being distant," he said carefully. "But I have quite a lot on my mind." He turned back to his desk once more.

But he heard the rustle of her skirts and knew she had come to stand directly behind him. He flinched when she put her hand on his back.

"Nathan . . . I thought we'd come so far in such a

short time," she said softly. "But now I think you will toss it all aside because of a conversation with Dunhill."

The mention of her lover's name grated; it felt as if there were a band tightening around his chest. "Please don't mention his name again."

"Will you not speak to me?"

"Evelyn . . . when I agreed to let you go to London, I was not so gullible that I didn't understand what I risked. I am no stranger to court and the things that go on there. But . . ." He looked at her. "But I suppose I was not prepared to be presented with it so boldly. I need time to let it settle. I need time to think some things through."

"*What* things?" she demanded.

It was impossible to explain it—he hardly understood it himself. He took her hand in his. "When we married, I never dreamed our lives would go as they did," he said softly. "But they did, and while a part of me understands what happened in London, another part of me is wounded by it. I thought we could repair our marriage, but now . . . now I need to think." It occurred to him that in the space of a fortnight, he'd gone from never wanting to think to needing desperately to think.

"But . . . I was never in his bed," Evelyn said, her cheeks coloring as she tried to put a brighter face on it.

She was only making it worse. "Don't say more, I beg you," he said, not unkindly. "I've heard all that I ever hope to hear of it."

"You find such fault in me, Nathan, but how is it any different than what you've done?"

There was no good answer for that, and he knew it. He looked at her hand in his, ran his thumb across her knuckles, marveling at the softness of her skin. "I suppose because I believe in my heart that my indiscretions were never more than that—indiscretions." A drunken tryst here or there to relieve himself physically, but he'd never stopped loving her. A part of him had never stopped wanting her home. He'd never been with another woman and actually *seen* that woman—he'd seen only Evelyn. "I never wanted anyone but you, Evie. But it would seem I was supplanted in your heart by another man." He looked up into her eyes. "I could see it in your face at Carlton House."

Her lashes flickered and she dropped her head guiltily. "We both behaved badly," she said roughly. "You forced me here against my will, and I hated you for it. But it made me realize how much you mean to me. I want to forgive and forget, Nathan, and I thought you wanted that, too. Why can't you want that?"

"I am trying," he answered honestly.

She looked up, her eyes shimmering with tears. "*Trying?* What does that mean?"

He didn't have to say it—she could obviously see it in his expression. A moment passed with her waiting hopefully. A moment later, she silently pulled her hand from his. Without a word, she walked to the door, her shoulders sloping as if they carried some invisible weight on them. She did not look back as she quit the room.

Nathan watched her go, feeling as if she were dragging his heart along behind her. When he could no longer hear her footfall, he turned back to his desk, his task completely forgotten now.

He *was* trying. With everything he had, he was trying. He just couldn't seem to rid himself of Dunhill's image.

From his perch in the woods, the rider had watched the countess return to the house in a carriage and emerge, sandwiched between two lanky footmen. Lindsey knew, then. The rider thought he should have taken his shot days ago, after the men the earl had hired to sweep through the woods had come and gone, finding nothing. That very afternoon, the countess had visited the grave of her son. It would have been so easy, and so poignant for Lindsey to find her body draped over the grave of her son. He might even have made it look like a suicide.

He'd been contemplating how, precisely, to do that when the boy had appeared. He'd been moved by the boy—he wanted to see Lady Lindsey dead, but he did not want to harm the boy.

Now, it seemed as if it might be too late, for somehow, Lindsey had discovered she was the target.

The rider glanced up; the clouds were as dark as ink. He would need shelter for the night and some time to think. His mission required a different approach. He retreated deeper into the woods to return to his shelter and to mull over his options.

chapter thirty

For two days, the rain fell in great long swaths, leaving the earth so saturated that water pooled on the ground. And for two days, Evelyn moped about the house, trying to find her way in the storm inside her.

Nathan's distance hurt her worse than she could have imagined possible. It was astounding to think how quickly her heart had turned back to his, as if there were a divining rod between them. After more than three long years of grief and abandon, something miraculous had happened. She had found, in the place that she least expected it, what was missing from her heart: her husband.

And now, he seemed as distant to her as Robbie did lying in his grave up the road. From where she stood at her window, Evelyn could just see the top of the cherub.

"This wretched rain won't let up a bit!" Kathleen groused as she entered Evelyn's room with a stack of damp linens. "It's a wonder we aren't floating out to sea just now."

If only she could float away, Evelyn thought idly. She'd seen Nathan precisely twice since he'd rebuffed her in his study. The first time at breakfast, when he had politely answered her questions, but had taken the first opportunity to escape.

The second time had been in the nursery. Oh yes, the nursery, the last frontier of her pain. She'd finally found the courage to face it. Granted, it had taken her a few rounds of standing and staring and walking away only to walk back again before she could actually put her hand on the knob. Then another few moments to find the actual nerve to open the door, but she'd done it, opening it slowly and carefully, holding her breath.

Which was why, probably, Nathan didn't hear her.

It shocked Evelyn to see him sitting there on a child's chair, his knees practically up around his ears, his face in his hands.

His head jerked up at her sound of surprise, and he stood quickly and surprisingly gracefully from that little chair, looking quite startled to have been discovered. He nervously ran his hand over the top of his head.

"I beg your pardon," Evelyn said hastily. "I had no idea . . . I didn't mean to disturb you."

"Please," he said. "Come in."

She peeked around the door, saw the baby's bed with the protective sides raised to keep the child from rolling off.

It was the very bed in which her soul had been scored by the devil's claw, where Evelyn had held Robbie as he drew his last breath.

Nathan followed her gaze to the bed, and sensing her distress, he walked forward, his hand extended to her. "Come," he quietly urged her.

His presence infused her with the fortitude she needed; she slipped her hand across the wide palm he held out to her, felt his fingers close around hers. He pulled her into the nursery and stood with her, hand in hand, in the middle of the room, as they both looked around.

It was just as they'd left it: Robbie's clothes still hung in the little wardrobe, his shoes and boots lined up beneath. The bed linens, faded yellow after all this time, still dressed the bed. His toys were neatly stacked on a shelf where he could reach them, and the bed for his nurse—his constant guardian—remained at the far end of the room.

In addition to a table and four small chairs in the middle of the room, there was a smattering of child-sized furniture and a fire screen painted with animals in front of the cold hearth.

It was just as Evelyn remembered it, every detail. Her knees felt a little wobbly, but she drew a steadying breath, let go of Nathan's hand, and walked to the shelf where Robbie's toys had stood silently for almost four years. "I'd forgotten how many ponies he had," she said with a smile. *Pony* was practically his first word.

She picked up a stuffed horse and looked out the bay of windows overlooking the small rose garden. The rain was falling steadily, sluicing down the panes of glass. "He used to climb up here and press his face to the window," she said, as she pressed her hand to the window. She stepped away, hugging herself, the horse dangling from her hand. "It seems damp in here," she said, looking at Nathan. "Do you suppose the dampness contributed somehow?"

"No," Nathan said quietly. "It is damp because the room goes unused."

Of course. *Of course.* "I have often wondered if there is something I might have done—"

"No," he said quickly. "His heart was weak from birth, Evie, and it was weakened further with ague and fever. He was never meant to have a full life."

It hurt her deeply to hear him say it, but she could not disagree. "Perhaps while I was carrying him, then. Remember, I had a bit of ague myself near the end—"

"God," Nathan said, and put his hands on her shoulders to stop her from saying more. "Look at me," he commanded her. "*Listen* to me. I have never in my life known a better mother than you, Evelyn. You did nothing to harm that child. Nothing! If you want someone to blame, blame me. It is far more likely that my years of drinking and God knows what contributed to his weak constitution."

"What?"

He dropped his hands. "I am to blame," he said tightly. "I suspected it from the moment he was born."

"No, Nathan," Evelyn said instantly. "No, no, I will not allow you to blame yourself!"

He shook his head, but Evelyn clutched his arm and forced him to look at her now. "Have you believed that all this time?"

He winced, the hard glint of his pain her answer.

Evelyn abruptly took his face in her hands. "I will not allow you to blame yourself," she said again. "You are a strong, virile man—you gave that boy what good health he had. Had it not been for your strength, he might not have had fifteen months on this earth—he might not have survived his birth."

Nathan looked at her skeptically; Evelyn nodded adamantly. "It wasn't you," she said. "Have you truly thought so? Oh no, Nathan, *no*. He fought so hard to be born, remember? That was your strength in him. And he fought so hard to *live*—that was your strength in him, too."

Nathan clenched his jaw. Evelyn's heart went out to him, for until that moment, she'd never suspected that he'd suffered the same unending, unanswerable, cruel questions that she had suffered.

"Oh Nathan," she said softly, and let her hands drift down his chest.

He made a sound deep in his throat and looked at the floor, but covered her hand with his, pressing it against his heart. "It would seem we've both been plagued with questions." Then he abruptly dropped his hand from hers and stepped back, away from her touch. "I will leave you to your private thoughts," he said.

"Nathan, please don't go—"

But he was already at the door. He glanced uncertainly at her as he went out, quietly pulling the door shut behind him.

Evelyn felt his absence in the draft that seemed to stream through the room. She hugged herself again and turned slowly, taking in every feature of the nursery.

It was more than an hour before she left, roused from her nap on the nurse's bed by the damp chill in the room. As she left the room, she gave it one more look, her eyes landing on Robbie's bed.

She had done it.

She had conquered the last of her old demons. She could, at long last, face and accept Robbie's death once and for all of time.

Now, she had only to face her new demons.

She was contemplating them when Kathleen came in

with the linens, complaining about the rain. As she listened to Kathleen puttering around the room and nattering on about the weather, Evelyn saw Nathan walk up from the river path. He was wearing a cloak buttoned at his throat and a wide-brimmed hat from which little waterfalls fell off the front and back.

"Lord, but he shouldn't be about!" Kathleen said disapprovingly as she looked over Evelyn's shoulder. "He ought to stay inside or he'll catch his death."

"Mmm," Evelyn said, and pressed her palm to the pane of glass. It was cold. He must be cold.

"You should tell him so, mu'um," Kathleen said. "He'll listen to you."

"Unfortunately, my husband is not interested in my opinion."

"Of the ill effects of rain?" Kathleen asked in a tone that suggested she thought it preposterous.

"Of anything," Evelyn said softly. "He has had a change of heart."

"*What?* Oh no, you must be wrong, mu'um," Kathleen huffed as she turned from the window. "If you don't mind me saying, I've seen the way he looks at you. There's not a man in England more in love with his wife, mark me."

"That was before he went to London earlier this week," Evelyn said, and traced a line down the glass. "And before he met Dunhill."

The silence was so great that Evelyn turned to look at Kathleen. The poor woman was gaping. "Oh dear," she managed.

Evelyn smiled sadly. "Oh dear, indeed."

"You apologized for it."

It was not a question, and Kathleen's disapproving

tone surprised Evelyn. A million retorts sparked in her brain, but she was struck by the fact she had *not* apologized for it. At the time, it had seemed an odd suggestion, given Nathan's conduct. She despised the way society turned a blind eye to a man's indiscretions, but crucified a woman for hers.

Nevertheless, it hardly mattered what Nathan had done—what mattered was what Evelyn had done and that she was truly sorry for her actions. She was truly sorry she'd ever left Eastchurch Abbey. She was sorry for everything that had happened to them, and sorrier still she hadn't been strong enough to weather it.

So when Evelyn encountered her husband later that afternoon—under the pretense of having him look at a nonexistent problem with the hearth in her bedchamber, for which she had begged Benton to send the earl— she apologized.

"I beg your pardon?" He was down on one knee inspecting the flue.

"I apologize," she said again, clasping her hands tightly together. "That is to say, I am very, very . . . *sorry* for . . . for everything," she stammered, casting her arms wide.

Nathan came to his feet and studied her a moment. "I don't quite know what you mean."

Lord, this was difficult! "I am very sorry, Nathan, for having hurt you."

He just looked at her.

"I am sorry that our son died and that I wasn't able to bear it properly. I am sorry that I went to London and . . . and . . ." She waved her hand at the words she couldn't bring herself to say. "I am sorry that our brief reconciliation didn't last longer than it did, for I . . ." She paused, trying to find the words that were significant and important enough to express what she was feeling, and finding none that suited, she foundered.

Nathan frowned lightly. "There is naught wrong with the flue, is there?"

She shook her head.

"I'll have Benton's fool head yet."

"It was my doing. Benton quite clearly wanted no part of it, but you know that I've always had the power to persuade him."

He was watching her, his expression stoic.

Evelyn shook her head, trying to clear it. "That is neither here nor there, really. I just wanted to speak to you, but I scarcely see you, and I . . . I forced him to do my bidding, and now you are here, and I should very much like you to know how sorry I am while I have your ear. *Truly* sorry," she said earnestly. "More than I can ever express, really."

"I see," he said simply. But his gaze went to the music box that still graced her mantel. Evelyn had forgotten it until this moment. She surprised herself by striding across the room, taking up the music box, and hurling it to the tiles before the hearth. It broke into several large pieces.

"Good Lord," Nathan said.

The dancing couple, still intact, rolled to a stop against the tip of Evelyn's slipper. She suddenly despised that dancing couple, and in a symbolic gesture, she stomped on it, crushing the porcelain as well as the heel of her shoe. "*Ouch, ouch, ouch*," she said with a whimper, and fell onto a chair to remove the offending shoe and rub her foot. "There, you see?" she demanded.

"I do indeed." With his hands on his hips, Nathan

looked down at the debris, and Evelyn hoped she was not imagining the hint of a smile on his lips. "Well then, I—"

Whatever he intended to say was interrupted by a knock on the door. Nathan moved to answer it before Evelyn could stop him and opened the door to Benton, who bowed apologetically.

"I beg your pardon, my lord, but the sheriff has come at last."

"About damn time. I shall be with him momentarily."

Benton nodded and quickly disappeared. Nathan glanced back at Evelyn. "We shall continue this conversation later," he said, and glanced at the broken music box. "Have a care where you step," he added.

With a groan, Evelyn sank back against her chair as he strode from the room.

chapter thirty-one

Having completed his morning chores, Frances Brady asked his grandmother, who looked after him most days while his father worked, if he might go and tend to the baby's grave. She made him wrap a scarf around his neck to ward off the chilly morning breeze, but sent him on his way, after extracting a promise that he be home at the noon hour.

Frances made his way through the woods along his favorite path. He found a limb that had fallen from a tree during the storm that made the perfect sword. He fought invisible enemies as he went, ducking behind trees only to lunge a moment later and spear his invisible opponent. By the time he reached the edge of the woods and the abbey church, he had lost interest in the limb and discarded it. He emerged from the woods with his hands in his pockets, and unwittingly allowed his long, forgotten scarf to trail behind him.

When he saw the man appear from around the corner of the church, he smiled. He'd seen him about often enough. The man smiled at him, too, and held up a hand in greeting. "Master Brady, is it not?"

"Aye, milord," Frances said. He had no idea if the man was a lord or not, but he had learned long ago, after one lord had boxed his ears for calling him mister, that it was safer to call all men lords.

"Lindsey said I'd find you here."

Frances stopped and peered up at the man. He had small brown eyes, wore a greatcoat of fine wool, and had a hat pulled low over his eyes. He clamped his hand on Frances's shoulder. "Lindsey has a task for you, if you are able."

"Aye, milord." Frances was always able to help the earl. He admired him very much and often wished he'd been born to him instead of his father, who toiled from sunup to sundown and was rarely in good humor.

"He would that you ask Lady Lindsey to meet him in the cottage at half past ten. He has a surprise for her."

"The lavender?" Frances asked, brightening.

The man smiled. "Can you be trusted with that important message?"

"Aye, sir!" Frances said, nodding enthusiastically.

"Very good." The man smiled at him again and turned away, walking back to the church and disappearing around the corner.

Frances thought that was rather odd, seeing as how there were no church services today, but he was too eager to deliver the message on behalf of Lord Lindsey to think about it for long.

As luck would have it, Lady Lindsey came a quarter of an hour later with a man dressed in the earl's livery. He stood at the gate as the countess walked across the graveyard, daintily lifting her skirts as she stepped over old graves. Frances was pleased to see her; it would save him a walk to the earl's house to deliver his message. "Good morning, mu'um!" he called cheerfully.

"Ah, there you are, Frances!" the countess called to him with a broad smile.

Frances could not help but smile in return. When Lady Lindsey had come home, Frances thought she'd seemed rather sad. Now she looked happy. And *beautiful*. He'd not seen a woman as pretty as she in all of Eastchurch. He had, however, seen some in London and supposed all beautiful women lived there. He fancied his mother had been beautiful, but he'd never seen her except when he was first born, and that, he didn't remember.

"I've a message from his lordship!" he announced grandly, proud to have been entrusted with it.

"Oh, have you indeed?" She brushed a strand of hair from her face with the back of her hand and looked at the baby's grave a moment. "Well then?" she asked, and tickled his ear. "Will you keep me on tenterhooks? What is the message?"

"His lordship should like you to meet him in the cottage at half past ten for a surprise."

She looked confused for a moment, and Frances fretted that he'd not delivered the message properly.

"I thought he'd gone to the village," she said.

Frances shook his head. He imagined if the earl was to give her a surprise, he was in the cottage, just as the man had said.

But then a smile almost as brilliant as the sun lit her face and she exclaimed with great delight, "A *surprise*! Do you know what it is?"

Frances really hadn't the slightest idea, but he didn't

want to appear not to know and said without thought, "Lavender. Perfume, I think."

Her eyes lit with pleasure. "Oh my, that is a special surprise, is it not?"

Frances didn't know if it was or not, but had the unnerving thought that she might mention to the earl that *he'd* said lavender when he really had no idea of the surprise at all. "But I'm not to tell you, mu'um. You won't tell him that I told you, will you?" he asked, panicking a little.

"Of course not," she assured him. She leaned over and caught his forgotten scarf, then wrapped it around his neck like his grandmother had done earlier. "You best keep this on. You'll catch an ague if you don't." She patted him on the cheek and, with a cheery wave, walked out of the graveyard with the earl's man.

Evelyn was cautiously hopeful that Nathan's invitation to the cottage signaled an end to their impasse. She eagerly changed from the drab day gown she had donned to visit Robbie's grave to a vibrant blue silk, which looked surprisingly nice with her thick leather boots, a necessity for walking anywhere today.

She looked at her reflection in the mirror to see what Nathan would see when she entered the cottage. Hopefully, he would see her true desire to reconcile. And that she loved him! Oh yes, she loved him—she'd realized she'd always loved him on some plane, but was only now beginning to realize how complex her feelings were. She could only thank God he'd come for her when he had—what might she have done if he hadn't?

Ah well, enough of that. She was ready to receive her

surprise—lavender! She chuckled out loud and picked up her cloak.

At half past ten, her spirits buoyed by hope, and a hopeful smile on her face, Evelyn slipped out of the house without Seth, her ever-present shadow, who had not heard her conversation with Frances, and really, why should she need him now? She'd be with her husband, and that was all the protection she needed.

Evelyn set out for the cottage, her stride long, her arms swinging.

The sheriff had brought the news last night that John, the man who had tried to kill Evelyn for fifty pounds— would be transported the following day to Cirencester to face a magistrate. The sheriff thought Nathan might like one last word with the criminal.

Nathan rode into Eastchurch very early to have that word, but when he arrived, the sheriff had some astounding news—he'd just discovered John had hanged himself rather than face the magistrate.

The discovery shocked Nathan—he quickly ran through the reasons why a man would take his own life, and the only thing that seemed even remotely plausible was that he feared something worse than death by his own hand.

Perhaps he feared the sort of death he might receive by another's hand more than his own.

The news left Nathan feeling at sixes and sevens— he rode hard for home, the sense of uneasiness growing in him. He knew Evelyn was in the company of his best men, but he had a prickly feeling beneath his collar.

As he rode past the church and graveyard, he saw Frances toiling away at Robert's grave. The lad saw him, too, and began to wave his arms, trying to entice him to stop. Nathan had no time for it, but he hated to disappoint the boy, and impatiently reined Cedric to a halt alongside the fence.

"I did what you asked, milord!" Frances said breathlessly, having run across the graveyard to meet him at the fence.

Nathan glanced at Robert's grave. "I see that you did, Frances, and what a fine job you've done." He smiled at him and lifted the reins.

"No, milord, I mean that I gave Lady Lindsey your message," he said brightly, and Nathan felt his heart drop to his toes. "I didn't mean to tell her the surprise, but she asked me what I thought it was, and I—"

"What message?" Nathan demanded.

Frances blinked. "That she was to meet you in the cottage—"

"Dear God," Nathan said. "Tell me slowly, lad. Who told you to give that message to Lady Lindsey? And when was she to meet me?"

The color bled from the boy's face. "The g-gentleman," he stammered. "He said I was to deliver the message for you, sir."

"What gentleman?"

"I . . . I don't know," Frances said frantically. "I've seen him round here, but I don't know his name."

"When? When was she to meet him?" he demanded roughly, causing Frances to shrink away from him.

"At half past ten, my lord."

Nathan quickly dug his watch from his pocket—it was just half past ten. He dug his spurs into Cedric's flank. Cedric jumped, startling Frances. Nathan heard the boy's cry of alarm, but he had no time to spare.

The river was running above its banks, the water rushing past, full of debris from the heavy rains. The path was pitted, too; Evelyn had to hop between shallow mud puddles. In the place where the path narrowed between the wall of a cliff and the river—which, she noticed, was dangerously close to the path—she heard the sound of an approaching horse.

Nathan.

She stopped in the middle of the road and looked up, smiling happily. She saw the rider and horse up the path, and her smile faded—that was not Nathan riding full bore for her.

Evelyn's heart stopped. She frantically looked around—there was no place for her to go except the rushing river. She whirled around and looked back the way she had come, but the path was too long and too narrow—she could never outrun that horse. She twisted about—horse and rider were coming straight at her. Panic filled her throat—she couldn't even scream. She was paralyzed with terror, could do nothing but stand and watch the horse's hooves clawing the ground as he raced toward her.

As the horse drew closer, something broke inside her; Evelyn screamed and threw her arms over her head, expecting to be trampled or knocked into the river.

The horse didn't run her down. She heard its bald neigh and opened her eyes. The horse had reared and the rider was trying desperately to rein him about on that narrow path.

Her initial thought was that the rider hadn't seen her until he was almost upon her, but he bent over the horse's neck and rode just as hard away from her.

It was then she heard another horse behind her and with a shriek of fear, she threw herself up against the side of the cliff, her arms splayed wide. The rider—Nathan—threw himself off his horse and lunged for her, catching her up in his arms. "God in heaven," he said breathlessly. "God in heaven."

"What happened?" she cried. "Who was that?"

"I don't know," he said grimly, and put his arm around her, forcing her along, while Evelyn tried to look over her shoulder.

"I don't understand," Evelyn said as Nathan lifted her up to his saddle. "He came so close to running me down! Did he not see me? Did he mean to frighten me?"

Nathan swung up behind her, put his arm tightly around her middle. "He meant to harm you," he said shortly, and started Cedric back to the house.

"*Oh my God,*" Evelyn whispered. She could no longer deny it—someone was trying to kill her.

chapter thirty-two

Evelyn was still shaking when Nathan helped her off the horse at the house, her eyes still wide with the frightening realization that she'd come close to death.

"Benton!" Nathan shouted. "Where in God's name are you?"

A moment later, the door of the house was thrown open and Benton came bounding down the steps, pointing a footman to Nathan's horse, another to the door. "Gather a search party," Nathan said to Benton as the butler took in a shaken Evelyn. "There is a man on horseback, probably deep in the woods by now. I want every inch of this property searched!"

Benton nodded and began striding briskly away.

"And have Frances Brady brought to me at once! Tell the men to bring me something!" Nathan shouted after him. *"Anything!"*

To Evelyn he said softly, "I will ring for Kathleen—"

"No!" Evelyn cried, and grabbed his lapel, looking up at him with terror.

"Calm down, Evie," he said, taking her hands in his and ushering her up the steps. "You are safe now—"

"No, no, I am *not* safe," she said wildly as they entered the foyer. "He meant to put me in the river! He meant to see me drowned! Frances sent me to that man—Frances *must* know who he is!"

"Frances is a boy, Evelyn," Nathan said as he ushered her into the nearest room. "He was duped. He would never wish you harm," he added once they were alone in the small receiving room.

"No, of course not—but he must know who did this!"

"You're right, he must know something," Nathan said. "I will speak with him at once, but in the meantime, I want you to stay here—"

"*No!*" she cried again, and launched herself at him, almost toppling them both. Nathan caught her with his hands on her waist as she threw her arms around his neck and pressed her face against his collar.

"Evelyn, darling, you are safe here, but I must go and look for the bastard who did this to you!"

"Let them find him," she pleaded tearfully. "Please, Nathan, please—promise me this time you will not leave me."

The way she said it brought back an ugly memory. He remembered another time she had pleaded with him to stay and he had gone—it was shortly after Robert's death, and she'd been standing in her bedroom, wearing a chemise and dressing gown. Her hair had been dull and straight, her eyes shadowed with dark circles.

For the life of him, he couldn't remember where he'd been headed, but she'd begged him to stay. "Promise me you will not leave me, Nathan," she'd said shakily. "I can't bear it if you leave me, too."

"You must get hold of yourself, Evelyn," he'd said

curtly, and had walked out, his eyes and ears closed to her tears.

At the time, he'd believed he could not bear her pain as well as his own, and he felt somewhat humiliated by those old fears. She'd needed reassurance and he'd refused to give it to her. He saw in her eyes now that same hopeless, frantic, wild look.

"Please, Nathan," she said tearfully. "Please don't leave me now."

He smoothed her hair with the palm of his hand. "I will not leave you," he said softly. "I will never leave you. You have my word." He kissed her forehead, then dipped down so that he was eye-level with her. "I want you to think again, Evie. Are you entirely certain you don't remember anything unusual or strange that you might have seen or heard in London? If you could but remember, it would help us find who is behind this. "Think back," he urged her. "Think back to your time with Dunhill—"

"I don't want to think of him!" she said, and twisted away from him.

Nathan wasn't particularly happy to, either. "Did you ever speak of the scandal?" he continued doggedly.

"No," she said with a wince, then, "I don't know. Perhaps." She closed her eyes and drew a steadying breath.

"Think," Nathan urged her.

"I *am* thinking," she said, and walked to the windows, her arms folded tightly around her.

But no amount of trying to jog her memory seemed to work—if anything, it had the opposite effect. The more questions Nathan asked, the more agitated Evelyn became.

Frances wasn't much help, either. He was frightened, and while he could say he'd seen the man before at Eastchurch, that he was one of the "hunters," he could not say anything more helpful than that. Nathan took "hunter" to mean one of the gamekeepers, but when he had them brought in, Frances swore it was none of them. The only thing Frances could say about the man was that he had small brown eyes, a woolen greatcoat, and a hat.

That described quite a lot of men in this shire.

Nathan sent the tearful boy home in the company of a groom.

It seemed impossible to Nathan that a man could attack his wife on his property and he could find no clue as to his identity.

That evening, the hastily assembled search party returned empty-handed. One of the men told Nathan that whoever had attempted to knock Evelyn into the river must have known the estate fairly well. "The horse's prints ended at the river's bend," the man said. "He left no trace."

"How could he leave no trace?" Nathan demanded.

"Only if he knows the pattern of the streams, sir, and went up into the hills," the man said. "He knew the lay of the estate fairly well."

Nathan felt completely impotent.

That night, after persuading Evelyn to take a sleeping draught and sending her up to bed in the company of Kathleen, Nathan discussed the matter with the sheriff and made a decision: If they couldn't find the culprit in Eastchurch, which, apparently, they could not, then the answers had to lie in London. Only this time, he would not leave Evelyn behind.

It was after midnight when he peeked in on her.

A snoring Kathleen had nodded off in a chair, and jumped when Nathan touched her on the shoulder. He quickly held a finger up to his mouth, cautioning her to be quiet. He then beckoned her to follow him.

In the corridor, he told her they would be leaving for London in two days and to have Evelyn's things readied. Kathleen seemed surprised by it, but nodded.

"You may return to your room," he said. "I will watch over her," he assured her.

With Kathleen toddling sleepily down the hall, Nathan stepped into Evelyn's room again. The fire was low, and in the dim light, she looked like a small lump beneath the bedcovers. He moved quietly to her bed and looked down at the golden tail of hair that spilled over her pillow. He had just turned away when he heard her speak.

He paused, wondering if she'd spoken in her sleep—and heard it again. Nathan eased down onto his haunches next to the bed and saw that her eyes were open. He tucked a strand of hair behind her ear.

"*I'm sorry,*" she whispered. "I don't know what I know, Nathan, I swear I don't. But you must believe me—if I knew, I would tell you."

He stroked her cheek.

"There is something I want to tell you."

"Of course."

"I am . . . I am afraid."

Something surged up inside him, something primal and raw. He had an innate need to protect, and to hear his wife tell him that she was afraid—for her life, of all things—twisted painfully inside him. It was the last thing he wanted to hear. It was the last thing he thought he would *ever* hear. He felt inadequate and weak, just as he had when Robert had died. "You are safe, darling."

Evelyn looked deeply into his eyes as she reached for the tails of his neckcloth and used it to pull herself up, lifting her face to his. "I am afraid of losing you," she whispered as her gaze moved to his mouth. Her lips parted and she pressed them lightly to his.

That small, simple kiss was as erotic as any he'd ever experienced. It surged through him like a current, inflaming every male instinct within him. He touched her hair, her face, and traced a line down her neck and then followed it with his mouth, to kiss the small hollow of her throat. "Don't leave me, Nathan," she whispered as she pushed her fingers through his hair.

"I would be mad to leave you," he said brusquely, and rose up, crawling over her on the bed. He pressed his lips to her hair and closed his eyes, breathing her in, the scent of lavender. "*Mad*," he murmured again as his hand ran down the side of her body.

Evelyn sighed deeply, her breath warm on his scalp. She moved her hands inside his coat, pushing it off his shoulders, helping him when Nathan paused to shake out of it, then pulled his shirt free of his trousers and slipped her hands beneath his shirt, sliding up to his chest. Nathan pressed his mouth to the open vee of her gown, in the valley between her breasts.

"I am the mad one," she whispered into his hair. "I should never have left you."

The regret in her voice floated around his heart.

"I would do anything to change all that has happened," she said as she slid her hand down his body, cupping him. "Anything."

God, he needed her. Her scent, the taste of her skin, and the love he'd always had for her was pushing him past his pride and into her arms. He took her breast in his mouth.

Evelyn moaned, grabbed his face, and forced him to

look up. She kissed him with surprising strength, her tongue sweeping into his mouth. She seemed to need him just as much, and Nathan was happy to oblige her. He moved over her, forcing her onto her back. "Love me," he demanded as his hands moved over her body.

She pushed him onto his side and kissed him while she stroked him with her hand. Nathan kissed every patch of skin, her neck and the curve of her shoulder, and the swell of her bosom above the bodice of her gown. He moved his hands down her back, her hips, and her legs, slipping in under the hem of her gown, moving up her thighs.

Evelyn groaned low when he caressed the soft flesh on the inside of her thigh and closed her eyes, reveling in his caress.

His desire was not of this earth—it was incomprehensible, far beyond his understanding. It was intense and filled every bit of space in the room, pushing at the walls, threatening to explode from its confines. Every stroke of his hands prompted another small sigh or groan, every stroke of her hands pushed Nathan closer to the edge of his control.

"I love you," she said breathlessly, lifting up to fill him with her breath and her tongue.

He was moved by the earnestness in her voice. He pushed her gown up to her neck, slipped his hands to her hips, and greedily took each breast into his mouth as she pressed against him.

He would never know the moment they had managed to cross the invisible chasm that had separated them, but it was beginning to feel as if they'd never been parted, as if they were still as bound to one another as they'd been when they stood before the king and queen and took the marriage vows.

He paused in his attention to her body to look into her eyes; Evelyn watched him as she pulled her nightgown over her head and tossed it aside. The hazel in her eyes was as deep as a well, and the look of them seductive, bewitching. This is what would guide him, he realized. To love her, protect her, defend her—it was what had been missing from him for so long. *This* was his guide.

"Nathan?" She touched the bit of hair that had fallen over his brow.

"I love you," he said hoarsely. "I *love* you."

She smiled with warm affection. "I love *you*."

He pressed his hand to the soft flat of her belly and caressed downward, to the springy tuft of hair at the apex of her legs. An ungodly fire was melting him inside out. He went up on his knees, shrugged out of his shirt, and unbuckled his belt.

Evelyn admiringly slid her hands over his shoulders and his arms.

He lay over her again, felt how small she was against him, felt her warmth seeping into his skin, filling him up. He moved his mouth down her body, to the softest place of her. "Oh," she gasped. *"Oh my."*

With a groan, Evelyn drew one leg up. His senses filled with the scent and the taste of her as he moved lower still. When his tongue slipped between the folds of her sex, she gave a strangled moan and her body jerked with pleasure. But Nathan was deliberately slow, his heart beating harder each time she bucked against him. When he closed his lips around the tiny core of her pleasure, her body spasmed and she gasped for breath, squeezing her legs around him, sinking away from him. A moment later, she rose up on her elbows and kissed him madly as he fumbled with his trousers, pushing them down over his hips, then sliding in between her legs. He kissed her roughly, passionately, possessively as he parted her legs with his thigh and lowered his body to hers, pressed the tip of his cock against her wet body, and slid deep inside her.

"I am enraptured," she murmured, and closed her eyes, letting her head fall back. She opened her eyes and slid her hand between their bodies, toying with him, and smiled seductively. "Take me, Nathan," she said breathlessly. "Ravish me. Seduce me until there is nothing left of me."

He smiled wickedly as he slid out again, to the very tip of him. "As you wish, Mrs. Grey," he said, and thrust into her again.

Her hands began to stroke his back as he moved fluidly within her, sliding deeper with each stroke, sliding closer to his release. He rolled onto his back, letting her take her delight on him, directing the pace, sliding up and down, sighing with ecstasy when he was buried deep inside her. When he could stand it no more, he rolled her onto her side, draped her leg over his hip, and began to move fast and hard.

Her body moved with his, her hands gripping his shoulders, her hips lifting with each stroke.

His breathing grew shallow as raging desire built in him and exploded inside her. He collapsed to her side and rolled onto his back.

Evelyn propped herself up on her elbow and pressed her hand against his wildly beating heart as if to hold it in place. "I have missed you," she said softly. "I had not realized how much I have missed you until I came home."

Nathan closed his eyes, put his hand on top of hers. He remembered the morning she had left for London. He remembered standing on the drive thinking he would never see her again, and that he hardly cared. But he'd been fooling himself. He'd been a broken man, he realized now, pieces of him breaking away each day, incapable of mending himself without her.

They slept wrapped in one another's arms until the early morning hours when Nathan finally untangled himself from her limbs and quietly dressed before Kathleen came in with her hot chocolate. When he had dressed, he sat on the edge of the bed and put his hand on her shoulder.

Evelyn, in the middle of the bed and buried deep beneath the bedcovers, groaned.

"Wake up, Evie," he said, and leaned over her, kissing the back of her neck.

"Don't want to," she muttered.

"You must. We've a lot to do before we depart for London on the morrow."

A moment passed before she seemed to understand him. She suddenly pushed herself up on her elbows.

"London?"

"Our answers are in London."

"But . . ." Evelyn scrambled to sit up, pulling the bedsheet over her breasts. "But isn't it dangerous?"

He leaned over and picked up her dressing robe and handed it to her. "It is the only way, Evelyn. Either we go and confront whatever it is, or we flee England." He leaned over and kissed her softly.

chapter thirty-three

They took Nathan's father's house in Mayfair and had not been in residence a pair of nights before engraved invitations began to flow in the door, piling up in silver trays in the foyer, all wanting Lord and Lady Lindsey to attend this function or that.

How Benton, who'd accompanied them to town, managed it all was beyond Evelyn's ability to understand. She felt completely overwhelmed by it.

Evelyn knew very well that after her infamous departure from London, everyone would be anxious to see the unhappy couple and feast on their misery. She looked with dismay at several of the more important invitations arrayed on a desk before her.

At Nathan's request, Mr. Nelson, the marquis's secretary, had been dispatched to London to help them navigate the social waters. The marquis and marchioness were beside themselves with joy that Nathan and Evelyn would re-enter society, as they saw it as a sign their relationship had changed and the scandals would be put behind them.

If only they knew the truth.

Mr. Nelson was happy to accommodate his employer's son—he had confided to Evelyn that he much preferred London to the marquis's county seat. "It can be rather rustic in the winter months," he'd said in a tone so nasal that it sounded a bit like a whine.

"Indeed," Evelyn said, and picked up an invitation. It was engraved on heavy vellum, and was requesting their presence at the Duke of Cumberland's for a small supper party. The duke had handwritten on the back that all of her "dear friends" would be in attendance. Evelyn was afraid of precisely that.

"It would not do to decline an invitation from the Duke of Cumberland, particularly given your association with his sister, Princess Mary," Mr. Nelson opined in that dreadful nasal tone, his pencil poised at the ready on a sheet of vellum.

Nathan had told her to accept all invitations. "The more we are in society, the more we will learn," he said to her over supper last night in response to Evelyn's complaint that he'd left her with Seth and Kathleen all day to visit his old haunts.

"Affirmative?" Mr. Nelson prompted her.

"Yes," she said simply, and pressed her hands to her belly.

She'd been feeling rather ill for a few days now.

"Here we have an invitation to join the Prince of Wales at the opera Thursday next, and a tea with the queen and the princesses for you, my lady. She requests the honor of your presence a week Friday."

"Yes, yes, to all of them," she said with a flick of her

wrist. Her stomach roiled; she felt as if she would be ill at any moment. As Mr. Nelson busily made notes, Evelyn stood abruptly. "Will you excuse me a moment, sir?"

The man quickly came to his feet, barely managing to hold on to his things in his haste. "Of course, madam."

She was already moving, walking quickly to the door that adjoined the sitting room with the grand salon, a room that was, fortunately, seldom used except when the marquis and marchioness were entertaining on a lavish scale.

She scarcely made it to an empty porcelain vase behind one of a pair of hand-painted Oriental silk screens before she was ill.

When she was certain she was through being ill, she turned her back to the wall in the salon and sank down to her haunches, the back of her head resting against the wainscot behind her.

She could no longer deny what was so obviously true—she was carrying a child. She had first begun to suspect it when they'd arrived in London, and she had realized, in looking at her appointments calendar, that her courses were more than a fortnight late. The nausea had begun in earnest in the last three days.

"What will I do?" she whispered tearfully to the painted ceiling. The thought of another child overwhelmed her. She had thought of the possibility, of course she had—but she had gone for several years before they'd conceived Robert and had supposed—oh, who was she fooling? She'd been enthralled with the renewed relations with her husband and had not been as cautious as she should have been.

Another child! What would Nathan think? Would he want this child? Would he fear another sickly boy? How many times could he lose an heir? How would she bear it if this one were ill? How could she bear to lose another child?

Evelyn pressed her hands to her abdomen as a tear slipped from her eye and slid down to her lip. She would just as soon die as lose another child.

She would just as soon die.

Finding someone who knew something about the Delicate Investigation and the matters purportedly revealed in the Princess of Wales's scandalous book was quite easy.

Finding anyone who actually knew something firsthand, and not via secondhand gossip whispered in salons across Mayfair, was quite another task. In the space of one frustrating fortnight, Nathan had heard from various and sundry that the Princess of Wales was carrying another love child (the father rumored to be any number of men, including Lambourne); that the Prince of Wales had fathered the child she supposedly bore out of wedlock, and that they were, indeed, secretly but happily conjugal; that the Princess of Wales had fled England for her native Brunswick, a German principality, in spite of the political trouble with France brewing there; that the king had engineered the entire scandal to keep his son and his Whig sympathies from the throne.

Nathan had heard these tales enough times now to suspect bits and parts of each story were true, but none of the stories were completely true, as he explained to Darlington one afternoon. "And there's nothing that would overtly point to Evelyn. It is a bit like looking for a particular leaf in a forest."

"You're looking in the wrong place," Darlington casually suggested as he sipped from a pint of ale at the public house where they'd met. "Ask after Dunhill—not the prince or your wife."

Dunhill. Nathan had tried so hard to forget him that he had overlooked the obvious.

"By the bye," Darlington said, "I happened to see Wilkes a day or so ago. Perhaps he can help."

"Wilkes?" Nathan said, surprised. "With Donnelly?"

"Donnelly is in Ireland," Darlington said. "I've had a letter from him. Wilkes said he'd just come from Chichester. Paid a call to his mother, apparently."

"Indeed? I would have sworn him motherless," Nathan said with a wink, and made a note to call on his old friend just as soon as he had a free moment.

That evening, they were to dine with the Duke of Cumberland. Nathan knew Evelyn was not very keen on attending. He worried about her health, in truth. A night at the opera had fatigued her, and she seemed so pale of late. He supposed it was the London air—thick as molasses and rather putrid in its smell.

As for himself, he was hardly looking forward to the evening, either. He'd never particularly liked Prince Ernst, the duke. He'd found him disturbingly odd. Rumors of an incestuous relationship with Princess Sophia only increased Nathan's wariness of him.

Evelyn was dressing for the evening when he entered her suite, lovely in a cream and gold gown. Kathleen was at her back, buttoning her gown as Nathan walked across the dressing room to kiss Evelyn's cheek. "How beautiful you are," he murmured appreciatively.

She blushed. "Thank you for that. I confess I've been feeling a little wan these last few days."

"Never," he said with a smile. "You are radiant. Will you join me in the green room later?" he asked as he continued to the door that adjoined their suites, where he paused for her answer. Her silhouette was elegant, almost regal, but she was uncharacteristically biting the corner of her lip. It seemed as if she hadn't heard him. "Evelyn?"

Her head came up and she looked at him wide-eyed, as if she'd been caught at some prank.

"Are you unwell?" he asked, looking at her curiously.

"Unwell? No, no, I am quite well," she said, and forced the smile again.

"You seem distracted."

"Oh." She fidgeted with her locket. "No, I . . . I suppose I was thinking of the evening. There will be so many people in attendance."

"Friends of yours, I should think."

She smiled wryly. "Surely you have been in London long enough to know that one never has *friends,* sir. I think of it more as if the vultures are circling."

He smiled sadly—she had him there. "I shall join you in the green room," he said again.

She nodded and watched him go out.

When the door had closed behind Nathan, Kathleen made a *tsking* sound of disapproval.

Evelyn sighed heavenward. "What is it, Kathleen?"

Her loyal ladies' maid, who had been with her for as long as Evelyn had been old enough to employ such services, finished buttoning her. "It's not my place to say," she said with much superiority, and walked into the adjoining room.

Damnation. Evelyn had not told Kathleen of her predicament, but Kathleen knew Evelyn's body and habits almost as well as Evelyn. She *knew*. Before long, everyone would know.

Evelyn couldn't avoid the inevitable. She had to tell her husband.

The supper party was a raucous affair with more than three dozen from the highest reaches of society in attendance.

Evelyn and Nathan were ushered into the grand salon and announced, then served wine before supper. Evelyn was quickly swept up into the ladies' inner circle with a cry of "Lady Lindsey! You've come back to us!" Several of the women looked at Nathan accusingly; more than one looked at him with a suggestive gleam in her eye.

Nathan kept his distance from that group of ladies and found himself standing with some of the men who surrounded Cumberland—men with whom Nathan was well acquainted from his own days of catting about the royal court.

Lord Moorhouse, a dandy with hair so meticulously curled that it had always annoyed Nathan, nudged Nathan with his elbow and tilted his wineglass in Evelyn's direction. "It would seem you have reined the filly to your will, my lord."

That remark startled Nathan; he looked pointedly at Moorhouse, who shrugged at his expression. "I beg your pardon if I have offended you, but there are no secrets in the royal salons. Your wife's interests are well known by most."

Nathan slowly turned to face him fully. "Is it your intent to provoke me, sir?"

"Not at all," Moorhouse said with a bit of a smirk. "I merely misjudged your marital attachment after all these years." He lifted his glass in a silent toast and wandered off.

Working to keep a surge of indignant rage in check, Nathan followed Moorhouse—he was well connected and Nathan needed men like him if he was to solve the mystery of who wanted Evelyn dead. When Moorhouse paused at a sideboard to pour more wine, Nathan forced down his pride and said with a derisive chuckle, "It wasn't easy bringing her round, I'll give you that, but I rather enjoyed the challenge."

Moorhouse glanced at him.

Nathan smiled. "Frankly, I shouldn't trust her in London at all, but seeing as how Dunhill has fled . . ."

Moorhouse snorted as he offered the bottle to Nathan, who had yet to take a sip of his wine. "You would flee as well, sir, if your life was threatened so openly."

Nathan smirked. "How many cuckolds have guns, do you suppose?"

Moorhouse laughed. "I gather you'd like to see the shooter find his mark. Have patience, Lindsey. The coterie will catch up to him eventually, I'd wager."

"The what?" Nathan asked, unfamiliar with the term.

"The coterie." Moorhouse grinned and clapped Nathan on the shoulder. "There is the duke. You will want to bid him a good evening." And with that, he sauntered away, leaving Nathan to wonder who or what was the coterie.

The question plagued him as he went through the motions of greeting the duke, who asked him bluntly if he intended to keep Evelyn in London among her friends, or in the country and away from any proper society.

And the question remained with him long after, when he had entered the gaming room for a round of cards and any bit of gossip he might glean, and even later, when Lady Fawcett sought his particular attention, hoping to soothe his tender feelings because of the well-known rift with his wife.

The coterie.

In the ladies' retiring room, Claire sat on a divan while Evelyn stood behind a screen, retching into a chamber pot. "Dear Lord, I hope you haven't come down with that awful fever that has circulated amongst the princesses," Claire complained. "I've managed to avoid it thus far."

"Something I ate, I think," Evelyn said hoarsely as she wiped her hands on a cloth. "How is Harriet? I was hoping to see her."

"I've sent her off to Italy for the winter with my mother to learn a bit of culture."

Evelyn looked at Claire.

"What?" Claire asked with a smile. "Did you think I was going to foist her on you again?"

"You've never foisted her on me, Claire. I sought her out. I enjoy Harriet's company and I am sorry I will not see her."

"Really, Evelyn, you should have children and plenty of them," Claire said with a sigh.

Evelyn didn't respond—another wave of illness overcame her, and she quickly stepped behind the screen.

When she was steady, she came from behind the screen and to the basin to wash.

"Such rotten food in the country! And I thought it so wholesome there," Claire said with disdain as she joined her at the basin to review her appearance in a looking glass. "You're not going to remain at Eastchurch, are you? It seems so . . . *rustic*," she said with a visible shudder.

Evelyn had thought so, too, a few short weeks ago. "I don't know," she lied. "Lindsey is very angry about . . . everything."

"He seems the sort to be angry," Claire said dispassionately. "I think the country suits him, however—he has that look of gentry about him."

Evelyn couldn't guess what that was supposed to mean, but she didn't care for the way Claire said it.

"Dunhill will return, you know," Claire said softly as she straightened the back of Evelyn's gown. "If you can think of a way to come back to Princess Mary . . ."

"Has she asked after me?" Evelyn asked.

"Of course," Claire said. "It's dreadfully dull for them all without us, and the queen is so *rigid*," she said irritably. "But the queen is quite displeased with *you*, Evelyn," Claire added with a smile. "I suspect you'll hear of it when you come to tea. She does not condone adultery."

Evelyn gasped and swung around to Claire. "I did not commit adultery!" she exclaimed.

Claire laughed. "Oh really, Evelyn! Didn't you? Thinking it is almost as criminal as *doing* it." She linked her arm through Evelyn's. "Oh, you mustn't fret! I've been very circumspect in my remarks when you are the topic of conversation. I have never told another breathing soul that you asked me the very morning you were taken away which one I would choose, were I you."

Evelyn glared at Claire. "I asked you which *ribbon* you would choose, Claire."

Claire smiled. "Did you indeed? How odd—I remember it quite differently."

Evelyn jerked her arm from Claire's and strode across the room.

"Oh, don't be in such a snit!" Claire said after her. "Everyone knew it! *Everyone!* Did you really think you had secrets?"

The door shut behind her, and Evelyn walked down the hall, her heart beating with anger and fury and shock. How had she ever believed she could be happy in this viper's nest? How had she ever counted these people as her friends?

In the grand salon once more, Evelyn looked about for Nathan, and spotted him having a very intimate conversation with Lady Fawcett. He was smiling charmingly, a smile that would melt Evelyn, just as it was undoubtedly melting Lady Fawcett.

She felt a twinge of jealousy and turned away. His laughing with Lady Fawcett made her irritable—not only was her life in danger, but he'd practically thrown her to the wolves when they'd entered, letting them swallow her up while he went off to do God knew what, and now, with—

"Wine, madam?"

The gentleman who addressed her was a smiling Lord Ramsey, a friend of Dunhill's whom Evelyn had met on a few occasions. "No, thank you," she said, and looked at the crowd again.

"The country air seems to have agreed with you," he said pleasantly. "You look very well."

Evelyn did not answer. If she so much as looked at him, she knew tongues would wag.

Ramsey inclined his head; she could see him from the corner of her eye. "I thought you might like word of our mutual friend."

"No," she said instantly.

He chuckled low. "Come now, madam, but wouldn't you? He was really rather saddened when you were so abruptly taken from our midst."

Evelyn swallowed, hard.

"He had to leave London rather suddenly himself, I'm sure you've heard," Ramsey continued unabashedly. "It would seem there is nothing delicate about the Delicate Investigation any longer."

There was something about the tone of his voice that curled uncomfortably around Evelyn's heart. She risked a look at him; Ramsey smiled at her, but his eyes seemed cold. She took a step backward. "I have no idea what you mean."

"That's the right answer, sweetheart," he said, his pleasant smile belying the rancor dripping in his tone. "Were I you, I would maintain that answer, and particularly with your husband. His inquiries have made some people rather anxious."

"What are you talking about?" she demanded, taking another step backward.

He laughed, caught her hand in his before she could jerk it away, and lifted it to his lips. *"Excellent."* He bussed the back of her hand and dropped it, looked her over once more with eyes cold as ice, and walked on.

Evelyn's pulse was suddenly racing, her face felt hot.

She whirled around—and nearly collided with her husband.

Nathan caught her with a smile. "Steady, love."

"Where have you been?" she snapped.

His smile faded. "Is something wrong?"

"Yes—everything!" she said, pressing her hand to her abdomen again.

His eyes darted to Ramsey. "What do you mean?"

"I mean that I want to go home, Nathan. I don't want to be here."

"We can't leave—"

"Can't we beg off? We'll tell Cumberland I am ill," she said, a little frantically.

"Are you ill?" Nathan asked, clearly concerned.

"*Yes!* No, no, not like that," she said again, and anxiously rubbed her forehead. "Perhaps just a *bit* like that—it's too warm in here, and I can't seem to think."

He took her by the elbow and steered her to a settee, signaling a footman as he took a seat next to her. "Water for the lady," he said when the footman appeared. "What is it, Evie?" Nathan asked, leaning slightly forward to look in her eyes. "What is it? Did Ramsey say something to offend you?"

"No," she said quickly. She wasn't certain *what* Ramsey had said to her. "It's just that I hate being here," she said, and glanced around the room at the people she had known these last few years. "These . . . these people are not my friends."

"I would guess they are not," he said with a sigh. "Very well, then. We will leave just as soon as the supper is done."

"Not before?" she begged him. "I can't eat a single bite, I swear it."

"You must do your best, Lady Lindsey. If we take our leave now, the talk will never end, you know that very well. We must put our best face on it."

She groaned softly. "I can't possibly do it if you are engaged with others, Nathan."

"Then I shall remain at your side," he said reassuringly.

She gave him a doubtful look as the footman returned with the water. "All night?"

Nathan took the water and handed it to her with a smile. "All night and forever more."

chapter thirty-four

Nathan was increasingly concerned about Evelyn. She was ill at ease, her color was pallid, and she hardly spoke at all through the course of the supper, which, thankfully, went unnoticed as Lady Copperley held court at their end of the table with a very extravagant tale of the misdeeds of Princess Caroline.

Nathan had made their excuses the moment he was, by society's standards, able to do so, and had bundled Evelyn in a fur-lined cloak and put her in the coach. On the drive home, however, Evelyn sat with her forehead against the window, staring bleakly out over the rain-soaked streets.

He could not help but wonder about her sudden despondency and if it was somehow due to Dunhill. He knew Ramsey was a friend of the prince and suspected he was a friend of Dunhill as well.

When they arrived home, Benton was there to greet them and held out a silver tray to Nathan. "Sir Wilkes has called this evening, my lord."

Nathan glanced at the card and pocketed it. "Some tea for Lady Lindsey—"

"No, please," Evelyn said, with a wave of her hand. "I couldn't." She pulled a sour face, as if the thought of tea made her ill. "I prefer to go to bed. Will you excuse me?" she asked, and started up the staircase.

Nathan followed her. Evelyn seemed not to notice or care.

In her dressing room, she wearily reached behind her and began to unbutton her gown. Nathan caught her hand. "You are unwell," he said, and pushed her hand away and began to unbutton the gown for her.

"I'm fine."

"I've never seen you look quite so peaked, Evie. Perhaps you have a bit of ague. I'll have Benton summon a doctor on the morrow—"

"I'm *fine!*" she snapped, and stepped away from him, continuing the unbuttoning herself.

Nathan slowly lowered his hands. "All right, then, Evelyn, what the devil is wrong? You've been in quite a state all evening."

"A *state?*" she repeated hotly. "Yes, I suppose I am, Nathan. My reputation is in tatters and there is someone who would like to see me dead!"

Nathan sighed impatiently. "I feel the strain, too, Evelyn."

"Do you, indeed, Nathan?" she asked crossly. "You didn't appear to feel any strain in your high-stakes card game or with a tot or two of whiskey, and certainly not with Lady Fawcett or Lady Copperley!"

"That is not fair," he said angrily. "I am doing my best to learn who would want to harm you. By the bye, have you ever heard of the coterie?"

"The what?" she asked, frowning at him.

"The coterie."

Evelyn made a sound of exasperation and threw her hands up in the air. "No, I've not heard of the coterie!"

"Moorhouse mentioned it and said the coterie would see to Dunhill."

"I don't want to hear his name!" she cried, putting her hands to her ears.

Her reaction angered him—they wouldn't be in this perilous situation if she'd turned a deaf ear to his name several months ago. "I am sorry for that," he bit out, "but you will hear his name until we get to the bottom of this."

"Then perhaps you should ask Lord Ramsey," she said, and Nathan realized tears were filling her eyes. "He seems to think I know something, too."

"What? Why didn't you tell me?"

"Because you weren't there!" she exclaimed. "You were smiling at Lady Fawcett at the time and besides, he threatened me if I told you!"

A different sort of anger soared in him, and Nathan quickly crossed the room, forcing her around to him. "What do you mean he *threatened* you?"

"Only that I would do well to repeat that I had no idea what I knew and to repeat it in particular to you, as your inquiry was making some people anxious."

Nathan dropped his hands from her and wheeled about, striding for the door.

"Where are you going?" Evelyn cried.

"Isn't it apparent? To have a conversation with Lord Ramsey."

"No!" she cried. "No, you can't, Nathan."

"You are *safe*," he said irritably, anxious to be on his way.

"You don't understand," she said as tears began to fall. "I am very frightened, I—"

"I know you are frightened, Evelyn, but I have the best men at your disposal. You are well protected, you *must* trust me."

"That is not what I mean!"

"Then what?" he exclaimed roughly. "For God's sake, *what?*"

"I am . . . I . . ." She collapsed onto a stool and bent over her knees.

"God in heaven!" Nathan cried angrily. "What is *wrong* with you, Evelyn? I am doing my best to mend this mess, but I cannot help you until I have! Stop *crying!*"

She sniffed loudly. "I can't seem to stop," she said tearfully, and looked up at him. "I want to laugh, but I cry. I feel sad, and I smile. I'm at loggerheads with myself."

Nathan groaned impatiently.

"I'm pregnant, Nathan."

The floor seemed to drop out from beneath Nathan's feet. The walls seemed to close in on him, then fall away again. He could see nothing but his wife sitting across the room on that stool, her expression full of fear and hope.

A *child*. The notion quickly swelled inside him, filling his heart with shock and elation and paralyzing fear.

"I'm sorry!" she said, and burst into tears, burying her face in her hands.

Nathan was moving instantly. He fell to one knee before her, cupped her face in his hands, wiped her tears with the pads of his thumbs, then dropped his hands to her arms and looked at her waist.

A *child*.

He understood Evelyn's fear—he feared it himself. Was it really possible they might have another chance? Could they produce a healthy child?

He placed his hand against her abdomen. "*Dear God*," he whispered reverently. "My God. Are you certain, Evie? It took so long . . ."

"I know," she said with a wry smile. "I don't understand it, either. Nathan, how will we endure it?" she asked, meaning, he knew full well, another sick child.

"We will," he said resolutely. But the ugly thought that someone wanted his wife—and now, his child—dead suddenly rose above all the myriad things Nathan was feeling. A very primal emotion overtook him—the need to protect and defend. Single-minded, he rose to his feet. Nothing would stand in his way now. He put his fingers beneath Evelyn's chin and tipped her face up to his. "All will be well, Evie. You have my word." He would protect her and the child she carried with his own life if it came to that. "But I must see Ramsey," he added, and leaned down to kiss her. "Sleep easy, love. The king's army could not penetrate this house."

With Evelyn behind a locked door, and Seth positioned outside of it, Nathan took up his cloak again and went out into the London night. He returned to Cumberland's house and waited in his coach, watching the guests as they trickled out over the course of an hour or more to their carriages.

Ramsey was one of the last to emerge, staggering a little in the company of a pair of friends. They boarded a coach with Ramsey's insignia blazoned on the outside; Nathan opened the vent between him and the driver. "The Ramsey house on Green Street," he ordered.

The coach lurched forward.

When Ramsey had divested himself of his friends and returned to his home, Nathan was waiting in the shadows for him. As the coach pulled out of the drive and around to the mews, Ramsey stumbled up the steps to his house. Nathan moved silently from the shadows behind him, and as the bastard reached for the door, Nathan lunged.

He tackled the drunken viscount, knocking him to the ground and rolling down the steps with him. He had Ramsey on his back, and Ramsey frantically began to fight. His inebriation affected his aim, however, and he swung blindly. Nathan swung only once, connecting with his jaw.

"Damn you!" Ramsey sputtered.

Nathan caught Ramsey's collar and yanked his head up. "Tell me what you know about the threat against my wife!"

"I don't know a damn thing about your *wife*," Ramsey said.

Nathan backhanded him, splitting Ramsey's lip.

"I will see you hang for this, Lindsey!"

Nathan was hardly moved by his threat—he caught the knot of Ramsey's neckcloth and twisted, choking him. "You will tell me what you know about the threat against my wife, or you will die like the dog you are here on the drive," he said evenly, and released the pressure on his neck.

"You're mad!" Ramsey managed hoarsely.

Nathan twisted again. "What do you know about the threat against Dunhill?" he asked angrily as Ramsey

frantically clawed at his hand. Nathan let go of his neckcloth. "Speak, you bloody scoundrel!"

"Dunhill . . ." Ramsey winced. "He knew of the plot
against the princess—"

"What plot?" Nathan asked, pinning the man's arms.

Ramsey coughed; blood dribbled from a cut at the
corner of his mouth. "Ask Dunhill," he spat.

Nathan was in no mood for games. He reached for
the gun in his boot and pressed the barrel of it against
Ramsey's forehead.

Now Ramsey's eyes widened with terror. "Do you
really think you can do this without consequence?"

"Someone would see my wife dead, sir. That is all
the consequence I need. The consequence to you, however, is death," Nathan said calmly. "What plot against
the princess?"

Ramsey swallowed. "All right, all right!" he said frantically. "Remove the gun and I'll tell you." When Nathan
withdrew it, Ramsey said, "The princess was involved in
a carriage accident in Leatherhead a month past. It was
intentional—she was meant to die, but unfortunately, it
was mishandled and her lady-in-waiting, Miss Cholmondeley, was killed instead. Somehow, the princess discovered the plot and told the king and now . . . now the
king's men are searching for the culprits, and they will
surely hang. I merely meant to warn your wife that if she
knew anything, she would do well to keep it to herself."

"Who was behind the plot?" Nathan demanded.
"Dunhill?"

"No," Ramsey said. "He was only privy to it. Men he
knew—"

"*Who?*" Nathan insisted, and pressed the tip of his
gun against Ramsey's forehead once more.

"I don't know!" Ramsey cried. "I only know that they are called the prince's coterie! They fancy themselves the power behind the prince, but I know nothing more than—"

"Who are they?" Nathan shouted.

"Look around you, Lindsey!" Ramsey cried. "They surround the prince and they surround you! Some you call friend!"

Stunned, Nathan could not react before the sound of men's voices coming down the drive reached him. They were running, he realized.

He dropped his gun in his pocket and stood up.

"You will pay for this, Lindsey," Ramsey said through clenched teeth.

"My lord!" someone shouted from behind.

Nathan began striding toward the street, uncaring of the commotion behind him, uncaring of anything but who of his friends was in this coterie, his mind running around all the inconceivable possibilities.

chapter thirty-five

Evelyn was awakened by Nathan's familiar weight as he crawled into bed with her. He moved close, his chest warm on her back, and put his hand protectively on her stomach. He sighed softly into her hair; Evelyn covered his hand with her own and gripped it tightly.

Neither of them spoke for several moments. "What if it is sick?" she whispered.

"What if it is healthy and beautiful like its mother?"

The tears, always present these last few days, filled her eyes again. "Or handsome and strong, like its father?"

Nathan kissed her shoulder. "Do you recall how Robert would say *peas* for *please*?"

Evelyn smiled in the dark. "I remember how he would laugh when you wrestled with him, Nathan. Oh how he *laughed*."

"And I remember the way he looked at you, Evie. He loved his mother very much."

She remembered, too. "I can't help but be afraid of

burying another child," she admitted. "I don't think I could survive it."

"I pray we never face such tragedy again. But if the child is healthy, imagine the joy it will bring us."

It was true, there was no greater joy. Evelyn twisted around to face him. "I want to hope, too."

He smiled, stroked her temple. "Then we shall hope. We will think only good thoughts and trust in the Lord that the child will be born healthy."

Yes, they could only trust . . . but before they could do anything, they had to end the danger to her life. Evelyn closed her eyes. "You found Lord Ramsey, then?"

Nathan stroked her hair. He seemed reluctant to speak, but at last said, "I did," and told her what Ramsey had said about the carriage accident.

Evelyn was horrified. "Who would do such a vile thing?" He didn't have to tell her it was the same people who would do it to her.

"I trust you never heard of the scheme?"

"Of course not! Had I heard it, I would have gone straight to the king and queen, you may be sure!"

"I believe you," he said. "I had hoped that Dunhill had said something, however vague."

She shook her head.

"Tell me who he considered a friend," he asked.

How she wished she'd never been involved with Pierce! "Ramsey, as you know," she said. "Beaverton, when he is in town—they liked to shoot. Eldingham, I believe." She thought back, to the soirées, to the balls, to the supper parties. He was friendly with so many people, quite popular as it were. "Is that what you mean?"

"That is precisely what I mean," he said, and kissed the tip of her nose. "We must rest now. You need to rest."

"I can't sleep."

"I'll get you something."

"I have a better idea," she whispered, and kissed him as she climbed on top of him.

Nathan left Evelyn sleeping deeply as only she could do, tangled in the linens.

He had an early breakfast and then took his horse to Darlington's.

His friend was breaking his fast as Nathan explained what he'd heard.

"The coterie," Darlington repeated thoughtfully.

"Would the prince be involved in something as vile as murdering Princess Caroline?" Nathan asked.

Darlington instantly shook his head. "He is a profligate to be sure, but not a murderer. And he was the first to offer he knew nothing of the princess's carriage accident when the plot was revealed."

"Oh?"

"The princess had heard the accident was no accident—one can only guess how; enemies of the prince, I should think—but she has threatened to make it public. Even if the prince is innocent, he won't be perceived so in the public's eye, and well the monarchy knows it. The king was so incensed that he vowed to see those who had planned it hanged. Perhaps Dunhill was involved?"

"No," Nathan said, shaking his head. "He was frightened when I saw him. My guess is that he knew of the plot, but did not participate."

Darlington looked at him over the top of his teacup. "Did your wife know of it?"

"No."

"It hardly matters if she did," Darlington said. "Obviously a member of this coterie believes she did, and believes she is a danger to their own fool neck." He glanced at Nathan. "You must be very careful."

Nathan thought of the child Evelyn was carrying. "I will. But I will not stop. I'll pay a call to Wilkes and see what he knows."

"Good luck with it," Darlington said, and stood with Nathan. "If there is anything I can do to help, you mustn't hesitate."

"Thank you," Nathan said, realizing that Darlington was one of the few men he could trust.

On the drive at Darlington's, as Nathan waited for his horse to be brought round, he withdrew the calling card Wilkes had left with Benton. On the back, Wilkes had written his location. He'd taken up residence in Donnelly's London town home until Donnelly returned from Ireland in the spring.

Nathan idly turned the card over and looked at the engraving. *Sir Oliver Wilkes*, it said. He was about to put the card in his pocket, but something caught his eye. He held the card in his palm and looked at it again. There was an elaborate scroll at the top of the card, with vines that trailed around the edges. But in that scroll, tucked in and scattered between the leaves and vines, were tiny letters: *T. P. C.*

T, P, C . . . he mused. *TPC*. The . . . "The coterie," he muttered, as that word was much on his mind, and then shook his head. Of course it wasn't the coterie. What would *P* stand for? "The prince," he smirked . . .

Nathan froze. *The prince's coterie.* Wilkes, a friend

who was in Nathan's company as often as he was in the prince's company. It was just as Ramsey had said. He blinked at the card. "No," he muttered. "It couldn't possibly be." *TPC. The prince's coterie.* But this was Wilkes! Wilkes would never be involved in a plot to kill the princess . . . or Evelyn, for God's sake!

But as Nathan thought more of it, his heart sank like a rock. It was at Wilkes's urging he'd taken that awful road from England to Eastchurch. Wilkes had been the only man besides himself to know he would take that road. At the time, Nathan had believed the attempted robbery of his coach a random occurrence, but it was possible that it had been the first attempt on Evelyn's life. Given the rift between Nathan and Evelyn, it is possible Wilkes did not think he would ride with her.

Moreover, on the day the orangery burned, Nathan and Evelyn met Wilkes dressed in a cloak in the foyer of the house when everyone else was fighting the blaze. Was it possible he had needed time to circle around through the forest and into the house to make it appear he had been within?

Wilkes knew the forest quite well, too, didn't he? He'd know the path of the streams. They'd certainly hunted that forest enough—

Hunted.

Dear God. Frances had said the man who had sent Evelyn to the river was "one of the hunters" and had "small brown eyes." Both descriptions fit Wilkes.

Mother of God. Nathan stared blindly at Cedric when the boy handed him the reins, his heart and head reeling with his suspicions. He could not fathom how a man who had been like a brother to him could plot to kill his wife.

He felt suddenly anxious about Evelyn. He swung up on his mount and headed for his father's house.

Benton told him she was in the marquis's study with Mr. Nelson. He burst into that room, startling them both. "Mr. Nelson, please leave us," he said.

"Nathan?" Evelyn said, rising to her feet as Mr. Nelson gathered his things and hurried out. Nathan looked at his beautiful wife. His pulse was pounding, thrumming in his throat, echoing through him. Wilkes had slept under the same roof as she. He deliberately took a breath. And another.

"Nathan!" Evelyn said again, clearly alarmed.

"It is *Wilkes*," he said, his voice incredulous.

"Wilkes?"

"It is Wilkes who has tried to harm you, Evie."

She gaped at him, as stunned and confused as he was. "*Why?*"

Nathan shook his head. "That, I cannot fathom." He proceeded to tell her what he suspected, showing her the card. Evelyn's eyes grew wider as she listened. When Nathan had finished, she hugged herself tightly and twirled away from him, staring at the window. "*Oh my God.*"

"I am going to him now," he said through gritted teeth. "I'm going to kill him. I'm—"

"Nathan!" Evelyn said, catching his arm. "No, Nathan, *wait*," Evelyn said. "If you are certain the prince is unaware of who has done this in his name, then he must hear it."

"That's impossible. Wilkes might admit his involvement when I confront him, but he would never admit it to the prince. That would be admitting high treason, and he would be hanged for it."

"Yet there is no proof," she wisely reminded him. "You cannot present mere suspicions to the prince. In the absence of proof, you must arrange for the prince to hear it from Wilkes's own lips."

What she said made sense, but for the life of him, Nathan could not imagine how they might manage it. He shook his head again. "It is impossible."

"No," she said, her eyes shining with determination. "No, it is *quite* possible. Come with me," she said, and reached for his hand. "I have an idea."

chapter thirty-six

As Nathan expected he would, Wilkes accepted his invitation to dine with him and Evelyn a few days later.

"Benton!" Nathan called out as he entered the grand salon to survey it.

"Yes, my lord?" Benton asked, appearing suddenly from behind one of the Oriental screens.

"Lord God, you gave me a start," Nathan said gruffly. "Everything is in order?"

"Yes, my lord," Benton said calmly.

"You best hope that it is, Benton. I would hate to see you hawking chickens at Covent Garden."

"Wine, my lord?" Benton asked, unfazed.

Nathan snorted. "Whiskey, please. A barrel of it if you have it."

With his whiskey firmly in hand, Nathan paced restlessly until Benton reappeared to tell Nathan that Wilkes's coach had just pulled into the drive.

Nathan drew a steadying breath. "Please see him in,

and send someone to tell her ladyship our guest has arrived."

With a nod, Benton went out to fetch their traitor.

Moments later, Wilkes strolled in behind Benton, a smile on his face. "Good evening, Lindsey," he said congenially.

"Ah, Wilkes," Nathan said, extending his hand. "Good evening. I know a look of thirst on a man—would you like a tot of Donnelly's devil whiskey?"

Wilkes laughed. "You know me well, old friend."

Nathan nodded to Benton, who walked to a sideboard at the far end of the formal salon and between the two Oriental screens to fetch the whiskey.

"There was quite a lot of traffic on the street," Wilkes remarked.

"Ah, yes. Fawcett is hosting a gathering this evening," Nathan said, and looked at Wilkes. "Perhaps after this interminable supper with my interminable wife, we might find a game there."

"Splendid," Wilkes said, his eyes lighting as he took the whiskey Benton offered him and a seat. "I've not seen you in an age, Lindsey. What have you been about? A fair young mistress, I hope, with silken hair and alabaster skin."

"Unfortunately, no," Nathan said, and hoped to high heaven he did not look as enraged as he felt as he sat directly across from Wilkes. "What of you, sir? How did you find your mother?"

"Exceedingly well. Have you word from Lambourne or Donnelly?"

"Not a word," Nathan said.

"I should hope Lambourne is deep in Scotland by now," Wilkes said with a grin. "The prince told me that it would be his pleasure to question him personally." He laughed.

"Indeed?" Nathan drawled. "You seem to know quite a lot about the prince these days, sir."

Wilkes shrugged and casually crossed his legs. "I only know what we all know of the prince—he likes his women and his drink. As a result, he's been rendered inept. He's in need of strong counsel, if you ask me."

A sound from near the screens drew their attention; Nathan slowly turned his head.

"I beg your pardon, my lord," Benton said, bowing low at the sideboard.

Nathan gave the butler a quick once-over and casually returned to his conversation. "It is interesting you mention the prince in that regard," Nathan said. "I've heard there is concern for the king's condition again."

"Yes, I've heard that as well." Wilkes sighed. "George is inept, but he'd make a better king, I should think . . . with the right people around him, of course. That is our king's failure, you know. He never had the right men," Wilkes opined.

An interesting notion. Nathan looked at him appraisingly and chose his words carefully. "Perhaps that is true," he agreed for the sake of argument. "He could use a good head such as yours, eh?"

Wilkes laughed. "I will not deny that I have much to gain if George ascends the throne. The same as you," he said, with a subtle wink.

Nathan smiled and raised his tot in response.

"The building of nations is tedious work," Wilkes added, settling back like some elder statesman about to impart his wisdom. "Perhaps too tedious for a prince who prefers laudanum to Parliament."

Nathan smiled. "I suppose—"

The door suddenly banged open and Evelyn, in high dudgeon, stepped across the threshold, clutching a piece of vellum.

Nathan and Wilkes instantly clambered to their feet.

"Good evening, Sir Wilkes," Evelyn said sweetly, then turned a murderous gaze to Nathan.

"Lady Lindsey, how well you look," Wilkes said, bowing. "The air at Eastchurch agrees with you."

"Thank you, sir," she said, and glided into the room.

"Wine, madam?" Benton asked.

"Oh, no thank you, Benton. I won't be staying."

"Pardon?" Nathan asked sharply. "We have a guest—"

"Because I found *this*, Nathan," she said, holding up the vellum. "A lovely note from Lady Fawcett—or, as she writes to you, *Beth*. How could you?" she demanded.

"Evelyn, it is nothing," Nathan said, glancing at Wilkes. "It is hardly cause for a scene."

"It's *always* nothing with you! Lady Fawcett, Lady Copperley—there is no end to them!"

"No *end*?" he shot back. "And what of you and Dunhill, my sweet? Is there any end to *your* perfidy?"

Evelyn gasped. "You are *half* the man he is!"

"My lady!" Wilkes exclaimed, alarmed. "Lindsey, perhaps we should sit—"

"Wilkes, help me," Evelyn said desperately. "Help me convince Lindsey to divorce!"

Startled, Wilkes looked at Nathan. "I—"

"There is no other option open to me other than death!"

"*Evelyn!*" Nathan snapped.

"It's true! I'd rather die than remain married to you!"

Nathan suddenly lunged and grabbed her arm. "Hush now, wife, or you may have your wish."

"Keep your hands off me," she hissed, and jerked her arm free of his grasp. She twirled about, marching from the salon as dramatically as she'd entered.

In the awkward silence that followed, Nathan ran a hand over the top of his head. "See after her, Benton," he said softly, and waited for his butler to leave the room.

Benton quickly followed, leaving the door slightly ajar. Nathan smiled sheepishly at Wilkes. "I beg your pardon, Wilkes. I am sorry you had to witness that."

"No apology necessary."

"There are times I wish I'd never laid eyes on her," Nathan added morosely. He picked up his tot and downed the contents. "She's an *impossible* wife . . . I have more in common with George than you know."

"Then perhaps you should consider divorce. Men cannot be so encumbered. Think of it, Lindsey—the woman has made you the laughingstock of London with her affairs. Rid yourself of her."

Nathan bristled. "I don't know if it is possible," he said tightly.

"There are many who have come to the conclusion that George would be a better king were he to ascend to the throne without the weight of Princess Caroline burdening him."

"A better king," Nathan drawled, working to restrain his murderous rage.

"A happier king," Wilkes clarified. "Perhaps even willing to reward those who helped remove the weight with a substantial boon."

"But the king seems unwilling to allow a divorce," Nathan reminded him.

"Perhaps—no one can judge his muddled mind, to be sure. Nevertheless, there *are* other options," Wilkes said. "Granted, George is too caught up in the gossip and talk to think things through clearly," Wilkes said, his distaste evident, "but that is why he needs good men around him, men who can look farther than the next meal or bout in the sack and think of what it is that Britain needs in a king. Men who can devise creative ways to reduce the prince's burden when a path is not clearly evident."

"And there are men who are thinking this way for him?"

"Throughout history, men have done as much for the Prince of Wales. It is a lord's duty to the crown."

"What lords?" Nathan asked.

Wilkes smiled. "Men who could help you as well, Lindsey."

Nathan's heart began to flutter madly in his chest. "Who?"

Wilkes considered Nathan a long moment. "Between you and me?"

"You and me and these four walls."

"We're calling ourselves the coterie," Wilkes said low. "Moorhouse, myself, Davis, Gillings, and Brockton."

"The five of you have the prince's ear?"

Wilkes chuckled. "We have his ear, all right. He's scarcely aware of it, he's so bloody thick at times, but yes, we have his ear. And when he is king, you might guess what favors will be bestowed on us—particularly if we can find a way to bring this Delicate Investigation to a mortal end once and for all."

Nathan was so stunned he could hardly speak. To hear Wilkes all but confess to treason without the slightest bit of conscience was staggering.

"So now I shall put the question to you, Lindsey— would you like to help shape the future of this nation and perhaps rid yourself of your own burdensome wife in the course of it? We've room for more."

Nathan couldn't tolerate another moment. The betrayal and disappointment was suffocating. "You bloody bastard," Nathan breathed, and watched the smile fade from Wilkes's face. "You tried to kill my *wife!*" he cried, coming to his feet.

Wilkes quickly came to his. "Oh, I see," he said, his eyes going cold. "This is some sort of revenge, is it? What the devil for, Lindsey? Your wife *cuckolded* you!" he snapped. "I meant to do you a favor and rid you of that whore!"

Nathan meant to respond with his hands around Wilkes's neck, but George, Prince of Wales, burst forth from behind the screen where he'd been hidden, knocking it over in his haste. "And what did you mean to do for me?" he asked sharply. "Enlighten me, sir! I am too *thick* to take your meaning otherwise!"

The color bled from Wilkes's face; he turned to the door, but Nathan was prepared for it. He lunged for him, catching him from behind and knocking him to the ground just as men listening on the other side of the door rushed in. But it wasn't until someone pulled Nathan off the bastard that he realized he was still hitting Wilkes.

Two footmen held Nathan to one side as men who had accompanied the prince brought Wilkes to his feet, forcing him to face the prince. "Have you any idea what you have done?" the prince asked angrily. "What you have *cost* me with your ridiculous scheme?" He looked at one of his men. "See to it that the others are rounded up at once!" he snapped. "And take him from my sight!"

"Your Highness!" Wilkes tried, but they were dragging him out.

The footmen let Nathan go. He kept his fists clenched at his sides—his heart was still racing, his rage still mushrooming. He could not see or hear anyone but Wilkes, wanted nothing more than to kill him.

It was the touch of Evelyn's hand to his arm that calmed him somewhat, at least enabling him to draw a breath.

"I cannot thank you enough, Lindsey," the prince said. "I had no idea such lying, traitorous jackals were in my midst."

"With all due respect, Your Highness, your thanks should be directed to my wife. It was her friendship with your sister, Her Highness Princess Mary, that brought this evening about."

"Ah, yes," he said, smiling a little. "I admit to being a bit skeptical when Mary told me I would witness a performance unlike any I'd seen."

Evelyn blushed.

"I beg your pardon, Lady Lindsey," the prince said, his smile fading. "I would that you had not had to see such an ugly side of Sir Wilkes."

"I was glad to hear it from the traitor's own lips, Your Highness. At least I know he's been caught and you will see that justice is done."

"You have my word. Now, if you will excuse me, I've a few more questions for Wilkes. Richard," he said, looking at one of his men, "I require an audience with the king at once."

"Yes, Your Grace."

The prince took his leave of them, and with their arms around each other's waist, Evelyn and Nathan walked together from that room and the awful betrayal. Nathan did not see Benton or the prince's men who lined the corridor. He could see nothing, think nothing, could feel nothing but a betrayal that cut so deep, it physically pained him.

"You heard it all?" Nathan asked Evelyn as they moved up the staircase.

"Every last word. Benton left the door adjoining the study open. We all heard it."

"It must have been difficult for you."

She smiled. "I was more relieved that he was admitting it, that we could at last put the scandal behind us."

"I wish I knew what made him turn against me," Nathan said.

"He didn't turn against you. He was never with you to begin with." Evelyn opened the door to his suite of rooms and looked up at him. "He will pay for what he has done, the king will see to it, I know he will." She walked across the threshold of his room and glanced at Nathan over her shoulder. "We're safe, are we not?"

"Completely," he said, and believed it.

She smiled.

Nathan suddenly laughed. "Madam, did you engage in acting lessons whilst in London? Your performance was disturbingly real."

"Mine?" She laughed. "Your tone was rather biting, as I recall."

"Oh no, love," he said, enveloping her in his arms, "*this* is biting." He nuzzled her neck.

Evelyn giggled as she twisted around in his arms. "I should punish you for grabbing my arm so violently."

He grinned and kissed the tip of her nose. "What did you have in mind?"

She shrugged as she began to untie his neckcloth. "I rather liked tying you up, actually. That seemed to torture you properly."

Nathan lifted a brow. "Lady Lindsey, are you suggesting what I think you are suggesting?"

She glanced up as she began to unwind the length of silk. "I'm not suggesting. I am *demanding*."

Nathan laughed and grabbed her up, walking with her to the bed as she continued to untie his neckcloth. "I've never wanted to receive my punishment quite as I do at the moment," he said, and tossed her on the bed, then pounced on her.

And as she tied his hand to the bedpost, her breasts just above his face, Nathan realized that with every slip knot she tied, they were rebuilding the foundation of their marriage.

And if she continued to tie them so artfully, he would never have cause to worry again that it might all come tumbling down.

chapter thirty-seven

A crisp wind blew across Eastchurch, making the day gloriously bright and blue. In the graveyard, Evelyn paused to rub her gloved hand beneath her nose before she finished planting the bulbs that would come up in the spring and mark the grave of her first child.

When she had finished, she sat back and looked across the yard. Frances was raking leaves from the graves of a pair of Lindsey ancestors. He still met Evelyn here two or three mornings a week, but he had given over the care of the grave to her. "He's your baby," Frances offered by way of explanation.

But Evelyn was in a bit of a rush this morning—their parents, having heard the news about her pregnancy, were filled with such elation they had blessed them again with a visit. This one was far less tiresome than the last, Evelyn had to admit, but she and Nathan had very little time to be alone.

This morning however, they had vowed to revisit the nursery and determine what was to be done for their new arrival. It was, they had agreed, another important step toward their future.

"Good morning, Frances!" Evelyn called as she gained her feet.

"Good morning, milady!" he called back.

She smiled and waved as she began the walk to the house. She was free to move about as she pleased now, of course. They'd heard that the coterie had been rounded up and all were awaiting trial. Darlington had sent word that he suspected Wilkes would be the one to be hanged, as he had been the one to carry out their dastardly deeds. If Nathan felt any grief or remorse for his old friend, he would not own to it.

The only thing that remained of the scandal for them was the shambles of Evelyn's reputation.

It was strange, Evelyn thought, as she marched briskly along, her arms swinging, taking in as much of the air as she could, that she hardly cared. The only thing that seemed to matter now was that she and Nathan had reconciled and that together, they were overcoming their past and were preparing for another child. She rather imagined she could be happy here at Eastchurch the whole of her life, with her family and the memory of her darling little boy.

Benton met her at the door of the house with a message. "His lordship has unexpected callers," he said. "He asks that you meet him at the appointed place in a quarter of an hour."

"Thank you, Benton," she said, and ran up the grand staircase to divest herself of her cloak and gloves.

A quarter of an hour later, she stood before the closed door of the nursery. She could hear Nathan below telling Benton he was going to sweep chimneys if he didn't send the marquis and marchioness to visit the DuPauls. She listened to the sound of his footfall up the stairs, and had the tingling sensation of that same footfall across her heart.

He smiled the moment he saw her, the skin around his eyes creasing in the corners. "There's a sight," he said, and kissed her temple.

"Who were you seeing?" she asked.

"Some of the prince's men," he said with a wink. "They are looking for Lambourne." At her look of concern, he smiled. "I had to give them the distressing news."

"That he'd fled to Scotland?"

"Was it Scotland? I rather thought it was Italy."

Evelyn laughed.

Nathan looked at the door of the nursery. So did Evelyn. "I wish Robbie were here," she said.

"He is," Nathan assured her, and opened the door.

Evelyn drew a breath, lifted her chin, and without looking at Nathan, she put her hand out. Just as she'd guessed, he knew her hand was there and took it in his, surrounding her fingers with his, infusing her with his strength. Together, they walked into the nursery and stood in the sunlight streaming in from the windows. Their family was together again.

Charles and Diana were not the first Prince and Princess of Wales to suffer marital woes.

More than two hundred years ago, in 1795, Prince George agreed to a marriage to his distant cousin arranged by his father, George III, in exchange for money from Parliament to pay off his debts. However, he and his bride, Caroline of Brunswick, a German principality, did not suit each other. Their vitriolic relationship, as described in this book, is historically accurate.

In 1806, the king established a council from the House of Lords to look into the allegations of Princess Caroline's bad behavior. Her friends and staff were suddenly hauled away to be questioned in the course of the Delicate Investigation. And because she was being investigated for treasonous charges, Caroline was not welcome in royal households and fell out of royal favor—particularly the king's, with whom she had managed, up to that point, to maintain a good relationship.

When the prince demanded a more thorough investigation, claiming at the very least he had grounds for divorce, Caroline countered that if she was not restored to favor, she'd publish correspondence between her and the king, as well as reveal the royal family's deeper, darker secrets.

The threat of publication of what was simply known as "the Book" hung over the king's head in late 1806 and early 1807. When Caroline claimed to have had five hundred of these so-called books printed, the king acted. Because Caroline had won the sympathy of the people, he went against his son and chose not to bring charges against her, and the Delicate Investigation came to an end.

In *The Book of Scandal*, I have condensed the timing and slightly rearranged key events that occurred over a year to a few months' time to mesh with the series story line. The people and events presented here, including the Lindseys, are fictional. In addition, I reference the carriage accident that took the life of the Lady Cholmondeley, a lady in waiting of the Princess of Wales. This was a true event, but there is no evidence to suggest the tragedy involved foul play.

If you would like to read more about this royal marital drama, I recommend *The Unruly Queen: The Life of Queen Caroline* by Flora Fraser, *George III: A Personal History* by Christopher Hibbert, *Princesses: The Six Daughters of George III* by Flora Fraser, and *George IV: The Rebel Who Would Be King* by Christopher Hibbert.

Don't miss the next installment
of the Scandalous series

HIGHLAND
SCANDAL

Available from Pocket Books!

Keep reading for a sneak peak . . .

chapter one

SCOTLAND
1807

From his vantage point in the middle of a brambly thicket—which, Jack noted gloomily, had torn his best buckskins—he could see the road through the branches. He'd ridden hard the last hour, pushing his horse to stay a mile ahead of the two men. He gulped down air as he watched them trot by, their hats pulled low over their eyes, their greatcoats draped over the rumps of their Highland ponies and wearing scarves about their necks that were definitely plaid.

Diah, they *were* Scots! The old man in Crieff had been right—the prince's men had hired Scots bounty hunters to help find him.

Bloody, *bloody* hell. He'd put himself in quite a quagmire this time, hadn't he?

Jack waited until he was certain they'd passed and moved down the road a piece before picking his way out of the thicket, cursing beneath his breath when another thorn caught his buckskins. He untethered his horse and tossed the reins over the mare's neck and swung up onto the saddle.

And sat.

Jack really didn't know where to go from here. He'd been running from the prince's men for more than a month, fleeing England the moment he'd learned he'd been accused of adultery with the Princess of Wales, running deep into the Highlands.

Adultery. Jack snorted as he rubbed the mare's neck. Imagine, taking the Princess of Wales to his bed! It was preposterous to believe he'd do such a thing! Yet Jack couldn't help the wry smile that curved his lips as he spurred the mare up onto the road.

He'd never taken the princess to his bed, to be sure—but he was guilty of participating in more than one vulgar activity at her residence.

In spite of his innocence, when Jack had been warned that men accused of bedding the princess were being rounded up for questioning and would likely face charges of high treason—a hanging offense—he'd decided to decamp to his native Scotland. That sort of accusation flung about in the midst of a royal scandal rarely played out well for a Scot in England, and Jack Haines, the Earl of Lambourne, who was no stranger to moral transgressions and shocking behavior, knew a bad scandal when he saw one.

On the road again, he paused to look up at the tops of the Scots pines that seemed to scrape a stretch of sky the color of blue China silk, and inhaled deeply. It was clean, crisp air that swept down the glens and hills that made up the Highland landscape . . . glens and hills that seemed endless and exasperatingly uninhabited.

Jack reined his horse north, in the opposite direction of the bounty hunters. He had four, maybe five hours of daylight left and would need to find a place to bed down for the night. *Diah,* he dreaded the thought of another night in a bloody cold barn. But a barn was a good sight better than the frigid forest floor.

The air was so still—he could hear the breathing of his mount above the clopping of her hooves.

The only thing he could recall this far north was Castle Beal, and that was several miles away across some questionable terrain, two days' hard ride from Lambourne Castle, just south of here. He was trying to recall the best route—it had been eleven years since he'd spent any time in Scotland other than the obligatory annual fortnight at Lambourne—when he heard the faint but unmistakable *clop clop* of another horse's hooves on the road . . . or worse, a pair of horses.

Jack reined up and listened. Damn their eyes—the bounty hunters had turned back. There wasn't a moment to spare. Jack dug his spurs into his mare, but she was fatigued and he spurred her too hard; he winced when she whinnied as loudly as if he'd stuck her with a hot poker and broke into a run. The bounty hunters had surely heard it and would realize they were on Jack's heels.

Indeed, they had gained ground on him throughout the day in spite of wretched terrain and the prime horse-flesh he rode. Christ Almighty, where had the prince found these men?

Jack sent the mare crashing into the woods and its thick undergrowth, leaping recklessly over the trunk of a downed tree. A deer path led off to the right; Jack reined her in that direction. The mare careered up the path, splashed through a running stream, but balked at a steep embankment. Jack quickly wheeled her around, pointed her toward the embankment again. "Move on, then— *move!*" he urged her, bending low over her neck and digging his spurs into her flanks.

The horse gave it all she had; she crested the top of the embankment—and reared at the sight of two men on horseback. Jack hung on and managed to yank her around with the intention of going back down the embankment, but saw the bounty hunters crashing through the stream and heaving up behind him.

He reined his horse tightly as four men encircled him. He quickly looked around for an escape, any escape, but saw only a pair of shotguns leveled at him. The mare's spittle was foaming and her breathing labored—she'd not sprint, and even if she did, she'd not get far.

Jack looked again at the shotguns leveled at him as his heart began to pound in his chest. There was no out—he'd been caught. *"Mary, Queen of Scots,"* he uttered irritably as he eyed the one with the largest gun. "I donna suppose we might have a chat, then? I am a wealthy man."

His answer was the cock of the gun's trigger.

"All right, all right," he said, slowly lifting his hands. "You have me, lads." And he braced himself as they closed in, entirely uncertain if today would be his last.

chapter two

If it was possible, Castle Beal was even drearier than Lambourne Castle.

When Jack realized where the men were taking him, and caught sight of the imposing, drab, gray structure, he mentioned, in a rather flimsy bid for better accommodations than might be given to a fugitive, that his great-grandmother had been born a Beal.

That clearly gave the four men pause.

He hastily added that she was of the Strathmore Beals, and hoped that was true—he was hard pressed to remember the tedious details of the family tree; his sister, Fiona, was the one who could recite it precisely—but it seemed to have the desired effect. Instead of a room in the dungeon, into which Jack knew very well he would have been tossed like a sack of tubers, he was put into a suite like a proper guest.

And there he'd been left to rot, apparently, divested of his gun and hunting knife. But Jack cheerfully reasoned that though he'd been in London quite a long time, he'd been born and bred a Highlander, and he knew how to fight his way out of a scrap.

The door was left unlocked. They considered him a gentleman, above escape. He debated whether or not he was, indeed, that sort of gentleman as he walked the length of the room, counting his steps for the breadth and depth, again and again. The room was approximately sixteen by fourteen feet, give or take an inch. There was a faint odor, too, a rather acrid smell that led him to believe something was rotting beneath the wood flooring.

Jack had no idea how long he'd have to wait, as they were a wee bit reluctant to discuss their plans with him. But they'd brought him something that passed as gruel, and had thrown a block of peat on the hearth when the sun slipped below the horizon.

By then, Jack was tired of pacing and lay on the bed fully clothed, including his greatcoat, on the chance an opportunity for escape should arise. He fell into a shallow sleep in which he envisioned himself floating on a cool green river near Lambourne Castle. The sunlight was dappled on the stern of his little boat, and a woman in a very large-brimmed hat was rowing. She had slender arms and elegant hands. She possessed a fine figure, but Jack could not see her face . . .

Something awakened him abruptly. He came up with a start and looked right into the eyes of a boy whose dark golden hair stuck out from beneath his cap.

Jack relaxed and idly scratched his chest as he observed the lad. "Who are you?"

The boy did not respond.

"You're a page, I'd wager, sent to attend me, aye?"

Again, the boy did not respond.

"No' a page? A spy, then?" Jack swung his legs off the side of the bed and stood, hands on hips, eyeing the boy.

"The blackguards sent you to ascertain my mood and whether or not I have any nefarious plans, is that it?"

"Who are you?" the boy asked.

"Ah! I asked you first. Who are *you*?"

"Lachlan," he said shyly.

"Sir Lachlan," Jack said, with a bow of his head. "I am Lord Lambourne."

Lachlan blinked.

Jack's brows rose. "What? You've no' heard of me? I am the Earl of Lambourne! I own a big, gloomy castle—no' as gloomy as this one, aye, but gloomy nonetheless—a wee bit south of here. Does that spark any recognition whatsoever?" he asked as he walked around to the basin.

The child shook his head.

"Then I would say," Jack said, pausing to dip his hands into the ice-cold basin to splash water on his face, "that your education has been sorely lacking." He glanced over his shoulder at the boy, who was studying him closely. He was wearing trousers that were too short by an inch or more, and his face was stained with the remnants of his last meal.

Jack calmly continued his toilette, aware of his audience. When he was done, he turned to the child once more. "Here we are, then," he said with a formal bow. "You may take me to your king."

"We donna have a king," Lachlan gravely informed him.

Jack shrugged. "Then take me to your squire. Everyone has a squire."

Lachlan pondered that for a moment. "I think it is me uncle Carson."

"He'll do," Jack said, and gestured toward the door. "Off we go, then."

They got as far as the threshold, where a pair of rather large Highlanders who'd most inconveniently just arrived, pushed Jack firmly back into the room. Behind them a dignified, silver-haired gentleman strolled into the room and eyed Jack appraisingly.

"Might I have the pleasure of knowing who is ogling me?" Jack asked.

"Carson Beal," the man answered. "I am laird here."

"Ah. So young Lachlan guessed correctly."

"Pardon?"

Jack smiled. "A private jest."

Carson Beal's brows knitted; he clasped his hands behind his back and walked deeper into the room as he continued to study Jack. "Who are you?"

"Jankin MacLeary Haines of Lambourne Castle," Jack said with a curt nod of his head. "Close acquaintances call me Jack. You may call me my Lord Lambourne." He gave Beal a bit of a smirk.

Carson Beal frowned. "Rather flippant for a man wanted by the Prince of Wales for high treason, are you no'?"

Jack's smile broadened—he was not one to let his true feelings be known, and he would never let this Beal fellow know how that pained him. "My good friend the prince has been woefully misinformed."

"Oh?" Carson asked, arching one dubious brow. "Is that why you ran like a coward from my men?"

That certainly got Jack's back up, but he said pleasantly, "Your men did no' identify themselves. As far as I knew they were bloodthirsty thieves, and I but one man."

"Mmm . . . be that as it may, milord Lambourne," Beal said with contempt, "I think you find yourself in a spot of trouble, aye?"

Jack laughed and said honestly, "I am in the devil's own scrape, that I am. But I rather think my loss is your gain."

"What might *I* possibly gain?" Beal scoffed.

"I'd no' even hazard a guess," Jack said congenially. "But you have no' yet turned me over for what is, I assume, knowing His Highness as I do, a generous bounty. Therefore, you must stand to gain."

Beal's eyes narrowed. "As it happens, I have a proposition for you."

Aha . . . they *were* thieves. They would give Jack the option of paying his way out of their clutches. Bloody good of them, and he, fortunately, was a man of means. "I'm listening," he said, folding his arms across his chest.

"You have one of two choices," Beal said. "We can hand you over to the prince's men—who, incidentally, have arrived to escort you to London."

That was a mildly alarming bit of news.

"Or, we can tell the prince's men you've escaped and point them away. To Lambourne Castle, perhaps. Insinuate that you had help, aye?"

An appealing alternative but one fraught with questions. "And why would you do that, Laird?" Jack asked casually.

Beal paused, tilted his head back to look up at Jack. "Because you would agree to a handfasting with one of our women."

Jack almost choked. "A *handfasting*?"

"Aye," Beal said calmly, as if it were perfectly normal to suggest that Jack engage in an ancient pagan ceremony with a complete stranger. "You will agree to a trial marriage of a year and a day. If, at the end of that year and a day, you and the woman do no' suit . . ." He shrugged. "You are free to go."

Jack gaped at him. "That's insanity!" he blustered. "Handfasting is no'—well, it's hardly legal, I'd wager, and it is certainly no longer a custom, sir! It is obsolete, passé, backward—"

"We have a vicar who will perform the ceremony."

"*Why?* Why would you ask this of me? Who is this woman? She must have the face of a horse and the body of a sow to warrant this!" he said bluntly.

"She's rather handsome, I'd say," Beal said casually.

Jack knew the man lied, of course. This was too drastic, too fantastic—there had to be something entirely odious about her. "Why me?" Jack demanded. "Surely you can command one of your henchmen to it."

"Ah, but I have something with which to persuade you, aye?" he said with a cold smile. "The prince seems rather determined to find you, he does. His men are combing every glen in search of you."

George was that angry, was he?

"In addition to his own men, he's hired teams of hunters to help them search the Scottish wilds for you, milord. I suppose I donna need to tell you that a royal bounty is quite attractive to a Highlander."

"Is it no' to you as well?" Jack asked.

Beal paused a moment, his eyes narrowing on Jack. "If you agree to the handfasting, you will have a place to remain out of sight for a time until the prince has lost interest in seeing you hang."

"He does no' really intend to hang me," Jack said unconvincingly. "And how will I be certain that one of your clan does no' find the bounty as attractive as the rest of Scotland?"

"Because Beals are fiercely loyal," Beal said smoothly. "And I will match the prince's bounty if one finds he canna live without it, aye?"

"Would you, indeed?" Jack said distrustfully. "This scheme means that much to you?"

"I have my reasons, Lambourne. But you need no' fear a Beal. We will keep you safe in Glenalmond."

Jack considered him. As much as he mistrusted this

laird, and as much as the suggestion of a handfasting repulsed Jack, Beal had a point: if he agreed to this insanity, he'd be tucked away until the scandal in London had passed like a bad winter storm. And he'd have the luxury of time to plot a proper escape. It was, surprisingly, the perfect situation for him in his present predicament. The woman might be as ugly as an old sow, but she might also be his saving grace. "A handfasting, is it?" he asked, studying Beal shrewdly. "A year and a day, and I may cry off?"

Beal nodded.

"Suppose I canna endure a year and a day."

"If you repudiate our woman and your troth, the Beals will act accordingly to avenge her honor."

An old clan threat to cut his throat, but a threat that would be difficult to carry out on a Mayfair street in London, where they'd have to go to find him.

"Once the ceremony is done, am I to be locked away?"

Carson Beal chuckled. "We are no' heathens, milord. Of course no'. We will depend on your word as a gentleman and an earl that you will remain on Beal lands for a year and a day and honor your vow. It will behoove you to do so, what with the prince so determined to find you, aye? But naturally, within our little glen, you shall be free."

Not bloody likely. The proposition was too outlandish to be true. Jack studied the gray-haired man, trying to think through all the angles.

"The prince's men are in the dining hall just now. I suspect they'll stay for a day or so unless I give them the unpleasant news that you've escaped and are headed for Lambourne Castle," the laird added far too casually.

That was enough. As mad as a handfasting sounded,

Jack would take his chances. "Well, Laird, I suppose we both gain something this day."

Beal's smile was slow and cold. "Take him," he ordered his men, and the two brutes grabbed Jack before he could change his fool mind.

chapter three

They kept him locked away in a dark and dank room, where he could hear what sounded like a herd of cattle being driven on the floor above. Beal said it was to keep him out of sight until the prince's men had left, but Jack was beginning to despair he'd ever see the light of day again.

At last a pair of large Highland men appeared wearing the Beal plaid. They roughly escorted him upstairs, dragging him into the bitterly cold night air.

A crowd had gathered in the upper bailey, Jack was chagrined to see. He was paraded through it like a fat Christmas goose to a cacophony of cheers and jeers. The laird had seen to it that the assembled throng had plenty of ale; the smell of it filled his nostrils, and his boots sloshed through more than one spill.

He was ushered through small wooden doors that deceptively marked a grand hall. Dozens of candles blazed inside and the hall was teeming with people. Frankly, Jack marveled that there were this many Beals and Beal tenants living in Glenalmond.

"Felicitations, milord!" someone shouted happily, holding a tankard aloft.

Felicitations, indeed.

Jack was practically dragged across the great hall toward a raised platform at the far end of the room, where musicians would sit during a ball. Tonight the platform was empty save the laird and a man of the cloth. Jack was deposited on that platform directly in front of Carson Beal. "You did no' make clear all the bloody Highlands would be on hand to witness," Jack complained.

"You'll be grateful to know that a small army assembled by the prince's men are riding hard to the south to Lambourne just now," Beal retorted, and leaned forward. "But a single word from me will bring them back."

Jack's reply was lost when a raucous cry went up. He turned to see what the shouting was about and saw a woman in a gray, homespun wool gown being dragged by two men to the dais. She was not dressed for a handfasting. She wore a plaid shawl around her shoulders, and her dark, auburn hair was tied up in a thin, long ribbon she'd wrapped around her head. As they reached the dais, one of the men grabbed her around the waist and bodily carried her up, putting her down next to Jack.

Jack was surprised—she was comely. Her eyes were blue, her lashes thick and black, and she looked at Carson Beal with what Jack instantly recognized as a woman's white-hot fury.

She was so furious, in fact, that she scarcely seemed to notice Jack or the vicar, who took her arm and held it out from her body, the palm of her hand turned up.

"Good evening, Lizzie," Beal said, as if she'd come for tea.

"Uncle, donna do this!" she said angrily. "I'll think of something, on my word I shall, but this . . . *this* is madness!"

Beal held up a thin strip of red ribbon. She tried to pull her hand away, but the vicar held it steady.

"It's no' legal!" she insisted as Beal quickly wrapped the ribbon around her slender wrist.

"I argued the same. Apparently it is," Jack said.

She snapped that stormy blue gaze at him, and Jack had the uneasy sense that she would have kicked him square in the knees if she could have managed it.

"Lass," Beal said as he knotted the ribbon, "the constable is here now. He's come to speak with you about your debts. I can send him away, or I can send him to Thorntree to speak with Charlotte."

The young woman froze.

"Sir," Beal said to Jack, indicating his hand. "Take her hand in your right hand."

Jack did not move as quickly as Beal liked; he was struck with a fist in his back at the same moment someone grabbed his arm and pushed his hand onto hers. There was no point in fighting it—he'd given his word, and Highland mercenaries surrounded him. He folded his fingers around the young woman's. Her hand felt delicate but rough, and if he weren't mistaken, there was a callus on her palm.

Beal tied the knot, binding them together. Satisfied with his handiwork, he stepped back, gesturing impatiently to the vicar. "Make it quick," he ordered.

"We stand here today to witness the handfasting of Miss Elizabeth Drummond Beal," the vicar said, "to Jankin MacLeary Haines, the Earl of Lambourne."

Jack heard the lass's small gasp of surprise as the man droned on, but she did not look at him. She was looking up, staring helplessly at a pair of ancient shields hanging above them. He could feel her pulse in her fingers—her heart was beating at a rapid clip. He hoped to high heaven she didn't swoon. He'd have this over as soon as possible and a dramatic swoon would only prolong it.

The vicar asked her if she agreed to the handfasting for a year and a day. Elizabeth Drummond Beal did not respond. Jack glanced down, arched a curious brow at the same moment Beal hissed, *"Lizzie!* The constable?"

She glared at him. *"Aye,"* she muttered.

The vicar looked at Jack. "Milord?"

"Aye," he growled.

It was done. A paper of some sort was thrust at them, and they were forced to put their names to it, at which point the vicar announced their troth plighted for a year and a day. They were turned about and their bound wrists lifted for the crowd to see. Cheers went up; tankards clashed, and from somewhere—the corridor, perhaps?—a pair of fiddles began to play.

The Highland brigade Carson Beal had assembled to enforce the handfasting pushed Jack and Lizzie off the platform and made them walk along at a rapid clip, causing Lizzie to stumble. Jack caught her elbow and held her up; she slapped his hand from her arm.

They were propelled through the crowd. "Well done, Lizzie!" one man shouted. "Who'd have thought it, Lizzie?" another called out with a laugh. "Is the hunting so bad in London, milord?" someone else shouted, earning the guffaws of several.

They were steered into a narrow corridor, and when Lizzie faltered, Beal barked, *"Keep on, keep on!"* from somewhere behind them. Several of the witnesses followed along behind them as well, breaking into a bawdy Gaelic wedding song. The men who swept Jack and Lizzie along picked up their pace when they reached a flight of stairs that spiraled upward, filling the narrow passageway with the sound of belts and boots scraping against the stone walls.

At the top of the stairs they came to an abrupt halt at a closed door. They were at the top of one of four turrets, Jack realized.

Beal pushed past Jack and stood on the top step, facing the revelers. "Join me, lads," he said, motioning for his men to turn Jack and Lizzie around to face the crowd, "in wishing the Earl of Lambourne and my lovely niece many happy nights in complete conjugal felicity!"

"Uncle, *no!*" Lizzie moaned at the very same moment Beal opened the door at their back. The crowd, facing the open door, let out a cry of glee. Jack glanced over his shoulder, as did his bound companion.

"Diah," she muttered.

Even Jack felt a flicker of surprise. The small, circular room was basking in soft candlelight. The brocade bed curtains had been pulled and belted around the bedposts and the bedlinens turned down. On a table in front of the hearth sat a dome-covered platter and decanted wine. Winter rose blooms were scattered on the floor and across the bed.

"There you are, milord!" someone shouted from the back. "A bit of romance to put her in a proper mood!"

"And a bit of wine if the romance does no' help!" someone else shouted to much raucous laughter.

"Oh, ye of little faith," Jack drawled, earning another round of laughter.

Lizzie closed her eyes.

"Go on, then," Beal said sternly, and pushed Lizzie into the room, and by doing so, forced Jack to follow her. He shut the door quickly behind them; a bolt on the outside slid into a lock. Jack could hear Beal tell the revelers that there was more ale and food in the banquet hall. More helpful and lewder suggestions were called through the door as the happy crowd began the trek downstairs.

It wasn't until he heard their voices far down the spiraling staircase that Jack looked at Lizzie.

"Get it off," she said, jerking their bound wrists up and holding them up under his nose.

"I thought perhaps we might at least introduce ourselves," he said lightly.

"Get it *off*!"

"What shall I call you?" he asked as he pulled her to the table and removed the silver dome on the platter. Mutton stew, by the smell of it. Not a single knife to be had. "Lover?"

"Rest assured you'll never need to call me anything at all!" she said with admirable conviction.

"You may reduce your rancor and save it for when you might need it," he said calmly. "I am as enchanted by this arrangement as you are. May I remove your brooch?"

"Pardon?"

"Your brooch," he said, looking at the small gold ring-shaped brooch that held her shawl on her shoulder.

Her eyes narrowed.

Jack knew that look and gestured to their wrists. "Rein in your thoughts, lass. I need something to *get it off*."

"*I'll* do it," she said tersely, and lifted her hands. Naturally, his went along with hers, and his fingers brushed against her breast. It was encased in thick wool, but it was a breast nonetheless, and little Miss Lizzie blushed furiously.

She quickly unfastened the pin and pushed it into his hand, managing to spear his palm in the process.

With a slight grimace, Jack took the pin and began to scrape at the sliver of red ribbon between their wrists. "Lizzie, is it?" he asked as he worked.

"Please hurry," she said.

"Perhaps you prefer Miss Beal," he said. "Although that seems rather formal, given that we've just been bound to each other for a year and a day."

"Here then, shall I do it?" she demanded, trying to take the pin from his hand.

"*Patience,*" he urged her, and lightly pushed her hand away with the back of his. He continued scraping until the fabric of the ribbon was threadbare. He then put his hand on hers and jerked their hands apart, ripping the last bits of ribbon and freeing them.

Lizzie Beal instantly rubbed her wrist, then put her hand out, palm up.

Jack looked at her hand, then at her. She really had remarkable blue eyes. The color of a Caribbean sea.

"My *brooch,* if you please."

He bowed unnecessarily low and placed it carefully in her palm.

Lizzie Beal spared him not as much as a glance. She marched to the single window in the room, shoved aside the heavy drapery, and then pushed the window open. She braced her hands against the casing and leaned over, looking out.

As it was black as ink outside, Jack couldn't imagine what she might possibly see. "It's quite cold," he said, and turned to the table. "Come and have some mutton stew. We may as well relax, for it looks to be a long night, aye?"

He expected a maidenly protest, but he heard what sounded like the scrape of a shoe against the wall. When he turned round, he started at the sight of Lizzie Beal crouched on the casing and fitting her body through the narrow window. "*Diah,* have you lost your mind?" he exclaimed. "Come down from there before you hurt yourself!" He surged forward to stop her, but Lizzie Beal never even looked at him—she just jumped.

Horrified, Jack lunged for the window and thrust his head through, expecting to see her crumpled form in the bailey below.

She was not the least bit crumpled; thankfully, she was crawling off a terrace below the turret's window. As with his own castle, additions and restructuring through the years had added a room just below the turret's window. From the roof of that room, it was but a short distance to the parapet walk, onto which Lizzie lowered herself like a wood nymph, disappearing from view.

"Foolish chit," he muttered, and straightened up. He had no idea where she was going, but it was hardly his concern. He'd held up his end of the bargain. Jack pulled the window closed and divested himself of his greatcoat. He was ravenous—he sat down at the table and ladled a generous helping of mutton stew into a bowl. "No doubt she's taken a stable boy as a lover and got herself into this predicament," he uttered aloud. "That's what is wrong with Highlanders. They've no respect for the natural order of things."

He ate quickly, and when he'd finished the meal, he stoked the fire, then propped himself on the bed, his legs crossed at the ankles, and folded his hands behind his head.

His belly was full, he was warm, and while he found himself in yet another unwelcome situation, he believed that he might at least have a proper night's sleep.

He'd think what to do on the morrow.

Unfortunately, Jack never managed to sleep. A commotion in the hall brought him to his feet. The door was thrown open before he could reach it, and the barrel of a shotgun was pointed at his head.

He sighed, put his hands on his hips. "*Diah*, what is it now?" he demanded of whoever held the shotgun.

In response, someone shoved a disheveled Lizzie

Beal into the room. She stumbled headlong into him; Jack caught her and quickly put her behind him as Carson Beal strolled into the room along with the very large fellow who held the shotgun. Beal's nostrils were flared, his jaw clenched. He glared at Lizzie, then at Jack, and pointed a long, menacing finger at her head, which, Jack realized, was peeking out around him. "If she escapes again, Lambourne, you will hang," he said tightly. "It is as simple as that."

All this talk of hanging tossed about willy-nilly was beginning to grate. And this wretched handfasting! Not an hour old and already a bloody nuisance!

Jack felt the lass move, and had an inkling she meant to make matters worse. He clamped a hand on her arm behind his back, squeezing just enough to warn her not to speak. He clicked his heels, said, "Aye, aye, Captain," and flippantly saluted Beal.

Beal's expression darkened. He stared at Jack, assessing him, but at last lifted one hand. His bear of a companion stepped out of the room. "Mind you keep her close, milord," Beal said ominously, and quit the room, slamming the door behind him and then sliding the bolt into the latch and locking them in once more.